Mavis Bone
And The
Fledgling Killer

B.P. Smythe

Matador
9 Priory Business Park,
Wistow Road, Kibworth Beauchamp,
Leicestershire. LE8 0RX
Tel: 0116 279 2299
Email: books@troubador.co.uk
Web: www.troubador.co.uk/matador
Twitter: @matadorbooks

ISBN 978 1800464 087

British Library Cataloguing in Publication Data.
A catalogue record for this book is available from the British Library.

Printed and bound in Great Britain by 4edge Limited
Typeset in 12pt Adobe Jenson Pro by Troubador Publishing Ltd, Leicester, UK

Matador is an imprint of Troubador Publishing Ltd

MAVIS BONE AND THE
FLEDGLING KILLER

By B.P Smythe

A fledgling killer whose evil roots were planted from a traumatic childhood. He makes an agenda to rob and kill women for financial gain. His crime spree is checked and eventually foiled by Mavis Bone, an Australian lesbian private investigator. And with her German lesbian secretary, Gertrude Stick, who was a former member of the Hitler Youth, they operate the Wimbledon Broadway-based Mavis Bone Detective Agency.

Mavis and Gertrude live above the agency office, and share the top two-bed flat. The walls of Mavis's bedroom are adorned with pictures of Mario Lanza. Being a true fan, she has all his old records. Gertrude's bedroom is full of Nazi memorabilia.

Gertrude's dislike for all Jews, stems from her horrifying experience nearing the end of the war. A Russian commissar wearing a Star of David pendant, raped her at the fall of Berlin. He said it was her punishment for stealing coal from the railway trucks. Her parets and small brother had already been killed by the commissar's Russian Jewish battalion, when they'd overrun their Belin apartment block. With no windows due to bomb damage, it was freezing.

Using a Russian motorcycle and sidecar, nicknamed *Lenin*, for their mode of transport. Mavis and Gertrude often turn up at a crime scene, wearing Hell's Angel's leathers and Stormtrooper helmets, Gertrude had recently purchased them from a Nazi memorabilia website. Included with her delivery was a giant swastika-patterned bedspread, and a black satin pillowcase set all decked out with swastikas and portraits of the Nazi leaders. Through the week, Gertrude rotates the pillows, so she can take it in turn to sleep on the faces of Hilter, Goebbels and Himmler.

Chasing the fledgling killer through his ingenious methodical killing spree is hands-on Mavis Bone, and she's not afraid to get those hands dirty. This involves the death of her husband, and a problem client who could send her secretary to prison for a war crime.

Dealing with her own personal issues through the years, Mavis has blood on her hands and sees it as justifiable, even though the police wouldn't. Her gender choices, along with her opinionated racist views, were moulded in her hard Australian outback childhood, and provided the twisted reasoning for killing her parents and philandering husband.

ONE

Coming Out

Born in Australia, Mavis Bone had grown up on her parents' outback sheep farm near Sydney.

In 1964 at fifteen years old, Mavis Bone attended the Sydney State Belonga School. The school was built in the nineteen forties, and had a high academic record. It was a mixed-sex establishment, consisting of a lower school and a sixth form. It was state-run and non-fee paying, which pleased her parents.

However, Mavis felt she never fitted in. That was until, as a fifteen-year-old, she met Ian Holmes one hot afternoon on a nature study field trip.

Ian Holmes, was tall for his age, a good-looking lad with fair hair, who'd just turned fifteen years old. By the end of the afternoon he was smitten with Mavis.

Mavis, who was medium height with frizzy dark hair, hoisted up her school uniform skirt to show a bit of leg.

For the older girls, miniskirts were the fashion. However, Mavis knew she had Ian hooked.

Being in the same class together, they became inseparable during breaks and lunchtimes.

While Mavis received some pocket money from helping out on her parents' farm, Ian worked the odd Saturday in his father's grocery store, which was a bus ride from the school.

Now and again they would pool their resources and go to the cinema. One such film was the old classic, *The Bonnie Parker Story*, which was about Bonnie and Clyde, the bank robbers. It made a real impression on them. On the way home on the bus, they talked excitedly about how good it would be to rob a shop or even a bank. Mavis told Ian about her father's guns. However, they decided to start small with Jessop's, the local newsagents at her bus stop.

That was it. Always needing money for cigarettes and booze, they thought they'd chance their arm. Jessop's seemed an easy score. Old Mr Jessop, since his wife had died, had run the shop on his own. The cigarettes were stacked at the rear of the counter, well out of reach of the opportunist thieving schoolkids that swamped his shop, mostly for candy and chocolate after school.

The plan was for Mavis to ask for sweets kept in the jars on the far opposite top shelf. Mr Jessop, with his back to them, would climb his set of steps. And then Ian, with his mother's shopping bag, would help himself.

Mr Jessop took pride in his top-shelf jars. They'd been handed down from his father and grandfather. Filled with

2

mint humbugs, acid drops, sherbet lemons, pear drops, liquorice allsorts and numerous sweets of a bygone era, they mostly attracted the elderly – at least those that still had teeth and could chew.

This mid-November, Sydney was experiencing a warm spell. It was too hot to go shopping. Most people this Saturday afternoon were either at Bondi Beach, or sitting in their gardens with a barbecue.

The high street was quiet as Mavis made her way into the empty shop. The door was open because of the good weather.

Mr Jessop, who was sitting behind the counter reading a newspaper, raised himself. He was dressed in his usual khaki work coat, and wearing a pair of half-rim spectacles. The overhead shop light reflected off his bald patch as he smiled at Mavis and said, 'Yes, my dear?'

Mavis with her dark frizzy hair tied back, and wearing a white skimpy blouse with matching shorts, pointed to the jars. 'A small cup of your sherbet lemons, and the same with the liquorice allsorts please.' She gave Mr Jessop a broad smile.

'Certainly.' He returned the smile, picked up the small set of steps, and moved to the far end wall with the jars above. Positioning the steps, he gingerly climbed up with the paper cup in one hand, and then carefully unscrewed the lid for the sherbet lemons.

Mavis, ensuring there was no wall mirror, signalled to Ian. He quietly appeared wearing a hooded tracksuit top, and then quickly started helping himself to five packets of cigarettes, a box of matches and a small bottle of Napoleon brandy.

Within twenty seconds, it was all in his shopping bag. And then he was gone, leaving Mavis still staring at the back of Mr Jessop as he fulfilled her purchase requirements.

Five minutes later, they met up at the bus stop along the high street. Both of them sucked on a sherbet lemon and inhaled deeply on a shared cigarette. They giggled at their first successful venture into the world of crime.

Mavis asked him, 'Do you want to come back to my place? My parents have gone to the big farm show in Sydney old town. They'll probably go on to eat, so they won't be home till late.'

Ian's face lit up. 'Okay, sounds great.' He took out the brandy. 'We can have a party,' he grinned.

Within forty minutes they'd taken the bus, and then it was a quarter-of-a-mile walk. Finally, in-between a swig of brandy each, they arrived at Mavis's parents' farmhouse.

Letting themselves in, Mavis immediately said, 'Did you bring any with you?'

Ian took the packet of Durex from his top pocket.

'Good,' she said. 'Let's go to my bedroom.'

*

While Ian had ensconced himself in the bathroom, Mavis had undressed and slipped into bed. Knowing it was her first time, she felt nervous. She'd let Ian breast fondle a few times, and done some pretty heavy petting with him, but that's as far as it had gone.

However, Mavis had made her mind up to moan and gasp in all the right places, to show she was enjoying it. She didn't want it getting back to Ian's school mates that Mavis Bone was frigid.

When Ian came out of the bathroom, he had his underpants on. He gave Mavis an embarrassing smile, and sat on the edge of the bed. In his hand he held the packet of Durex and took out a rubber. And then Ian began to read the instructions on the back.

Mavis saw the funny side and poked him in the ribs. 'Haven't you used one before?'

'Err, no.' Ian tried to act cool. 'Always rode bareback.'

Mavis prodded him again. 'You're a virgin, aren't you, Ian? Come on, be honest?'

He flushed up. 'No-no, it's just… I'm not too sure how they fit.'

Mavis sat up and placed her hand on his crotch.

Ian stiffened automatically.

She swung her legs out of bed and sat next to him.

Ian held his breath. God she was beautiful with her black frizzy hair. He looked at the little vee Mavis's pubic hair made, and then at the gorgeous nubs of her little breasts.

Mavis helped him out of his underpants. 'Here, let me have a go.' She peeled open a rubber, and then rolled it down over his erection.

They kissed and fondled each other. Mavis guided his hand down between her legs.

5

Ian stroked her and could feel she was wet.

And then Mavis took the initiative and pulled him on top, guiding him inside her.

Within a minute and a half, while Mavis moaned and shrieked on cue, Ian had shuddered to a grand halt, and then slumped lifeless on top of her.

'Jesus. That was great,' he said. 'Was it good for you?'

She kissed him. 'That was fantastic. Let's lie back and smoke a cigarette like they do in the films.'

With his arm around her, Mavis felt complete. She wasn't a virgin any more. She could join in the conversations at school with the other girls now, when they bragged about getting laid. And at this moment in time, she loved Ian more than anything else. She couldn't imagine life without him.

It was after they'd tried it again, a little more measured this time, that Mavis said, 'I'm starving. Sex makes you hungry.' They both laughed, climbed out of bed and got dressed.

Downstairs, they sat at the kitchen table, making up French bread rolls with slices of ham and cheese. And then with their mouths full, in-between slurps of brandy mixed with Coca-Cola, they belched. At which they both laughed, and then Ian said, 'So where does yer dad keep his gun?'

'In his strongbox out in the pantry,' Mavis confirmed, turning serious. 'But that's out of bounds.'

'Oh, come on, Mavis, just a peek,' he pouted. 'Your dad won't know.'

She thought for a second. 'Okay, but you can't mess with it. Just a look and that's all.'

She knew where the spare key was kept. On top of the cupboard.

Unlocking the narrow steel door, the sight of the gun made Ian gasp. 'Jesus, is that the real thing, or what? Let me just hold it, Mavis', please.'

'Okay, but that's all.' She lifted it out and handed it to him.

Ian raised the Remington 1100 shotgun to his shoulder, and pretended to take aim. 'Wow, this could do some damage.' He looked at the boxes of cartridge shells on the strongbox shelf. 'Any chance I could fire it outside, Mavis, just to see what it's like?'

'No chance. What if my parents come back? I'd really be in the shit.'

'You said they'd be back late. And you're always telling me how good you are shooting rabbits and foxes. Or is that all talk?' Ian mocked.

Mavis defended herself. 'I am good,' she said, all serious.

'Are you now?' he mocked again.

Ian picked up some cardboard targets from the shelf. 'Still reckon I can get nearer the bullseye than you.'

Mavis scoffed. 'You, you've never fired a rifle before.'

'I tell you what, Miss Annie Oakley. I bet you a Wimpy meal tonight, using two bullets each, I can get nearer to the centre than you.'

Mavis corrected him. 'They're not single bullets, you know, but lots of small lead shot.' She checked her wallet. She had three dollars and some change. Mavis nodded. 'Okay, Mr Wyatt Earp, you're on.'

Ian and Mavis walked around to the rear of the farmhouse, out of sight from the road. In the three o'clock afternoon heat, they set up a target pinned to the side of a barn. From that, Mavis measured fifty feet back, and set down a mat.

'Okay, let me fire first,' she said, 'so you can see my stance and how my shoulder buffers the recoil. Or you could end up with a very sore shoulder sprain. And remember, in target shooting, don't pull, just squeeze the trigger.'

Ian saluted her and joked, 'Yes, Ma'am.'

She ignored him and continued, 'Most important of all, when not firing, always carry it upright or over your shoulder. Never point it at anyone.'

He saluted again. 'Yes, Ma'am.'

Mavis sneered at him, 'You can joke, Mr Wyatt Earp, but we'll see just how good you are.'

She loaded four twelve-gauge shells into the tubular magazine, and put on a pair of safety glasses and earmuffs.

Taking up the stance, Mavis fired two off immediately.

Ian rubbed his ears. 'Jesus, Mavis', you looked like Bonnie doing a bank job.'

Mavis moved to the target. The centre was spattered with small lead-shot holes. She handed it to him. 'Now see if you can do any better.'

'Wow, some shooting, Mavis.'

With another target pinned up, Ian, now wearing the safety specs and earmuffs, took aim and then fired. The instant recoil made him jerk back, and he dropped the rifle uttering a loud profanity.

Mavis creased up laughing. 'Not bad, but I wouldn't hold a shootout with a top gunslinger at the moment.'

Ian picked up the rifle and unknowingly pointed it in her direction. 'Sorry, what did you say?'

Mavis froze and then reacted. '*UP! UP!* Don't point.' Waving to him frantically. '*UP! UP! Fuck's sake!*'

Ian lifted the earmuffs with a puzzled expression. 'What did you say?'

Mavis crouched and moved towards him, gesticulating with her arms. '*UP! UP! Point the bloody thing up!*'

Suddenly Ian realised. 'Oh, Jesus, I'm sorry.' He quickly raised the barrel, as Mavis reached him and snatched the rifle out of his hands.

She bent over with sheer exhaustion and shook her head. 'Don't ever do that again, you dumb fuck!' she shouted.

Ian playfully saluted and repeated, 'Yes, Ma'am, I mean no, Ma'am.'

Mavis ejected the last cartridge from the rifle magazine.

Ian saw the funny side of it, and began to laugh. He put his arm around Mavis and started mimicking her. '*UP! UP! Point the bloody thing up!*'

That made her laugh, and they both exploded into convulsive shrieks, while she tried to say, 'You silly prat! You could have killed me.'

*

With the rifle back in its strongbox, and still early and hot for the afternoon, they decided to take the bus to the popular Sydney fishing reservoirs, which were near Port Jackson.

The Port Jackson reservoirs were private, and accessible to fishing permit holders only. There was a warden who came round by van to check the permits from time to time, but past experience showed that Sunday afternoons were his time off.

One reservoir that was particularly popular was Clifton Gardens with its overhanging trees. From one large tree, someone had made a swing with a tied rope and a car tyre attached to it.

From the bus stop they took a short walk across a field, until they reached the trodden-down part of the perimeter fence to Clifton Gardens, no doubt caused by non-permit holders, game poachers and teenagers like themselves who wanted to cool off.

On the reservoir bank they changed, Ian already wearing his trunks underneath, and Mavis in her sexy cutaway thigh-high one piece.

With no one else around, apart from a set of youngsters further down on the opposite side of the bank, they took the plunge and dived in, knowing the water was deep enough even at the very edge. And now, with all the awkwardness out of the way, they embraced, with Mavis wrapping her legs around Ian's waist while he doggy paddled.

After a further twenty minutes of embracing and kissing, punctuated by a lot of splashing and larking around, they clambered to the bank. Checking their money and watches were still safely hidden away under their clothing, they climbed the tree with the swinging tyre.

After crawling along the thick bough, it was Ian who first slid down the rope and stood upright with his feet positioned on the inside rim of the car tyre. And then, slowly working up a momentum, he generated a big swing and leapt off with a loud Tarzan howl.

As Ian hit the water, Mavis heard a loud smack like a belly flop. She waited for him to reappear. As the seconds ticked by, it began to seemed like he was taking a long time. Mavis called out, 'Ian, stop messing around.' She crawled nearer to the dangling rope and shouted again. 'Ian, you okay? Ian, for fuck's sake, you're making me scared.'

Mavis hesitated. She was in two minds whether to crawl back down again or jump in. She scanned the water. She shouted again. 'Ian, you okay?' She waited a few seconds. 'Shit, if you're messing me around.' Mavis put on her goggles and took a deep breath, and then, holding her nose, she jumped off.

Mavis hit the water clean and nearly went to the bottom. Coming up she strained to see through her goggles, but there was no sign of Ian. She doggy paddled and frantically shouted again. 'Ian, where are you?' She dived down again, pulling herself as deep as possible, while scanning the murky floor until she was about to burst for air. As she surfaced, she gulped and coughed and felt sick. Mavis composed herself and then swam further out to have another go. Holding her breath she dived again, deeper still this time, until her lungs were bursting once more. Still no sign of Ian. And the cold was getting to her. Mavis began to shiver.

She feverishly breast stroked her way to the bank and clambered out. And then she saw the fishing warden and his van. She raced over to him in panic, shouting, 'Help me, get someone, my boyfriend's drowning. I can't find him.'

He responded immediately and called for an ambulance on his two-way radio.

Mavis yelled into the offered phone, 'Yes, we're at Clifton Gardens, Port Jackson Reservoir. He dived in, but there's no sign of him. I've tried to look myself.' And with that, Mavis burst into tears.

*

Within five minutes, the wail of an ambulance could be heard. Twenty minutes later, the area was crawling with police frogmen, while Mavis was being comforted by a policewoman.

For a further two hours, after refusing to be taken home, Mavis stood on the bank with a blanket wrapped around her shoulders drinking coffee. Frogmen dived from rubber dinghies and surfaced repeatedly.

Suddenly a frogman raised his arm from the inky waters with a shout.

Mavis approached the edge of the bank with the policewoman.

Two frogmen were holding something large. It was white. And then it was being hauled into the boat.

Mavis realised they'd all stopped and were edging their way to the bank. As the dinghy slowly motored nearer, she had a horrible gut feeling. And then she saw the body bag.

The frogman reported the body was face down on the reservoir bed. He'd had to untangle the reeds from around the ankles.

With the policewoman's hand on her shoulder, they unzipped the body bag for identification. Ian's chalky white body stood out against the frogman's black rubber suit.

Mavis flinched back and began to sob uncontrollably. A few minutes later she watched the ambulance take him away to the mortuary.

*

Mavis dreamed of Ian that night. Trying to swim under the dark reedy water to save him. In the murky distance, he was ghostly white, waving to her. His eyes were upturned as though he was unconscious. The harder she swam, the further he moved away.

A week later, after Mavis's statement at the inquest, the coroner gave a verdict of accidental death. The local newspapers had stated that Ian had drowned after hitting the water awkwardly, and most probably became disorientated while getting tangled in the reservoir weeds.

On the day of the funeral, Ian's parents had his open coffin set out in their living room. Anyone was allowed to attend.

Mavis, dressed in her school uniform along with many classmates, clutched a white rose, supplied by the parents. As they filed past, they each dropped the flower into the coffin.

The mortician had done a good job. It looked like Ian was asleep, and there was colour in his cheeks, unlike the last time she had seen him. Mavis hovered before she dropped her rose. She wanted to touch him, wake him up.

Outside in the hallway, Mavis sobbed with her classmates.

During a quiet moment, knowing their Ian had been close to Mavis, the mother had retrieved Ian's East Sydney football scarf from the coffin, and gave it to her. Mavis promised herself she would cherish it for the rest of her life.

At the funeral, held in the North Sydney Parish Church of St Mary the Virgin, every pew was filled to capacity. The service, including a eulogy, was conducted by the Reverend Dr Kayhill, along with tributes from Ian's schoolteacher and two of his friends. This was followed by the interment, which Mavis couldn't watch. She was content to stare at the backs of the mourners and listen to the service.

For the next six weeks, Mavis visited Ian's grave and knelt by the headstone talking to it. She'd saved up and brought along souvenirs from the East Sydney FC club shop. She laid out club-coloured pendants and rosettes amongst the fresh flowers that his parents replenished.

Gradually, Mavis's visits became more infrequent, as the memory of Ian began to fade, like the colours of the club mementoes that had been left.

*

And it was a year later that Mavis Bone met sixteen-year-old Hayley. And then romance blossomed.

Mavis knew lesbian relationships were against the law in 1965 Australia. However, this wasn't an issue, because they were both in love. So deep in love, a love they thought was only possible in novels. And for Mavis it was exciting. They just acted as friends in front of people. Eventually they were spending a great deal of time in each other's houses.

And it was then that Hayley's mum caught them, naked, cuddled up in bed.

After a horrendous row, Mavis was slapped out of the house and called a filthy perverted bitch.

She was banned forever from seeing Hayley. But this didn't stop Mavis.

From then onwards, Mavis knew her life was mapped out to be a lesbian. And there was to be no hunky Tab Hunter lookalike for a husband. Or the stereotype white picket fence, surrounding a husband, wife and two point three children, with the community support for normal, heterosexual people.

And a few weeks later, in the midst of this eye-opening lesbian whirlwind revelation, Mavis shouted out at the top of her voice, to the gathered congregation at Hayley's confirmation, which included her mother, "I am a lesbian, so fuck the lot of you!"

TWO

The Fledgling

Vincent Pollack had grown up in Rainham, Essex. He remembered how he and his dad had done everything together. They were keen football fans. His father used to take him and his friend Rupert to all the Arsenal home games. He didn't have to pay for Rupert, as Vincent smuggled Rupert in under his jumper. By the mid-1970s, when Vincent was a young lad, his father Tom was in his forties. People would say they looked so alike with their slim build, ginger hair and similar features.

It was easy to spot they were father and son.

It was later in the year, after his father had remarried, that Tom started getting the stomach pains. They gradually became worse. After visiting his doctor on and off for two months, he was referred to a hospital consultant. With tests and treatment, they eventually diagnosed bowel cancer. It was terminal.

When nothing more could be done, the hospital sent him home.

However, the National Health Service could only do so much. Vincent remembered the toilet smell in the back bedroom was unbearable. Doreen, his father's second wife, never went in; she'd lost interest. She was just counting the days.

Doreen had been a forty-five-year-old widow with no children; she hadn't wanted any. However, she was looking for security. And under sufferance, she was willing to put up with young Vincent in tow. His father had first spotted her serving in his works canteen. She was a bit overweight with a round face, and kept her brown hair tied back in a bun. At five-foot-six inches tall, in her dinner lady off-white stained coat, she wasn't exactly a stunner. Nevertheless, his father was dead keen. And after a registry office wedding, Vincent stayed a few days with his aunt Maureen, while Tom and Doreen had a weekend honeymoon at Canvey Island.

Doreen was a strict no-nonsense evangelist, and tried to impose her late husband's blinkered faith on Vincent and his dad. Sunday evening mealtimes consisted of a stern-faced Doreen, hair in curlers, sucking the bones of her oxtail stew. Wearing a housecoat, she'd concentrate on tonight's new sermon, already stained with gravy, while getting herself ready for another hell-fire evening service down at the Pentecostal Hall.

Doreen knew she was wasting preaching time with her new husband. However, ten-year-old Vincent, young and impressionable, was an easy option, because he was afraid of her. With religious zeal, Doreen instilled into Vincent how he would suffer fire and brimstone in hell for his sins, unless he was punished on earth. She ordered him to scratch himself on the arms and chest, for his salvation, where it didn't show. This was achieved using the pruned cuttings from their rose trees. Vincent obeyed her, hoping it would save him and have his sins forgiven.

It was over the next four months that his father's stomach pains first surfaced. Vincent watched his father melt away. He'd forego school dinners and come home to sit with him. He'd watch the daytime nurse with her syringe. The morphine brightening his dad's face – dulling the pain. The nurse would change him, mornings and lunchtimes. Near the end, it was easy, as if she were changing a baby. She'd roll him over, pick him up – he only weighed six stone.

It was during one of these lunchtimes that his father pointed a trembling finger to the wardrobe door. 'Vincent, in my blue suit top pocket. There's something for you.'

He went over as his dad instructed, and reached for the fine-linked chain. It was a beautifully engraved silver fob watch.

'I want you to have it, Son. It was given to me by my parents on my twenty-first birthday.'

Vincent was overwhelmed; he looked at the watch and then at his dad. 'But – but, I can't take…'

'It's yours, Son; something to remember me by.'

It was the first time Vincent had really accepted his

father's situation. He broke down sitting on the edge of the bed and wept. His father, with great effort, put a very thin arm around his shoulder.

He kept his father's fob watch in the top pocket of his school blazer, which he wore over his grey jumper that hid Rupert. He imagined Rupert keeping guard over it.

And then, one Monday morning, Vincent's world shattered. He came running in, just before leaving for school. 'Have you seen dad's fob watch?' He was panicking, breathing fast while searching his pockets.

Doreen looked at him, a little annoyed. She said with no emotion, 'I'm sorry, Vincent, I had to pawn it. Your father was sick. He didn't know its true value.'

'But – but it was my dad's. He gave it to *me*?' Vincent's face had gone white with shock.

'He just lent it to you,' she said. 'It's far too expensive for a young boy like *you* to have.' She turned away, ignoring his pleading stare. 'Those sort of things are for you when you're grown up. Now get to school.'

'But it was mine, you shouldn't have —'

'*Shouldn't have!*' Doreen turned on him, her face blazing. 'Shouldn't have! Just remember who puts food on the table, Vincent! It's better off in hock than in your blazer pocket. At least it's paying its way, which is a lot more than can be said for you.'

The arm of his blazer stemmed the tears. With a pang of remorse, she added, 'Don't worry; you'll have it back by the end of the week. I've just loaned it to get some money. It's helping to purchase a new stair lift for your father.'

The daytime nurse had advised Doreen to get a stair lift fitted. This would be free of charge, paid for by the NHS. However, she didn't tell Vincent it was free.

His father's sister Maureen had visited, a bubbly slim woman with short dyed auburn hair and an engaging laugh. She'd lived locally, so Vincent had gone there sometimes for tea after school. Maureen had remarked to Doreen that Vincent was getting thinner, not eating properly, probably worried about his dad. That's when they fell out. She'd exploded, telling Maureen to mind her own business.

His stepmother wasn't stupid. Doreen had it all worked out. His father had never thought of making a will. Truth was, until he'd been terminally diagnosed, neither had Doreen. So, with his father on morphine and medication, she wasted no time in drawing one up, and getting him to sign. She'd planned it right; his father died three days later.

At the funeral, Doreen and Maureen ignored each other. They sat well apart. This also sat well with Doreen and her plans.

The next few months were hard. His father's pension didn't transfer to Doreen on his death, and his small life insurance barely covered the funeral costs.

Doreen had become bitter and snappy with Vincent, because she still had to work at her canteen job, while drawing a small widow's state benefit. However, it wasn't nearly enough, as there was still a mortgage to pay on the house they were living in.

Not long after, without telling Vincent, Doreen had put the house in the hands of three estate agents, looking for a quick sale. Trouble was, it was winter, and greed had its clammy arm around Doreen's shoulder, and she wasn't dropping the price. So with no offers, and to make ends meet, she took a charring job.

She'd answered a card placed in a local post office window: *Cleaner required for general housework (mornings). Twice a week i.e. polishing, dusting, vacuum cleaning.* It didn't quote hours or wages, but it would fit in nicely before her daytime job. She went for the interview. For Doreen it was just a short walk through the park, and then into a manicured residential area.

She took Vincent with her, while he still had Rupert concealed under his jumper. After ringing the doorbell, they were confronted by Mrs Crackston, a short, thin and white-haired elderly lady with a hook nose and very few teeth. As she let them in, they were curtly reminded to wipe their feet, and were shown into a house with large rooms that contained lots of expensive knick-knacks.

Doreen had picked the right neighbourhood, as these residents, with their comfortable trust funds and pensions, were the only ones around Rainham that could employ regular cleaning staff.

Mrs Crackston was roughly in her late seventies, and apart from Winnie her yappy cocker spaniel, lived alone. Her expensive inlaid French polished sideboard was festooned with silver-framed photos of her late husband and their children and grandchildren.

Doreen had checked out the cleaning rates, and before Mrs Crackston could utter a word she made it clear what she wanted, which was fifty pence an hour over the standard wage.

On hearing this, Mrs Crackston's lips pursed and seemed to cave in on her toothless gums. Even Winnie the dog yapped, and then hid behind her rolled-down stockings. She finally nodded in agreement, but made it clear she expected a first-class job.

Walking home, Doreen spelled out to Vincent that she wanted him to help, so she could be finished in half the time.

The next morning, Doreen woke Vincent up at 7.00am before school. Ignoring his protests, she marched him off to help with her charring job.

Doreen kept him busy. He was assigned general dusting and helping with the washing up, while she covered the wiping down, polishing and vacuum cleaning.

Vincent never received any pocket money for helping – just the occasional slap if the old lady whined out a complaint. And she was pretty fond of that.

Mrs Crackston and her cocker spaniel took an instant dislike to Vincent. She would shuffle behind as he dusted, muttering, picking fault. Frequently she'd call Doreen away from her duties, wiping her finger along an edge to show where Vincent had missed bits. For that, he received another slap from Doreen, while Winnie yapped at him and then bolted behind the old lady's blue-veined legs.

On one occasion, without the old toothless crone being present, Vincent pulled out Rupert from under his jumper and waved it at her dog. Winnie bared her teeth and then shot out of the room in a yapping frenzy.

One of his jobs was dusting a beautiful and highly polished yew corner table. In the middle of it sat an engraved silver trinket box. Vincent did peek into it once and jumped, as the ballet dancer sprang into action, to the chimes of the 'Sugar Plum Fairy'. Before he closed the lid, however, he did notice a gold fob watch, dull with age, sitting in the deep blue satin, amongst some tiepins and cufflinks.

It was about a week later when, with Doreen, Vincent was on his way to the cleaning job. They slowed at the sight of a police car in Mrs Crackston's drive.

Using the spare key, Doreen let herself in as usual, with Vincent by her side.

All of a sudden, a hand came from behind the door and grabbed her wrist. 'I'll take that, Mrs Pollack.' The key was snatched from Doreen's fingers, and returned to Mrs Crackston. She was leaning on her stick, with the arm of a sympathetic policewoman supporting her.

'Thank you, constable,' the old lady said, smiling briefly at the uniformed young man.

Doreen looked at them, mystified. 'What's all this about?'

'You know what it's about,' Mrs Crackston hissed. 'Your son's a thief.'

'What do you mean he's a thief?' Doreen whirled round on Vincent, and then looked back at the two of them. 'What's he supposed to have stolen?'

The old lady, ignoring the constable's gesture to let him handle the matter, continued, 'He stole my husband's fob watch.'

'Now let's calm down, shall we?' The constable turned to Mrs Crackston, with another wave to cast off her remark, while Winnie yapped out her little protest at the policeman's feet. 'We can't just start accusing people, Madam, until we have evidence.' The constable turned back to Doreen and Vincent. He spoke to them quietly. 'Look, just to clear this up, eliminate yourselves.' He glanced cautiously at the old lady, and then back again. 'Could you both empty the contents of your pockets, and your handbag, Mrs Pollack, on the table?'

Without hesitation, they did as they were told. Rupert stayed well concealed. No one noticed the bulge.

'Just because it's not on him, doesn't mean he hasn't hidden it somewhere. I bet she's in with him, probably sold it herself?' She waved her stick at them, followed in succession by three yaps from Winnie.

The constable raised both hands to quieten her. 'We can't go accusing, Mrs Crackston, unless we have evidence, I've told you.' The policewoman patted the old lady's shoulder to pacify her.

Doreen answered back in a mocking smirk. 'She's probably mislaid it herself, the old fool.'

With that, Mrs Crackston raised her stick again and said, 'I want you out of my house, *now*. You can collect your stuff and go.' She looked at the constable. 'I want you to wait here until they're gone.'

The constable raised his hands to quieten her again, and then offered a nervous smile to Doreen and Vincent. 'I'm sorry, but you'll have to do as she says.'

'Okay, that suits me,' Doreen said abruptly. 'Vincent,

get our things from the broom cupboard and we'll be off. I don't like being accused of being a thief.'

A minute later, with a clatter, Vincent emerged with a broom, bucket and mop, and dusters stuffed in his pockets.

Mrs Crackston started up, 'And make sure none of that's mine. I know exactly what's in that broom cupboard.'

Doreen matched her with, 'I can't say it's been a pleasure, you old cow. But I hope you, and your husband's fob watch, rot in hell.' With that retort, Doreen slammed the door behind them.

Outside, Doreen gave Vincent two hard slaps on the back of his head. 'You stole it, didn't you?'

'No I didn't – honestly!'

'Yes you did, you little brat, just to get back at me for your dad's watch.'

Vincent shouted at her, 'No I didn't!' He rubbed the back of his head, the tears welling up.

'All you had to do was keep your nose clean. *You* knew the old bag didn't like you. Now I'm out of a job. And you– you!' She faced him with an intense look of dislike. '*You* can go to bed without any tea tonight.' With that, she turned and walked off in a huff.

Poor Vincent, out of favour with Doreen once again, glumly followed her all the way home.

It was then the idea came to him.

While Doreen made herself a cup of tea and a sandwich from the cold meats in the fridge, Vincent moved swiftly up the stairs, two at a time. At the top, he pulled out Rupert from his grey school jumper, and kissed him affectionately on the head. And then he threaded Rupert through the balustrades and waited.

Ten o'clock was the time Doreen went to bed. Vincent looked over the landing rail, as she made her way to the stair lift.

Having put on more weight, her knees were suffering, and so climbing stairs made them painful. The stair lift was there to be used, and so she made full use of it.

Vincent looked down and watched Doreen carefully manoeuvre herself into the mobile chair. As she pushed the control to ascend, she slowly began to move up the stairs.

Vincent crouched and hid himself, just as the chair reached the right-angled bend. This was exactly the position where Rupert had slid down the balustrades, and was peering over the top of the landing.

Doreen let out a scream when she saw the black mamba. She cowered half out of her seat and leant away. Panicking, she forgot the stop control and began to stand, leaning away and screaming.

As the long, olive grey body of the black mamba's gaping mouth came nearer, Doreen lost her balance as she lunged at the newel post of the handrail.

Missing her grip, as Vincent watched she tipped out of the stair lift and rolled over and over, screaming, down the stairs. Her face smashed into the wall at the right-angled bend, leaving a bloody smear, and then she somersaulted down the remaining stairs.

As she hit the bottom, he heard the brittle snap of her neck as it echoed through the quiet hall.

Vincent made his way down the stairs and winced at the scene; Doreen's staring eyes, her twisted head at right angles, with blood oozing from her mouth and nose.

And it was then something burned into his brain. He picked up the rubber snake and said, 'Well done, Rupert,' and then stuffed it under his school jumper.

Vincent knew he had to be punished for Doreen's death. This meant stripping to the waist and gritting his teeth while falling into a rose bush. God would see the blood and scratches he endured for true salvation.

Vincent was pleased when Doreen's cleaning job was finished so abruptly.

A few days later, while living with his aunt Maureen, he'd smuggled a local newspaper into his bedroom. Underneath the covers that evening using his torch, he read the headline. WOMAN FALLS TO HER DEATH.

Vincent smiled. He fumbled under his pillow and felt the cold, smooth roundness. He pulled it out one more time, and shone the torch on the inscription. *Presented to George Crackston on his retirement by E. F. Cole &Sons (Accountants).*

Vincent rolled Mrs Crackston's gold fob watch in his hand, and then rubbed it against his cheek. The touch, the sensation made him close his eyes in brief ecstasy.

*

And from then on, even years later as a young man, Vincent Pollack still couldn't separate his stepmother from other women. She represented them all, an evil bitch who had conned his dad while he suffered in pain; similar to the nurse who had the power with her needle, treating his dad without dignity, like a baby who'd messed its nappy.

That's when Vincent made up his mind. When he was older and had the means, they would all pay, those bitches. And one day they would suffer, and he would con them.

THREE

Snake Eyes

Forty-seven-year-old spinster Maureen Pollack, could never forget how her sister-in-law Doreen had died in that supposed tragic accident while falling down the stairs. Still wanting justice after ten years or more, she arrived at the entrance of the Mavis Bone Detective Agency on Wimbledon Broadway, South London.

Maureen Pollack wanted Mavis Bone to investigate her sister-in-law's accident. How she could have fallen to her death from the chairlift?

Years earlier, an investigation had been carried out on behalf of Doreen's mortgage protection life insurance company, and the stair lift was found to be in working order. Their maintenance report was used at the coroner's inquiry, which delivered a verdict of accidental death.

Maureen was not satisfied, and was rather bitter because she hadn't been a beneficiary in Doreen's will. Providing after-school meals and teas for her stepson all those years ago, and that's all the thanks she got. 'I know it's been a long time, but if you *can* find some clue that leads to Vincent Pollack, her stepson, I know my money won't be wasted, Mrs Bone.'

Wearing a mustard-coloured two-piece suit that complemented her slim figure and bobbed auburn hair, she pressed the third button down on the business list. Instantly, she heard a buzzer that unlocked a door stencilled with **The Mavis Bone Detective Agency – An eye for an eye makes the whole world blind.** From there she pressed another button which allowed her through to a small and cluttered outer office.

In the outer office, she was immediately confronted with a collection of stuffed animals. A glass-eyed tawny owl, suspended by twine, slowly twisted above her head in full flight. A grey squirrel was being chased by a fox on top of a bookcase, as two ominous black crows watched.

Sitting at a desk strewn with files, and a small bronze paperweight bust of Adolf Hitler keeping a pile of papers in check, was a smart but sad-faced secretary.

Wearing a blue trouser suit with big gold earrings, and a chic, lavender blue headscarf to hide her platinum blonde dyed hair, she introduced herself as Gertrude Stick.

The forty-eight year old secretary immediately announced through an intercom to Mavis Bone that her client had arrived, and then she ushered her through to another office.

Maureen Pollack apologised for being late, and explained it was a train delay.

Gertrude Stick told her, 'The tvains are 'opeless in this country, vun delay after ze other.' She continued, 'All people do is moan about it. They need another Adolf Eichmann. He made the tvains vun on time. You never heard the Jews complain about tvain delays.'

All at once, the forty-year-old Australian private detective appeared.

Wearing a red trouser suit, Mavis Bone extended her hand. With a stocky build, standing at five feet nine inches tall in flat sensible shoes, her jet black hair of tiny curls, was comparable to a guardsmen's busby. She immediately pulled out a compact mirror, touched up her faint pink cheeks with rouge, and then added some heavy red lipstick and a smidgen of black eyeshadow.

Mavis adjusted her thick, black-framed reading glasses, and then fingered her big chunky pearl necklace, as well as the matching pear-drop earrings. A habit she always carried out while preparing herself when meeting new clients.

After introductions, Gertrude Stick, with a notepad, took her usual position for client interviews, which was at the end of Mavis Bone's desk.

She reassured Miss Pollack that client discretion was uppermost, informing her everything she wrote was fully confidential and would not be disclosed to anyone.

'I'm sure it wasn't an accident, Mrs Bone. That little shit, Vincent, the stepson of hers at the time, was the only beneficiary. I'm sure he was behind it. Even now, as a young man, he's evil, believe me. My next-door neighbour found her cat writhing in agony from burns last Guy Fawkes

Night. Someone had tied a rocket to the poor thing. It could only have been him.'

'We'll investigate thoroughly for you, Miss Pollack,' Mavis confirmed. 'It will have top priority. Please be assured, if any foul play has been committed, we will find it.' Mavis smiled, 'I always say, no sin is hidden to the soul.'

'As I said before, if you can find some clue, one that leads to Vincent Pollack, I would be very grateful, Mrs Bone.'

Taking her on as a client, Mavis Bone and Gertrude Stick set out and explained their investigation charges. After shaking their hands, Maureen Pollack signed the standard agency client investigation contract.

Setting a date, and receiving Doreen's house key from Maureen, Mavis Bone reassured her, 'We'll call at Doreen's house to investigate the stairlift, and the surrounding stairs and hallway.'

*

Two days later, Mavis and her secretary made their way carefully down the outside steel steps of the agency fire escape. This brought them to the up-and-over door of the small garage situated at the rear of the building.

Mavis, with some exertion, lifted it up, and then wheeled out *Lenin*, their nickname for the Russian Ural K750 motorbike and sidecar they used as their means of transport.

While Gertrude climbed into the sidecar, Mavis

checked the ignition and turned on the gas. Setting the fuel to full choke, she straddled the seat and then pushed down on the kick-start lever. The bike uttered a throaty roar and a puff of exhaust smoke, as Mavis checked her goggles and gave a thumbs up to Gertrude.

They put on their Hell's Angels studded jackets and Nazi helmets, which they used as a make-do for proper biker clothes. And then they adjusted their helmet chinstraps and zipped up the jackets, with a last-minute check in the mirror.

After a twenty-six-mile journey, they arrived at the small end-of-terrace house in Rainham where Doreen Pollack had died.

Letting themselves in through the front door with the key Maureen Pollack had provided, they were immediately confronted with the stair lift. As their client had mentioned, the house had never been decorated since the accident. Maureen Pollack, over the years, had wanted to preserve any incriminating evidence that might catch her sister-in-law's killer. This included Vincent Pollack's childhood bedroom.

Gertrude immediately poured two hot coffees into the plastic thermos cups she'd brought with her. While Mavis blew on her drink, she slowly climbed the stairs and began taking photographs. At the sharp bend of the staircase, she noticed the bloodstained wallpaper which had been left by the deceased while falling. After all these years, it still looked fresh.

Mavis continued scanning the carpet, and then noticed

something in the pile, near the landing balustrades. She picked up a small, coloured glass bead, and thought it must have come from some cheap ring or brooch perhaps.

In one of the bedrooms, Mavis spotted a pink satin-covered jewellery box. Assuming it had belonged to the late Doreen Pollack, she opened the lid and checked out the contents. Sifting through a collection of cheap costume jewellery items, she inspected them for missing stones.

Looking around the landing, she came upon what appeared to be a boy's small bedroom, the giveaway being the walls adorned with pictures of the Arsenal football team, while some shelves displayed numerous Meccano and Lego models.

Mavis became more inquisitive, and looked through a chest of drawers, which contained items of clothing and various football programmes and schoolboy magazines.

With difficulty, she crouched down and knelt on a pillow, while peering under the small single bed. Mavis spotted and pulled out a cardboard box containing a Scalextric track and cars. Hidden behind that, she could see a biscuit tin that had been well tucked away. Having to reach further for it, Mavis swore under her breath, as her fingers eventually pulled it nearer herself.

Prising off the lid, she flinched when she saw the rubber black mamba snake. Lifting it out, she could see one of the eyes was missing.

Now things began to make sense. Taking the snake, she climbed the stairs to where she found the glass bead. It seemed the ideal position to frighten someone, especially if they would lose their balance as a result. A fall from there down the stairs would have been fatal, and for Doreen Pollack it was.

After the ride home, they reached the agency by mid-afternoon, and then settled down and took stock. Mavis was thinking. 'You know, Gerty, this Vincent Pollack may have got away with the perfect murder. He might even try his luck again, you mark my words. If he was evil at that young age, he could be a fledgling killer in the making. And it's unlikely he'll ever stop, that type never does, they always want more. And then they get sloppy. Perhaps that's where we'll come in, you never know.'

Gertrude took out her bottle of Bailey's, the one she kept in her desk drawer, and offered Mavis a slug.

Mavis declined and busied herself with her own afternoon pleasure. She unscrewed the sterling silver snuff necklace, and cautiously tapped out the cocaine powder onto the attached silver spoon. After making two lines, followed by two hefty sniffs, she sat back and relaxed. Mavis had picked up her cocaine habit in Colombia, while backpacking as a student around South America during her mid-twenties.

*

A few days later in her office, while her secretary was out shopping, Mavis Bone showed Maureen Pollack her findings, and shared her theory of what had taken place. 'I'm sure her stepson hid the snake somewhere on the

35

stairs to frighten his mother. I found the rubber snake, with a missing glass eye, in a biscuit tin under his bed. And the glass eye I found in the carpet, at the top of the stairs.' Mavis sighed. 'However, with no witnesses or CCTV to support these ideas, it's not enough to prove foul play and involve the police. But I'm sure that's how Doreen Pollack met her death. She must have panicked when she saw the snake, and fell from the chair of the stair lift.'

Mavis tried to console her client. 'I know it's no comfort, but at least we found out for you how your sister-in-law may have died.' She patted her arm affectionately. And that's when their eyes knowingly met.

Mavis had suspected and, as they say, it takes one to know one. However, eyeing Maureen up in her mustard-coloured two-piece suit, and her slim figure and bobbed auburn hair, Mavis came to the conclusion that forty-seven-year-old spinster Maureen Pollack was screaming *I'm a closet dyke*. And the sofa in the office waiting room did look inviting.

Mavis tried to lighten the mood, and so she put on the office hi-fi system, her favourite Mario Lanza CD, *Be My Love*. Mavis mouthed the words and swayed to the song,

'Such a great singer.' Mavis dabbed her eyes with a handkerchief. 'I always play it, and get emotional when I hear him sing.'

'Me too,' Maureen agreed, and affectionately put her arm around Mavis's shoulder.

That's when Mavis seized her chance and pulled Maureen towards her. She unbuttoned her shirt.

36

Underneath, she was wearing a lace tank top. And then they kissed, ferocious tongue-in-the-mouth kissing, chewing-each-other's-lips kissing, as horny lesbians do.

Mavis said to Maureen, 'Have you ever fucked on coke?' Maureen declined. 'You should try,' Mavis added. 'It makes your blood scream when you climax.' She unscrewed her sterling silver snuff necklace, and cautiously tapped out the cocaine powder onto the attached silver spoon, making two lines. Mavis gave two hefty sniffs, and then licked her finger after using it to wipe off the excess from her nose.

And then they both stripped off, embracing one another, kissing passionately, while their nails dug into one another's fleshy arses. Mavis pulled her strap-on dildo from a filing cabinet and carefully rolled down a rubber on the silicone-veined erection.

On the sofa, Maureen lay on her back while Mavis climbed on. Instantly, Maureen wrapped her legs around Mavis's waist, missionary position.

Mavis felt her warm soft body underneath, and Maureen's firm tits with surprisingly dark and beautiful nipples. And then Mavis was inside her, with a guttural screech from Maureen.

They kissed and writhed with passion, biting each other's nipples amongst gasps, while tangling fingers through each other's hair. Mavis was so turned on, to see the saliva on Maureen's breasts, shining on her pale skin, gleaming on those dark nipples of hers.

And then Maureen began to climax, starting with a soft moan, and she started to buck underneath Mavis, her body and hips going crazy as her pussy screamed with pleasure, squirting hot juice between them. They both groaned and came to a shuddering halt.

After their mutual passion had been spent, they kissed and cuddled gently.

And then, as they got dressed, an uneasy silence prevailed, both feeling slightly embarrassed at what had taken place.

Later that afternoon, Maureen thanked Mavis and settled the agency investigation costs. At the office door they said their goodbyes and promised to meet up again. Both knowing it was never going to happen.

*

The following day, Maureen confronted Vincent Pollack with the snake eye evidence. As expected, he denied everything.

However, with Maureen being so bitter because of his inheritance, Vincent knew she wouldn't give up prying and sniffing around, trying to prove his involvement.

Vincent Pollack had to find a way to silence her; perhaps a chance would arise later. And that would go for all the other bitches just like her.

FOUR

Pretty Woman

Vincent Pollack had lived in Rainham, Essex all his life, haunted by the tragic death of his father from cancer, and then the guilt of causing his stepmother's death, both occurring when he was a child. This had been compounded with the loss of his aunt Maureen from a severe stroke two years ago. Now living alone, he was faced with tackling bereavement in his own way.

Nothing gave Vincent Pollack more pleasure than dressing up in women's clothes. He'd often wondered what it would be like to parade in front of men as a girl, like those Thai ladyboys. It must be fantastic. Only Vincent wasn't keen on having all that surgery to make the change official. He'd read the books and seen the documentaries on the procedure. It made him shudder and cringe.

Vincent knew he was different, standing naked in front of his full-length bedroom mirror. With great effort, using a spatula as he didn't like touching them with his hands, he would push his genitals through his legs to hide them. And then he'd take up a swimsuit pose, wearing his late Aunt Maureen's stockings and red lipstick, along with her green eye shadow and blonde wig with its flick-ups, and her bra stuffed with cotton wool. Her gaudy pearl earrings finished off the look of a young man who wanted to break free of conformity.

Vincent pushed the button of the music player for 'Oh, Pretty Woman' by Roy Orbison. He began to gyrate and sing along in front of the mirror.

He slowly stopped and looked at himself. The face took on a vacant expression. And then he broke down weeping. Roy Orbison carried on: *'Pretty woman won't you pardon me? Pretty woman I couldn't help but see. Pretty woman that you look lovely as can be-eeeee… Are you lonely… just like me-eeee?'*

Vincent Pollack didn't have much luck with girls. He couldn't bring himself to indulge in all that petting and sweaty fumbling in the back seats of cars or the cinema. Girls didn't interest him sexually, and they soon tired after the first or second date, when he'd said goodnight after a polite handshake. No matter how pretty they were, he just didn't fancy them. In fact he thought he should have been a girl.

Despite his gender confusion, Vincent Pollack still liked the company of the lads. As an older student he was popular with them at college. When they talked about their sexual conquests, he'd pretend and make stuff up.

Being average height and with wavy ginger hair, he was a good-looking young man, and they believed him. However, Vincent Pollack felt ashamed about his transvestite ladyboy desires. He knew he was in no man's land and worried how he was going to be sexually fulfilled. And then a chance presented itself on a Friday afternoon in November.

At this time of the day, the local woods of Spring Park Farm were a popular meeting place for queers, as his mates called them, especially around the public toilets. He'd often thought of visiting with his camera, and then chickened out. The Polaroid photos would make for possible masturbation material.

It was bad enough with girls – what to say at introductions, the nervous handshake, suggesting where to go, the cinema or a pub. This might be different, he hoped. They were there for a purpose. That purpose was sex. Pollack was on a mission to find his true gender feelings.

However, he was in a quandary. The thing that worried him was rejection. He had read in gay magazines that there were givers and receivers. What was he? Pollack decided that the only thing to do was make himself appealing as a receiver. He'd read they dressed more femininely.

This Friday, it had just turned 2.30pm. The weather was surprisingly mild on this November afternoon in 1994.

Thirty-year-old Pollack had thought about even wearing a dress. However, he decided he didn't want to look like a drag queen. He'd studied gay magazines for cross-dressing pictures, and decided to wear a pair of pink slacks. With his late Aunt Maureen's blouse and blonde wig, he finished off what he hoped would be a look of allurement, and sealed it by wearing her Alice band, with lipstick and eye make-up.

*

Perspiration was already forming on Pollack's forehead as he made his way along the wooded trail to the public toilets. The smell of wood and dry earth was filling his senses.

Pollack's mouth was dry. He stopped and pulled out a can of Coca-Cola from his stepmother's handbag. The seal hissed off, and he quenched his thirst with a nervous smile. A plane faintly droned overhead leaving a fluffy trail.

Vincent Pollack looked up. It was quiet, and he felt claustrophobic, surrounded by the tall trees. It was as if they were whispering overhead. Their secrets contained in a majestic stillness, constantly exchanging what they'd seen, witnessed over the long years.

Pollack had moved off the popular walking trail, in case he passed ramblers or a family out for an afternoon stroll. He didn't want to draw attention, especially dressed as he was.

As he softly crunched his way over dry twigs and earth to the public toilets, he suddenly heard voices and then saw movement. Pollack froze. His hand went to his late aunt's handbag. Inside it, he'd brought with him a small kitchen knife. Just for self-protection, even though he knew it was an offence to carry one. He'd read the local newspapers about the gay-bashing gangs that frequented the common.

Suddenly Pollack's head jerked towards the muffled cry and panting to the left of him. The dense bushes gave no indication of what was happening.

Wincing as the ground crunched under his feet, he tiptoed forwards. He wiped his forehead, the nervous perspiration now running down his face. The odour of earth and grass had become nauseating, heavy and thick with humidity. The panting and moaning grew louder. Pollack carefully parted the fern leaves, and held his camera ready.

It was two men, half-naked. One was lying on top of the other, their trousers down to their ankles.

Pollack was spellbound, and quickly took a picture. He'd never seen sex acts or been this close up before. Of course, he'd purchased and read, with a box of tissues, the banned backstreet magazines with the pornographic pictures.

However, this was a whole new world for him. To be here among it all. The Polaroid photo he'd taken made him excited, and would be useful wanking material.

All at once Pollack recognised the man on top. Although he was dressed effeminately, it was Mr Jenkins, a tutor at his mortician training college. In fact, he'd taken Vincent's class for embalming, in mortuary science for his bachelor's degree. The other younger man he knew from college as Colin Dance, a mortician training assistant.

Now he had to be discreet. Move away without being seen.

As he turned to go, the bushes suddenly parted. Mr

Jenkins was staring at him, and his face had a look of thunder.

Jenkins was well-built, and in his early forties. He visited a gym, and played rugby.

'Pollack, what do you think you're doing?' Jenkins had recognised him through his disguise while hastily hoisting up his trousers. The *Vincent* tattoo on his wrist was unmistakeable. He brushed himself down, and then realised his young male acquaintance, was gone and had done a runner.

'Oh my God, Sir. I'm sorry. I didn't mean to...' Pollack knew he had to get away. He started to run, and then panic set in. What if Jenkins was going to harm him, because of what he'd seen? Wanted to silence him? Perhaps there was some gay code of conduct he didn't know about. Pollack's mind was racing. He sprinted off with his late aunt's handbag swinging on his arm.

And then he remembered. The knife. He fumbled for the catch, but dropped the handbag. Pollack stooped to grab the knife, and the wig fell off. 'Shit!' He could see Jenkins running through the trees, about a hundred yards away.

Pollack knew he had to get back to his house. He had around four hundred yards to run. He ran in blind panic. His temples were now pounding, and his eyes seemed to pulse in their sockets. A hot stitch pained his left side, from the bottom of the ribs up to his armpit.

Running and gulping for air, he could now taste blood, and something like metal shavings in the back of his throat.

Just then, Pollack tripped and fell sprawling, twisting his ankle. He tried to get up on one knee, but it was no use.

Jenkins was upon him, and knocked him to the ground. He put his foot on his chest.

Pollack noticed the foot had a woman's shoe with straps. As he looked up, he saw the floral trouser suit and make-up Jenkins was wearing.

The white mask of a face, with heavy red lipstick and beads of sweat, looked down on him and grinned. In his hand, he held an aluminium baseball bat. Jenkins said, 'I always carry this with me, when I'm over here. You can never be too careful, not with these gangs around.'

Pollack winced from the pain in his ankle. It throbbed as he pleaded, *'Let me go, please. I won't tell. I haven't seen you.'*

'Oh but you have, Vincent,' he replied. 'And knowing lads like you, it will be all over the college by tonight. And then I'd have to face the dean and his board of governors.'

'I swear I won't tell anyone.' Pollack tried to sit up, but Jenkins' foot pushed him back down.

He said with menace, 'I know you won't tell anyone.' Jenkins pressed his foot more firmly on Pollack's chest. He looked around to make sure they weren't going to be heard, and raised the baseball bat. 'One of the gay-bashing gangs must have caught you. My perfect alibi, when they find your skull caved in. You see, Vincent, I've got too much to lose. There's no way out.'

This was it, Pollack thought. His mouth was dry. There was nothing he could do. *'Don't kill me, please. They'll know it was you. Your friend will know.'*

Jenkins was unimpressed. 'Oh, he's a mortician training assistant, and a student of mine. I mark his degree coursework. He'll say anything I tell him to say.'

And then Pollack realised, *the knife, it must have fallen out of the handbag.* Something was prodding him under his shoulder. It could be a stone, but there were only seconds to find out.

'*Behind you!*' Pollack shouted, pointing to divert his attention.

As Jenkins turned, Pollack pushed the foot off his chest and rolled over. That's when they both saw the kitchen knife with the black handle. Pollack grabbed it, while Jenkins smashed down with the baseball bat, missing his head by a fraction. Pollack with all his might, raised his shoulders for leverage and plunged the knife into Jenkins' foot, pinning it to the ground.

'*AARRGH! You Bastard.*' Jenkins dropped the baseball bat and fell on one knee. '*AARRGH! You fucking cunt.*' He tried to pull the knife out. His foot and shoe were soaked in blood.

Pollack saw his chance. He raised himself, wincing, hopping on one foot. His ankle felt like someone was pushing a hot poker through it. He grabbed the baseball bat.

Jenkins was moaning and whimpering, pinned to the ground, trying to pluck up courage to pull out the knife. His face and hands were covered with bloody smears from wiping away sweat and drools of phlegm.

Pollack stood behind him. With an almighty swing, he

brought the baseball bat down on the back of Jenkins' head. The loud *Pock!* sound echoed through the trees.

Jenkins gave out a muffled gasp and collapsed in a heap.

Pollack looked around. It was still quiet. *Was he dead?* He gingerly felt Jenkins' wrist for a pulse, and then the neck. There was a faint throb. Pollack knew he had to finish him off.

Raising the baseball bat, Pollack gritted his teeth, and smashed it down onto the back of his head again.

And then panic gripped him again. What to do with the body?

Pollack surveyed the scene. It was getting dark. People on the common were thinning out. And then, where the common dipped down into a grassy recess, he saw the huge pile of wood, covered by a large tarpaulin.

He smacked his head for not realising, tomorrow was November 5th. The banner spread out between two posts stated it all. THE RAINHAM ROUND TABLE FIREWORKS DISPLAY.

Buried under a huge pile of wood, was a dressed-up Guy Fawkes sitting in an old rusty wheelchair that was no doubt used for wheeling it around while collecting donations.

The scene brought a knowing smile to Pollack's face. This was his chance to get rid of Mr Jenkins, all trace of him.

Pollack then realised something was missing. The handbag. He must have dropped it in the chase. He had to go back for it. There might be something traceable inside. He was leaving nothing to chance.

Finding the handbag after a few minutes, and in the early-evening darkness on the deserted common, Pollack dragged Jenkins' body over to the bonfire.

Now was the tricky part, climbing through the wood to remove the old guy from the wheelchair. It was made up of a broom handle with rags and stuffing, and conveniently wore a large witch's mask with a hooked nose. He carried it all away into the undergrowth.

It was then he noticed that some fireworks had spilled out from the guy's old clothing. No doubt for the display pyrotechnics, and the amusement of the gathered crowd.

Manoeuvring Jenkins' body into the wheelchair, Pollack had an idea where to place the fireworks. In case the remains were discovered, especially the smashed-in skull, he had to be assured that no trace would be left for police forensics. The only way to guarantee this was to fill the mouth of the corpse with fireworks. This would make the head explode and let the bonfire take care of the rest.

Pollack fitted the mask to the face of Jenkins and stood back to admire his work. No one would know, and hopefully no one would find out.

*

Back at his small, end-of-terrace house in Rainham, Pollack was on a high.

Nursing a large Jack Daniel's on ice for Dutch courage. Pollack prepared himself.

He stripped to the waist and took out the knife. He

48

carefully pressed the knife tip into his chest, and drew a crucifix.

With his chest dripping with blood, Pollack dropped to his knees in front of the red neon-lit crucifix, and asked for forgiveness, while chanting, 'I have placed my trust in false teachings and substitutes for God. I have broken a solemn vow and promise. I have neglected prayer for a long time.

'I have abused drugs and alcohol. I have killed and discriminated against others because of race and gender.

'I have not been chaste in thought and word.

'I have used sex outside marriage and not to procreate life.

'I have given myself sexual gratification.

'I have deliberately looked at pornographic films and magazines.

'I have permitted sexual thoughts about someone, to whom I am not married.'

Vincent Pollack closed his eyes in a trance-like state of self-gratification, knowing he had cleansed himself before God.

*

The following night, November 5th, it was like a war zone. Dressed for a cold night and wearing gloves, Pollack made his way across the common on Spring Park Farm.

Confronted with *zings! bangs! wizzes! whooshes! flashes!* together with every other conceivable starburst of

49

fireworks above his head, he saw the glow of the bonfire in the distance. A massive crowd had gathered, fenced off safely from the bonfire and fireworks.

A barbecue was in full swing, with a long queue waiting to be served, while a stall was busy dishing out soup and jacket potatoes. Pollack helped himself to a hot dog and watched the crowd, as they *oohed!* and *aahed!* to the display.

By nine-thirty in the evening, the bonfire had really taken off. Being a dry night, the flames were thirty feet high.

All at once, there was an almighty explosion of sparks and cinders from the bonfire. People nearest the perimeter fence cried out and ducked back. Some, standing near Pollack, laughed nervously. He smiled with satisfaction as the wood began to burn with even greater ferocity.

Pollack could see that the guy had been completely destroyed, and the head was missing. Hopefully all that remained of Mr Jenkins would be his skull fragments, lost amongst the burned-out wood ash.

FIVE

A Shot in the Dark

Born in Australia, Mavis Bone had grown up on her parents' outback sheep farm near Sydney in the 1950s. However, Mavis harboured a terrible secret. A secret so terrible she would have to take it to her grave.

At an early age, Mavis had learned to use her father's Remington twelve-bore shotgun. While out on the farm, shooting vermin and rabbits, it was part of her chores, which also included sheep shearing.

*

Mavis had been fostered out at two years old, when the authorities had taken her away from her real mother, who was a nineteen-year-old drug addict, and died later of an overdose.

Her new farm-labouring parents had adopted her when

they couldn't have any more children, after their daughter Caroline was born.

The girls grew up on the farm together. However, it was Caroline who the parents doted on. She was the clever one who went to boarding school, and then on to university.

While Mavis was groomed to be a farmer's wife, Caroline had met up with a lad at university with good social connections.

Jonathan Paul Barkworth came from a well-heeled family, and his father was a wealthy building contractor. Eventually, at twenty-four years old, Caroline married her twenty-five-year-old fiancé.

For a while, Caroline lived in a seven-bedroomed house on an estate in Dover Heights, north of Sydney. This came with its own swimming pool, tennis courts and horse-riding stables.

Everything seemed perfect at first for Caroline and her new husband. However, the situation began to become tense.

Jonathan's parents disliked Caroline, and thought their son had married beneath the family status. They were counting on a marriage to the likes of a chairman or banker's daughter. Not a farmer's daughter. That's when Caroline's depression first took hold.

The following year, the couple had a baby girl, who they named Amy. Although Jonathan was over the moon, his parents still regarded Caroline and her farming family as gold diggers. She was just about accepted, but only under sufferance.

Gradually it all became too much for Caroline. Her

depression became more severe. She began to neglect her baby. And then chinks in the marriage started to appear. The little rows became big rows, until Caroline decided to take the baby and return to her parents' farm, in the outback near Sydney.

Although Jonathan was heartbroken, his parents persuaded him it was for the best. Arrangements were made that he would come to visit Caroline and the baby once a month.

Caroline's parents welcomed her and the baby with open arms. However, this wasn't the case for Mavis. The parents once again began to dote on their daughter, now with the addition of their granddaughter as well.

By now in 1973, twenty-five year old Mavis was helping full time on the farm, and soon felt her nose was being pushed out again. Caroline spent most of the time in bed, drugged up on depression pills.

The cruncher came when Mavis decided to come out of the closet. She told her parents she had a girlfriend and was in love. A huge row followed, in which they said they wanted to disown her and cut all family ties. Mavis tried to explain her feelings. But her parents wouldn't listen. After that, relations with them became frosty.

Sometime later, Mavis's parents visited a solicitor in the town. Being nosey, she steamed open the letter from the solicitor that she found on the doormat.

Mavis began to think about her parents' will. She knew where it was kept – in a reproduction walnut bureau in the lounge. A key hung down the back on a piece of string. Her father kept his whisky there for a quick snort, away from the prying eyes of her mother, who was teetotal.

One Saturday morning, as she watched her parents leave for the local market, Mavis seized her chance. With that lazy bitch of a sister Caroline still in bed, and her baby not yet awake. Mavis unlocked the bureau and quickly found the folder marked Marsland and Barber and Co. Solicitors.

Mavis thumbed through the copy of the will, dated three weeks earlier. She read quickly through all the herewiths, aforesaids, henceforths, notwithstandings and power of attorneys, until she came to the nitty-gritty. She leaned close and read. *And we leave seventy-five per cent of our estate to our first-born daughter Caroline Lucy Barkworth. The remaining twenty-five per cent of our estate, we leave to our second daughter Mavis.*

Reading on, it stated Mavis would only get the full inheritance provided she survived them all.

Mavis was seething. She hated Caroline and her baby. And now she hated her parents. She banged her fist on the bureau table, shouting, '*Shit! Shit! Shit!*'

And then Mavis calmed down in case she was heard. 'Seventy-five per cent to that lazy bitch. No way,' she mumbled.

*

Mavis had it all planned for the last weekend of the month. Jonathan, as usual, would be coming down to visit his wife and child.

On that late Saturday afternoon, the parents were watching television in the lounge. Caroline and Jonathan, with the baby, had discreetly made themselves scarce, and were upstairs in the bedroom. Her parents always hoped Caroline and Jonathan could work things out and get their marriage back on course, and thought it best they be left alone.

Mavis had told her parents she was off to the cinema for the evening.

At 6.10 p.m., with the television blaring out a game show, Mavis crept up the stairs with her father's twelve-bore Remington shotgun.

On the landing she saw Caroline's bedroom door was closed, and it was quiet. Mavis moved forwards and gripped the door handle. She slowly began to turn it. The door inched open, and she saw Caroline and Jonathan in bed together, with the baby asleep in its cot by the far wall. It was good; their backs were facing her. Mavis crept in; she had to get up close if she was going to make it look like suicide. She didn't have to worry about the noise of the gunshot. The next farmhouse was three miles away.

Mavis spotted the remains of a half-smoked joint in the ashtray. That was good. It would make them feel heady. Perhaps numb the senses.

She checked the baby. It appeared to be sound asleep. With one eye on the cot, she tiptoed nearer. Mavis knew she was at the point of no return. As the barrel of the rifle came within an inch of Caroline's mouth, Mavis began to shake. She pulled it away and took some deep, silent breaths. And then she focused again, bringing the barrel down. Mavis steadied herself.

Just then, the baby snuffled and fidgeted. Mavis froze and waited. After ten seconds all was quiet. She checked Jonathan; he was sound asleep.

Mavis swallowed hard. She nudged Caroline's chin with the rifle barrel.

Caroline instantly opened her eyes, and as she began to scream, Mavis forced the barrel into her mouth. She motioned for her to sit up. With the barrel in her mouth, Caroline gave out a muffled cry. And then Mavis squeezed the trigger.

The blast was deafening. The back of Caroline's head peppered the pillows with bone and blood, with some spattering on Mavis's face.

The baby started crying, and she knew she had to be quick. As Jonathan woke and half raised himself, Mavis took aim and shot him between the eyes. The blast sent him spiralling out of the bed.

He lay there on his back, his dead eyes staring at the ceiling.

With the baby screaming its head off, Mavis reloaded. Now she had to be quick. Mavis could hear her parents calling out. They must have heard the gunshots over the television. As she moved out onto the landing, her parents were coming up the stairs. Mavis levelled the rifle. They stopped halfway up in amazement.

She fired off two clear headshots. Her mother and

father were dead before they'd toppled back down to the bottom of the stairs.

Mavis had to arrange the grisly scene to look as though Caroline had lost control of her depression, killing them all and shooting herself through the mouth.

Returning to the bedroom, Mavis carefully wrapped Caroline's dead hands around the rifle, leaving as many of her sister's fingerprints on it as possible. And then she laid the shotgun on Caroline's blood-spattered nightdress, with the barrel pointing towards her face, and the thumb of her right hand still resting on the trigger.

She took a step back. It looked realistic enough, and the gunshot residue on the trigger hand would be an added confirmation. Satisfied, Mavis moved into the bathroom and took a shower.

Thankfully the baby had stopped crying. And then she carried out a thorough clean-up of the shower tiles and tray. After one last scan of the bedroom, she made her way to her own room to get dressed.

Holding a bin liner containing her bloodstained clothes, she carefully stepped over her parents' bodies to reach the front door. With a last-minute glance over her shoulder, she closed the door behind her, and pretended to wave and say goodbye, in full view of her waiting girlfriend. Mavis waved again to support her alibi, and then sped off in her girlfriend's car.

Returning home from the cinema, she practised her hysterical Triple Zero emergency call in the kitchen, many times over. 'Emergency! – Emergency!' she shouted. 'Oh

Jesus! They're all dead. Quick, get someone to the house. They've all been murdered.' Gulp – Sob. 'There's blood everywhere,' she blabbed.

Within seconds, the Sydney emergency operator had transferred Mavis to the local Force Control Room. In-between calming her down, they began to take details. Mavis explained she dare not stay in the house, in case whoever did it was still around. She told them she'd be waiting at the end of the farmhouse drive.

*

The killings were in the news for weeks. In the meantime, she stayed with her girlfriend until the farm was sold. But the big shock came at the reading of the will. Unbeknown to Mavis, her parents had taken out equity release on the farmhouse for a loan to finance Caroline's education. That meant after expenses and the costly funeral headstone that had been pre-ordered, Mavis was left with only a third of what she'd hoped for. The baby, just like Mavis herself, was taken into care and then fostered out to another family.

SIX

A Ménage à Trois

Later on, in 1976, as a twenty-eight-year-old, Mavis Bone met Henry Walker in a Sydney singles bar. Henry and Mavis married two years later.

*

And now in 1991, after thirteen years of marriage, they live in a semi-detached house, on the outskirts of Sydney, Australia.

However, life for forty-three-year-old Mavis Bone had become boring, and she had already met Charlotte. Charlotte was exciting and fun to be with. The lesbian sex was good with her. In fact the sex was far better than it had ever been with dull old Henry Walker. Of course, Henry never knew about Charlotte, or Mavis's preferences.

And he could be so annoying, as he was a man who

always planned carefully. He thought everything through one step at a time. In fact, Henry never made any choices, until he'd carefully worked out every possible option. It used to drive Mavis bonkers. It drove her almost as bonkers as his snoring. She joked with Charlotte that he'd probably have RIP SNORING on his gravestone. While adding, with a laugh, he'll probably even die snoring, with any luck.

Henry Walker at forty-four years old, hiding his bald spot with a comb-over, already had a pot belly. And being a diabetic, he wasn't in the best of health. While Mavis in her early forties was plump, with a double chin. When they had first met, Mavis had thought Henry was handsome and dashing. Henry had thought Mavis was sex on two legs.

The three-bed semi they lived in had views across Rushcutters Bay. And they could see the green slopes of Bay Park, which had first attracted them to the area.

However, most of the time these days, when they were at home together, they spent arguing. When they weren't arguing with each other, they argued with their neighbours. Henry had fallen out with all the neighbours they'd ever had. It was one of the many things about him that drove Mavis mad. She got mad at him several times a day, on most days.

Yesterday she had been mad at him for buying a television so big it took up half their living room. He was even madder at her for spending a fortune on a new oven. Their old one was quite all right, in his opinion.

Later that evening they had another row, because she

wanted to put down a new kitchen floor. He was happy with the one they had. There were years of life left in it, he told her. And then, during the night, they had another row. This time it was because of his snoring.

In the early days, Henry never used to snore. Now, almost every night, she would wake him with a nudge, to stop his snoring. Sometimes it worked, sometimes it didn't.

For Mavis, it was like sleeping with a sodding elephant or walrus, she'd joke with Charlotte. More and more often, she would have to go into the spare room, just to get some sleep. Mavis would drag herself out of their bed, wrap herself in a blanket, and crawl onto the hard single bed in there.

When Mavis first met Henry, he was doing a course in computers at Sydney Tech, while living with his widowed mother. Mavis was working as a dispatch operator for a taxi company, and lived on her own in a rented room. It was then that a girlfriend told Mavis that gay singles bars were a great place to meet up and have fun. And Mavis became a closet lesbian, unbeknown to Henry.

However, Henry had seemed a very suitable partner, if a little shy and clumsy on the dance floor. 'Two left feet, you've got!' Mavis had teased him, when he went over and chose her as his dance partner for the next set. At first sight, Henry himself had been thinking, *Great tits you've got, and a stonking pair of legs*, as he struggled to keep his stiffy from nudging into her.

Mavis thought he was funny, and sweet, and very handsome. He seemed to have a bit of a spark about him.

In her view, he was a man who would go places. She ignored the opinion of her gay friends, who thought Henry looked lazy and had greedy eyes. And then again, her friends were naturally biased against a straight-looking Joe. Whereas she couldn't afford to be that choosy, while living on her own on a single wage. Mavis was looking for long-term security, which in 1970s Australia wasn't often affordable amongst the painted-up lesbians on Sydney's gay pride marches.

Henry thought Mavis was the loveliest creature he had ever set eyes on. She looked like a pin-up girl. When he was a teenager, he used to stick photos of glamour girls on his bedroom wall and lust over them. Henry couldn't believe his luck when she agreed to go on a date with him.

On their wedding day, Mavis imagined that in ten years' time Henry would be a high-powered businessman. She thought they'd have four children, two boys and two girls. They would live in a grand house with a swimming pool. For his part, Henry imagined that in ten years' time Mavis would still be slim and gorgeous, and they would still be having wild sex twice a day. He thought kids would be nice, as long as they didn't interfere with their lives too much, especially their sex life!

*

In 1991, the idea of divorcing Henry, did not come to Mavis Bone straight away. She saw it as the only way out of a boring, unfaithful marriage. This was compounded by his philandering, regularly visiting the prostitutes at Sydney's poshest whorehouse, the Kitten Parlour. Mavis had found their business card in Henry's jacket pocket while taking some of his clothes to the dry cleaners.

In leaving Henry, there was one thing she wouldn't miss. That was his incessant snoring. Mavis considered that to be out of earshot from the fat snoring walrus she'd married would be heaven on earth.

And then something else had convinced her to make the decision to leave Henry. Mavis wondered if she was being paranoid, from seeing too many TV crime documentaries, but she had this feeling that Henry was planning to kill her.

Because of his past indiscretions, Mavis steamed open Henry's mail from time to time. One such intercepted letter contained a copy of their joint life insurance policy, which Henry had increased to the sum of one hundred thousand Australian dollars. She thought of confronting him, wondering how he could afford the premiums.

And then another bombshell from the postman fell onto the doormat. It was a loan agreement taken out by Henry, which would be more than enough to cover the life insurance costs.

From then on, Mavis increased her level of suspicion. Which was ironic, considering her enrolment in a private investigator course. Unbeknown to her husband, she was trying to achieve her lifelong ambition to become a private detective. The TV crime dramas she'd watched had planted the seeds. Crime and investigation fascinated her, and she devoured books on the subject.

Part of the mature student coursework was researching

what would make the perfect murder. With help from her books, she carefully covered the common mistakes murderers make, and the typical forensics that catch a killer.

*

Henry was a modest IT manager, they had been stuck in the same modest, boring house for thirteen years, and no children had come along. They lived alone with their ginger cat, Gregory. The cat didn't like either of them, and would walk past with its nose in the air.

Mavis did not like to face the real prospect that life might always be like this. They would both be unhappy. What kind of future would that be? They disagreed on just about everything. They even argued most nights on whether to have the bedroom window open or shut. Henry said he couldn't sleep in a room that was warm and stuffy. Mavis said she couldn't sleep in a room where the air was cold.

The worst thing of all for her was when they went to a restaurant. Going out on Saturday nights had long been a ritual for them, and Mavis dreaded those evenings more and more. Mavis always made sure they went with another couple, Ron and Phyllis. Sitting with them, at least they didn't bicker at each other. However, those evenings still always eventually turned into slanging matches between herself and Henry.

And so, over the years, their friends dropped away, all

except for Ron and Phyllis. At every restaurant, Henry would spend several long minutes reading the menu, and then ask the waiter to explain each item in detail. After that, he'd normally ask for something that was not listed. It was the same thing each time: prawn cocktail followed by steak and chips. That was all he really liked to eat. Even if they went for a Chinese, which Mavis and Phyllis were keen on, or an Indian, which Ron liked even more, Henry would still order his sodding prawn cocktail, followed by steak and chips. He would make racist remarks under his breath, if they couldn't do it. 'Got to have things you can't get at home!' he would say loudly. And then, with a wink at Ron, and nudging Phyllis with his elbow, Henry would add, 'Shame they don't have blow jobs on the menu, because I can't get one of those at home, either!'

Ron would guffaw and rub Phyllis's thigh under the table, and say, 'We don't have that problem, do we, love?' Phyllis would go bright red and say proudly, 'He's a randy sod, is my Ron!'

Mavis Bone would apologise to the waiter. She would have liked to add, *Sorry I'm here with this fat, balding, smug little man with his horrible comb-over, and his loud suit and nasty tie. He was actually thin and quite handsome when I married him!* Of course, she never dared. Instead, Mavis would hiss at her husband, 'Why can't you try something else for a change? Be bold for once!'

'Because that's what I like,' Henry would always reply. 'Why risk having something I won't like? I could be dead tomorrow.'

Oh God, yes please, Mavis would think to herself, more and more often.

It was the same for Henry with books and with television. He only ever read detective stories, and only ever watched detective shows. Sherlock Holmes was his favourite. He had read every Sherlock Holmes story several times, and seen every film and TV adaptation of his hero. His obsession with detective shows, and the workings of forensics, further increased her suspicions that Henry was planning to kill her.

Henry had strong views on everything, including driving. He would never talk and drive at the same time, because, as he would tell Mavis, over and over again, that was dangerous.

'Slow down!' she would tell him all the time when he drove.

'Shut up, woman!' he would snap back. 'How do you expect me to drive with you talking? That's what's dangerous!'

Henry smoked cigars at home, but for some reason he didn't consider smoking cigars to be dangerous. He would state, 'Cigarettes, yes, but not cigars!' He didn't worry when Mavis told him that cigars made his breath smell like a dragon's. In the early years, when they were in love, that had not mattered to her. She used to tell him then that he was a horny creature, and that she loved his smoky breath. In later years, it was worse on Sunday mornings when he hadn't shaved since Friday. She'd joke to her lesbian girlfriends, 'It was like making love to a fire-eating porcupine.'

As for Henry, none of the pretty girls in Sydney's Kitten Parlour ever complained about his breath. They were more than happy to give him all the blow jobs he could ever want. They'd tie his hands while being spanked, and tell him over and over that he was a naughty boy. After each visit to the Kitten Parlour, he would arrive home and crawl into bed beside a sleeping Mavis, who was putting on weight by the day; and, unbeknown to him, reading more and more perfect murder stories by the day.

Henry would think about the books on poisons he'd read, and go to sleep every night dreaming of a happy future. Henry's first job had been with a firm in Sydney that made paint for the car repair industry. Cyanide, a deadly poison, was one of the chemicals used in this process. One night, when he was working late, he'd stolen a bottle of cyanide. For years, Henry kept it hidden among the cans of weedkiller and other bits and pieces in his garden shed.

Recently, as he became more and more fed up with Mavis, he would sit in his shed and stare at that bottle. He would dream of using it on her. This was how the idea to murder his wife evolved, not over days, not over weeks, not even over months, but over a couple of years.

Their marriage had started to turn sour when Mavis failed to produce a child. They tried for some years, and that part of it at least had been fun. And then they started on a round of seeing doctors. The problem, they were told, was that Henry had a low sperm count, and Mavis had hostile mucus. Each blamed the other. Mavis taunted Henry that he wasn't really a man. She sneered that real men had dicks that worked properly. He taunted her back, saying real women did not need sixty-five million sperms, because one would be enough. They made love less and less often, until they finally stopped making love.

Henry looked for relief at the Kitten Parlour. Mavis had found thirty-seven-year-old curvy, tall, blonde Charlotte Elliot, her lesbian lover. When her lover wasn't around, she'd binge on chocolate and cream cakes. Sometimes she got drunk on the white wine she brought home from the supermarket where she worked.

The first clue Henry might have picked up about Mavis having a new lover in her life was her new hairstyle. At first, he didn't even notice when she changed her hair. Since she began putting on weight, he'd started looking at her less.

Sitting in front of the TV, beer can in hand, with the cat looking at him sourly from across the room, he was watching Miss Marple in *Murder at the Vicarage* when Mavis came in and sat down. She began reading one of the trashy romantic novels she liked. For a good half-hour, Henry thought there was something different about his wife's appearance, but he couldn't put his finger on it.

And then it clicked! Her long, dark brown hair, which she'd worn at the same length, and in the same style since their wedding thirteen years ago, had gone. Now it was cut short and dyed black in a mass of tiny curls. A, guardsman's busby at Buckingham Palace came to mind. Henry told her she looked butch. Mavis replied he was out of touch, and this was the modern fashion. The second clue, which Henry also missed, at least until he got the credit card statement at the end of the month, was the purchases of expensive silky underwear. Her private investigator course fees were thankfully hidden amongst her clothes expenses. Henry was blissfully unaware of these as well.

And then Mavis started buying all kinds of new clothes. He began spotting the items every month on their joint credit card statement. Or more correctly, his credit card statement, as it was all paid for with money from his IT manager's job. Her part-time one at the supermarket checkout till didn't pay a lot.

Henry moaned about her spending. Mavis lied that she had decided to do part-time work for charities, because she wanted to put something back into the world. And she needed to look smart for the meetings – she told him there were endless meetings, night after night. Doing good for the world, she told him. Charity work, helping deprived people.

When, in fact, Mavis was spending these evenings with Charlotte Elliot, her newfound lover. And Mavis was so in love. She couldn't wait to cuddle up to Charlotte at her flat, where they would share the strap-on and the double-ended dildo. She often wondered what stuffy old Henry would say if he saw them together. He'd probably have a heart attack.

However, it meant Mavis would stay out late more and more, and leave Henry with ready meals to stick into the microwave while he watched his detective shows. That suited him fine. What did not suit him fine were the bills. She was spending more than he earned. And he was having to dip into his savings. That was not his long-term plan at all. He had in mind something far better to do with his savings than pay for her new clothes.

Mavis had told him it was good for a couple to have separate interests. She patted his head lovingly, and told him he should enjoy his television shows, while she went out to help save the world. At first it all worked well, apart from her spending of course.

Henry's current job was the IT manager at Norman Mantle & Sons, the ninth-largest makers of egg boxes in Australia. Now that Mavis was busy in the evenings, he could leave the office and go to Kelly's bar for a couple of leisurely pints of Foster's. He would step outside with the other smokers, puffing and chatting away to his heart's content.

Twice a week, when he was drunk enough not to feel shy, he would pop along to the Kitten Parlour, just off Silkwood Street. And then, after a bit of rumpy-pumpy, he would head contentedly home.

While waiting for his ready meal and the ping of the microwave, he would check his blood-sugar level, and give himself his evening jab of insulin. Henry would watch a re-run of *Morse*, or a *Poirot*, and feel content.

There was one special girl at the Kitten Parlour he was growing sweet on. She was Polish, and her name was Christine. She had a tangle of blonde hair and a slender body. She told him she had run away to Sydney to escape from her boyfriend, Ricky, who beat her up.

In the tiny boudoir, with the pink bedspread and the

price list on the wall, detailing hand jobs, blow jobs, full sex, with kissing extra, porno movies played on the little square television.

While Henry lay next to her, after their ten minutes of banging away, he listened with a sympathetic ear to Christine's tales of woe. He told Christine he'd like to help her. She told Henry she liked him. He made her feel safe, and she liked the way he was so manly. That made Henry feel good. Mavis never told him he was manly. On the contrary, he knew Mavis rated him as a wet haddock.

Henry wanted to give Christine more money to help her start a new life in Sydney. He wanted to keep her safe from her bully boyfriend, Ricky. He planned a new life for Christine, with him. Before Christine started on each blow job, she told him that a new life with him would be her idea of paradise.

On his Kitten Parlour visits, Henry started giving Christine bigger and bigger tips, a habit that was making his money worries even worse. He was already stretched to keep up the mortgage payments on the house. His overdraft was going up, because of the credit card bills and the housekeeping money Mavis demanded. She was spending so much these days on sexy underwear and new clothes, including a fancy hairdresser.

It had been all right until recently, because his bank manager had been helpful to him. He'd been particularly helpful ever since Henry had bumped into him one day in the Kitten Parlour. Now he'd left the bank to move to another branch, and the new manager had told him, sorry, there was no more money, due to the credit crunch. Henry pondered over his choices, one of which would involve fewer visits to the Kitten Parlour and no more big tips for Christine. The alternative was to stop Mavis spending his money.

It was a no-brainer. He cancelled their joint credit card without telling her. That night, Mavis came home and shouted at him, saying the card had been declined and she had never been so embarrassed in her life. She called him a big fat lazy turd. She told him her friends had been right about him looking shifty, and she should have listened to them!

Henry ignored her ranting. He was watching Agatha Christie's *Sparkling Cyanide* on the television. He wondered what it would be like to give Mavis a glass of cyanide. To watch her collapse and die on the floor in agony, the same way the actress on TV was doing right now.

Little did he know that Mavis was thinking exactly the same about him?

Mavis already knew that her secret lesbian lover, Charlotte Elliot, was in a platonic live-in relationship with a girlfriend called Debbi, and she wanted to finish it.

Charlotte was a taxi driver, and so her girlfriend never knew where she was. That was just as well, because much of the time these past months Charlotte had been in bed, screwing Mavis, at Mavis's house, while Henry was at work. They screwed during the day, and sometimes at night, taking time off to fit in their busy work schedules.

Charlotte made Mavis feel young again. She couldn't

get enough of her, and nor could *she* get enough of Mavis. Charlotte liked her plump body, and she liked her big boobs, telling Mavis she was just ripe, like a juicy bunch of grapes.

As her love for Charlotte grew, Mavis began to hate weekends more and more, especially Sundays. She knew Charlotte was at home with Debbi, while she was stuck at home with boring Henry. She couldn't find a way to make the weekends pass faster.

These past couple of years, Henry had hated Sundays every bit as much as Mavis did, because it meant he couldn't see Christine. He would spend some of the day pottering around in the garden, or with his vegetables in the greenhouse. He would sit in his shed, staring at his dusty bottle of cyanide, killing time. In his mind, he was killing Mavis. For him, the only good thing about Sundays was that he had Monday to look forward to, which was a blow job day.

On this particular Monday morning in February, Henry woke up as usual at half past six. Mavis was still asleep, as he showered and shaved, humming the *Dam Busters* tune to himself. The theme from the old war film was his favourite piece of music, and he always hummed it when he was in a good mood. On Monday mornings, these days, he was always in a good mood. He carefully applied some roll-on under his armpits, and sprayed cologne all over his flabby white body. He adjusted his comb-over, put on fresh underpants, and wore his best suit and smartest tie. He knew that, for some reason, the *Dam Busters* tune always annoyed Mavis, more than any other tune. This made him hum it even more loudly as he brought her a cup of tea in bed. And then he switched on the portable television. Henry told her, in no uncertain terms, she would have to cut down. No more spending. They had to make ends meet. He left for work still humming, before Mavis was awake enough to argue back.

SEVEN

Prussian Blue

The Norman Mantle & Sons egg box factory was a two-storey building on an industrial estate in the north of Sydney. Henry greeted a few of his colleagues when he arrived, and then poured a coffee and helped himself to a biscuit from a packet that had been left out. And then he trotted along happily to his little office. Alone in there, quietly and without Mavis's knowledge, he used some of the last of his savings to buy a life insurance policy for her. It would produce a nice cash lump sum on her death. Enough to pay off his debts, with plenty left over for a new life. A new life with Christine!

Although Henry's business card read IT Manager, that was a grander title than the job deserved. He was the costings clerk and the payroll clerk. He produced the monthly accounts. Much of the time, he didn't actually have anything to do at all. Most of the egg box production was done by machines. Most of the people who worked for the company were there to look after the machines. No one noticed that he had plenty of spare time in his job. Because Henry was always careful to look busy. He was spending most of his days reading about case histories of fraud on life insurance companies. It quickly became clear to Henry that life insurance companies were not stupid.

If a husband took out a big policy on his wife, and his wife died a few weeks later, the insurance company would investigate. Most people who had tried that kind of scam ended up on trial for murder. Henry realised it would be smart to wait, however hard that might be. He would have to be patient. He decided that he would wait a year before killing Mavis.

Christine would have to be patient as well. The big plus was that it would give him plenty of time to think of a plan. One whole year to plan the perfect murder.

So every day, after he'd dealt with any urgent business to do with his job, Henry would read up on perfect murder stories in crime magazines, as well as books on poisons, and detecting poisons. Everything he wanted was right there. He made careful notes, building up a file. Finally, he had a long list of rules that needed to be kept to commit a perfect murder.

There were fifty-two rules in all. These were some of them: Rule One: Don't have a criminal record. Rule Two: Don't have a motive that is clear for all to see. Rule Three: Plan carefully and leave no tracks. Rule Four: Bloodstains are hard to remove completely, so avoid creating them.

Rule Five: Most poisons can be found in post-mortems and autopsies, so avoid using them. Rule Six: Suffocation with a plastic bag is clean and quick, and leaves no mess. Rule Seven: Get rid of the body, because, no body, no proof. Rule Eight: Don't brag or boast to anyone, how you did it. Not ever! Rule Nine: No pangs of conscience or regret, so be ready to deny anything. Rule Ten: Act as if you are missing her. Rule Eleven: Don't appear with your new lover too quickly, after the murder.

Henry was eagerly looking forward to ticking each box when the time came. The plan was taking shape nicely inside his head. He began to write it down, bit by bit by bit. Each time he read it over, he hummed proudly to himself. It was a good plan. A genius plan. He named it Plan A.

And then, one day, without any warning, his boss came into his office. His boss was the son of the founder of the Norman Mantle & Sons egg-box-making factory. Rodney Mantle was a big, unpleasant tosser, who drove a gold-coloured Porsche. According to office gossip, he was screwing his secretary. Mantle told Henry that he was sorry, but as sales were down, and costs were up, and savings had to be found, Henry would have to be made redundant. He would get severance pay, based on the time he had worked for the company. He would get one and a half weeks' pay for each of the thirteen years he had served. That worked out at around five months' pay.

Henry was so shocked that after work he drank five pints and four whisky chasers at his Sydney local, *The Font and Firkin*. He had intended to keep the news a secret from

Mavis, but, arriving home blind drunk, he blurted it out. That night, Mavis screamed at him in rage, and told him how useless he was.

At his desk the next morning, Henry had a bad hangover. He worked out how many visits to the Kitten Parlour he could make with five months' pay and the remains of his savings. He realised he could make more visits, and give bigger tips to Christine, if he didn't have to pay housekeeping money to Mavis.

To save his money, Mavis would have to be removed more quickly than he had planned. There was no option. There simply was not enough time for Plan A. He would have to revert to his unfinished Plan B. But that was the problem: he didn't yet have a complete Plan B.

But Mavis did.

The solution came to Henry that night. It just so happened that his creativity seemed to blossom during the nights. And suddenly he was woken at about 2am by Mavis hitting him on the chest and hissing, 'Stop snoring!'

At 4am Mavis woke him again, climbing out of bed saying, 'Good God, Henry, you're worse than ever! What do you keep up your nose? Trumpets?'

Henry mumbled a sleepy apology. He heard her leave the room and slam the bedroom door behind her. And then he heard the spare-bedroom door slam. All of a sudden, he was wide awake with excitement. He had an idea. Mavis was always moaning about the little spare room where she went to sleep when his snoring kept her awake at night. It was grotty, she said, and she was right. The walls were the colour of sludge, and the thin curtains had moth holes in them. It was the one room they had never bothered to decorate after they bought the house. To begin with, they had planned it to be their first child's bedroom. But they'd had no children. So it still had the old single bed, which the previous owners of the house had left behind. It was a sad little room. Every few weeks, Mavis would have a go at Henry about it, telling him it was high time to decorate the room. She said he should make it look nice in case they ever had an overnight guest. He could at least make it nice for her to sleep in, when she couldn't stay in their room because of his snoring. This feud had been going on for years and years.

Now he thought he had the answer to it. The answer to solve two problems at once! Make the room nice for Mavis, and fulfil his Plan A after all!

Unable to sleep any more, he put on his dressing gown and went into the kitchen, quietly, not wanting to wake Mavis. He made himself a cup of tea. He was so excited, he went up to his den, and found his book on cyanide poison. Henry steadily narrowed down his search to cyanide vapour, and then cyanide gas. He read every word, greedily lapping it all up. The more he read, the more excited he became. Some things he read over several times, because it was better to remember things, rather than to write them down. That was Rule Three: Plan carefully and leave no tracks.

This is what he remembered. The extent of poisoning caused by cyanide depends on the amount of cyanide a person is exposed to. Breathing cyanide gas causes the most harm. Cyanide gas is most dangerous in enclosed places, where the gas will be trapped. To some people, cyanide smells like almonds. Cyanide is present in some paints, such as Prussian blue. Henry had to smile. Prussian blue had long been one of Mavis's favourite colours.

Mavis wondered what had come over Henry. That weekend, he didn't watch his detective shows or potter around in his shed or his greenhouse. He spent the whole of Saturday and Sunday in the spare bedroom. He was busily decorating it for her.

'For you, my angel!' he told her. 'You're quite right. This room has been in an awful state, far too long. Now I'm going to make it beautiful for you.'

Henry wouldn't let her in while he was at work. He wanted to surprise Mavis. He told her she couldn't go in until it was finished.

From time to time, he came out coughing and spluttering. He had a breathing mask, pushed up onto his forehead, while he wore a white, hooded, paint-spattered boiler suit. His appearance reminded Mavis of the forensic scene of crime officers in a television murder documentary. 'It's your favourite colour!' he told her.

Mavis exclaimed, 'What, Prussian blue?'

Henry beamed at her. 'How did you guess? Have you peeped?'

She simply pointed at him. 'It's splashed all over you!' she said with a scowl.

'I'm putting up new blinds too,' he told her.

'They'll probably fall down,' she scoffed. 'Everything else you put up usually falls down after a while.' *Just like your tiny weeny dick*, she nearly added.

Henry did not react to her rudeness. It no longer mattered. After a few nights sleeping in the spare room with the windows shut, she wouldn't be saying anything rude to him ever again.

They would find the cyanide in her at the post-mortem, of course. But the makers of the paint would be blamed. They would be in trouble for making a rogue batch of Prussian blue, with too much cyanide in it. The cyanide he'd added.

On Sunday night, when he'd finished, he left the spare-bedroom window wide open. He told Mavis it was to let the paint dry. She would be able to start using the bedroom from Monday night onwards – whenever he snored, he joked. And Henry was planning to snore tomorrow night! He would snore like he'd never snored before.

Mavis watched Henry drive off to work the next day in his usual cheery Monday morning mood. He was even more cheery than usual, she thought, despite the fact that this was the start of his last week at work. She had too much on her mind to dwell on this. And so she busied herself with the household chores. Later it would be time to catch the bus for her afternoon shift at the supermarket. She needed to put on a good show of normality, and so she gathered all of Henry's dirty underwear from the laundry basket to do a wash. She was a little surprised that his boiler suit was not in there. She hunted everywhere, wondering where he might have left it. However, she still couldn't find it.

Never mind, she thought, with a wicked smile. With *her* plan, he wouldn't need it again. Not where he was going. Every human being has a weak spot. Henry's was his diabetes. Mavis knew that, give him too much sugar and he would fall sound asleep. And then he would snore like an elephant, keeping her awake all night. Her plan was simple. All she needed to do was swap the insulin in his needle for sugar, and he would go into a deep sleep. A very deep sleep. And then she would inject some more sugar, until he was still, and stopped snoring. Still enough until he stopped breathing, she hoped. Mavis had it planned, to sweet perfection.

She told Charlotte her plan, and being so in love with each other, they knew deep down they would spend their whole lives together after Henry's death.

Charlotte added, 'You know, Mavis, if we're going to live together, we should take out some life insurance, like most couples do. Especially if we move into my flat together. Perhaps we could tie in the life insurance with a joint mortgage protection policy on my flat.

'It would make sense, God forbid, if anything should happen to either of us. Although it's too horrible to think about, at least the surviving one of us wouldn't be lumbered with a whopping mortgage to pay off. And saying that, we should also see a solicitor to make a will each, and make each other the beneficiary, like couples do.'

Mavis agreed with her. 'You're right, Charl.'

On this Monday evening of his last week at work, Henry arrived home and opened the front door with his latch key. He was surprised by what he found. Reclining on the sofa, in the lounge, was Mavis, stark naked except for a black lace bra and matching thong. She reeked of perfume.

Henry looked astonished. 'Aren't you cold?' he said.

Mavis replied, 'I thought you might like a blow job, my darling husband.'

He mulled it over, and then added, 'Actually, not really.' Henry did not add that he'd just had one at the Kitten Parlour. 'I think I'd prefer a beer. You look cold. You've got goose pimples.'

'We can warm each other up, my darling,' she replied.

'I'm warm enough,' he said. 'But I'm worried about you.'

Mavis brushed up sexily against him, and pressed her fingers against his crotch. 'Let's go to bed, my angel,' she said.

Looking at his watch, he answered, 'Thanks, but *Poirot*'s on at nine o'clock.'

Mavis rolled her eyes and said, 'We can record it.'

He replied, 'I'd rather watch it now.'

She kissed him. 'Tell me, my angel, if you were to be hanged in the morning, what would your last meal be?'

Henry didn't have to think, and answered immediately, 'Prawn cocktail, rib-eye steak, mushrooms, tomatoes, chips and peas. Followed by hot chocolate pudding with hot chocolate sauce. Why?' he asked.

'Well, that's a coincidence!' Mavis said. 'Guess what's for supper?'

He looked at her, astonished, 'Don't tell me you have all that?'

She said, 'For my darling Henry, nothing less would be good enough!' Mavis thought the hot chocolate pudding with hot chocolate sauce would mask the extra amount of sugar she'd added. Every little bit helps!

Henry wondered if she'd been drinking, or perhaps taking drugs. Or perhaps she had a motive? She wanted a car of her own, instead of having to share his? *In your dreams!* he thought.

Soon after finishing the meal, Henry fell asleep on the sofa, with Poirot busily solving a crime in front of him. Mavis texted Charlotte, as planned.

Twenty minutes later, Charlotte arrived at the front door. They kissed and embraced, but Mavis saw the frown and asked, 'What's up?'

'There's a problem,' Charlotte said. 'I've just been watching that *Blue Heelers*.'

'I like those Crime Scene Investigation episodes,' Mavis added. She liked it because Henry didn't. It was too modern for his taste.

'Well, you wouldn't have liked this one tonight,' Charlotte explained. 'It was about diabetics.'

Mavis was curious. 'Tell me about it.'

'Several diabetics had been murdered by this serial killer, who injected them with a sugar overdose. In some cases he gave them too much sugar, and was caught because they have new forensic ways of testing. We can't risk it! Mavis. We're going to have to just kill him, and then get rid of the body. Make out he'd run off somewhere. Clear out his belongings. Bury him somewhere remote, with his clothes and suitcases.'

'No!' Mavis said. 'That's not the plan! We agreed I would call the doctor in the morning, after we found him in a blood-sugar coma, nice and cold. That's the plan.'

'It doesn't work any more,' Charlotte replied. 'They'll know he's had a massive sugar overdose.'

'I could tell them he's been depressed since losing his job. I could forge a suicide note.'

'It's too dangerous.'

'No one will know!' Mavis replied. 'How will they know?'

Charlotte rolled her eyes. 'Handwriting experts!' She looked down at Henry, and was startled to see his eyes struggling to open. Charlotte hastily stepped back, out of sight.

'Doing it your way, where would we put the body?' Mavis asked.

'Did you say something about a blow job?' a bleary-eyed Henry slurred out.

'A blow job, my darling husband? Coming up!' Mavis said. 'Just wait two minutes for the blow job of your life, my darling!' She hurried into the kitchen and pulled on her yellow rubber gloves. And then Mavis dashed into the connecting garage, where Henry's tools were hanging neatly from their hooks. She selected a medium-weight claw hammer, and hurried back into the lounge. Holding the hammer behind her back, Mavis said, 'Would you like your blow job now, my darling?'

Henry nodded. 'Yerrrr.'

Mavis handed the hammer to Charlotte. And then Charlotte brought the hammer down hard on the side of Henry's forehead. She'd never hit anyone on the side of the forehead with a claw hammer before, so she didn't know what to expect.

Seeing Henry with his skull cracked open, like a broken coconut, blood spurting in all directions, with his eyeballs bulging, unseeing from their sockets, terrified Charlotte. His tongue had shot out and stayed out. An orange and grey goo of brain matter leaked through his shattered temple.

Charlotte's stomach heaved, and shockwaves pulsed through her. She took one more look at him, ran into the kitchen and threw up in the sink. She went back, and peered at him again.

Charlotte stood still, her eyes wide open, her mouth open even more. 'Bloody hell,' she gasped. 'What have I done? I think he's brown bread.'

'I think you're right, Charl,' said Mavis. 'He looks fuckin' carked.'

There was hair and blood on the end of the hammer. Charlotte quickly rinsed it in the sink.

Mavis now realised she had a dead husband on her hands. A dead husband who was leaking blood and brains onto the sofa. Leaking forensic evidence. Charlotte put the hammer down on the floor and started shaking wildly, as she began to fully realise just what she had done.

Mavis looked at Charlotte in desperation. She was staring at Henry, wide-eyed. His eyeballs still bulged from their sockets, while his tongue stuck out like a slaughtered cow.

Shaking her head from side to side, Mavis said, 'Oh God! Oh Jesus!' And then she looked at Charlotte. 'Why – why did you have to hit him so hard?'

Charlotte was annoyed. 'You'd have hit him softer, would you? It's what we agreed, Mavis.' After some moments, she calmed down. 'This is probably not the time for an argument.'

EIGHT

Missing Persons

In the utility room off the kitchen, Mavis had a big chest freezer squeezed in next to the washing machine and tumble dryer. Henry had got angry when she'd bought the freezer. He'd told her it was a waste of money, and where the hell were they going to put it?

Mavis had replied it would pay for itself, because of all the bulk-buying supermarket discount offers.

And now she stood over it, with the lid open and the icy vapour rising. Mavis started pulling out all those bargains she had been piling into it for the past year. Out came a packet of lamb cutlets with a special offer sticker. And then came a big bag of frozen peas, and a huge tub of Streets vanilla ice cream. There were three chocolate cheesecakes, which she'd been planning to eat by herself. She'd reasoned they were too good to share with Henry!

Mavis handed each item to Charlotte, who placed them

on the floor. Every few moments, Mavis would peer out of the window. They had drawn the curtains and blinds on all the other windows, just in case anyone happened to look in.

However, the blind on this window had fallen down months ago. Lazy Henry had never bothered to put it back up again. She could see the lights of the houses in the valley below, and the dark outline of the hills in the distance. She could see the stars and the rising moon. It was almost a full moon. In the light from it, she could see the little greenhouse in the garden. She thought for a moment about the tomatoes Henry had planted. He was never going to see them, or eat them. Henry wasn't even going to see daylight ever again.

For a moment, just for a tiny moment, Mavis had a choking feeling in her throat. *Henry wasn't so bad*, she thought to herself. *Not really so bad, was he? He had his good points, didn't he?*

Charlotte's voice cut harshly through her thoughts. 'Come on, keep it coming, nearly done are we?'

Mavis stooped over and reached down to the bottom of the freezer for a frozen sponge cake in its box. And then she pulled out some Special Reduction pork chops.

'Okay, Charl, that's it.' Mavis peered in nervously, all her thoughts in turmoil. What if he did not fit?

Five minutes later, Mavis and Charlotte had removed all of Henry's clothes. They also took off his watch and wedding ring. 'No point letting anything go to waste or be traceable,' Mavis said. And then they struggled to carry his fat, blubbery body, through the kitchen and into the utility room. They left a trail of blood spots and brain-fluid droplets on their way.

It was lucky Charlotte was so strong, because Mavis felt she had no strength left in her. With some pushing and shoving, they lifted Henry up over the lip of the freezer. And then, to her relief, he slid down easily to the bottom. She just needed to arrange his arms and legs so they would not obstruct the lid. All the time, Mavis avoided looking at his bulging eyes. In fact, she avoided looking at any part of him. She couldn't help glimpsing his tiny penis, though. *That's the bit of you I'll be missing least of all*, she thought. And then she began to pile the frozen foods back on top of him.

'Hope he doesn't wake up feeling hungry,' Charlotte said, as they finally slammed the lid down.

Mavis scoffed. 'With those bulging eyes, he's as brown bread as they get.'

*

They spent the rest of the evening cleaning. They scrubbed the downstairs carpets and kitchen floor. They had to scrub the living room walls as well, because they found spots of blood and brain spatter. There were more on the ceiling and on one of the lampshades. There was even a spot of blood on the television screen. 'Hope Poirot doesn't notice this one,' Charlotte joked, wiping the tiny fleck off.

Mavis did not smile. She was now totally exhausted

from cleaning, and shaking from too much coffee. Charlotte told her she had to go home, and she would be back first thing in the morning.

Mavis stayed downstairs for a long time. She stared at the dents in the armchair cushions, where Henry had been sitting at the time Charlotte had hit him. The house was silent. The air felt heavy, as if it was pushing down on her. She could hear the occasional tick of the freezer. But she didn't dare lift the lid, certainly not tonight while it was dark. just to check Henry was really in there. Or if it had all been a horrible nightmare.

It was nearly 2am as Mavis went upstairs. The bathroom smelled of Henry's colognes and aftershaves. The bedroom smelled of him as well, but not so strongly. There were a couple of strands of his hair in the basin. That was another thing that annoyed her about him. He was always leaving hairs in the basin, the lazy bugger. He could never be bothered to clean up. Mavis scooped them up with a tissue. She thought with some small joy, as she dropped the tissue into the pedal bin, it was the last time she'd have to do that.

The lid shut with a loud clang that startled her. *God, I'm jumpy*, she thought. *Hardly surprising*.

She drew the bathroom curtain, and did the same with the bedroom curtains. She hoped none of the nosy neighbours were looking out of their windows. They might think it was odd she was closing the bedroom curtains at this hour. She and Henry were normally in bed by eleven.

Mavis took off all her clothes and put them in a black bin liner, as Charlotte had instructed. She was going to take them to the municipal tip in the morning, along with Henry's clothes. The hammer she used was put into the bottom tray of Henry's toolbox, which was stored in the garage.

After pulling on her nightdress, she swallowed two aspirins. And then she removed Henry's striped pyjamas from his side of the bed, and put them on the floor.

Mavis climbed into the empty bed, which smelt of Henry, and then switched the light off. She immediately switched it back on again. The darkness scared her. There was so much buzzing in her head, with a list of things worked out that she had to do tomorrow with Charlotte.

Mavis stared at the blank portable television screen on the shelf, just beyond the end of the bed. She looked at Henry's brown leather slippers on the floor, and at the Sherlock Holmes novel on his bedside table. She listened to the silence of the night. It seemed so loud. She heard the distant wail of a siren from a police car, or from an ambulance, or perhaps a fire engine.

And then the piercing screech of two cats fighting, knowing one of them was probably her Gregory. Mavis watched her bedside clock, displaying 2:59am. Then 3:00. Then 3:01. She couldn't sleep. And then she turned on the bedside portable television. There was a medium she recognised, talking to a studio audience. 'I have someone with me called Mary,' he said. 'Is there anyone here who has recently lost someone called Mary?'

Normally, Mavis liked these shows. But tonight it made her uneasy. She switched channels and saw two young men and a fat blonde girl, sitting in a lounge, smoking. She listened to their rubbish chatter for some minutes, and then switched channels again. An old black and white movie with Laurel and Hardy was playing. Mavis hastily switched channels once more, and then looked at the clock again.

She needed to pee. All that damned coffee! Getting out of bed, she padded out of the room and into the bathroom. Mavis went to the basin to rinse her hands, and then froze. Two long, black strands of Henry's hair were lying there.

*

'You imagined it!' Charlotte said when she came round at nine o'clock in the morning.

'No, Charl, I didn't,' Mavis said, her hands shaking so much she could hardly open the tin of cat food. 'I didn't imagine it!'

'Of course you did. Your nerves are all shot to hell!'

Mavis's eyes felt raw from lack of sleep. 'I didn't imagine it! I looked in the pedal bin, and the hairs I took out were still there in the tissue.' She scraped the stinky cat food out of the tin into Gregory's bowl and put it on the floor. As usual, the cat glared at the bowl, and then at her, as if suspecting poison.

'You must have missed them, love,' Charlotte said. 'We were both tired!' She put her arms around Mavis and hugged her tightly, and then nuzzled her ear. 'Let's go to bed. I'm feeling really horny.'

Mavis, despite her exhaustion, was feeling randy as well. She eyed Charlotte in the tight-fitting summer shorts that barely covered the legal minimum of her sturdy, tattooed legs and arse. Her tissue-thin blouse was tied in a knot just below her chubby cupcake tits.

Mavis snaked her arm around Charlotte's narrow waist, and then guided her to the bedroom. They kissed. She cupped her ample backside in both hands and then lifted Charlotte onto the bed.

Mavis unscrewed the sterling silver snuff necklace that she wore, and cautiously tapped out the cocaine powder into the attached silver spoon. She made two lines on the glass of her bedside table. Charlotte acknowledged a line, and gave two hefty sniffs. She relaxed and watched Mavis do the same to the other line.

And that's when Mavis seized her chance. In a matter of breathless seconds she had Charlotte bent over the bedside table, with those tiny shorts around her ankles. Mavis knelt down behind her, hungry but wanting to enjoy the scenery. In that moment, her arse was Mavis's world. Voluptuous, pear-shaped cheeks that begged to be slapped. Charlotte's full pink lips, peeking out between them, begged for something else, and Mavis was happy to oblige.

Mavis spread them wide and buried her face, tongue stretching to tease her fat clit that smelt of raw sugar and fresh girl sweat. Charlotte let out a gasp that swiftly melted into a happy purr, as Mavis slid her tongue slowly backwards and forwards, through slick folds of pink, salty, hairless flesh. She started working her clit in earnest with her middle finger, and then slid a thumb into Charlotte's pussy.

Homing in on a g-spot using her tongue, while circling Charlotte's back door at the same time, Mavis found her rhythm. She could feel Charlotte build up to an orgasm, her strong meaty thighs starting to tense up as she wrapped her legs around Mavis's waist and pulled her in closer. From there she went from kittenish sighs to deep throaty grunts, and finished with a gurgled moan.

Mavis knew from experience that this was far from the end of the show. They were both getting warmed up and she was ready to go the distance. Mavis glanced at her desk drawer. In the Mickey Spillane hard-boiled pulp novels she used to read as a teenager, Mike Hammer always kept a snub-nose and holster in his desk drawer. Mavis kept a strap-on in hers, just for emergencies.

Taking off her trouser suit and panties, she handed Charlotte the strap-on tackle. She fixed it around her hips and then rolled an offered condom down the length of the silicone shaft. Charlotte finished off with a middle finger coating of Vaseline.

As Mavis bent over the desk, she looked over her shoulder at Charlotte with wide eyes and flushed cheeks. Charlotte started slowly, with deliberate thrusts. Mavis bucked with her own demanding rhythm, daring her to keep up.

Not about to be outdone, Charlotte gripped Mavis's plush, fleshy arse, and went at her double time. Mavis responded by jacking one leg high onto the bedside table, to allow easy entry. Sweat was everywhere, running into her eyes and down between her tits, pooling in the hollow between her shoulder blades.

Charlotte started off teasing with gentle side-to-side rhythm, while Mavis climaxed and yelled, 'Fuck me, cowboy!'

With both of them completely worn out after their juices had been spent, they kissed and hugged for a while. And then, tired out, they decided to take a nap.

Looking at her watch, Mavis reminded her, 'We can't sleep too long, Charl. Remember, I've got to go to the police and report Henry missing, as we agreed. I have to show my face at work, to support our alibi. Like you said, we have to act normal.'

Half an hour later, Mavis drove to Sydney police station on Day Street, using Henry's yellow Toyota Corolla. She parked at a meter, and went in through the front door. There was a second door marked IN, with a short queue on the far side of it. She joined the queue, and as she waited, she read some of the notices on the walls. One was headed MISSING PERSONS. There were several photographs, close-ups of faces, with the same wording at the bottom of each one: IF YOU HAVE SEEN THIS PERSON PLEASE CONTACT YOUR NEAREST POLICE STATION.

Mavis didn't recognise any of them. She read another notice, warning about alcohol abuse, and another about drugs. Finally, she reached the front desk. A policewoman in her thirties, wearing a white shirt and black tie, asked if she could help. Mavis was glad the woman couldn't see her trembling knees. 'I want to report a missing person,' Mavis said.

'All right,' the woman responded. 'Can you give me some details?'

'It's Henry, my husband. He didn't come home last night. I'm worried because this is very unusual for him. He has never in his life not come home in the evening after work.' Mavis felt her face burning. She felt hot and confused. 'He doesn't ... you know ... I mean ... he always does ... come home ... my husband ...' There was a brief silence. Suddenly, in this silence, all Mavis could think about were the two hairs in the washbasin.

'I see,' the policewoman said. 'And you are?' She picked up a pen.

'His wife,' Mavis said, dumbly, her voice trembling. She could feel sweat trickling down her neck.

'Your name?' the woman said patiently.

'Yes, yes. I'm Mrs Walker.'

The policewoman wrote it down. 'If you could step aside and wait for a moment, I'll get an officer to come and take down some details.'

The woman went over to the phone. One of her colleagues attended to the next person in the queue behind Mavis, she was a young girl looking spaced out because she'd been mugged and had her mobile phone stolen.

Mavis took some deep breaths, trying to calm down. She watched several more people in turn step up to the counter. But she wasn't listening to them. She was trying to rehearse what Charlotte had told her to say.

'Mrs Walker?' Mavis turned at the sound of her name, and saw a tubby young policewoman with short fair hair. She was wearing a black uniform waistcoat over a white shirt and black trousers. The officer was peering at the people in the room.

Mavis raised a hand. 'Yes, that's me.'

The officer had a radio sticking out of her breast pocket. A badge on one side of her chest bore a police crest with the words SYDNEY CITY POLICE AREA COMMAND.

'Would you come this way, please?' she said. Mavis followed her through the door, along a corridor into a cramped, windowless room. There, a metal table and chairs were set out. 'I'm Constable Watts,' she said politely.

'Nice to meet you,' Mavis replied. She was now drenched in sweat, hoping it wasn't noticeable.

The police officer asked her to sit down. She opened a large notebook with a printed form on it. 'Your husband is missing, is that right, Mrs Walker?'

Mavis nodded.

Constable Watts picked up a biro. 'Right, let's start with his name.'

'Henry Walker,' Mavis said.

The officer wrote this down, very slowly. 'And his age, Mrs Walker?'

'Forty-four.'

'And you're worried because he didn't come home last night, is that correct?'

Mavis nodded. She didn't like the way the officer was looking at her, studying her face intently. It felt as if she was looking right through her. 'It's very unusual,' Mavis said. 'I mean, more than unusual, if you see what I mean?'

The officer frowned and said abruptly, 'I'm afraid I don't.'

Mavis explained, 'Henry's never done this before. Not come home. Not ever in all the time we've been married.'

'Which is how long?' the officer asked.

'Thirteen and a half years,' Mavis replied. She could have added, three weeks, four days, sixteen hours and seven minutes too long.

'And you say he didn't take his car. Which makes our job harder, without a number plate to trace.'

Mavis thought, *That's how we planned it, mate.*

For the next quarter of an hour, Mavis felt like she was on trial. The officer fired one question after another at her, including whether Mavis had contacted any of their friends.

'Yes, Ron and Phyllis,' replied Mavis. 'But they'd not seen or heard from him.'

'What about Henry's relatives?'

'All he had was a sister, in Melbourne,' Mavis said. 'I telephoned her yesterday,' she lied. 'But again, she hadn't seen or heard from him in ages.'

The officer wrote each answer down, painfully slowly.

Mavis did her best to talk about Henry in a way she thought any loving wife would talk about her husband. He was the perfect man in every way. She adored him. And he adored her.

'We'd never spent a single day apart in all the years of

being married,' she informed the officer. 'Of course, we had our ups and downs, like any other couple.'

And then Mavis told the officer, 'Mind you, he was feeling very low after being made redundant. Very, very low. I'd never seen him that low before.' She reminded PC Watts again, 'But he had never, ever, not come home.'

The police constable was kind and full of sympathy. 'Have you tried phoning his mobile?'

Mavis went white for an instant. She felt her stomach churn like a cement mixer. The officer went in and out of focus. Mavis thought, *That stupid fool, Charlotte! Why the hell didn't she tell me to do that? How could I have been so stupid not to have thought of it?* 'Oh yes,' she said. 'I try all the time. I keep phoning and phoning him.'

'Are you worried about the effect of losing his job might have had on him, and on his pride?' PC Watts enquired.

'He's a proud man,' Mavis said. She thought that was better than saying he was an arrogant tosser.

'Do you have a photograph of him we could circulate?' PC Watts asked.

'I could find one,' Mavis said.

'That would be very helpful.'

'I'll drop one in.'

'Look,' the officer said, 'I know this might be difficult for you, but is it possible that Henry is having an affair?'

Mavis shook her head. 'No. He loves me. We are very close. We are very, very close.'

'So, you are worried about his state of mind after losing his job?'

Mavis pulled a handkerchief and tearfully sniffled into it. 'I'm very worried,' she said. 'Henry is such a proud man. He came home in tears and sobbed his heart out, the day he heard the news.' That was a big fib, of course. He'd come home blind drunk, telling her he'd just told his boss where to stick his job! Charlotte had told her to focus on this. She'd told her to try to make the police think he might have killed himself.

'Are you worried that he might have killed himself, Mrs Walker?'

'Yes I am,' Mavis said, breaking down in tears, sobbing into her wet hanky.

NINE

Too Shallow

As she drove away from the police station, Mavis was pleased with herself. She thought she'd come across rather well as the desperate, sad wife of a missing person.

However, PC Watts had a different opinion. *Not too happy about this person,* she'd written in her report.

Yes, Mavis thought, she did feel pleased with herself. She decided she'd handled it well, all things considered. She'd given a great performance, worthy of any Oscar-winning film actress.

The police officer had believed her. That was important. It was also important that the officer had said she was marking Henry down as high risk.

Success!

Mavis couldn't wait to tell Charlotte. But first she had to do her afternoon shift as usual, at the supermarket. Her mind wasn't on it, and she kept making mistakes at the checkout. And then at six o'clock, on the dot, she left and drove home in Henry's yellow Toyota Corolla. Not having to wait for the bus was a luxury in itself.

When she turned into her road, the sight of a white van in her driveway sent a bolt of fear through her. The van was backed right up against the garage door. Mavis parked in the street, hurried to the front door, and let herself in. Charlotte was standing in the hall, in grimy jeans and a filthy T-shirt. Sweat was pouring off her. She was covered in grey dust, looking like a ghost.

'How did it go?' Charlotte asked.

'What's the van? Whose is it?' Mavis blurted anxiously.

'Calm down, love. Don't I get a kiss?'

Ignoring her, she repeated anxiously, 'Whose van is it?' As Mavis asked, she was looking at the hall table, to see if Henry's mobile phone was there.

'Relax! I borrowed the van from a mate. I'll show you what I used it for in a moment. So, how did it go at the cop shop?'

'It was a breeze!' Mavis said.

'See, you're a star.' Charlotte hugged her and tried to kiss her on the lips, but Mavis turned her face away. Charlotte kissed her cheek instead. And then Mavis pulled away from her.

'You're all sweaty,' Mavis said.

'I've been working, while you've been acting the star!'

Mavis didn't feel like a star. She felt in need of a drink. She wanted a glass of wine. After that, she thought she'd want another one, and then another. 'I need to phone Henry,' she said.

'You'd get a shock if he answered!'

'That's not funny,' Mavis replied. 'The police officer asked if I'd phoned him. We should have thought of the phone. That was stupid. Why didn't you think of it?'

Charlotte shrugged her shoulders. 'Dunno, must have slipped my mind.'

'Great,' Mavis said. 'What else didn't we think of? You had it all under control, you told me. You had it all planned. The perfect murder!'

'I did,' she nodded. 'That was before I saw the *Blue Heelers* episode on forensics, how they determined someone died from an injected sugar overdose.'

'You should have found out about the sugar sooner,' Mavis said.

'Yeah, well, now we have to deal with things as they are,' replied Charlotte. 'Don't worry, I have it all worked out.'

Mavis took out her mobile phone and dialled Henry's number. His Nokia, on the hall table, rang six times and then stopped. She listened, and moments later she heard his voice message. *Hello, this is Henry Walker. I'm sorry I can't take your call at the moment. I'm not available, so please leave me a message and I'll call you back.*

It was strange hearing his voice. It made her feel all tingly, in a bad way. Feeling very self-conscious, Mavis said, 'Hello, Henry. Where are you? Please call me. I'm so worried, I love you, and I'm missing you!'

'Liar!' Charlotte said, when Mavis hung up. 'You didn't love him!'

Mavis's face was burning, as if it was on fire. *It must*

be a guilt thing, telling a lie to a dead person, she thought.

'We need to hide his phone,' Charlotte said. 'Remind me to take it later and ditch it somewhere. You shouldn't have left that message. That was stupid. That was really stupid.'

Mavis snapped, 'It would have been even more stupid not to. I told the police I'd phoned him.'

'It was stupid,' Charlotte repeated. 'You didn't call before you reported him missing – they can check – so it'll look to the police like you were panicking. And we mustn't panic.'

'I need a drink,' Mavis said.

Charlotte insisted they went to the garage first. They had work to do, she said.

Mavis followed her through the door that led from the hall to the garage. It was draughty in there, and the concrete floor was cold under her feet. The air was so thick with dust she could barely see. It prickled her throat and she coughed.

Normally, Henry's Toyota Corolla was parked in there at night, but there was no room now. In the centre of the garage there was a hole that Charlotte had been digging. It was about six feet long and three feet wide. Concrete rubble and earth were scattered either side of it. Stacked against the far wall were several sacks of ready-mixed concrete, a pickaxe, two garden spades and several more tools.

'There we are,' Charlotte said proudly. 'I've been busy today. I'm a one-man HDT.'

'HDT?' Mavis asked. 'What's that?'

'Henry Disposal Team!' she replied.

'That's not funny,' Mavis said.

'Come on, love. You're the one who wanted to do away with him. You asked me to help you. So I'm helping you.'

Mavis looked down into the grave. It was about two feet deep. 'It's too shallow,' she said.

'I'm not finished yet. We're going to have to put him down a good six feet. Don't want the smell to start getting out when he decomposes.'

Henry was the man she used to love and sleep with. Mavis's stomach suddenly churned at the thought of him rotting. 'You're not – you're not serious? You're going to bury Henry here?'

'Too right,' Charlotte replied.

'In my garage?'

'It's perfect! Remember, I used to be a bricklayer's mate in my teens, to help out with college fees. That was good, for looking like a butch dyke with cropped hair, wearing dungarees and steel-capped safety boots. On a building site, I could pass for a bloke. I can also do a perfect concrete screed. No one will ever know.'

'What about me?' Mavis said. 'I will know.'

And then the front doorbell rang.

They both froze, looking at each other.

'Who's that?' Charlotte said.

'I dunno.' Mavis raised a finger to her lips for her to keep quiet. She went out into the hall, closing the internal garage door behind her. She coughed again from the dust. As she went nearer the front door, the bell rang again. She hurried up the stairs and into the room that Henry used as his den. She peered down through the window, and saw two police officers standing outside her front door. They were both male, wearing their black uniform waistcoats and police caps with chequered bands. She studied them for a moment and could see they were getting impatient. Mavis hurried downstairs to tell Charlotte to wait quietly in the garage.

As Mavis opened the front door, her nerves were jangling. 'Sorry to keep you waiting, I – I was on the loo.'

'Mrs Walker?' said the older of the two officers, holding up his warrant card. 'Detective Sergeant Palmer and Police Constable Remington from the Sydney City Police.'

'Yes,' she said. 'Oh, err, hello.' Quick as a flash, she added, 'Have you got any news about my husband Henry? Have you found my husband?'

'No, I'm afraid not, madam. We presume you've not heard from him either?'

Mavis answered in a bewildered expression and shook her head. 'No, I haven't.'

'May we come in, Mrs Walker?'

'Yes, yes, of course.' She moved so that they could come into the hall. Both men took their caps off. Detective Sergeant Palmer looked in his mid-forties. His hair was short and black, with some grey. He had a pleasant face, and a brisk but friendly manner. His younger colleague, PC Remington, looked in his mid-twenties. He was tall and rather gangly, with short fair hair. As she led them through into the lounge, she noticed Henry's phone sitting on the hall table. For a moment Mavis felt panic, and then she realised they wouldn't know it was his.

She pointed at the settee, and the two policemen sat down holding their caps, while nonchalantly looking around and taking everything in. Mavis sat opposite them in an armchair and did her best to look sad.

Detective Sergeant Palmer took out a notebook, and the constable did the same. 'Is that your van in the driveway, Mrs Walker?' the DS enquired.

'The – the white one?' Mavis said, trying to keep calm.

The two police officers exchanged a brief glance, which made Mavis even more uneasy. 'The white one, yes,' the DS said.

'No – err – that's not mine – ours – err – that's the plumber's van.'

'Got a problem with your drains, have you?' the constable asked.

Mavis felt herself breaking out into a sweat. Rising panic tightened her throat so much that her voice came out as a squeak. 'No. No, nothing like that! Just – err – new bathroom taps and a new shower. Henry and I were ... err ... I mean are having a bathroom makeover.' She thought, *You stupid cunt for tripping up on that. The difference between were and are, to the police, meant dead or alive.*

The sergeant nodded. There was silence for a few moments. And then the constable added, 'For a workman, your plumber's very quiet.'

'He is,' Mavis said. 'Good as gold! You wouldn't know he was here.'

108

'Apart from the van outside,' Detective Sergeant Palmer wryly added.

Mavis nodded. 'Yes, well, of course, apart from that!'

There was another silence, longer and more awkward than the last one. And then the DS said, 'We've come round, Mrs Walker, because we have some concerns about your husband.'

Mavis did her best. 'Oh, dear God. You think something bad has happened to my Henry?' She took a handkerchief from her handbag and dabbed her eyes. 'I feel so useless, not being able to help find him.'

The DS glanced down at the writing in his notebook. 'On the missing persons report, you stated that your husband is diabetic. Do you know if he had his medication with him?'

'I – I would think so,' she said. 'He always made sure.'

'Have you checked whether he took it with him yesterday? Sunday evening was the last time you saw your husband, correct?'

'Err, yes,' Mavis said. 'Sunday evening was the last time.'

'Can you repeat the events of Sunday for me, Mrs Walker?'

Mavis felt the heat burning her face. The back of her neck felt slippery with sweat. She needed to make sure she said the same thing to these officers as she had said to the officer at the police station. 'I wasn't feeling well. Henry was home. I went to bed early and left him downstairs watching television. In the morning, he was gone. At first I thought he'd left for work early, but it was strange because he always brought me a cup of tea before he went.'

'What was his state of mind after losing his job, Mrs Walker?' the sergeant asked.

'Terrible. He was in shock. He'd given the best years of his life to those sods at that company. It destroyed him, being let go like that. He was a broken man. He just sat here weeping in this room, night after night.' Mavis paused, feeling a little more confident. She was calming down and getting into her stride. 'He told me several times in the past few weeks that he didn't want to go on living. He couldn't face not being wanted any more. He was broken, totally broken.'

The DS frowned. 'We went round to the premises of Norman Mantle & Sons on the Kookaburra industrial estate this afternoon. That's where your husband is, or was employed, isn't it?'

Mavis nodded, not liking the sound of this.

'We talked to several of his colleagues, trying to find out the state of his mind. Everyone we spoke to said he seemed very happy.' The DS looked down at his notes again. 'One of them said that on the first day of his last week with the company, he was humming and smiling a lot. In fact, he was telling them he felt free for the first time in his life. He said that he was going to enjoy himself. He said that life was too short to spend it all in an office.'

'That's my Henry,' she said, pressing her eyelids tightly together. Mavis was trying to make herself cry, or at least squeeze out a couple of tears. 'He was such a proud man.'

'Was?' said the Detective Sergeant, sharply.

'What am I saying? See what a state I'm in! My

darling Henry is such a proud man. He wouldn't let those sods think they'd won!' She dabbed her eyes with her handkerchief. 'Oh yes, he gave them all a good show, trying to let them think he didn't care. But inside, he was churning up and broken. He just came home and wept and wept and wept. Please find him for me. Please find him. I'm terrified he might have gone and done something rash. My poor darling. My Henry. I couldn't live without him.'

'We'll try our best, Mrs Walker,' they promised. And then they left.

At that moment, Henry's mobile began to warble. Mavis closed the door and went to the table to pick it up. It was ringing and vibrating in her hand. *Private Number* showed on the display. She didn't want to answer it, and so she let it continue for several more rings until it stopped. And then Mavis checked to see if the caller had left a message. But they hadn't.

*

Downstairs, in the basement of the Kitten Parlour, was a rest room. It had comfy chairs and a television, so the girls could relax while they were waiting for clients. At seven o'clock in the evening, blonde-haired Christine put down her mobile phone. She lit a cigarette, and took a sip of her coffee. She was worried about Henry. He hadn't called or texted her for two days. He was constantly phoning, and leaving her text messages. He would usually send two or three texts during the night, and he always called her from his office in the morning. This was not like him.

Christine badly needed to speak to Henry. Ricky, her boyfriend, had found out she was in Sydney, and he knew where she was living. He'd left threatening messages on her voicemail. Henry had promised to take care of her. She liked Henry. He was funny, and he made her feel safe. The most important thing was that he was a rich man! He would be able to get rid of Ricky. He'd told her he had contacts in high places and promised her that Ricky would be history. But now Henry had vanished. She did not dare to leave a message, because Henry had told her never to do that.

Nervously, Christine smoked her cigarette down to the butt. She was about to light another, when the bordello madam called her name on the intercom. 'Christine, you have a client!' She hurried up the stairs, hopeful that it might be Henry. When she saw it wasn't, her smile slipped a notch.

TEN

Tricks of the Mind

After the police left, Charlotte drove off in the van. She couldn't leave it in the driveway all evening, or the neighbours would wonder about it. And so she parked it a couple of streets away, and walked back. She was dressed in black and barely visible in the darkness.

At eleven o'clock, Mavis came into the garage with a tenth mug of coffee for Charlotte. By then her head could hardly be seen as she continued digging. Earth was piled high on either side of Henry's makeshift grave. The smell of dust was less strong now, and instead there was a musty smell of damp soil.

Mavis, covered in dirt, was cold and exhausted from helping Charlotte. Her hands were blistered from when she'd taken over the digging a couple of times. She was still not happy about burying Henry in their garage.

'It's the best place,' Charlotte said. 'Trust me! If you

look at how most murderers get caught, it's because a body turns up somewhere. A body is found in a shallow grave in the woods, or washed up on a beach. Or they get caught trying to get rid of the body. If there's no body, then there's nothing for the police to go on. They've no reason to suspect you, have they?'

'No,' Mavis agreed. She did feel the police were just a little suspicious. But what Charlotte said made sense. And so she watched as Charlotte dug deeper and deeper, slowly but steadily, getting there, bit by bit by bit.

A few minutes past midnight, Mavis helped Charlotte heave her husband's body out of the freezer. Henry was hard and cold, and his flesh was a grey colour with specks of frost on it. She avoided looking at his face. She didn't want to catch his eye. They half carried and half dragged him into the hall, and then into the garage. And then they hauled him over the mounds of freshly dug earth into the long, narrow hole. For one horrible moment, Mavis thought the hole was too narrow. Henry's body fell a couple of feet, but his shoulders and stomach got wedged. Charlotte gave him a shove with her foot. Henry slithered and tumbled, like a huge Guy Fawkes dummy. He landed with a hard thud into the wet earth at the bottom.

'Have some respect,' Mavis said. 'You shouldn't have pushed him with your foot.'

'Pardon me,' Charlotte said. 'Why don't you phone the sodding vicar, and ask him to come round here? He could hold a proper burial service.'

Mavis said nothing. She just stared down at the naked,

ungainly heap that had once been the man she loved. She felt a whole raft of emotions. She felt sadness, fear and guilt.

But she felt no joy. She had thought she would feel joy from the moment he was dead. She had expected her love for Charlotte would be so much stronger. But she didn't feel any love for Charlotte at all right now. In fact, Mavis wished she would go away and leave her alone. She wanted to say a private goodbye to Henry. She knelt, scooped up a handful of earth and dropped it onto the corpse. And then she whispered, so quietly that Charlotte could not hear, 'Goodbye, my love. It wasn't all bad, was it?' And then she stood up and helped Charlotte to shovel the earth back in.

It was after one o'clock by the time they'd finished. Mavis was almost asleep on her feet. 'Isn't your girlfriend Debbi going to be wondering where you are?' she asked.

Charlotte glanced at her watch. 'That soppy cow will be asleep. I told her I was cabbing and working late, doing an early-morning pickup from Sydney airport. That thick twat will believe anything I tell her.'

Mavis all at once began to wonder how long it would be before Charlotte's love for her would be discarded, like her friend Debbi.

Charlotte gave Mavis a peck on the cheek. 'Don't worry, love, I've got it all in hand.'

Mavis swept all the loose soil onto the mound of the grave, while Charlotte walked up and down, flattening it. Finally, the mound was level with the garage floor.

Charlotte cut open the first bag of ready-mixed cement.

Mavis went to fetch a bucket of water from the kitchen. And then Charlotte started mixing up, and steadily began to trowel and screed the entire floor with cement. Bit by bit, she floated the screed to a professional mirror finish.

By four o'clock in the morning, the job was done. After clearing up, all her tools and empty sacks of cement were in the hall. Charlotte was going to bring the van round later to collect and dispose of them. 'What do you think, love?' she said, putting her arm around Mavis.

Mavis peered through the garage door at the glistening wet cement. It was impossible to see where the grave had been dug. The whole floor was perfectly flat and even. 'Yes,' she said. 'It's very good.'

'Mustn't walk on it until tomorrow,' Charlotte said.

'No, okay,' Mavis mumbled. 'I'll have to remember.'

Charlotte tried to make light of the situation. 'I don't think Henry's going to walk on it, not where he is!' They stared at each other, and then Charlotte gave Mavis a hug. 'It'll all be fine,' she said. 'Just stay calm and no one will be ever be the wiser. Tomorrow afternoon, after you finish work, we'll have a drink. Yeah? In bed, yeah?'

Mavis bit her lip. With Henry under the garage floor, she didn't know how she felt. She nodded, and gave a thin smile.

Charlotte opened the front door and slipped out into the night. Mavis closed the door and pressed down the latch lock. And then, feeling a strange sense that she was being watched, she turned round. Henry was standing halfway up the stairs, looking at her. Mavis screamed, but only silence came out of her throat. She screamed again, but still her voice wouldn't work. Her whole body was shaking. She was in a dream. She had to be sleepwalking. She closed her eyes and backed up against the door. She fumbled with the latch to open it. And then she opened her eyes.

Henry had gone. Upstairs? Had he gone upstairs? Her heart was crashing around inside her chest. She was gulping down air. She looked up at the dark landing and listened.

And listened.

But only silence prevailed.

Suddenly a loud clatter in the kitchen made her jump. Mavis realised it was just the cat flap. Gregory slunk into the hall and glared at her, as if he wanted to know what she was doing up so late, and in his space.

'Henry!' Mavis called out. To her relief, her voice was suddenly working again, but it was very shrill. 'Henry?' she called again.

Only silence remained.

Of course there was silence. She reasoned with herself, *You stupid prick, what else would there be? With him five feet deep.* Mavis muttered to herself, 'It's just your imagination working overtime, you silly bitch.' She went through into the kitchen, deciding she was far too wide awake to sleep. Mavis did not dare go up the stairs. She needed a drink, badly. She took a bottle of wine out of the fridge and poured herself a glass. She drank it straight down and poured another. She was about to start drinking the second glass, when the cat pawed at her leg. 'What is it?' she said, talking in a whisper. 'Hungry, are we?' The cat just looked at her. She had never liked the way Gregory looked at her, and she liked it even less now. It was as if the cat knew what she'd done. Mavis opened a tin of food, scooped some of it into a bowl, and placed it on the floor. Straight away, Gregory turned and began staring at her again. Mavis drained her glass of wine, and then poured a third. Within a few minutes, as the alcohol began to kick in, she started to feel better.

She had simply imagined Henry. That's all it was. Her mind was playing tricks, because she was tired. She'd been through a lot in the past twenty-four hours.

Suddenly, she smelt cigar smoke. The familiar smell of Henry's cigars. It was getting stronger by the second. And then there was a strange, ghastly hissing sound. It sent a bolt of fear through her like electricity. It was coming from Gregory. The cat was standing with his back arched and his fur raised on end. He was baring his teeth and hissing at the open door to her left. A large blue ring of cigar smoke was drifting in from the hall.

Mavis ran out of the house, down her front garden and into the street. As she did so, the front door slammed behind her. She stood, panting, in the faint yellow glow of the streetlight. Her heart was hammering, and she was gulping air. And then she heard a vehicle. For a moment she was tempted to run into the middle of the road. She could shout for help and flag it down. It was a police patrol car. Mavis stepped back hastily into the shadow of a bush.

She was aware that questions would be asked. She knew the police might want to know what she was doing up at this hour. Why had she run out of her house?

Christ, she thought. She stared at the house. She looked at the windows. It was as if she was expecting to see Henry peering out at her. Henry didn't believe in ghosts. She liked to watch shows about mediums, but he always pooh-poohed them. He used to say, *Tricks of the mind, that's all ghosts are. They're tricks of the mind.* Had it been a trick of the mind when she saw Henry standing on the stairs? What about the ring of cigar smoke? What about his hairs in the basin yesterday?

The tail lights of the police car vanished around the corner. She shivered. An icy wind was blowing. A spot of rain struck her cheek. She was locked out, she realised. Locked out of her house by a ghost! 'Bugger – Damn – Blast,' she muttered. Her phone was inside. Everything was inside. She didn't want to go back in, but where else could she go, especially at this hour? She could go round to their old friends, Ron and Phyllis, but they lived about three miles away. And then Mavis remembered the spare key! Henry kept one under a brick by the back door. At least he used to. She just hoped it was still there. She squeezed past the dustbins, opened the side gate and reached the step to the kitchen door. In the darkness, she found the brick, lifted it and felt around on the ground. To her relief the key was there. She scooped it safely into her palm, went back around to the front of the house, unlocked the door and went in. She locked the door behind her, saying loudly, 'Tricks of the mind. That's all. Tricks of the mind!'

Mavis was too afraid to go upstairs, so she rushed into the kitchen and shut herself in. The cat had run off somewhere, back into the night. The night was where he belonged, she thought. Mavis switched on the television for company, and sat down at the table. Over the next twenty minutes she finished the entire bottle of wine.

*

Christine had only gone to bed at 4am. At 8.30 she was woken in her bedsit by the ringtone of her mobile. She opened one eye and stared through her fringe of blonde hair at the phone. She hoped it was Henry. Or was it Ricky? Please don't let it be Ricky, she thought. It's too early. I can't put up with his anger so early. No numbers showed on the display. It simply said: Call. She answered nervously. Was it Henry calling from a new phone? Was it Ricky hiding his number? A male voice she did not recognise said, 'Hello, this is Detective Sergeant Palmer from the Sydney City Police.' Christine felt a stab of panic. Was she in trouble for working at the Kitten Parlour?

'Yes?' she said anxiously.

'We are looking for Mr Henry Walker, who has been missing since Monday evening. Calls to his mobile phone are being monitored, and it was reported to us that a call was made to his phone from your number at 6.55pm yesterday. Are you the person who made the call?'

'Henry is missing?' she said.

'Yes. We are concerned for his safety. Are you a friend of his?'

'Yes,' Christine said in her broken English. 'I very good friend.' Henry was missing? She closed her eyes for a moment, feeling gutted. What did this mean? Had something happened to him?

'We'd like to talk to you,' the DS said. 'Can we come over to see you? If you'd prefer, you could drop into Sydney City Police Station.'

Christine walked past the police station every day on her way to work. She always walked, to save the bus fare. She had to be at work by midday for the lunchtime trade. 'I can come about half past ten. Is okay?'

'That will be fine. May I have your name?'

'It's Christine Baltacha,' she told him.

'At the front desk, ask for me, Detective Sergeant Palmer.'

'Please, can you tell me, is Henry ... is he okay?'

'We don't know. We are anxious to find him. We are concerned for his safety.'

Christine thanked him, and then ended the call. She lay on her bed staring at the ceiling. She was far too wide awake to sleep any more. Not with Henry's safety at risk. Henry was the only man who had ever been kind to her. The only person who offered her an escape from the horrible life she was stuck with. Now the police were concerned for his safety. She would do everything to help them. Christine stared at the phone again, and pleaded. 'Please call, Henry, please call!' And then a thought struck her. Henry often talked to her about his wife. He said she was a bad person. That she made him very unhappy. She wondered if she should tell the police this.

*

'You look like shit,' Charlotte said to Mavis.

'Well, thank you. You certainly know how to make a girl feel great!'

Mavis sat at the kitchen table with a blinding hangover, and no make-up on. She'd had about one hour's sleep. She felt like shit. There were three messages on her mobile phone. They were all from Phyllis, who'd phoned last night. Mavis had been busy in the garage with Charlotte, and hadn't heard her phone ring. Phyllis said that she and Ron had received a visit from the police, who told them that Henry was still missing. Phyllis asked if she was okay? Why hadn't she called them? Would she like them to pop round?

Mavis decided she wouldn't. But she had to tell Charlotte about her sighting of Henry. 'Charlotte, Henry was here in the house last night. It was after you left,' she said.

'Then he should change his name to Houdini,' she mocked, 'if he's capable of getting out from under six feet of earth and a concrete screed!'

'No joke, Henry was here, Charl.'

'Was the Pope here too?' she asked.

'I'm serious, Charl.'

Charlotte affectionately stroked her hair. 'It's going to be tough, love, but we have to keep calm. And keep cool, right?'

'Easy for you to say. You weren't here.'

'Ghosts don't exist, love,' she said.

Mavis stared at Charlotte, sitting across the table. She was angry that she doubted her. And then she realised Charlotte wasn't the big powerful hero that she had seemed only a few days ago. She looked so weak.

Mavis Bone looked at the lawn Henry had tended, and at his shed. She looked at the greenhouse, with Henry's tomato plants. She looked at the flower beds. And Mavis realised that she hated Charlotte now, and knew their relationship was finished. The thought of what she had done to Henry, it could never be the same. However, Mavis knew she was an accomplice in crime with her. And the thought of sharing her life with Charlotte suddenly didn't fit into Mavis's plans.

Charlotte could incriminate her. She had to disappear, and quick.

It was time to switch on the charm. Mavis sidled up to Charlotte and said, 'Charl,' fancy staying the night? I don't want to stay in this place on my own, you know, it gets so spooky. You've got your overnight bag and things here. We could send out for a takeaway and watch a video.'

Charlotte weighed up the offer. 'Okay, you're on, I fancy Chinese tonight, you up for one?'

'Chinese would be great for me as well, Charl.'

*

That evening, after watching *Rain Man* with Dustin Hoffman, they'd devoured five Chinese takeaway dishes, along with a bottle and a half of Rioja, Charlotte's favourite. Towards eleven o'clock, while halfway through the second bottle and on her third glass, Charlotte began to doze on the sofa in front of the television.

Mavis Bone had crushed up two of her strong sleeping tablets, the ones she'd used to stave off Henry's snoring. Mixing them up into Charlotte's glass of wine, she watched them slowly take effect.

Within an hour, Mavis was leading Charlotte up to the spare bedroom that Henry had decorated. With Charlotte feeling dozy, Mavis sorted her out and tucked her in. Finally, Mavis kissed her goodnight, and made sure the windows and door were shut.

Mavis smiled knowingly at the faint smell of almonds. She had easily sussed out Henry's motives for decorating the spare bedroom, and checked out the ingredients that made up Prussian blue, finding cyanide to be a prominent one. With this in mind, she'd soon found his top-up cyanide bottle in the garden shed.

Closing Charlotte's door, she whispered, 'Sweet dreams.'

*

One month later, Mavis Bone heard the clatter of the letterbox, and picked up the buff-coloured business envelope. Her hand shook as she held Charlotte's life insurance payout cheque for fifty thousand Australian dollars.

Who would have thought such a tragic accident could have happened. Asphyxiated by cyanide paint vapour. Of course, the paint manufacturer was to be prosecuted for producing a rogue batch of Prussian blue paint.

Thankfully the police had swallowed her suggestion that Henry must have run off with his Kitten Parlour floozy, Christine. Conveniently the girl had disappeared in fear of her life from boyfriend Ricky.

Delving deep into Henry's mobile messages, Mavis had discovered his illicit dalliance with Christine. Of course she'd known about his trips to the bordello for years, after finding the Kitten Parlour business card in his dry cleaning. Some of his messages to Christine had suggested that they could run away together somewhere warm and sunny. After she showed the police this evidence, they temporarily relaxed their criminal investigation on Henry's disappearance.

Mavis Bone decided she needed a fresh start. A move to the UK seemed the best option. The decision was made easier by the idea of starting up her own private detective agency. She had studied for it as a mature student. And she was sure the Brits would take a female private investigator more seriously than the Australians would.

ELEVEN

Harry

Mavis Bone and Gertrude Stick were sitting in the agency office, thumbing through an old photo album. Mavis enthused, 'That was one of my best holidays, Gerty, that 1993 Mexican sightseeing tour of Querétaro with its Aztec temples. And it was all down to Harry Pritchard. To think I was sweet on him once. No wonder I'm a lesbo,' she joked.

Gertrude said, 'e vos probably a cunning Jew, vunning off vith your zyndicate vootball pools win. I tell you. They're all tied to the same bvush.'

Mavis laughed. 'Now-now, Gerty. He could have been a crafty stinking Abo. I remember one family of Abos on my parents' farm who did our labouring, cleaned out and sold off all our furniture while we were away on holiday. When my dad caught up with the Abo father, he took a riding whip to him. I'll tell you what, Gerty, the wheals on his back looked like a map of the London Underground. Of course, back in the fifties, you could do that sort of thing to an Abo. Not now you can't. Too many do-gooders telling folk they've got to be treated like human beings. As if?' Mavis mocked a laugh. 'I remember my daddy, God bless him, always said you gotta have discipline, that's the key to the Aboriginal problem. You must treat the Abo's like you treat a stray dog that you give a home too. You feed it to make it trusting, and then you beat it if it's unruly, to instil fear and respect for its master.'

*

Mavis Bone and Gertrude Stick had never told anybody the whole story of how they managed to finance, and purchase outright, their agency office and the flat upstairs. This scheme had included the purchase of various buy-to-let flats around the Wimbledon area. Like most things they kept the story to themselves.

*

It had been around 1992, at Preston Engineering Ltd, when Mavis Bone and Harry Pritchard first met. Mavis had joined the company after arriving from Australia, just after her husband's tragic disappearance.

Preston Engineering Ltd were recruiting for cheap female labour. Working in the capstan machine shop, Mavis was grateful for the job as there was very little of Charlotte's windfall left. The company had been founded in the early 1950s, during the pre-war manufacturing boom period.

It was a family-run company based in Rainham, Essex. Its initial bread and butter was manufacturing precision components for the auto industry. Over the years, it had diversified into other commercial markets including domestic appliance mouldings.

Preston was a survivor. They had weathered all the slumps – competing with foreign suppliers and the rising costs of manufacturing. Now it was April 1993 and the order book was looking good, good enough to carry it through the next six months.

Not many people left Preston Ltd. They had a good reputation for looking after staff, so most of the shop-floor lads and girls were now in their mid-forties.

'We're all lifers in here, but we might get parole,' Mavis Bone the Australian capstan operator would sometimes joke, usually when the factory buzzer signalled the seven-thirty morning start.

Stocky forty-four-year-old Mavis Bone, her jet-black hair full of tiny curls, worked the capstans along with forty-five-year-old Harry Pritchard, the supervisor. Now it was tea break, and in the green-walled canteen the free vending machine was going into overdrive – churning out teas, coffee, hot chocolate, soup and anything else to satisfy the gathered queue of blue overalls. Elsewhere two microwaves were busy humming their boring tune as sausage rolls, pies and pasties gently revolved, while workers looked on, waiting with anticipation for that audible *ping*.

Mavis Bone, Alf Hubbard and Harry Pritchard always sat together during tea breaks. They'd gone through various phases to pass the break time. Some days they'd play cards, and then it was crosswords.

Now they were into reading, with Mavis digesting her sausage roll and flicking through the pages of her monthly magazine on Maya, Inca and Aztec Civilisations. As a student in her teens, Mavis had backpacked around South America on a charity sponsorship, doing missionary work in hospitals and orphanages. Since then, her fascination for these ancient cults had grown. She'd also picked up a cocaine habit along the way in Colombia. However, due to her financial situation, that avenue of pleasure had been cut off for the last few years.

Harry Pritchard would sit with his football pools coupon, filling in the crosses while he busied himself in-between with sandwich bites. He never got lucky, however, along with thousands of others, he probably kept Littlewoods boss John Moores well stocked in cigars.

Harry had a strange way of holding his pen. He'd lost his left-hand index finger at the lower joint in a machinery accident some years ago. He was awarded a small amount of compensation, but it mostly went on the football pools, filling out numerous coupons per week.

The injury certainly didn't give him any handicap playing snooker. The hideous skull and crossbones biker ring he wore on his finger stump was used as a bridge to rest his cue on. It seemed to work, and he'd been Preston's social club snooker champion for the last five years running. A framed photo of him holding the trophy proudly recorded last year's win, and took pride of place on the wall above Harry's workbench.

Alf Hubbard, at sixty-four, was the oldest of the three, with his white bushy beard, baldhead and weathered face. He was also in his last year before retirement. Healthwise, Alf had been unlucky with his angina and arthritis in both legs. He was one of the originals at Preston and had started with the firm as an apprentice. He'd been there ever since, apart from his seven-year spell in the merchant navy, a subject everybody carefully avoided after being collared once, and forced to listen to tales from his naval career. He still tried to look the part, wearing his seaman's cap and baggy duffle coat.

On his toolbox was a large photo of him with three mates, all stripped to the waist, suntanned and with unkempt beards on board some boat in Durban. '*From me last cargo trip*,' he starts telling any unfortunate who's glanced over while walking past.

The management had been good to Alf. They'd given him a sitting-down job as a deburrer in the finishing department, but kept him on the centre-lathe rate.

George Preston the managing director, always had a little chat with Alf when he made his rounds on Friday mornings. Alf could remember him when he was just a kid, when his dad, Walter Preston, the company founder, used to bring him in on Saturday mornings to kick a ball about in the yard.

After George Preston had nodded a goodbye to him,

Alf would be met by a flurry of derisive remarks. '*How's your friend getting on?*' and '*You invited for Sunday lunch?*' his mates would taunt above the clatter of machinery.

Alf would reply, with a two-finger salute, 'Yer only jealous.'

Nowadays, Alf was into crosswords, but he'd never been very good at them, this particular tea break being no exception, 'Audience response to a comic, something – something U something H…?'

Harry looked up and quickly said, 'Its *laugh*.'

'You clever old sod,' Alf replied.

'Well, it was a tricky one,' Harry explained, catching Mavis's eye with a sarcastic grin.

Alf carried on intently scanning the clues, while at the same time holding a bitter expression as he rolled an angina tablet in his mouth, and then dispatched it with his last dregs of tea. 'God, I hate taking those,' he said. 'You'd think by now they'd make all tablets taste decent. Now, if I 'ad a choice, I'd ask for navy rum flavoured.'

'Of course you would, you old soak,' Harry chuckled.

'You can't beat a decent drop of rum,' Alf said seriously. 'Now, when I was in the merchant they used to give us…'

Mavis and Harry quickly buried their heads in whatever they were reading. No eye contact meant Alf wouldn't ramble on too long. They'd learned the hard way.

'It's cordial,' interrupted Harry, 'the clue for the fruit-flavoured drink. You said you had R and L.'

Alf stopped and went back to his paper. 'That fits!' he shouted over the end of the tea break buzzer.

'Before you lot go,' Harry said, 'can I have your pools money? A pound each from you please.'

Harry received the usual groans from the others when it was time to cough up.

'I wouldn't care if we *won* something,' Alf moaned, getting his small leather purse out. 'We 'aven't won anything in years.'

'Don't worry,' Harry said, counting his change. 'Our day will come. The first thing I'll do, if we win the big one, is to book a Caribbean cruise for my Pat.'

'How is your missus, Harry?' Mavis asked with a sympathetic expression.

'Not too good. She's been off work for nearly a month with the pain. Her doctor's referred her to a back specialist up at the General. I think they're going to do some tests and X-rays.'

'Doctors!' Alf chimed in. 'I wouldn't give a thank you for any of 'em. They couldn't do anything for my Pauline, God rest 'er soul. Watched 'er suffer for six months before she died.' Alf's voice quavered.

Harry muttered to himself, 'Thanks for cheering me up, Alf, you're all I need today.'

On cue with the machines starting up, Harry folded his racing paper and stuffed it inside his overalls. He carefully looked around and did his usual slope-off to the toilet. This gave him an extra ten minutes of peace and quiet. His routine included flushing the toilet now and again and running the tap water – just in case management had their ear to the door.

Harry put the paper on the side and looked into the mirror. He was forty-five years old, married and had lost interest in life, while cheating on a wife in poor health.

He'd been a machinist at Preston for seven years, but now he was really pissed off with it all. The job was dirty and boring – turning out the same auto parts, day in and day out.

Harry wasn't too badly off, considering. He had his own two-bed flat on the second floor of a block in Basildon, just off the A1235. And with it a small mortgage, small enough so as not to keep him awake at night, should the overtime ever dry up.

He sniffed and winced at his blue overall sleeve. The strong smell of soluble oil clung to his work coat. The smell was the first thing that hit you in the morning, when you started your shift.

Harry carefully parted his dark, wavy hair in the mirror. 'No grey yet,' he muttered to himself. He leant closer, stretching the skin around his blue eyes and then under his chin. 'No wrinkles either.'

Harry Pritchard was good-looking and knew it. With his six-foot-one-inch frame he was a dead ringer for Pierce Brosnan, his past girlfriends used to say. He would sometimes reply to them, scoffing, 'I wish I had his money instead of his looks.'

One of his past girlfriends was Mavis Bone. Even though, she secretly declared herself to close friends, she was a lesbian and swung both ways. Mavis in her day was pretty, fun loving and vivacious. She had been dancing with

133

Harry over the past year, unbeknown to Pat, Harry's wife. They'd go every Saturday evening to the Preston social club dance with its five-piece band. The place was always packed. That's where Harry and Mavis hit it off. They danced many times together. Harry's wife was always poorly, kept indoors by her bad back. Harry became infatuated with Mavis, asking her to live with him, promising to leave his wife. Mavis, with some of her old-school values still intact, wanted him to divorce Pat.

Harry told her he couldn't, what with Pat under the hospital and having tests. So they planned their meetings while he was working. Harry used to take mornings or afternoons off work. It used to make him feel guilty, but he couldn't help himself.

One time, they sneaked a weekend away at a B&B in Weymouth, while Harry was on a three-day supervisor's course. Just for a laugh, they went into a passport booth and had their pictures taken. Harry kept the photos, although Mavis had told him to throw them away in case his wife found them.

Eventually, Harry and Mavis stopped seeing each other, and they both realised their relationship had played itself out. However, they still remained friends.

It was three months later, after many hospital tests and visits, that Harry tearfully told Mavis and Alf that Pat had died of bone cancer.

They'd attended her funeral, along with a few friends from Preston Engineering. George Preston, the MD, had thoughtfully sent a nice wreath from the company.

*

And then, suddenly, came a bombshell. There was a buzz around the firm. Harry Pritchard had handed his notice in. Mavis and Alf were gobsmacked. When Harry told them, they looked like a couple of goldfish – mouths opening and shutting in astonishment. That morning tea break, they cornered him.

'But you've been here seven years, Harry. What you gonna do?' Alf asked while chewing on a tuna and cucumber sandwich.

'I'm going to Newcastle to live with my sister,' Harry replied. 'She hasn't been well for a long time, and she's just come out of hospital. She lives on her own, there's no other family, so I'll be packing up work for good and looking after her.'

Mavis smiled and said, 'I wish you all the luck, Harry, we'll miss you.'

'I never knew you had a sister,' Alf said, looking puzzled. 'You kept that one quiet.'

Harry explained, 'We were never that close. Mainly cos I never got on with her husband. He could be an awkward bastard at times. But he died a couple of years ago, and she's got no one else.'

'Don't let it break yer back, son,' Alf said with a worried look. 'Looking after people can take it out of yer. I remember looking after my Pauline when she was alive – God bless 'er. Up and down those stairs. Weekends were the worst when 'er carer wasn't there.'

'Don't worry, you two. I'll be okay,' Harry said with a grin. 'She's had one of those women's operations, and it takes a long time to get over, so the doctors reckon.' Harry changed the subject. 'I even managed to find a buyer for my flat. Nice couple, they move in next week.' Harry considered, and then said, 'When my sister's better, we might even start up a bit of bed and breakfast at her place. You can both come and visit when I'm settled in; I'll forward you her address.'

'Long as you know what yer doing, Harry,' Alf said with a concerned look.

'I'll be okay; they say a change is as good as a holiday,' Harry replied. 'And I've had years of this place – or prison,' he said with a chuckle, looking around the drab machine shop. 'More than enough, thank you. It'll feel like being released on good behaviour.'

All three of them laughed.

That Friday lunchtime, after their weekly thirty-six-hour shift had finished. Harry took Mavis and Alf with a few others, down to the King's Head for a final pint and some sandwiches, for his leaving day send-off.

They'd all clubbed together, including management, and bought him a snooker cue with a case. Harry thanked them all and made a little speech in the public bar. After a lot of vigorous handshakes and pats on the back, he waved them a last goodbye.

With his toolbox and suitcases in the boot, he climbed into his old Sierra and drove off to his sister in Newcastle.

*

Mavis heard the postman. She picked up the buff-coloured A4 envelope from the mat, and walked back to the kitchen of her rented one-bed flat in Rainham.

After five minutes of reading, a smile spread across her face. It was to do with her private pension plan. The letter informed that her pension company, Cape Mutual, had just been floated on the Australian stock exchange. And as a holder of a pension plan, along with other loyal policy holders, she had been awarded a flotation bonus of five thousand pounds. Mavis fingered the enclosed cheque and had to re-read the letter to make sure.

A telephone call to the London office confirmed the good news.

Five thousand pounds; what to do? She carefully thought it through, and then decided.

Mavis was a hoarder of magazines, mostly to do with Aztec, Inca and Maya history. She never threw them away. She had so many, with piles of them tucked away under her bed. As a student in her teens, her fascination for these ancient civilisations had increased while backpacking around Mexico and South America.

At this moment, her latest magazine was spread out on the kitchen table. The back pages always advertised expensive sightseeing coach holidays of Mexico, to trace the Aztec civilisation. These holidays were way beyond Mavis's budget; however, her pension cheque had changed all that.

Mavis flipped to the back page and began to study

the tour photos of Aztec temples, supported with luxury hotels and air-conditioned coaches. The magazine gave the booking details, and with the money in her hand, the temptation was too great to resist.

After five minutes, she finally circled the seven-day Mexican sightseeing tour of Querétaro with its Aztec temple itinerary. The cost with flight was £1,120. Not cheap, she thought, but hell, why not? Mavis hadn't had a real holiday abroad for years, certainly not since her student shoestring backpacking ones.

Mavis decided, with the remaining money from her windfall, she'd buy a second-hand Ford Fiesta, and stick what was left over in her building society.

The holiday was for mid-August 1993, and they only wanted a deposit. The final balance had to be paid two weeks before departure from Gatwick.

Mavis filled out the deposit cheque, and then licked and stamped the envelope addressed to Global Tour Holidays. Before leaving to post it, she made out a small shopping list. She preened herself in the mirror above the fireplace in the small front room. Harry Pritchard looked up at her from a framed portrait on the mantelpiece. It had been over nine months since he left. The framed photo had been taken in a studio and given to her by Harry as a birthday present. At the bottom he'd written, *To Mavis with Love from Harry*.

Mavis stared into the hall mirror. Her mind wandered to the fleeting days and weekends breaks they'd spent together. Now she was going alone. She remembered how Harry was always bubbly and laughing. Those were the good times, being with friends at the company dinner-dances. It felt so right her being on his arm. They were distant memories, especially now, since Preston Engineering had folded earlier in the year due to cash flow problems and fierce competition that had forced them into liquidation.

Her reflection darkened when Mavis remembered the time Harry told her he wanted to finish their relationship. It seemed so sudden, and she never saw it coming.

TWELVE

Eight Score Draws

Mavis never heard from Harry Pritchard. His sister's forwarding address in Newcastle never arrived. 'Perhaps too busy making loads of money doing bed and breakfast,' she'd told Alf Hubbard over the phone.

Alf, although suffering with his angina and arthritis, was now busying himself with a little painting and decorating retirement job. Mavis made a point of keeping in touch with him. As well as phoning, she'd pop over to see him every couple of months with his favourite tobacco and a bottle of rum.

Alf's unemployed son, Brian, visited now and again, but that was only to borrow money. His wife, Viv, couldn't stand going round there, even though they lived locally. She didn't like the smell of the place, or Alf's mangy dog. She said it had fleas. She wanted Brian to get him into a home, so they could sell Alf's house. Brian had suggested this to Alf, but

Alf had flatly refused. He was having none of it. In fact, his heated words to Mavis on her last visit, as he downed a large rum, were, 'The only time I'm leaving here will be in a box.'

Mavis put down Harry's photo and swallowed hard, wiping her eyes. She took one last look in the mirror, and knew she was being silly.

Mavis had a lot to be cheerful about. For starters, there was her pension company cheque, and now she was about to go on a fantastic holiday.

Feeling a bit cheered up, she closed the front door and set off with a brisk walk to the shops and post box.

*

It was day three of her holiday coach tour itinerary. Mavis had two seats to himself, so she could spread out and stretch her legs.

After landing at Mexico City airport, and then spending a day and a half touring the city's sights, she was glad to be on the move. It seemed as though she'd walked a hundred miles around museums and galleries, full of Aztec artefacts. This Wednesday morning, they were off to see an Aztec temple near the city of Querétaro.

Mavis leant back in the luxury padded seat with its headrest and built-in headphones. With the seat belt fastened, she felt like she was flying a jet. She adjusted the air-conditioning blower above her head. It was only 10.30am, but outside it was already seventy-eight degrees and climbing.

Taking a swig from her bottle of mineral water, she began to read the schedule. It stated that Querétaro was a 135-mile drive north-west of Mexico City, and had a population of 800,000 residents. Founded by the Spanish in 1531, it was originally a silver mining city, but now, through commerce and industry, it had become one of the wealthiest cities in Mexico.

Mavis felt the tap on her shoulder. She turned and saw that it was Doris and Jack, the elderly couple from Ramsgate she'd wined and dined with last night. They'd walked into the hotel dining room together, and asked her to join them for dinner. Both were in their late sixties, still looked trim and were very smartly dressed. Doris, a dyed redhead and heavily made up, was just slightly shorter than her husband, who sported a full head of white hair and a thin trained moustache.

They'd hit it off straight away because, like Mavis, they were Aztec buffs as well. They drank and talked all evening. Mavis was grateful for their company, and it saved sitting alone like Billy no-mates.

After exchanging pleasantries and chatting about the day's schedule, they settled back as the double-decker tour coach started up.

Mavis had her camera out ready and laid it on the seat. She had a good position for taking photos, which sitting on the top tier by a window.

Passing through the smaller villages, Mavis was surprised at the poverty. The shanty town shacks with dirty shoeless children playing amongst chickens, and goats running around. Gritty, dusty roads, religious paintings daubed on rundown apartment buildings.

And always the markets, as they approached the tourist areas; selling belts, Aztec symbol T-shirts, stitched leather jackets with feathers, leather hats with feathers, Aztec masks and headdresses with feathers, and crude wooden carvings of condors and eagles, as well as an endless supply of tatty bracelets and neck charms.

The two-hour journey was interrupted frequently by the young, pretty tour guide. She was sitting at the front in uniform, near the driver, explaining into her microphone the history and industry of the area, including many snippets about the numerous picturesque baroque churches they passed.

Finally, they pulled into the main plaza of Querétaro. With Mavis's stomach rumbling for something to eat, she agreed with her friends Doris and Jack to find a place to lunch at the coach stop, and then to go sightseeing afterwards.

Before the pneumatic doors opened, the tour guide briefly pointed out the large fountain to the left of the coach that was built in tribute to German Patiño Díaz, the famous artist and engineer. She explained how he had brought water to Querétaro by constructing the seventy-four-arch aqueduct that overlooked the city, a twelve-year project from 1726 to 1738.

The tour guide asked everyone to meet by the fountain after lunch, at 2.15pm sharp, so they could swiftly move on to the beautiful town of San Juan del Río. This would be to see its temple and the volcanic hot springs.

As they stepped off the coach, the eight-six-degree lunchtime heat hit them.

'Can see why they use air conditioning,' Mavis joked to Doris and Jack. They nodded, quickly pulling out handkerchiefs and dabbing at their perspiration.

The sky was a perfect blue and so bright that they had to shield their eyes from the white glare of the plaza granite floor and its stone walls.

As they approached the edge of the square, restaurant smells of tacos, tortas, tamales and sweet potatoes rose up and sharpened their appetites. A grinning waiter stepped out to greet them, and nodded to one of the few remaining empty tables.

'This looks as good as anything, and it's busy,' Mavis suggested to the couple, as they stooped to sit down under the parasol.

'Good afternoon, would you like some drinks first?' the waiter inquired, grinning at them again, and handing out three menus.

At two o'clock, after a full lunch and a light stroll around the square with its market, they settled back into their coach, with appetites satisfied and feeling content.

As they pulled away, their tour guide came over the microphone. 'Good afternoon, ladies and gentlemen. Before we arrive at San Juan del Río, we shall be passing through the small and wealthy town of San Luis Potosí. Like Beverly Hills is to Los Angeles, so San Luis Potosí is to Querétaro.' She added, 'We shall be seeing some beautiful colonial mansions. Many are owned by wealthy businessmen including famous film stars and pop singers, so have your camera ready.'

The enormous mansions were set back in their own grounds, and being on the top tier, Mavis had a good view over the high walls.

A couple of times the coach stopped to allow for photographs. The tour guide would briefly explain if the mansion belonged to a celebrity, the type of architecture and when it was built. Most of them, she informed, were occupied for only six months of the year, and this was usually during the winter, when it was cooler.

Mavis couldn't believe how one family needed to live in such a huge house. Especially with all the people she'd seen sleeping rough in the shanty towns.

It was then the coach had to slow down. This was to allow the van ahead, towing a trailer full of gardening tools, to turn right into a massive colonial mansion.

The van driver climbed out and spoke into the security box. With that, the mansion gates slowly opened.

Just at that moment, someone was coming out from the entrance. Mavis had a good view. She could see a gleaming powder blue Bentley Continental, open-topped, with its suntanned driver wearing dark glasses. He was waving for the van to reverse, so he could pull out of the entrance.

In the coach there was a buzz. Some of the passengers pointed and said it looked like the actor Pierce Brosnan. People raised their cameras and snapped away. 'Could be someone famous,' Mavis muttered to herself as she quickly zoomed in and took a few pictures.

Within seconds the Bentley had roared off, and the gates closed.

Mavis turned to Doris and Jack and rolled her eyes. 'How the other half live, eh?'

'I know,' said Doris, laughing. 'Makes yer sick, dunnit?'

They relaxed and sat back for the rest of the journey. It was going to be a long day with more walking and a guided tour to follow. Mavis closed her eyes and tried to catnap, but her mind was turning something over. She couldn't put her finger on it. She'd seen something, something familiar she'd recognised.

It was annoying. Had she dreamed about this place or seen it on the television? Was it from one of her magazines?

Within minutes, Mavis was quietly sitting back in her seat and snoring away.

*

It had been three months since the holiday. Mavis had kept in touch with Doris and Jack, and they had promised to invite her down to Ramsgate when the weather was a bit kinder.

It was then, after some consideration that Alf Hubbard, with his angina and arthritis in both legs, decided to ditch his part-time retirement job, and put away his ladder and paint tins. With his small savings and pension, while drawing on some housing benefit, he was able to keep his head above water after retirement.

It was a chilly November morning, and Alf was sweeping some leaves off his front lawn.

'Excuse me, are you Mr Hubbard? The painter and decorator?'

Alf turned to see an elderly lady standing by his front gate. She had a walking stick in one hand and a small canvas shopping trolley in the other.

'Yes, I am. Can I help you?'

'I'm Mrs Hockington, from number ninety-two up the road. I saw your decorating card in the post office window.'

Alf quickly interrupted. 'I'm sorry, my love, I should have taken it out. I don't do jobs any more.'

Her face dropped. 'Oh, I see. It's just that... I need two bedrooms decorated by Christmas. My son and his family are coming over from Canada. I've tried the local paper, but everyone's busy – I expect the job's too small.'

Alf felt sorry for her. He remembered the old lady now. She'd lost her husband some years ago, and lived on her own. From the way her fingers clutched the walking stick, he could also see she had problems with arthritis.

As she was about to turn away, Alf had second thoughts. 'Look, um, if you're really hard pressed, Mrs Hockington, I could come along and take a look.'

She beamed at him. 'Oh, thank you, Mr Hubbard.'

'Call me Alf,' he said. 'As you're only up the road, I could pop along this afternoon and give you a price, cash only if that's okay, say around three pm?'

'That'll be fine,' the old lady said. 'I'll have a nice cup of

147

tea and a slice of Victoria sponge waiting for you.'

Alf laughed and thanked her.

After agreeing a price, including paint and wallpaper, she was happy to let Alf start.

By the second day, he'd stripped the walls and was painting the skirting board and doors. Alf liked painting more than wallpapering. With painting, his brain could go into neutral. He didn't have to think too hard; just backwards and forwards with the brush. Unlike wallpapering, where there was always that urgency – because the paste was drying – or smoothing out the bubbles – or cutting around fiddly bits – or trying to line the pattern up. Painting allowed the mind to rest, or vegetate, as he called it.

Alf looked out of the window; it was raining. Mrs Hockington had left him a spare key. She'd gone to the library, and told him she was going to have a coffee there with an elderly friend.

He looked at his watch; it was eleven-thirty, time for his morning tea break and favourite radio programme. Alf twiddled the knob of his old paint-stained portable, when suddenly, Jonathan Dimbleby burst into life, chairing *Any Questions?* Alf poured himself a coffee from his thermos, and then unwrapped his cheese and tomato sandwich.

'Damn,' Alf mumbled. He'd forgotten his morning paper. No point now, going back for it in the rain. Alf sat on the bedroom stool and listened to his radio. He glanced at the old newspapers sticking out from under the rolled-back carpet. People years ago, including his own parents, had lined their floorboards, before underlay was introduced, with newspapers, to stop the dust from coming through.

Out of curiosity, Alf stooped and slid out an old *Sunday Mirror*. He smiled to himself: the date was April 1993, nearly a year ago.

He shook it and blew off some of the dust, and then he slowly turned the pages, starting from the back. Alf always read a newspaper from back to front, because of the sport pages. That was the first news he looked at. Football results, rugby, cricket in the summer. Old habits die hard, even reading a year-old newspaper.

As Alf turned the pages, his eyes scanned some of the football action photos, together with holiday adverts, crossword puzzles and of course the football results.

After twenty-five minutes, that was it. Alf decided there's only so much old news you could read – and he'd read enough.

He tucked the newspaper back under the carpet. On the radio, Jonathan Dimbleby was arguing with a backbench member of parliament. Alf looked out of the window again. It was still raining.

He was about to dip his brush when he suddenly stopped. Something in Alf's memory stirred. What the hell was it? A face, a saying? He racked his brains, but it wouldn't leave him alone. It had to be the newspaper. Alf pulled it out, and quickly flicked through the pages again. He suddenly stopped at the easy-check, weekend football pools results. That was it, listed below were the eight winning draw numbers

4...9...17...25...32...37...43...47. Alf knew them off by heart. He'd kept a copy of the coupon in his old works diary. Harry Pritchard used to do the same line with those same numbers every week. He remembered that Harry always did the treble chance, which included three lines of eight from eleven chances. Harry would hand in the filled-out coupon every Wednesday to the pools agent, who owned a corner newspaper shop. At the same time, Harry would buy his fags and a newspaper there, and then pick up a new pools coupon for the following week.

Alf, by now, was in deep and confused thought. He tore out the football results page, folded it and put it in his pocket.

By 5pm, he'd had enough. Alf cleaned his brushes, checked everything was tidy, and told Mrs Hockington he'd be back tomorrow morning to finish off the painting.

She thanked him at the door, and waved Alf off.

Back in his kitchen, Alf changed out of his overalls. He washed up and put his favourite dinner in the oven – cottage pie, chips and beans. He set the oven timer, and sat down with today's newspaper, the one he'd forgotten to take with him.

While reading, Alf's eyes kept wandering to his overalls pocket. He stood up and pulled out the old, crumpled football results page. He looked at the numbers again.

Alf remembered now that he'd kept some copies of the football coupons in one of his old diaries up in the loft. They were with his toolbox gathering dust. He'd planned to sell his toolbox at a car boot sale one day, but it was the hassle of getting it all down, and it being covered in dust.

Many years ago, he was going to have the loft lined and get a proper access ladder fitted, which would have been a relief to his arthritis, while clambering up and down. However, the estimate was too expensive, so it was all forgotten about.

Alf thought for a moment. Was he being silly about all this? The chances of winning the football pools were something like umpteen millions to one. And, if they had won, they'd have been notified.

Alf dismissed it, screwed up the page and chucked it into the waste bin.

After dinner, he sat at the kitchen table finishing off his newspaper; but he just couldn't concentrate. His eyes seemed to drift to the waste bin.

That was it, he decided, he just had to know.

Alf stood up and gingerly picked the crumpled page from the bin. Stained with the remains of his cottage pie, he could still make out the winning numbers.

'You just can't leave it, can you?' Alf cursed to himself. 'Now I've got to trudge down the bloody garden in the rain, to get the stepladder in the garage. And then come back, climb up into the loft, get covered in dust, and for what? A fool's errand, to satisfy your stupid curiosity.' Alf finally convinced himself it wasn't worthwhile. However, as always, curiosity had its way.

With some further light-hearted cursing, he retrieved his stepladder, and positioned it on the landing. Alf climbed up and opened the loft hatch carefully, while closing his eyes to avoid the dust.

His fingers felt for the light switch, and then, with a lot of effort, he pulled himself through the hatch, panting and puffing. Alf crouched in the poor light of the bare bulb for a couple of minutes, until he got his breath back.

The toolbox was near the hatch, with his diaries piled on top. He pulled out the old newspaper and checked the date. He was looking for last year's diary.

He blew the dust off each one, and then held it up to the light. 'Bingo!' Alf exclaimed. There it was. He opened the diary at the front, to reveal photocopies of the football pools coupon. Carefully, he matched up the results with his newspaper.

Alf stared for quite a long time before it really registered. He kept saying to himself, 'It can't be... it just can't be.' He read the numbers, again and again, and there it was, the winning line of twenty-four points, eight draws from eleven.

Alf double-checked the results date from the Sunday newspaper. He then flicked through the diary to the date.

Alf was a stickler with his diaries. All the workforce at Preston Engineering were given diaries as a token Christmas present by the management.

Alf kept it on top of his toolbox. He used to put almost every day-to-day detail in his diary. This included reminders of who borrowed his workshop tools. His car mileage to petrol quantity fill-ups. And of course his horse-racing form notes, and bets placed.

And finally, Alf came to the diary page dated Wednesday 14 April. It clearly showed *pools paid* in his own handwriting.

Now his mind was swimming. He stared and stared at the diary, the dates, the copy of the pools coupon, the newspaper clipping.

From the back page of the diary, a paper fell on the floor. Alf stooped to pick it up. It was their pools syndicate agreement with the three signatures – Harry Pritchard, Alf Hubbard and Mavis Bone.

That night, Alf couldn't get any sleep. He tossed and turned, his mind going over all the possibilities. There must be a reason why he hadn't been notified of the winnings. Surely Harry must have known. He just assumed Harry checked the pools results each week. He always collected their money and handed in the coupon. All of them just relied on Harry, relaying if they'd won anything, which was pretty much never.

In the morning, Alf telephoned Littlewoods customer enquiries. After putting him through to the results department, they briefly explained there had been one jackpot winner, collecting a cheque for £986,000. Alf asked them for the winner's details. They declined to give any information, stating their customer confidentiality policy. They also highlighted to Alf that the winner had wished to remain anonymous.

Later that following morning, Alf telephoned Mavis Bone.

'Alf, nice to hear from you. How's it going, mate?'

'Legs are giving me gyp, Mavis, you know, the arthritis. Angina's been playin' me up as well. 'Ad a couple of dodgy turns a fortnight ago. Reckon it was the ticker. Doc put me on these big red tablets. I think a horse would 'ave troubles swallowing 'em.'

Mavis laughed, 'Does your boy Brian still come round and help out?'

'Yeah, now and again, but only when 'e's short of money. Never see 'is missus though. 'Er and me don't hit it off, so to speak. I think she's waiting for the day I drop dead.'

Mavis laughed again, and told him a little about her holiday in Mexico.

And then Alf relayed what he'd discovered and found out. Mavis was stunned into silence, and then said, 'Come on, Alf, you've got to be joking. Won the pools, us for Christ's sake?' she scoffed. 'Bit early to start on the rum, Alf; take it easy and pace yourself.'

'Listen, Mavis, I'm tellin' yer, and the winner collected the jackpot, all £986,000 of it. As God be my judge, we won the pools. Littlewoods confirmed it, I phoned them. And they said the winner wanted to remain anonymous.'

After a slight pause, Mavis said, 'I don't believe it, Alf, there must be some mistake.'

'No mistake, my love. We got twenty-four points on eight draws on our coupon. I still kept old Harry's copy coupon in me works diary, including the syndicate agreement what we signed, remember?'

'Good God!' Mavis said. 'That means we would have won over' – she started to calculate in her head – 'three hundred and twenty-eight thousand pounds each.'

Alf replied, 'That's exactly what I made it.'

Mavis gasped. 'But it can't be true, Alf. I thought you and Harry checked the results each week?'

'Not me, my love,' Alf replied, 'I just left it to old Harry boy.'

'I get the feeling, Alf, maybe we were a little too trusting with our Harry.'

Alf moaned, 'We even bought him a bloody present for his send-off, and all the time he had our wad under his belt. So, what now?'

Mavis asked him, 'Did you know the pools agent where he used to collect and hand in the coupon? Maybe they might know something.'

'Hardy's, the newspaper shop, not far from the old firm,' Alf remembered. 'I used to get my paper and fags there. You went out the factory, took a left, then left again, and it was along the parade of shops. It just so happened, I queued up behind Harry once, when he handed in a coupon and collected a new one.'

Mavis inquired, 'Is this Hardy's still there now?'

'Dunno,' Alf replied, 'You're talking some time ago. I remember they used to be next to a fish and chip shop.'

Mavis said, 'Look, Alf, you take it easy, what with your arthritis. I can do the leg work, and see what comes up, and then I'll pop round to visit you. I'll bring a bottle of rum, and bore you silly with some of my holiday photos.'

Alf laughed, 'Okay, Mavis, best of luck.'

*

By 11.30am, Mavis had found *CHIPS ARE US*, the fish and chip shop Alf had highlighted. Next door was now Patel's, a mini-supermarket. As Mavis expected, Mr Singh Patel, a lean man who wore a sherwani with churidars and a Gandhi cap, expressed his ignorance of the previous owner. He explained that he and his family had taken on the lease after the shop had been empty for three months. Mavis thanked him, and went next door to the overpowering smells of the fish and chip fat fryer.

The chippy, a fat man with a sweaty, rosy face, wearing a batter-stained striped apron, was more helpful. After quickly serving two customers, he returned to Mavis's questions. 'I remember Don and Maggie Hardy next door, who had the newspaper shop. Nice couple, used to get my paper and fags there. What about them?'

Mavis lied, 'Oh… it's just someone I met on holiday who now lives in Cornwall knew them. They were friends and lost touch when they retired down there. Asked me to pop in and say hello from them. But like you say, I can see they've moved.'

'You're right, love. Indians have got it now. Don and Maggie have been gone…' He squeezed his chin in thought, '… at least ten months ago.'

Mavis asked hopefully, 'Would you have an address?'

'Sorry, love. All I know is they moved in a hurry. One minute they were here, next minute they were gone. There was a rumour, though.' The chippy looked pensive and squeezed his chin again. He leaned over the counter to Mavis, to be more intimate. 'Don't quote me… but my ex-missus at the time was talking to her hairdresser, who also styled Maggie Hardy's.

'Apparently, Cristiano, or whatever his name was, had told my ex that Maggie and her hubby had come into a lot of money, fifteen thousand pounds to be exact. Maggie had been told to keep quiet about it. But you know what women are like – can't keep their mouths shut. Soon afterwards, the Hardys are driving around in a posh Merc. Then all of a sudden their shop is up for lease. Never even said goodbye.'

Mavis was getting a sinking feeling in her stomach. What had started out as a silly passing thought was now gaining a horrible ring of truth? Had herself and Alf been well and truly shit-on from a great height?

Mavis asked the chippy, 'Is it possible to have a word with your ex?'

He laughed, 'Be my guest, love, wherever she and wotsisname, Cristiano, her hairdresser boyfriend are. My last solicitor's letter highlighted Liverpool, where *he* came from. That was six – no, nearly eight months ago.'

Mavis thanked him.

At the door, the chippy shouted, 'Don't forget, love, we give ten per cent discount at weekday lunchtimes.'

Mavis thanked him and gave him a wave.

THIRTEEN

Mr Hernandez

Three days later, Mavis received a phone call. It was from Alf's son Brian. She listened in silence as a teary Brian told her Alf had died from a heart attack in hospital the previous night.

'He was admitted yesterday evening, complaining of chest pains. I went to see him last night, and he was in and out of consciousness. Wanted me to phone you.' Brian sniffled a bit and then carried on. 'At the end, he wasn't making much sense. Said he'd won the football pools... kept on saying he'd won the pools.'

Mavis exhaled a sigh. 'Poor old, Alf, he was a nice man, your dad,' she offered in comfort. 'It was our standing joke when we were workmates – what we'd do with the money if we won the football pools.'

'That's what I told the wife, the silly bitch,' Brian sniffled. 'Wanted me to go through his house looking for the winning coupon.' He laughed and sniffled again at the nonsense of it all.

Mavis asked, 'Do you know when the funeral will be?'

'Sometime next week. It'll be a small affair. A cremation, and then a drink and sandwich at his old local across the road from where he lived,' Brian sniffled out. 'I'll let you know the arrangements.'

Mavis thanked him and replaced the receiver thoughtfully. She looked at the sideboard and the lonely bottle of rum, with the green pouch of shag tobacco, and the wallet of holiday photos she was going to take along when she visited Alf. Now they were the only reminders of her old workmate.

As Mavis picked up the holiday photos, they slipped from her hand and spilled out onto the floor. 'Shit! You silly bastard,' she said to herself. Picking them up one by one, she blew off the static carpet hairs that had stuck to the glossy surface. And then her hand froze. Mavis stood transfixed. If she hadn't had her camera on zoom, she wouldn't have noticed. It was the photo of the man in the powder blue Bentley – the very suntanned Pierce Brosnan lookalike, with his hand raised. She'd snapped him while passing through the town of San Luis Potosí. That was it, what she'd seen on the coach. Now it came back to her, the glimpse she'd caught of his left-hand index finger and the ring.

Mavis went to her sideboard drawer and grabbed a magnifying glass. 'My God,' she said under her breath, 'but it can't be.' In the photo she could clearly see the missing finger and the skull and crossbones biker ring at the stump. The face was half hidden, but the remaining portion: could it really be Harry?

To the left of the raised hand, just behind, was a sign on a board. Mavis squinted into the magnifying glass, where she read: For Sale. Contact Realty World Real Estate, Blvd, Bernardo Quintana No.113, Local 3 Plaza Centrum, Villa del Parque, Querétaro C.P. 76140, Tel: 52 (442) 248-3504.

From the sideboard drawer, Mavis pulled out a Michelin street map she'd picked up on her holiday. Using the magnifying glass, she traced across it with her finger. She knew the house was near the Querétaro Plaza, where the coach had stopped for lunch. San Juan del Río with its Aztec temple was after the town of San Luis Potosí. That must be it, San Luis Potosí; the tour guide had called it the Beverly Hills of Mexico or something.

Mavis sat down, her mind buzzing. She had to have a plan. Pretend to be somebody else. Get some business cards printed.

Two days later, she picked up the telephone and asked for the operator. After she'd repeated the number twice, for Realty World Real Estate, Mavis heard an international ringing tone. And then someone answered in Spanish. Mavis quickly replied with a false name. 'This is Mrs Sandra Gladden speaking from England, I'm interested in one of your houses for sale, can someone help me?'

The Spanish changed to broken English. 'Good Morning, Madam, this is Realty World Real Estate, can I help you?'

Never in Mavis's wildest dreams had she ever expected to be back in Mexico within three months. After an uncomfortable eleven-hour flight to Mexico City, and then a 135-mile, fast-track coach ride along the tolled highway to Queretaro, she finally reached the offices of Realty World Real Estate.

A secretary led Mavis through into a sumptuous air-conditioned office to meet Mr Ricardo Espinoza, the estate agent dealing with properties in the San Luis Potosí area. The office smelt of coffee and cigars. Mavis, now disguised in a brown-haired wig with heavy tanned make-up and over-the-top white sunglasses, was grateful it was cool. The outside afternoon temperature had reached ninety-six degrees.

Mr Espinoza was a big, rotund man. Wearing a light beige suit which looked a size too large, and a white shirt with a flamboyant kipper tie, loosely knotted, his smile flashed a gold front tooth. Mavis remembered the old Warner Bros movies – he could have been Sydney Greenstreet, straight out of *The Maltese Falcon*.

He introduced himself with a half bow and shook her hand vigorously. 'I hope you had a good journey?' He looked at Mavis's business card. 'Mrs Sandra Gladden – yes?' Mavis nodded.

She'd given the estate agent a fake business card, in case the seller, if it was indeed Harry Pritchard, smelled a rat and wouldn't see her. Mavis eased herself back into a comfortable leather sofa, while Mr Espinoza sat behind a large carved mahogany desk, from which he visibly drew authority.

He reassured Mavis, in what was clearly a well-rehearsed opening sales pitch, 'Realty World is one of the top real estate brokers in Mexico, catering for the needs of expatriates looking to buy property or invest in real estate. Our highly trained bilingual agents provide detailed advice on a wide range of topics concerning the real estate market in Mexico.'

Mavis Bone showed him the photograph, with the FOR SALE sign, which he recognised immediately. 'Ah yes, the Hernandez property, the Villa Casa Nova in San Luis Potosí, a very good choice, Mrs Gladden.'

'Is it still up for sale?' she asked.

'Yes it is,' the estate agent smiled, flashing his gold tooth. 'We did have a buyer, but they dropped out – couldn't raise the money. The price is 2.3 million US dollars.'

'Is that negotiable?' Mavis asked.

The estate agent smiled again. 'I'm sure we can come to a compromise, Mrs Gladden.'

As it was a Wednesday, Mavis's luck was in. Only Wednesdays and Mondays were viewing days. A further twenty-minute drive in the estate agent's car brought them to the beautiful town of San Luis Potosí.

After speaking into the security box, they finally stood outside the massive ornate front door of the Villa Casa Nova.

The estate agent pressed the bell, and a smartly dressed

maid wearing an immaculate white uniform and cap came to the door. After a few words in Spanish with the agent, they were led through a heavily ornate oak-panelled hall into a study. After another brief exchange, the maid departed.

'I suggest we start in the west wing,' the estate agent said, handing Mavis a copy of the sales brochure, 'and then move on around the ground floor. We can view upstairs and the bedrooms after the maids have tidied up.'

Mavis nodded in agreement. She'd never seen a house so beautiful. As she was led through each magnificent room, her head turned and twisted to take in the tapestries, Chinese rugs, Aztec-patterned textiles, French inlaid bureaus and writing desks. There were also various dark and ominous paintings of Conquistadors, who looked down on expensive dining room furniture, Spanish style with high-backed and ornately carved chairs, and long tables all set out with silverware.

'Now, this is the games room.' The estate agent held the door open for Mavis. Before them stood a magnificent snooker table with the balls roughly placed, as though a match had been interrupted. The green baize cloth stood out in contrast to the dark panelled walls and oak flooring. 'Mr Hernandez, the owner, had the table made especially to match the antique drinks cabinet.' He nodded to the cabinet over in the corner. 'For many years it was in the family of Napoleon Bonaparte. As you can imagine, it is extremely valuable. Might I add, the furniture is not included in the sale of the property? The price of course reflects this.'

'Of course,' Mavis quickly said, making out she was an old hand at negotiating at this level.

'Now, over in the far corner we have a range of fitness machines and…' The estate agent tapered off. He was looking at Mavis.

Mavis stood mesmerised, rooted to the spot. It was the picture on the wall she'd just noticed. There it was in all its glory, the framed photo of Harry Pritchard holding the winner's trophy at the Preston Engineering snooker final. The same photo he used to keep on his toolbox. 'The bastard's still got it on show,' Mavis murmured under her breath.

'I'm sorry…?' The estate agent looked puzzled.

'Oh, err, the picture,' Mavis added. 'I thought I recognised a famous snooker player.'

'Ah, I think it's a picture of the present owner, taken some time ago in his snooker days,' the agent informed her with a smile.

At that moment, the door opened and a tall slim, tanned and good-looking man entered. 'Ah, Mr Hernandez,' the agent said and bowed with the greeting, 'let me introduce you to Mrs Sandra Gladden, one of our prospective buyers.'

Mr Victor Hernandez flashed a set of expensive porcelain crowns that a Hollywood film star would have been proud of, and said, 'Welcome to the Villa Casa Nova.' He shook Mavis's hand. His left hand remained at his side, but now, up close, Mavis could clearly see the missing finger and the ring.

Victor Hernandez never recognised Mavis – and why

should he? Wearing her wig and the large white sunglasses, Mavis would've had trouble getting her late parents to recognise her.

And it had been almost ten months now. Mavis had put on a bit of weight, which made her face slightly fuller. Now it was a different time and a different place.

On the other hand, the past months had been kind to Harry Pritchard, Mavis thought. The spotless complexion with a possible facelift – he certainly looked younger, and he now had a physique you could only get from lots of workouts. No doubt fine food, expensive health farms and a country club lifestyle of spa treatments, personal fitness trainers and tennis lessons had contributed.

He simply oozed wealth in his casual Versace clothes; the silk shirt and beige corduroy trousers displayed discreet designer labels. Gucci loafers and a Rolex Oyster watch, helped to finish off the look of a man who'd done well for himself; either that or won the football pools.

'I'm pleased to meet you, Mrs Gladden. I hope you had a pleasing trip?' Harry's forced, smooth, Spanish-style accent, with just a hint of broken English, had been well rehearsed over the months.

Mavis nodded with a smile.

'I hope we're not disturbing you, Sir?' the agent asked with a deferential frown.

'No – no, please carry on,' Mr Hernandez replied with a nonchalant wave. 'I will be in my study if you need me; I have some work to do.'

Victor Hernandez moved to the door, and then said,

with another flashing smile, 'I hope negotiations will be fruitful and mutually agreeable, Mr Espinoza.'

The estate agent bowed as Hernandez departed and said, 'Thank you, Mr Hernandez.'

'He sounds a very important man, your Mr Hernandez,' Mavis said, trying to avoid sounding too sarcastic.

'Ah, you must remember, Mrs Gladden, Realty World Real Estate is a very exclusive and prestigious company. We sell and manage property for many top businesspersons and politicians,' he proudly boasted. 'Mr Hernandez' – he leaned forward and lowered his voice, as if imparting confidential information – 'is a high-profile entrepreneur and sponsor. He wants to sell this house and move to Querétaro, where he hopes to be the mayor of the city.'

'Wow! The mayor of Querétaro,' Mavis, said trying to look interested. It was obvious the estate agent liked to stress the importance of his clients, and that he also loved the sound of his own voice. *Just try to keep him talking*, Mavis thought. She asked him, 'So what does he sponsor?'

'Mr Hernandez is a kind benefactor and sponsor of numerous projects. He sits on various trade councils, and has donated to museums and hospitals. In fact, he sits on the city council for research and development, and is on one of the boards of governors for the University of Querétaro. He is also the borough mayor for San Luis Potosí,' the estate agent said with a glow of pride.

Mavis had a feeling this was one of Mr Espinoza's selling tactics. The more he praised his clients, the stronger the incentive to buy their property.

The estate agent shifted through his papers until he pulled out a monthly industry magazine. He handed the *América Economia* to Mavis. She was gobsmacked. On the front cover was a picture of a smiling Harry Pritchard.

'Of course, as he's one of our top clients, we have to be discreet. But I can tell you' – the estate agent leaned in close to Mavis once again, with his eye on the door – 'as I mentioned, he hopes to be appointed mayor of Querétaro. This means he will be in charge over the other seven boroughs and mayors covering the city. But most of all' – again he preened himself for being so fortunate to have such an illustrious client on his books – 'he is shortlisted to receive Mexico's highest award for industry.'

'And what is that?' Mavis asked.

'What is that!' the estate agent repeated in astonishment, as if Mavis should have known. He said with pride, 'It is the German Patiño Díaz medal, of course, named after Mexico's great artist and engineer.'

'Wow, that must be something special,' Mavis said with false interest. 'He does sound a respectable pillar of the community.' Looking again at the snooker picture of Harry on the wall, Mavis asked, 'So how did he make his money?'

'His profile is in the magazine, but briefly, he moved here about a year ago, and invested in food processing. With the profits, he bought some cheap land for farming. Just after that, to his good fortune, the giant multinational companies moved in, like Gerber and Nestlé. He sold out to them, using his land, and made a killing.' The estate agent nodded at the magazine. 'It says in there, his estimated fortune is now worth five million dollars, with his yacht and various properties.'

Mavis interrupted, 'My God! He *is* a rich man. I'll have to ask him for a loan.' She laughed at her little joke, but the estate agent didn't seem to have seen the funny side.

Mavis had heard enough; it was now or never. Before he started prattling on again, she asked, 'Mr Espinoza, may I use the washroom?'

'Yes, of course,' the estate agent said. 'It's through the door, past the study and the first on the left. Forgive me my manners, let me show you.' He moved towards the door.

'No, no, it's quite all right, Mr Espinoza.' Mavis held up her hand with a smile. 'I can find it myself.'

She remembered Hernandez saying he would be in his study. Mavis moved along the oak-panelled hallway until she came to a door that stood partially open. She peered in and saw Hernandez reading at a huge leather-topped desk, peppered with expensive ornaments. A brass lamp with a green shade illuminated the document in front of him.

Mavis knocked politely.

Hernandez looked up. 'Do come in, Mrs... err...'

'Gladden, but please call me Mavis.'

Hernandez's eyes swept past Mavis to the door, expecting to see the estate agent.

She told him, 'Oh, Mr Espinoza had to visit the washroom, I was just taking a stroll; sorry for being nosey.'

Hernandez said in his smooth Spanish accent, 'That's all right, Mavis, it's a big house if you don't know your way.'

He stopped abruptly. 'That's funny, I thought Mr Espinoza said your name was Sandra?'

Mavis closed the study door and smiled. She walked over to Hernandez and took out her own copy of the signed football pools syndicate agreement. She placed it on the desk in front of him.

It took a few seconds to register. And then the blood drained from his face. He was speechless, with a look of disbelief. Never-but-never in a million years was he ever going to see Mavis again, he'd made sure of it. With a new name, a new identity, plastic surgery and even a hair transplant.

'My my, Harry. You have done well for yourself. How's that sister of yours in Newcastle?' she asked him.

With a look of astonishment he said, 'But how did you find…?'

'It's a long story, Harry. I won't bother you with the details. Don't try tearing up the agreement. Alf Hubbard has the original nice and safe; remember, you gave it to him. By the way, I like your snooker picture in the games room, nice touch. Don't worry, I haven't let on to Mr Espinoza.'

Mavis made herself comfortable on the chesterfield sofa. 'How life changes, Harry. I thought you and me had a good relationship once. And then you finished it, and just upped and left.

'Oh, that reminds me, Harry, the chippy next to Hardy's the newsagents, told me about Don and Maggie's little windfall from you.'

Harry's face changed to a sneer. 'You can't prove

anything, it's been over a year or more.' He reached for the fancy brass telephone on his desk. 'I'm going to call security, have you thrown out.'

Mavis reached across and held down the receiver. 'I wouldn't do that if I were you, Harry. Think about it.' She held up the agreement with the signatures. 'I checked it out with a solicitor. This document is still valid, and *you* could be prosecuted for fraud, and making a false syndicate claim on Littlewoods football pools.' She hastened to add, 'Okay, so perhaps not over here in Mexico. But think what the newspapers would say, Harry.'

Mavis reached to her inside pocket and produced a half page from a British newspaper. The headline of the *Daily Mirror* read, SYNDICATE CHEAT RUNS OFF WITH FOOTBALL POOLS WINNINGS. The picture underneath the caption was the same one, showing Harry with the snooker cup. Mavis reminded him, 'Remember, you gave me a copy of the photo at the time. Can you imagine the Querétaro newspapers with this story? How you did all that wheeling and dealing with donations and sponsorships, all from stolen pools money.'

Harry slowly replaced the receiver.

'Now, a little birdy told me you were in line for mayor – even getting some fancy gong. An award for industry or something. What do you think your chances would be for election, if I went to see the current mayor? Or the board of governors for the various trade councils you sit on, including Querétaro University?'

Harry looked surprised to find that Mavis knew so much about his new life.

'Been doing my homework, Harry boy. Now, this is how we're going to play it.' She showed Harry the magazine, *América Economia*. 'Says in there you're worth five million dollars.'

Instantly, Harry jumped on the defensive; he knew what was coming. 'I'm worth nothing like that. That's pure newspaper speculation.'

'Oh, come on, Harry, you must have a few bob tucked away. Myself and Alf just want what's rightfully ours, we won't even charge you interest,' she said with a smile. 'The payout was £986,000. So I reckon that makes £328,666 each.' Mavis moved herself intimidatingly to within inches of Harry's face. Wearing a mean look, she said, 'Now listen, chum. You will follow the instructions on this piece of paper, or else.'

The paper showed details of Mavis's UK building society. 'I want my cut and Alf's share put in my UK account. Alf knows I'm out here,' she lied. 'He'll get his share when I get back. It'll be a nice little nest-egg for him, he deserves it. That's what friends are for, Harry – sharing. You've got a month to do it.'

'You're joking, I can't get that sort of money together in a month.'

'You will, if you sell this house within the month, and I strongly suggest you do. Otherwise this page with the headline, and your picture, will be sent to the press over here.'

Mavis knew she had him over a barrel. She just hoped he wasn't going to call her bluff. 'When the two shares, amounting to £657,333, have been transferred in full, I'll send you the original pools syndicate agreement with your signature, and you'll never hear from me again.'

At that moment the estate agent entered.

Quickly stepping away from Harry, Mavis apologised and told him, 'I'm sorry, I got a little bit lost, but I'd still like to see the rest of the house.'

Mr Espinoza asked Mr Hernandez if he would be joining them on the tour.

'I expect he's too busy writing cheques,' joked Mavis.

*

Three months later, Mavis preened herself in the hall mirror. Her executive limo was due in five minutes. She picked up her savings account statement, and looked again at the new balance of £657,333 – minus the £5,000 of course for the first-class flight and Mexican holiday she was about to take, plus spending money.

No doubt the taxman would be after her at some time or another, but for now she dismissed this possibility with a shrug, while adjusting the time of her Rolex watch.

In the hall, Mavis made a final check of her cases and travel bag. She glanced at the three new picture frames above the telephone table. Mavis leaned in, and smiled to herself at the suntanned Harry Prichard in the powder blue Bentley, with his arm forever raised. And then the snooker final with Harry holding the cup. Finally, the *Daily Mirror* front page: SYNDICATE CHEAT RUNS OFF WITH FOOTBALL POOLS WINNINGS. 'What you can do on a home PC these days,' Mavis said to herself smiling.

It had crossed her mind to give Alf Hubbard's share to his son and his wife. However, Mavis didn't think they deserved it. Alf always said they couldn't wait for him to pop off so they could sell his house.

Instead, she'd bought herself a flat and office space on Wimbledon Broadway. It was an ideal location to start her new private detective agency. Something that Mavis had always wanted to do, and now she could share it with Gertrude Stick, her new German secretary and lover. They'd met at a lesbian bar in Soho, and they were already smitten with each other.

FOURTEEN

Modom

As Mavis Bone sat back on the Tube, passing the time between South Kensington and Knightsbridge, she flicked through the latest fashions in this month's *Vogue*.

Right now, she was travelling to the West End for a good old spend-up. And why not. Having won the football pools, she felt she deserved a treat. And Gertrude Stick, her secretary, had taken a couple of days' holiday leave to Eastbourne.

*

Mavis had been to Harrods a number of times, but only to browse. Now she had money, and there was a spring in her step. Shopping meant something, it was purposeful.

She pushed through the heavy swing doors and caught a glimpse of the store guide. Mavis ran her thumb along, until it stopped at Women's Fashion. And then she headed for the first floor.

Christian Dior, Yves Saint Laurent and André Courrèges were her favourites. She wasn't a King's Road or Carnaby Street person. Mavis wasn't into the 1960s Mary Quant or Ossie Clark, with their revolting psychedelic black and white pop-art patterns. In 1994, she was a traditionalist and proud of it, wearing red trouser suits, to go with her jet-black hair of tiny curls.

In the fashion magazines, Mavis loved Vivienne Westwood's trouser suit collections. And for the hair, it had to be Vidal Sassoon. She had made her mind up to have a cut and blow dry makeover.

After a couple of hours' shopping and clutching four designer bags, and a new Dior cream-coloured handbag, Mavis made her way up the escalator to the Harrods Georgian Restaurant.

It looked bloody expensive – Mavis eyed up the suited maître d' who was standing on the podium in his roped-off area, with the afternoon menu opened up in front of him. He looked like an orchestra conductor with his sheet music.

'Just the one, modom?' Mavis nodded as the maître d' clicked his fingers.

Passing faces looked up at her, as she followed the waiter to a fancy decorated middle table.

Leaving Mavis with the menu, he came back after a few minutes and flipped his pad.

'A camomile tea with the smoked salmon on brown,

and a selection of pastries, thank you,' Mavis said. 'Oh! And a glass of champagne.'

The waiter made his notes, nodded indifferently and said, 'Thank you, modom.' And then disappeared through the swing doors.

Mavis sat back and surveyed the customers. It was easy to pick out the business tables from the special occasions. Male domination and the lack of smiles gave the game away.

Although the restaurant was nearly full, the service was surprisingly quick, as the waiter came back juggling three plates on one arm, while holding a fluted glass with his free hand.

The presentation looked fantastic, especially the selection of pastries, which were all gussied up with icing sugar and chocolate bits and bobs.

Mavis sipped her champagne and nibbled the smoked salmon. She sat back and took it all in. The Georgian silk drapes with the bullion windows; the matching rococo chairs and table clothes with the tulip-folded serviettes. The gleaming silver cutlery. She knew she deserved this. And she'd worked hard to get it.

Mavis glanced at her new Omega wristwatch, thinking, *Plenty of time, might even get in a bit more browsing before heading off to Vidal Sassoon's for the 4pm hair appointment.*

'Everything to your satisfaction, modom?'

With the agility and stealth of a panther, the waiter had appeared from nowhere and startled her. Mavis turned sharply towards the voice, and knocked over the glass of

176

champagne. 'Oh shit! I'm sorry...' She half got up, and quickly dabbed the dregs on the table that were spilling onto her red Biba trouser suit.

'I'm sorry, my fault,' the waiter said, as he helped her by dabbing here and there with another table serviette.

'That's okay... I'll be all right, thank you. No damage done...' A few other tables were looking over and then lowered their heads as she glanced around. Mavis felt embarrassed at the fuss she'd caused.

'I will get modom another glass and a clean tablecloth; again I'm sorry...'

'No... No. My fault... I'll just pop along to the ladies to freshen up.'

Mavis pushed her bags under the table. She stood up as nonchalantly as possible, and then made her way to the white and pink washroom door.

There was only one other person, who looked up as she entered. A smartly dressed mature lady, who carried on titivating her hair in the mirror.

Mavis moved to an elaborate wash-hand basin with gold taps, and started dabbing at the stain on her suit jacket. She took in the opulence. Certainly a better toilet than the one she shared with Gertrude in their Wimbledon Broadway agency flat.

On the vanity unit there was a selection of perfumes and freebies, with the store's compliments. Mavis delicately puffed a bottle of Chanel behind each ear. And then, after a bit more fussing in the mirror, she finally moistened her lips and applied a very red glossy lipstick.

She closed her new Dior handbag and took one last look. Mavis straightened her red jacket, fluffed up the lapels and then moved to the door. Before leaving, she put fifty pence in the tipping saucer as she passed the lady concierge, sitting idly on a stall, reading a magazine.

When Mavis arrived back, there was a new tablecloth, and sitting on her silver drinks mat was a fresh glass of champagne. Mavis took a sip and reached for a smoked salmon sandwich. She delicately took a bite, trying to keep it as refined as possible, and picked up the serviette to dab the crumbs.

And then she froze.

Mavis slowly unfolded the pink, tulip-shaped serviette. There was a message on it in biro.

Her eyes swam over the blue scribble before they focused. It read, I've kidnapped your secretary Gertrude Stick. Be at Knightsbridge tube station phone booths at 4pm sharp today, and await a telephone call. Don't be late, and make sure to be there, or I will kill her.

She read it again to take it all in.

Mavis slowly folded the serviette, looking around furtively as she placed it in her handbag. Everything seemed normal. Everybody carrying on with their business. Nothing out of the ordinary.

The waiter came up behind her again, but this time she recognised the voice.

'Is everything to your satisfaction, modom?'

Mavis half turned and looked at him. *He certainly had the opportunity*, she thought. He wouldn't have looked out of place fussing around her table. The waiter's age was around the late forties, and he sounded a Londoner by his accent. But that was it.

Mavis didn't recognise him from anywhere. He didn't look like an old agency client, someone with a grudge?

'Yes, it was very nice. Did... did you see anybody at my table while I was away?'

He shook his head, puzzled. 'No, modom, is there a problem? Does modom have anything missing?'

'No, no, it's okay.' She searched his face once more and then said, 'I'll just have the bill please?'

'Thank you, modom.' He politely nodded and then was gone.

Three minutes later, he came back with a silver tray and a smart leather pouch emblazoned with the gold Harrods motif on the front. The waiter discreetly left, while Mavis checked the amount. They hadn't charged for the champagne.

*

It was 4pm, and only one of the four phone booths was occupied at Knightsbridge tube station. Mavis hovered, clutching her bags. She'd pushed the three remaining booth doors open, so she could listen for the ringing.

And then a couple approached. 'Scuse me, honey,' he asked her. They were of course American. Early fifties – in age and dress style. Him with his loud check jacket and a Panama hat, with a camera dangling from his neck. Her with the leopard-skin jacket, alligator handbag and half a dozen gold bracelets. 'Can yer tell us, honey, which entrance for Harryards?' The wife stood by him with an impatient look.

Mavis took her eyes off the booths, half-listening. 'I'm sorry... what?'

'Come on, Walt, let's ask someone else.' The wife was tugging at his arm.

'Hold on, Rhoda.' Walt held his hand up to quieten her, and then produced a street map. 'We want to get to Harryards,' he said pointing, 'you know, the store the Queen uses. Is it the Bromhampton Street exit, honey?'

'Err... yes,' Mavis said, 'you need the exit for...'

Somewhere in the back of her brain, she heard ringing. It didn't register at first, with all the station noise. Mavis half turned to the sound, and realised it was coming from the left-hand booth.

Mavis lurched away like a gazelle that had been spotted by a cheetah. Leaving the American couple with their mouths open, she exploded into the booth, clutching up the receiver and panting hard.

'Yes, yes, it's Mavis,' she said, while waving to the American couple through the glass and mouthing, 'Sorry.'

'Where were you? I said don't be late.'

The voice sounded muffled, she thought. A man's voice, probably talking with a handkerchief over the mouthpiece.

'Who are you?'

'Shut up! Now listen. Your secretary will die unless you carry out these instructions.'

'So, what do you want?'

'One hundred thousand pounds in used notes. You've got four days, otherwise your secretary Gertrude Stick will die, I promise you.'

'Three days. Where am I going to get that sort of money in three days?'

'The same bank where you put all the money you obtained from Mr Hernandez in Mexico City. He is a very angry man, although he can afford it. However, I'm not that financially blessed. So I wouldn't mess with him or go to the police. Your secretary will die if you do.'

Mavis replied, 'But I can't just…'

'You get the money and your secretary will be safely returned. Now listen carefully, and I suggest you get a pen and paper.'

Mavis fumbled in her handbag. 'Okay.'

'This Thursday evening, you will take one hundred thousand pounds in used notes and place it in that cream-coloured Dior bag you've got with you.'

Mavis spun round and realised she was being watched. She scanned the commuters and the station for anything suspicious. But nothing stood out. It all looked quite normal.

'Now listen,' the voice continued. 'This Thursday you will take the nine-forty-five evening train from Basildon to West Horndon. You must get on in the end trailing carriage, and sit near a left-hand carriage door, forward-moving position. At a certain point during the journey, the train will stop. It won't be at a station. And then you have to push down the carriage door window, and throw out the bag of money onto the track. After that, the train will proceed to West Horndon station. Get off there and go to the phone box just outside the station, and wait for it to ring.'

'And when do I see Gertrude, my secretary?' Mavis asked.

'We will be holding her in a car. And provided we pick up the money, she'll be returned to you safe and sound.'

'How do I know you won't try it again? Next month or next year?' Mavis shouted down the phone.

'You'll just have to trust me, like I trust you to get the money, and not go to the police. Remember, her life is in your hands, believe me.'

Mavis closed her eyes in submission, wondering what Gertrude was going through. 'Okay – okay, I'll get your money,' she said.

'I just knew, Mavis, you'd see sense.'

*

By nine-forty in the evening that Thursday, Basildon station was winding down for the day. The diesel with its four carriages was at the platform. Mavis made her way past four seated people, and sat as near as possible to the carriage door. She eyed two gentlemen and an elderly couple. The couple smiled as she took her seat. The compartment smelt of stale cigarettes and pipe smoke. Opening a discarded newspaper, she quickly buried her face in it, pretending to read.

Mavis clutched her bag thinking *Why the shit did he ask*

for my new Dior handbag for the drop? Why not an old carrier bag or something? He must have been watching me when I bought it in Harrods. She'd spent ages shopping for it, to match the shoes and gloves she'd bought. And now having to part with it, as well as the money, was like rubbing salt into the wound.

Mavis had managed to scrape together two thousand pounds. She'd spent four nights scanning and printing twenty-pound notes on A4 paper, and then cutting them up into bank note sizes. With elastic bands, she fastened the fake cash bundles either side with real money, to make it look good. And hopefully this would allow her some extra negotiating time with the hammer she'd brought along. Mavis clutched the handle, deep in her coat pocket, making sure it was in easy reach.

Mavis Bone mulled it over as she rocked with the motion of the train. Whoever it was had her arse nailed to the barn door, and knew it. This slippery bastard would probably want more. And the worrying thing? He knew who she was. Where she lived. Had followed her. Made the telephone call – probably in a disguised voice.

Mavis put a hand in her pocket, and felt the hammer. It reassured her.

At Laindon station, the last of the four passengers exited. The carriage was now empty apart from Mavis. As it continued, she stood up and slightly swayed with the train's motion. She moved to a seat near the door. She sat down thinking, and then shifted uncomfortably. Would he go through with it? Hand back Gertrude after the swap?

Suddenly there was a blast on the driver's horn, and Mavis lurched sideways as the train braked sharply and then slurred to a halt. She got up tentatively and moved to a window. Mavis shielded her eyes from the reflected light and tried to look out, but it was too dark to make anything out.

Before she parted with two thousand pounds, she had to make sure this was the right spot. She pushed the carriage door window down and leant out. There was a level crossing up ahead, all lit up. A man with a torch, probably the driver, was playing the beam around, surveying something at the front of the train.

Mavis turned as the interconnecting carriage door opened, and the ticket inspector walked through. He was a large fat man wearing a cap and reeking of stale tobacco. He had a waist that could easily have burst his British Rail uniform trousers. He looked around, and then spoke loudly, in a well-prepared reassuring little speech. 'Just to let you know we have an obstruction on the line, and the matter is being dealt with. Please do not make any attempt to get off the train, and don't worry, we will be moving shortly.' With that, he closed the door and was gone.

FIFTEEN

The Drop

Mavis was convinced. This had to be the drop. She took the bag and leant out of the carriage window, looking into the darkness. She swung the cream-coloured Dior bag backwards and forwards in an exaggerated motion. She wanted to stand out, wanted him to see where she was going to throw it. With a heave she let it go, and it bounced and rolled, and then came to rest across the opposite line.

'Shit!' Mavis muttered. She stared down into the darkness and could make out the cream shape, sitting smack on the polished steel strip. Then Mavis looked up, startled. In the faint distance she could see the lights of an opposing train approaching. Mavis's expression turned to horror. Instant thoughts flashed through her mind. *The train could be derailed, the money all chewed up under the wheels.* She had to do something, get it off the line and quick. *Mustn't let him see me. Don't want him to think I'm taking the money back.*

Mavis crouched down and made her way to the other side of the carriage. She got to the door and pushed the window down. At the same time, she put her hand through to turn the handle. The carriage door swung open. There was a steep embankment directly opposite, with no space for movement.

In that split second, Mavis was grateful she'd worn sensible shoes. '*Jesus!*' Mavis cried out as she jumped, hitting the steep grass embankment. And then she rolled back under a large steel train wheel. She frantically scrambled out from underneath the carriage, thinking it might start moving again at any moment. Mavis hauled herself up while brushing herself down. She listened out; all quiet apart from the rumble of the diesel engine up front. Using the carriage as support, she carefully made her way to the rear of the train.

Suddenly, there were crunching noises. Someone nearby walking on the gravel ballast under the sleepers.

Mavis crouched, and as she peered around the end carriage she could see the cream bag, and a figure approaching. The silhouette of a rotund man appeared, picking his way along the track, stopping, looking around, moving on, and then stopping again.

Now that she was outside, away from the glare of the windows, it was a clear night. Mavis wasn't sure if it was just a railway worker doing his job? Last-minute checks before moving off? But if it was, where was his torch? Even so, once he clocked the bag, the money would be gone. She knew what she had to do.

Mavis looked behind; she had to be quick, as the lights of the oncoming train were getting clearer and brighter. And then a horn sounded and she realised her own train was about to move off. And now she knew for sure, because the man stopped.

At about thirty feet away, he spotted the bag. The man began to move quickly, coming towards her. And then the horn of the approaching train sounded. The man checked, looked at the oncoming lights of the train and continued faster. Mavis felt in her pocket. She took out the hammer and held it down by her side.

The man tripped and half stumbled to one knee. 'Shit! You mother…' She was near enough to hear his cursing.

The man got up and brushed himself down. Up front, the horn sounded again, and Mavis's train started moving off. Her cover was gone. She crouched in the dark, but the man's eyes were only for her cream-coloured Dior handbag, containing all that money.

On the opposite line, the chugging of the leading diesel carriage was getting louder. And now he was at the bag. The man stooped to pick it up, and then tried to open it. He was having trouble with the clasp.

Mavis had twenty feet to cover. She looked behind. The diesel was getting nearer; looming out of the dark like a giant angry serpent, all lit up, spewing out its rage.

He opened the bag and got out the money; standing there totally oblivious, feverishly tearing at the newspaper she'd wrapped it in.

The approaching noise drowned out her footsteps.

With the hammer at shoulder height, Mavis moved in with a fixated and purposeful look. Like a lioness that had crept behind a wildebeest on its knees at a waterhole she was upon him, swinging the hammer to the back of his head. He half turned as the blow glanced off, and then she hit him again above the right eye. He swore at her, *'You fucking bitch!'* And then he grabbed her arm, pulling her down.

Mavis was on top, trying to hit him, but he had hold of her arm. And then with her left hand she threw gravel in his eyes. Wincing and blinking, he let her go, yelling out as she smashed the hammer into his face.

Sitting astride him, Mavis swung the hammer again, and then froze. She recognised the fat Mexican estate agent, Mr Ricardo Espinoza, from Realty World Real Estate.

She knew this man, even with blood pouring down his face. *Espinoza, what the fuck…?*

'Get off me, you bitch!'

The noise behind was deafening. Mavis could feel the approaching heat – smell the hot diesel oil. They were lit up in the train's beam. The horn sounded again.

He reached inside his jacket but got his hand tangled up as he tried to pull out a gun. She caught a glimpse of steel and instantly grabbed at it. It went off, and then fired again with his finger on the trigger and her hand clutching the barrel – Mavis yelled out, the heat scorching her hand.

Still astride the man she wrestled with him, both her hands holding his hands with the gun. She let go with one hand, feverishly clawing at the gravel, until her fingers reached the hammer's wooden handle. She grabbed it and swung it down into his face once more. Blood from his broken nose sprayed over her. He screamed with pain and dropped the gun. Again, Mavis tried to get up, but he was pulling her down on top of him.

Even with his injuries, Espinoza wrestled with her, shouting at her, 'You bitch! You fucking bitch!'

She rolled with him between the rails, dropping the hammer again, trying to kick him away, break free. Mavis could feel the vibration of the giant steel wheels on the track as they bore down on them. Espinoza wasn't going to let go. Out of the corner of her eye, she saw the gun, just beyond reach. Mavis stretched for it, but her fingers clutched at nothing. The train was less than thirty yards away. The ground was shaking like an earthquake.

Espinoza began to cough up blood, which was clogging in his throat. He relaxed his grip just a little. Mavis took advantage and strained as her fingers wrapped around the gun barrel. She looked behind; the steaming monster was nearly upon them. She wasn't going to make it.

With one last exhausted lunge, Mavis smashed the gun handle into his forehead. Blood spurted out of Espinoza's nose and mouth as she tried to push him away. Mavis rolled and rolled in the gravel across the sleepers, crying out in pain as her head and knees hit the steel rail.

It was as if the devil had invited her in. Hell's door had opened; the heat, the wind, the roar and the burning stench of diesel as the train thundered past, taking Espinoza and her money with it.

Mavis lay there on her back, not quite believing;

breathing in deep snatches as she looked up at the stars. All of a sudden, she felt cold and started to shiver. She held up her hands, mesmerised by them; they were covered in blood.

Mavis pulled herself up. She swayed a little, unsteady, taking in what happened, where she was. She took a step, stopped, hesitated, and then straightened herself, and slowly walked over to her Dior handbag. She reached down for it, and buffed it up under her arm, wanting to get rid of the scuffmarks, as if that were the only thing that mattered.

Proudly holding her cream-coloured Dior handbag, Mavis walked slowly along the track; it was surreal, as if she was strolling down Bond Street on a Saturday afternoon.

She spotted the hammer. Close by it was the gun. Picking up both items, she wiped them on her sleeve. Mavis now recognised the gun, a Smith & Wesson 10 military .38 revolver. Her late father had owned one on their Australian outback farm. It was his pride and joy, shooting beer cans for target practice as well as the occasional rabbit and fox that wandered too close.

Mavis remembered how, when her mother was working, her father would sit in his wicker chair on the farm veranda, wearing just his vest and braces, with a tumbler of Johnnie Walker at his side. He'd suck the stub of a wet cigar while polishing the steel barrel, and then hold it up occasionally, to admire his work.

Her father, being an Australian sheep farmer, used to keep the gun under his pillow. It was to keep the filthy Abos in line, he'd say. Saturday night they'd get drunk and come into town looking for white girls. And then he'd squeeze up his cheeks, and spit chewed tobacco onto the floor.

*

Mavis checked the chamber; there were three bullets remaining. She carefully wrapped the gun in a bit of newspaper she found by her feet, and then she put it in her handbag.

The first part of Ricardo Espinoza she came across was his severed left leg. Mavis nudged it with her toe, as if it might still be alive; perhaps start moving of its own accord.

She carried on another fifteen yards, and then on the edge of the right-hand rail, she saw a severed arm, cut off at the elbow.

Mavis stepped over to look at it. The left-hand little finger twitched nervously, as if beckoning her to come closer; the remains of a newspaper still clutched between the thumb and forefinger. Again, she carelessly poked it with her foot, and then turned and slowly walked on.

Mavis had gone another twenty yards when she saw the shape. It was the moaning, as it dragged itself along over the railway sleepers, that attracted her. Leaving a glistening trail of smeared blood, it looked like a giant early-morning slug. Mavis walked ahead and then blocked its way. The pitiful thing in front of her stopped. It stared carefully at her shoes, recognising them, and then lifted its head.

'Please help me?' Espinoza said weakly, with pleading eyes. 'Look... look, take the money.' He rolled over onto

191

the stump of his left arm and bellowed out with the pain. With the remaining hand, he opened his jacket, giving Mavis access.

With relish, Mavis told him, 'I conned you. The bundles of money are fake, just like your tan, Mr Espinoza.'

Espinoza could hardly speak; he was losing blood and fast. He managed to whisper, 'Don't leave me here, please help me.'

Mavis crouched and asked him, 'Where's my secretary?'

She kicked his leg stump and Espinoza screamed, 'Ahhh!!!... She's in the car – she's in the car... Please God, don't, I beg you.'

'Where are the car keys?' She didn't wait for a reply. Mavis took a deep breath and fumbled through his bloody, ripped jacket, wincing, until her fingers felt the key ring. She pulled them out. Attached to the bunch was a Mercedes key and tag.

'What's the car and colour, and where is it? And don't lie, otherwise you'll know real pain.' Mavis made as if to kick his stump again.

Espinoza, with great effort, raised himself to a half-sitting position. He put up the arm he had left, and pleaded. 'No, please. I'll tell you anything. It's a white Mercedes, registration CMP 35H.' He had to pause to get his energy, and then he said weakly, 'It's parked on the left side of the crossing up ahead, about fifty feet from the gates.' He collapsed back, exhausted, turning to cough up blood, and spitting on the side of the track.

Mavis sighed with relief, pushing her hair back and

leaving a bloody scuff on her forehead. Espinoza, in desperation, bellowed out again as he rolled onto his stomach. His remaining hand clutched the bottom of Mavis's coat. He looked up at her, whining, begging her to get help, call an ambulance. But Mavis wasn't looking at him. Her eyes were focused on the distant lights. Espinoza's eyes followed hers. He saw the approaching train.

He shuffled and slithered towards her, slipping and slopping in the blood. 'Don't leave me here,' he begged, 'I'll give you anything... Pleeeese...'

Mavis stooped and patted him on the head. 'Goodbye, Mr Espinoza. It's been nice doing business with you.'

She moved off along the side of the track amid his last desperate cries. Mavis headed towards the flashing warning lights of the level crossing gates that were now swinging open, as if allowing her a grand entrance – like some Cleopatra or Boudicca, coming home after a great battle.

Espinoza's last scream was drowned out as the ten-forty-five to Basildon swept past and directly over him. And then there was nothing. It was as if Espinoza had never existed, as if he'd been swallowed up.

Mavis ducked down out of the glare of car headlights as she approached the signal box. The gates were now closing to allow cars. Some, quick off the mark, slowly bumped their way over the raised crossing. Mavis crouched until the traffic had gone, and then she moved into the country lane, keeping close to the hedges.

After a while, the white apparition of a Mercedes

saloon slowly appeared out of the dark, with a CMP 35H registration plate. Mavis fumbled with the car keys, and then eased herself back into the luxurious leather seats. It was then she heard the moaning and banging. Mavis realised it was coming from the car boot.

Raising the boot lid, she discovered a trussed-up Gertrude Stick. 'Zank God you vound me. I thought I vos a goner.'

Helping her out, Mavis joked, 'I could never be that lucky.' And then she gave her secretary a big hug and a kiss. 'I tell yer what, Gerty, that Espinoza froitened the shits out of me. He had a face like a fuckin' bunyip; worse in fact.'

Mavis checked her watch. 'Come on, Gerty, let's find a late-night colonel for a suthy fried chooky with large chips, and lashings of dead horse. On the way we can grab a few cold tins to wash it down.'

Gertrude beamed, 'If you're paying? Zat is a good idea.'

SIXTEEN

Tears for Souvenirs

Vincent Pollack could relax this afternoon. At the July barbecue he was on his third glass of Sancerre, and Jonathan had just handed him a full plate of ribs, chicken legs, French bread and salad.

'There you are, old chap, get stuck in.' Jonathan put his hand on his shoulder. 'What you drinking, Vincent? No, don't get up. Sancerre, wasn't it?' Jonathan, the host with the most, brought him back a full glass. 'So glad you and Olivia could make it this Sunday. Not often we get an office get-together.'

Vincent Pollack's wife Olivia was driving back, so he could let his hair down for once. The weekend house-warming barbecue consisted mostly of people from his wife's office, including thirty-four-year-old Jonathan, who was also her boss and managing director of The Jonathan Bower Advertising Agency.

The weather was glorious this 2006 July afternoon. Olivia chatted as she moved from couple to couple. With Jonathan she used a polite smile and a nod, and then bypassed him. Not surprising.

In his late forties, Vincent Pollack, with his wavy ginger hair now combed over a gradually receding forehead with early worry lines, eyed Jonathan with a twinge of jealousy. Taller than him, single, good-looking and younger, with his blonde, fashionably unkempt hairstyle, *and* shacked up with a beautiful girlfriend, who was mingling with guests somewhere in the garden. All compounded with his clever and astute selection of advertising contracts, to such an extent he'd become a millionaire thrice over.

Jonathan's five-bedroom holiday home was near Lulworth Cove in Dorset. Swigging from a bottle of lager, and wearing an apron with a crude design of stockings and suspenders, he waved his barbecue fork around, explaining to people his concept of what the house would look like once the builders had finished. 'I plan to let it out and use it myself now and again in the summer. Long-term though, I'll probably turn it into a bed and breakfast and sell it as a retirement investment.' Sounding like an estate agent, he added, 'Its tourist location near the B3070, and its clifftop seclusion with the fantastic views out to sea, make it a desirable purchase.'

Jonathan explained to them, pointing, that over the years there had been a slight subsidence on the south-facing wall of the property adjacent to the cliffs. This had resulted in a quarter-inch gap underneath the downstairs windows that side. However, he'd had a full survey before purchase, and they'd assured him nothing was going to drop into the sea. Hopefully not today at least. He laughed, and the waiting barbecue diners holding their plates laughed in response.

*

Pollack had known, of course, for the last three months. They'd redecorated, and he'd used Olivia's Fiesta to take some rubbish to the council refuse dump. While closing the hatchback, he'd accidentally dropped the keys down the side of the boot-well. Cursing while lifting the cover to reveal the jack and the toolbox, he found her second mobile phone.

Thirty-nine-year-old Olivia Pollack was going to get her finances in order first, by emptying the savings and bank accounts. And then, using a solicitor's help, take her husband for half the house, and his share in her father's plastics company, which had been set up at the time she and Pollack had first met, with her father making Pollack the financial director.

The texts from his wife to Jonathan revealed she was going to divorce him, and he was going to elbow the girlfriend. And then they'd shack up together and eventually get married. He was even going to make her a director, and give Olivia the prestigious Northway contract.

However, the house was the cruncher. The savings and bank accounts he could just about suffer, but not the house, or his shares in the family company, which he'd help to build up. No way, José.

The one-hundred-and-twenty-five-mile journey back to their home in Marryat Road in Wimbledon, had taken two hours and forty-five minutes. Pollack liked living where he was, in the affluent part of Wimbledon. The five-bedroom house with its rear extension onto a beautiful sweeping garden, and the sunken half-indoor, half-outdoor floodlit swimming pool. He'd worked hard at her parents' family business to get it, even though she'd been the cash cow. Yes, that would just about sum her up, he thought.

Olivia had come from well-off parents who lived in Reigate, on a smart gated estate called Pilgrims' Way. With a paid-for education at Cheltenham Girls' College and then achieving a BA at Cambridge, she moved easily into a career in advertising, and was all set to climb the ladder in one of the media conglomerates. Her parents hoped she would eventually find herself a man from a pedigree family, of equal financial stability as her own. Instead, while booking a skydive, she met a young Vincent Pollack at Redhill Aerodrome where he was a keen tandem skydiver. With love being at first sight, there was no way the parents could change her mind. Still – Pollack had to give them their due – they coughed up for their one and only daughter, a seventy-thousand-pound wedding bash that could have been fit for Princess Diana herself.

While Olivia had been driving back from Lulworth Cove, Pollack had nonchalantly checked out the mileage and made a mental note. He'd also made a mental note of their joint five-hundred-thousand pounds mortgage protection policy, to be paid on death to the surviving spouse. And another mental note of her employment death benefit, which paid out a lump sum of three times her annual salary. With the ISAs and savings, provided she kept her grubby little paws off, that was another two hundred and twenty thousand pounds in the kitty.

Most important of all was the mental note he'd made of the gas canisters for the patio heaters, which were stacked against the wall next to Jonathan's barbecue.

With Olivia out of the way he stood to clean up. The problem was, at only thirty-nine years old, blonde and very attractive, still in good shape, and having never smoked, she epitomised the embodiment of good health, with visits to an expensive health club gym twice a week. Meaning she was hardly the type to keel over from a heart attack. And he knew he'd be in the frame if she did.

Pollack could imagine they'd be all over her at the autopsy. Looking for poisons, needle marks, DNA trace evidence, stomach contents, or anything else they could pin onto a grieving husband who stood to inherit two million pounds, including the house and business.

Pollack contemplated. He would have to have a watertight alibi.

After he'd found her mobile, things fell into place. When she had to be away at an advertising launch, which was usually a two-day affair, he'd ring the following morning and he always got her answer phone. Later on in the day she'd ring him back. This was the usual pattern, with her apologising she'd left her mobile in the bathroom, or she'd gone to the hotel gym for an early morning workout and forgot to take it with her. He now realised from recent developments, it was probably an early bedroom workout with lover boy.

It was when he read her mobile message from him, finalising a tryst for the Friday after next at his Lulworth Cove love nest, a plan began to materialise.

*

Two weeks later, on the Friday, he kissed Olivia goodbye after breakfast, and she confirmed she'd be back late Saturday evening after the advertising launch. She took the Fiesta, and as she was pulling out of their drive, he was already on the internet, holding his Ken Dodd ticket and checking out the Wimbledon theatre seating plan. He'd read that Ken Dodd shows often ran for more than five hours. That should be enough time to get to Lulworth Cove and back. The theatre would be a suitable alibi, but he had to make sure he was noticed going in and coming out late. That would be one of the first things the police would check.

At first he'd thought of using his own car, but that would be too risky, especially with cameras now standard on motorways and the main A roads. He could imagine the police trawling through CCTV footage looking for his number plate. A rental car was out of the question as well. They'd want a credit card for payment, as well as for insurance.

It was while returning home from work three days earlier he saw the minibus turn into a neighbour's driveway. Pollack slowed his silver-coloured Audi A3 1.6TDI and pulled up at a discreet distance. From there he watched the family with their suitcases all pile in, and the minibus driver close the sliding doors. Pollack watched them pull out into the road and disappear, off to some airport no doubt. What remained on their driveway interested Pollack. Although a different colour, it was the same make and model as his own car.

From the amount of luggage they'd loaded onto the minibus, the family looked as though they'd be gone a few days. He would come back tomorrow night to double check, and if the car was still there he'd switch the registration plates with his own. And then, later at night, switch them back again after coming home from the theatre. He'd have to take the chance the swap wouldn't be spotted by a nosy neighbour.

*

With Ken Dodd grinning at him from a poster. Pollack, wearing a second set of clothes under his top clothes, and with a wig and cap tucked inside his shirt, queued in the foyer of the Wimbledon theatre. As the attendant tore off the ticket stubs, Pollack inched his way along until his turn came.

Pollack searched his pockets and apologised. He turned around and apologised to the people behind. He feverishly opened his wallet and took everything out, and apologised again. And then at last he made a show of remembering where he'd put his ticket.

To the growing impatience of the attendant, Pollack went to his back pocket and breathed a fake sigh of relief. 'Jesus! Thought I'd lost it. Sorry about that,' he grinned as he handed it over. The attendant tore off the stub without a smile, and waved him through.

With an end-of-row seat booked, which saved the need to clamber over people, Pollack watched the show for five minutes, and then sneaked off to the men's washroom. Locking himself into a cubicle, he swapped his clothes, put on the wig and cap, and as a finishing touch applied a stick-on moustache. Now he was all set.

The woman in the box office was reading a book, and the couple at the ice cream, popcorn and soft drinks counter chatted with their backs to him. Pollack saw his chance and quietly left the foyer.

Striding down Wimbledon High Street to where he'd parked the car, his eyes quickly adjusted from the dark theatre to the bright summer evening. Pollack made his way into a side road to the ticket parking bays. The time was 7.18pm as he climbed into his Audi. And then he moved off, and was soon on the A3 heading towards the M25 turn-off.

To get himself there and back before Ken Dodd took his final encores, he had to maintain an average speed of at least sixty miles per hour. If he could maintain seventy-five to eighty miles per hour on the motorway, and everything went to plan at Jonathan's love nest, he should then be able to get back before twelve midnight. He shouldn't have many problems that time of an evening, and he'd done an AA road check for holdups and roadworks. There was just one stop he had to make. He needed to buy some extra gas canisters to pull off his plan. Wearing his disguise, that should be no problem.

*

By 9:33pm he'd just come off the B3070 and was making his way along Lulworth Cove's Main Road to Jonathan's turn-off. This would take him along the deserted clifftop road. A few minutes later, the holiday home came into view.

Pollack switched off his lights and coasted to within seventy feet of the property. With the car hidden by a clutch of roadside bushes, he opened the boot and took out two large carrier bags.

It was a warm, dry evening, and the sky was an earie deep purple, which was getting darker as he made his way along the rough path that led to the house. At the drystone wall entrance, his heart missed a beat in elation. Olivia's Ford Fiesta was parked next to Jonathan's top-of-the-range 4x4 BMW. So much for her advertising launch business trip.

The upstairs bedroom lights were on. They hadn't even bothered to pull the curtains. There was no need, they must have thought, being in such an isolated location. Pollack pulled out his binoculars and adjusted the focus.

At that very moment, a stark naked Jonathan came out onto the upstairs balcony facing the sea. He leaned on the rail smoking a cigarette. Olivia, also naked, sauntered up behind him and put her arms around his waist. And then she dropped them, and started massaging him. Jonathan turned and, discarding the cigarette, he picked her up in his arms and they disappeared into the bedroom again.

That was good. With their attention diverted, it allowed him to continue unnoticed.

The barbecue with the patio heaters was still in the same place, directly under the balcony, with the gas canisters stacked against the wall. Pollack had brought along three more small canisters as a backup.

From a carrier bag he took out a pack of coals, and laid them out on the lower shelf of the barbecue. Pollack withdrew the top food grill and laid it to one side. Using a blowtorch, as it was quicker than firelighters, he played the flame over the coals until they'd all taken hold and were covered in white ash. And then, using a thin cardboard tube from striplight packaging, he began to Sellotape the tube end onto the nipple of a patio gas canister. The other end of the tube was poked through the quarter-inch settlement crack in the wall, just below the window. As he opened the tap, a hiss of gas began to escape. Propane, being heavier than air, would slowly collect at the bottom of the house, without the lovers even noticing the smell. Hopefully in the explosion the cardboard tube would burn away, leaving no trace.

With the coals becoming a dull red colour, he had to be careful. Pollack laid the food grill over five patio gas canisters that were lying on their sides against the wall. And then, using a tin shovel, he collected the burning coals and laid them out on the food grill that was resting on the canisters. Finally, and quietly, he overturned the barbecue that was facing the canisters, and laid a patio heater on top of it, to look as though it had flipped over accidentally from a strong wind in the night.

Pollack didn't quite know how long it would take before the canisters would explode from the heat of the coals, but what he did know was he had to get out of there quickly.

Collecting up all his things and double checking there was nothing left behind, he moved swiftly to his car. The time was 9.57pm and he was well on schedule.

A minute later, as he was making his way along Main Road to the B3070, there was a sudden and almighty bright flash in his rear windscreen. Pollack stopped the car and got out.

With a view over the clifftop, he stood transfixed at the eruption in the distance. Exploding gas canisters catapulted into the night sky, like miniature cruise missiles. All of a sudden came a massive fireball, followed by the delayed rumble of an explosion. Burning debris shot upwards and then began to rain down like a firework display. Even from this distance, helped by the remaining afterglow, he could see the house, with its lovers, was no more.

Pollack made better time on the journey back. It was five past midnight as he parked the car in an empty bay behind the Wimbledon theatre. With the ticket clutched in his hand, his only fear was the show had ended.

At the entrance he gave a furtive glance. The foyer was deserted apart from a security guard who was on his mobile phone and not looking his way. The problem was that the door into the auditorium was in the man's eyeline.

Pollack crept around to his rear and, holding his ticket in view, tapped him on the shoulder. 'Sorry to disturb, the men's washroom?'

The young security man half turned and pointed to a side door, without taking the mobile from his ear. Clearly a little agitated from the intrusion, he ignored Pollack and carried on talking. Pollack relaxed and realised that if the show was over and the theatre was closing, the toilets would have been off limits.

Ken Dodd was winding up the show with his old 1965 hit record 'Tears', and had the audience singing along with him. Pollack was able to make his way to the men's washroom without being noticed and discarded the disguise. Double checking in the mirror, he carefully peered out from behind the door to make sure all was clear. And then he made his way back to his aisle seat. Nobody seemed to notice, they were too busy singing.

As the final curtain came down, the lights came up and people began to gather up their coats and belongings. Pollack sat fast in his chair while they edged past his legs, some even apologising if they trod on his foot.

Within minutes the theatre was empty, but Pollack stayed seated with his eyes closed, pretending that he'd dozed off.

A hand shook him from behind and said, 'Excuse me, sir, time to leave. The show has finished.'

Pollack jolted and turned to see an apologetic young security guard in uniform, holding a torch and a walkie-talkie. 'I'm terribly sorry,' Pollack laughed. 'I must have dozed off. Too much wine in the break.'

The guard forced a smile, while Pollack gathered up his jacket and made his way up the aisle to the entrance. He stopped halfway and asked, 'Is it okay if I visit the toilet first?'

With a stern expression, the security guard was quite clear. 'I'm sorry, sir, the toilets are now locked. But there are the station toilets at the top of the high street.'

Pollack was satisfied that if push came to shove and he was hauled into a police line-up, or the theatre staff were shown his photo, he'd be remembered.

By 12.50am he'd swapped back his neighbour's registration plates with his own. Now he was chilling out on his sofa, nursing a large Jack Daniel's on the rocks, while watching a late-night TV movie. Pollack was concentrating and not concentrating as he smiled to himself, thinking of his wife and Jonathan. He raised his glass to no one and said, 'Did the earth move for you, Olivia?'

Pollack chuckled and took another swig.

*

It had been more than six weeks since his wife's tragic death. Of course the police had fussed around, poked and prodded, until it appeared they believed it to be a genuine accident, confirming and supporting the coroner's verdict of accidental death.

Vincent Pollack managed to inherit from his deceased wife over two million pounds in shares, savings and property. He even fulfilled a long-held ambition and bought a small hotel on the island of Majorca, as well as treating himself to a brand new Mercedes E-Class Cabriolet, all £41,000 of it.

SEVENTEEN

Lennin

The woman arrived at the shared business entrance for the office of the Mavis Bone Detective Agency on Wimbledon Broadway SW19.

Mrs Joan Clifton pressed the third button down, and heard a buzzer as the door unlocked to allow her through to an entrance lobby. From there she climbed to the first floor as indicated by a business list board.

At a half-panelled glass door stencilled with the words **Mavis Bone Detective Agency – An eye for an eye makes the whole world blind,** she pressed another buzzer. Immediately Gertrude Stick, the agency secretary spoke through the intercom. 'Can I 'elp you?'

'It's Mrs Clifton. I have a three o'clock appointment to see Mavis Bone.'

'Come through please.'

Another buzzer unlocked the door and Mrs Joan

Clifton entered a small and cluttered outer office. She was immediately confronted by a mature looking smart sad-faced secretary, wearing a blue trouser suit and big gold earrings. A chic, lavender blue headscarf hid her platinum blonde dyed hair. She was sitting at a desk covered in files.

Mrs Clifton couldn't help noticing that high above, strategically placed between empty spaces on dusty shelves filled with files and ledgers, sets of glassy eyes peered at her from two stuffed squirrels, a fox about to pounce, and a suspended tawny owl that twisted slowly in flight.

The secretary nodded to the animals. 'Our last office tenant was a mortician, and liked to keep his vinger in.'

The German secretary's heavily lined, tanned face, which was mostly the result of visits to a sunbed salon, was further made up with pink lipstick and green eye shadow. She indicated to Mrs Clifton to take a seat, while she spoke into the intercom. 'Mrs Joan Clifton to see you, Mrs Bone.'

'Please show her through, Gertrude.'

Gertrude Stick came round from behind her desk, and escorted the prospective client to a larger, brown-carpeted office, containing three large sash windows and four filing cabinets. There she was greeted by the private detective.

Australian-born Mavis Bone, with her jet black hair full of tiny curls, was wearing a smart red trouser suit. She raised herself from behind a leather-topped desk and extended her hand. 'G'day. Please take a seat, Mrs Clifton.'

After introductions, Mavis said, 'Would you mind if my secretary sits in on this and takes notes? That way we make sure to capture all the vital information.'

Gertrude Stick sat herself down with a notepad at the end of the desk, and reassured Mrs Clifton. 'Everything vot I write is fully confidential, my dear. It vill not be disclosed to anyvun else.'

Mavis rolled her eyes, knowing Gertrude always trotted out her same introduction line. 'Yes, thank you, Gerty.' She turned to Mrs Clifton with a big, cheesy grin. 'I wouldn't know what to do, without my Gerty. She's my Girl Friday, as you poms call it.'

Gertrude chimed in. 'Vot to do? You could give me a 'vise for a start if you *vont* to do something. I 'aven't 'ad a—'

Mavis interrupted. 'Yes – yes, thank you, Gerty.' She turned to Mrs Clifton. 'You indicated on the phone, you wanted to see me about the death of your daughter.' Private Investigator Mavis Bone, wearing white make-up with faint pink cheeks, black eye shadow and heavy red lipstick, adjusted her thick, black-framed glasses and fiddled with her chunky pearl necklace as she prepared to listen.

Mrs Clifton added bitterly. 'Yes. I'm sure her death wasn't an accident. That smug bastard she married had something to do with it. They'd been married three years when she died.'

Mavis asked, 'So who was that?'

'His name is Vincent Pollack.'

'I know that name from an investigation some time ago. He was young then. A fledgling killer, but it was never proved. And you think she was murdered by him?'

'Yes I do, Mrs Bone. I'd like you to find out if he was involved.'

'Mrs Clifton,' Mavis sighed. 'I'd like to help you. But you must face facts. The police have already carried out a thorough investigation concerning your daughter's death.'

'That bastard is too clever for the police. He's very methodical,' Mrs Clifton added. 'No doubt he planned it to the finest premeditated degree. However, someone like you, Mrs Bone, could find something the police have missed or overlooked. I read the fantastic reviews on your agency website.'

Mrs Clifton's eyes were pleading. 'So will you take the case on, Mrs Bone?'

'Call me Mavis, me Darlin', and you'd better know my agency rates before you commit yerself.' She turned to her secretary. 'Gerty, can you tell this lovely sheila our current rates, and I'll put the billy on. Would yer like a tea or coffee, me darlin'?' she asked Mrs Clifton.

'A tea would be nice with milk, no sugar, thank you.'

Gertrude chimed in. 'And I'll 'ave my usual. Black coffee and strong vith three sugars.'

'Yes, I know,' said Mavis, taking the kettle to the outside office sink to fill up. 'How could I ever forget you,' she said with a sigh.

Mrs Clifton smiled at the office banter and enquired, 'If you don't mind me asking, how long have you been in business together?'

Gertrude pondered and then said, 'It was before zee year tvoo zousand, around six years ago. My deceased 'usband was a private investigator, and I vas 'is secretary. Vhen 'e died seven years ago, 'e left me comfortably off. I alveady knew Mavis when she 'elped out from time to time with private investigations at my 'usband's agency, usually vhen ve vere overloaded. Then Mavis was looking to strike out on 'er own, and so ve teamed up. I do the accounts and filing, vhile she does the investigating. We even share the two-bed flat above the agency building. It vorks vell.'

'So you're partners then?'

Gertrude laughed, 'Yes, partners in crime, you could say.'

'Well, the reviews on your website were full of praise,' Mrs Clifton informed her. 'That's why I'm here.'

Gertrude assured her, 'Mrs Clifton. Ve can never guarantee success, but you vill receive from our agency a first-class thorough investigation for your money.'

Mrs Clifton's face darkened. 'All I want you to do is find out how my daughter came to be killed by a gas canister explosion. The police have come up with nothing.' She dabbed her eyes with a handkerchief. 'I still reckon it was that bastard she married. I should have taken the rumours about Vincent Pollack seriously.'

'And what were they, me darlin'?' asked Mavis, returning from the other office.

While Gertrude scribbled away, Mavis listened intently.

'Twenty years ago, Vincent Pollack was dating my neighbour's au pair. She was a pretty young blonde German girl called Anna; this was when he'd just met Olivia, my daughter. And then the au pair disappeared. He said at the time she'd upped and left and gone back home to Germany. My deceased husband had employed him as a driver at his plastics company, delivering drums of plastic pellets to moulding companies. Rumours started to spread that she'd been sealed up in one of the drums. Of course, I thought it was nonsense. That sort of thing only happened in murder films or books. And then, years later, this Pollack moved up the ladder in my husband's company, and qualified as my husband's accountant. He eventually became financial director.'

'Any children?' Mavis enquired as she sipped her coffee while Gertrude carried on making notes.

Mrs Clifton responded. 'Only adopted. My Olivia couldn't have kids. Helen is her name. She must be around eleven years old now. She's living with Vincent Pollack in Majorca. Although he never showed her much affection, well never in my company.'

Mrs Clifton said bitterly, 'I suppose he doesn't have the time, managing the hotel he bought in Majorca with the money from my daughter's life insurance policy. That's why I think the bastard had something to do with her death.'

'Ve vill do our best. Now, my dear.' Gertrude pulled the folder and took out a client contract sheet. 'Vates of pay are as follows.' She put on her expensive pair of Prada leopard-spotted glasses that dangled around her neck. 'Now our daily vate is one 'undred and twenty pounds per hour, plus expenses. Investigation standard time is eight hours per day, with a minimum time of vour hours per day, for a minimum of three days. After eight hours per day, the overtime vate is at time and a 'alf, which includes through the night. Our car usage vates are fifty pence per mile.'

Gertrude sipped her coffee and then continued. 'The client vill be updated verbally every veek on the progress of the investigation, culminating in a full vitten veport at the end of the investigation. Veports vill only be veleased to the client upon full payment of final invoice. You are vequired to give us tventy-four hours' notice to terminate the agreement or forfeit any vemaining monies in the client's account. Upon engaging into an investigation contract with the Mavis Bone Detective Agency, the client vill open and credit an expenses account for five 'undred pounds. You are to ensure the account is always in credit by three 'undred pounds.' Gertrude slid the contract across to Mrs Clifton. 'You vill sign vare I 'ave marked vith a cross. Yes?'

Mrs Clifton briefly checked the page and then signed where indicated. She took out her cheque book and made one out to open the expense account.

Mavis and Gertrude stood up and offered their hands. Mavis assured her, 'We will be in touch as soon as we have something concrete, me darlin', I promise you. Oh! Just one more thing. Where does this Vincent Pollack reside?'

Mrs Clifton pulled out her address book. 'While managing his hotel in Majorca, he still retained his house at number twenty-three Marryat Road, which as you know is in an affluent part of Wimbledon.'

Mavis replied, 'Thank you, me darlin''. She turned to her secretary. 'What do yer reckon, Gerty? Shall we take *Lenin* for a spin? Check out what we can find about Mister Vincent Pollack. Ask around a few of his neighbours, that sort of thing. Maybe do a stake-out on him? Making sure not to attract the wrath of Detective Inspector Eric Faversham, of course.'

Her secretary laughed, 'Heaven forbid. Vhy not? It's verth a try. He's probably a slippery yid this Pollack, and vill come a cropper vun day.'

Mrs Clifton winced at the racism and said, 'What makes you think he's Jewish?'

Gertrude responded, 'If I vemember, the name Pollack is an Ashkenazic name for somevun coming vrom Poland. The name is a veference to a person of Hebrew origin vrom Poland.'

Mrs Clifton raised her eyebrows in enlightenment and said, 'Ah, I see.'

*

Donning their flying jackets and stormtrooper helmets, they wheeled out *Lenin*, their Russian motorbike and sidecar, from the garage. Mavis straddled the seat and pushed down on the kick-start lever. The bike uttered a throaty roar with clouds of exhaust smoke. And then Mavis checked her goggles, and gave a thumbs up to Gertrude, who looked comfortable in the sidecar, with a tartan blanket over her knees.

It was just gone five-thirty this warm August Friday afternoon, and the rush-hour traffic was building up. They chugged along Wimbledon Broadway and up the hill to Wimbledon village, stopping for an altercation at the oncoming roundabout with a commercial goods driver, who ranted his disgust as Mavis cut him up.

She throttled *Lenin* across his path, shouting, 'Roll up a bridge, mate, and fuck off, you cocksucker.' Gertrude compounded the insult, poking her hand through the flap of the sidecar window with a stiff one-fingered salute for the driver to sit on.

Moving on towards the edge of the common, and then taking a right into Marryat Road, they eased up as number twenty-three came into view. And then they carefully surveyed Vincent Pollack's five-bedroomed house, with its manicured front garden and sweeping drive. Mavis discreetly parked *Lenin* out of view onto the secluded footpath of Dairy Walk.

Gertrude made herself comfortable sitting in the sidecar. Wrapped in the tartan blanket, she had her flask of coffee, plus two rounds of garlic sausage and mustard sandwiches for company. Mavis waved her goodbye, and set off to find a side entrance for number twenty-three Marryat Road. The double garage at the rear of the property, protected by a row of high conifers, seemed the most suitable prospect for an unlawful entry, without being seen.

Using the oldest knock-down-ginger trick, Mavis tied a length of extra thin fishing line to the door knocker and waited, keeping out of sight. After a couple of tugs, it was obvious no one was at home.

She made easy work of the padlock to the side door of the garage with her set of lock-picking tools. In the dark, she fumbled for the pull-down light switch, and scanned the walls for an alarm or movement sensors. The overhead strip light revealed a white van. She tried the side and back doors, but as expected they were all locked. There was an internal wall with a door into the house. Mavis picked the lock and edged her way into a dank-smelling interior. She pulled a pencil torch from her shoulder bag and played it around. The floor and walls were damp, as if they'd been hosed down. A giant crucifix was attached to the wall, and below it sat a couple of silver vases filled with flowers. And then Mavis whispered, 'Dear God,' as her eyes fell on an RSJ that stretched across the ceiling with a line of meat hooks and wire nooses hanging from them.

A video camera on a tripod stood a short distance away. Mavis whispered again, 'Dear God.'

She instantly thought of the July plot. The failed attempt on Adolf Hitler's life, where the conspirators had been sentenced to death and were filmed suspended from meat hooks while choking slowly from piano wire nooses. It was said that Hitler watched the film for his amusement later that evening after dinner.

Mavis Bone wondered. Would Pollack have done the same? Filmed some poor wretch, suspended, choking and gasping their last breath, while he grinned and captured it on film. And then later, reclining on his sofa with a few hors d'oeuvres, sipping a glass of wine, he'd watch his little movie play out. Was that the reason for the crucifix? Were they religious sacrifices?

Mavis pushed the thoughts away. She took out her mobile phone to take pictures of the grisly scene.

Playing the torch around, she spotted a circular shape in the floor. Kneeling down, Mavis discovered it was a wooden cover, around four feet in diameter. There was a metal ring handle. Using both hands she tried to lift it. The cover didn't budge. She needed some sort of lever.

Mavis shone the torch and found a crowbar on a shelf.

She slipped it through the metal ring, and with legs apart for balance, she levered it up until she could get her fingers under the lip. And then she slid the cover away, to reveal what appeared to be a large manhole.

Mavis peered in and shone her torch. There was an iron ladder going down, fixed to the concrete wall. At the bottom, her torch picked out what appeared to be two filing cabinets and a large oil drum. Mavis descended the iron ladder.

Reaching the concrete floor, she pulled the drawers of the filing cabinets. They were unlocked, and filled with DVDs. Picking them up one by one, Mavis cringed. The DVD covers showed scenes of flogging, S&M and bondage. One drawer showed DVD covers of filmed executions, snuff movies Mavis guessed. And now the gruesome film set above with the meat hooks and nooses made sense.

Her torch picked out the oil drum. The lid was sealed. Mavis looked up the steel ladder, and wondered how anybody could have got it down here, and for what reason? With difficulty she tried to read the painted stencilled markings around the drum, but they had become illegible with rust. Using her handkerchief, she rubbed away the dirt and grease that had collected, and peered in close adjusting her glasses. Mavis could just make out a 1994 date stamp, and a Clifton's Plastics manufacturer's label, stating it was a forty-five-gallon type. She checked again for hazard markings, and couldn't see any skull and crossbones for poisons or toxic waste.

Using both hands and all her weight just to move the steel drum a couple of inches, Mavis realised it was obviously full up with whatever it was intended for. She examined the sealed lid more closely. It looked well and truly pressed home. And then she picked up the crowbar. Using the flattened end, she pressed it hard into the edge of the lid, and then levered it up. After two attempts and a great deal of cursing – 'Come on, you cocksucker, don't fuck with mamma' – she felt it move slightly. And then at the third attempt, a little portion of the lid popped up. Mavis blurted out, 'Fuckin' champion!'

She pulled out her mobile phone and called her secretary. 'Gerty, how's it goin'?'

'Vare are you? I'm bored shvitless sitting 'ere in *Lenin*.'

'Listen, I managed to get into the Pom's garage, and found a lot of weird shit like torture stuff. I reckon this Pollack is into snuff movies. Even Blind Freddy can see that. He's got the camera all set up to film it.'

'You be careful and take pictures for evidence. Zat vay ve vill stitch up zis Jew boy.'

Mavis laughed. 'Okay, Gerty. I'll keep in touch, see you soon.'

'Shall I still vait here?'

'No, Gerty, you take *Lenin* back to the agency, and I'll meet you there.'

'Okay, be carevul though.'

'I will; see you soon.' Easing the lid off the steel drum, Mavis leant back, not knowing what to expect. Using the light from her pencil torch, she could see it was filled to the brim with particles of some description. She gingerly fingered the small granules, and examined a handful. They appeared to be made of plastic and coloured green. Mavis swished her fingers and then dug down and grabbed more handfuls. Noting the manufacturer's label, Clifton's Plastics, it all made sense. This was probably the raw material that was melted down for the moulding machines.

As she was about to replace the container lid, her eye caught something protruding. Mavis swished the granules around it. And then she tugged at what appeared to be the heel of a shoe. Using the torch and digging down further, she uncovered another heel. Mavis grabbed it and pulled harder, until a woman's high-heeled shoe came off in her hand. She held it up astonished, and then realised she had disturbed the granules around a woman's stockinged foot.

Mavis swished around some more until she felt another shoe. To her horror she uncovered another foot. Her mind began racing. Could this be a mannequin? One of the products that the company moulded? There was only one way to find out.

She pushed the drum with both hands, using all her weight, until it tipped over and spilled out some of its contents.

Playing her pencil torch over it, Mavis flinched back at what she saw. Half in, half out of the drum, lay a body. It looked mummified and well preserved, almost like her original thought of a mannequin. At that moment, Mavis spotted an identity charm necklace, and moved in closer. It was engraved with a name: Anna. The same name as the missing au pair her client had mentioned. Using her mobile phone she took pictures. Under her breath, Mavis said with satisfaction, 'That should provide enough evidence for Detective Inspector Eric Faversham, and warrant my illegal break-in.'

EIGHTEEN

Four Sided Coffin

Mavis froze, as above her she heard a door slam. She killed the pencil torch and waited in the darkness and silence. Feeling her way to the ladder, she slowly climbed the iron rungs until her torch picked out the circular hole above her head.

Standing on the top rungs she listened intently, and then reached out to slide the wooden cover to leave an inch gap.

Mavis craned her neck and spotted a man in the overhead strip lighting that had now been switched on. She assumed it must be Vincent Pollack. He was holding a whip. Through the gap, she could see him go to the video camera and switch it on. And then he proceeded to tear off his shirt and vest, while all the time mumbling religious gibberish.

Mavis Bone was mesmerised by the scars on his back.

In history books back home, she'd seen terrible photos of Aborigines who had been flogged under the British colonial system, while in captivity as slaves. Vincent Pollack's back wasn't far off those..

He held out what appeared to be a leather cat of nine tails with sharp metal thongs at the ends. And then he proceeded to whip himself and chant at the same time.

'I have placed my trust in false teachings and substitutes for God.' *Thwack!*

'I have broken a solemn vow and promise.' *Thwack!*

'I have neglected prayer for a long time.' *Thwack!*

'I have abused drugs and alcohol.' *Thwack!*

'I have killed and discriminated against others because of greed, race and gender.' *Thwack!*

'I have not been chaste in thought and word.' *Thwack!*

'I have used sex outside marriage and not to procreate life.' *Thwack!*

'I have given myself sexual gratification. I have deliberately looked at pornographic films and magazines.' *Thwack!*

'I have permitted sexual thoughts about someone to whom I am not married.' *Thwack!*

Blood was now running down his back as the thongs bit deep into his skin. And then he fell to his knees in front of the crucifix.

Pollack eventually stood up and put on his vest and shirt, wincing as he did so. Taking the whip and the video camera, he exited through the door.

Mavis hauled herself over the edge of the manhole and

lay sprawled out, exhausted. She realised her red trouser suit was ruined, or maybe a decent dry clean might salvage it.

As she pulled at her shoulder bag, she lost her balance as the strap caught on the iron ladder, making her nearly fall headlong down the hole. The contents of her bag spilled out onto the concrete floor. 'Shit! Shit! Shit!' she cursed under her breath. 'Yer could have come a gutser there, Mavis.' As she crouched to pick up the items, she became instantly confused. A pair of men's sandals stood neatly side by side in her field of view. She couldn't remember packing those. And then, at the full realisation there were feet inside them, she felt a sharp pain in her head with coloured dots as blackness took over.

Pollack put down the crowbar, and tied Mavis to a porter's sack barrow. He wheeled her through the garage side door into his hallway and lounge.

Twenty minutes later, Mavis came round to find herself laid out on his rug. The blurring in her vision slowly began to sharpen until she could focus on Vincent Pollack. He'd made himself comfortable with a chair, and was looking down at her, holding a large steel carving knife.

The back of her head was sending slow waves of pain to the front. With each wave, it felt like someone was squeezing her head an extra turn in a cider press.

He put the knife to her eye, just in case she screamed, and then pulled the handkerchief from her mouth.

And that's when Mavis spotted the *Vincent* tattoo on his wrist. Now she knew for sure that it was Vincent Pollack at her side.

'You awake? That's good,' he said. 'How did you find me?'

'Your old mother-in-law, Mrs Clifton told me where you lived,' Mavis replied, looking at the blade out of the corner of her eye.

'Who knows you're here?'

'No one, I swear.' Her answer came without hesitation.

Thwack! He hit her across the face so fast she never saw it coming. Her head snapped to one side, white dots exploded in front of her eyes, and she tasted blood as her lower lip burst where the inner lining had been cut by her teeth.

Pollack looked crazy. He told her, 'I spotted you earlier snooping around my garage. Figured it was only a matter of time for you to make your move, and here we are.'

Mavis was shaking; she blinked as she looked at him, and tasted blood.

Pollack leaned over and bellowed into her face, '*Who knows you're here?*'

Mavis pleaded with him, 'No one, no one, please, honestly.'

He looked at Mavis's frightened face. The old bitch knew too much, she could incriminate him. And then he searched through her pockets, and emptied out the contents of her shoulder bag.

He picked up from the carpet the engraved silver identity charm necklace, and looked at it thoughtfully. Pollack smiled at Mavis. 'We have been busy investigating haven't we? Me and Anna had a good thing going, until the silly cow got pregnant and threatened to tell my employer. I was sweet on my employer's daughter Olivia at the time, and didn't need Anna lousing it up, with all the prospects of me marrying into a wealthy family.'

Pollack checked out Mavis's mobile phone and found the pictures she'd taken. He picked up the crowbar, and Mavis leant away, fearing the worst. He smashed up her mobile phone and threw the broken bits at her in rage, while she flinched back.

Thwack! He hit her across the face again. Pollack put the tip of the carving knife onto Mavis's lower eyelid. It dimpled the sensitive area and pushed up her eyeball into the socket. 'Tell me who else knows you're here, and don't hesitate. If you hesitate I'll know you're lying, and I'll flip your eye right out of its socket onto the floor. I can do it. Believe me?' He leaned in, pushing the knife painfully deep, until a tear of blood appeared on her lower lid. 'So who else knows?'

'Please, nobody else knows I'm here, please believe me,' she blurted out with her lower lip swelling up. Mavis felt blood spilling down her chin in a small stream.

Pollack walked to a fancy antique bureau in his lounge, and took out a Glock 19 pistol. With the oily rag it was wrapped in, he slowly buffed up the barrel. It was clear he was thinking that she could drag him down. He had to get rid of her, and quick.

Mavis cringed as Pollack raised the pistol. He pressed the barrel of the gun to her head. 'I'll ask you one more time, who else knows you're here?'

Mavis pleaded again, 'Okay, okay, please don't kill me. My secretary knows I'm here. If I don't return within an hour, she'll go to the police.'

Pollack levelled the gun at her head once more. 'Where is she?'

Mavis tried to look honest and sincere. 'She's waiting for me in the sidecar of our motorcycle, at the Crooked Billet pub car park on Wimbledon Common.'

Pollack guessed she could be telling the truth. He'd seen the pair of them set off on that smoking Russian contraption when they'd left the agency on Wimbledon Broadway. That was after he'd followed his ex-mother-in-law Mrs Clifton there.

Thwack! Pollack hit her round the face again with the back of his hand, '*You fucking bitch, for giving me all this trouble.*' Mavis flinched at the sting, and fresh blood oozed from her lip. Before she could say any more, he stuffed the handkerchief back in her mouth, and made his way to the laundry room. He came back with a roll of washing line in his hand.

With the knife, he cut off a length and gagged Mavis with it, to keep the handkerchief in place. As it cut into her mouth, he tied the knot at the back of her neck extra tight. And then he tied her hands and feet behind her back with a single length, so they pulled against each other. Moving to the side door, he came back a few minutes later, wheeling an old wardrobe on the barrow. He patted it affectionately and informed Mavis, 'Your little prison for the time being. Ideal for transporting you to Hampton Court Bridge, where you'll have an unfortunate accident sinking to the bottom of the Thames,' he mocked.

'Now, I'm off to check out your secretary at the Crooked Billet pub. See if I can persuade her not to call the police.'

Amongst Mavis's protests, while she kicked and moaned through her gag, Pollack, with great effort, dragged her to the wardrobe and then bundled her inside. As the wardrobe door slammed shut, she realised this could be her coffin.

Mavis heard the van door slam and the engine start up. She knew she had around forty minutes, time for him to drive to the Crooked Billet pub and return. Flexing her calf and thigh muscles, she strained and threw her head back, baring her teeth as fresh blood from her swollen lip leaked out of the sides of the handkerchief and down her chin. As her bound feet kicked against the wardrobe door, the cords on her neck stood out through her skin. But it was no good, she was too scrunched up to get any leverage. Hot pain bloomed suddenly in her right calf, tightening it more. She had to be careful.

She rested for a while. Then Mavis managed to turn her weight to one side and kick backwards at the door. But that was no good either, there wasn't enough room to give it a full good thump. The wardrobe rocked away and then steadied itself. After three more futile attempts, she knew the door was a non-runner. She lay back, breathing hard. Her wrists were sore. Every time she kicked, the plastic washing line pulled on them.

It was when Mavis rolled slightly that she noticed a

tiny sliver of light at the bottom of the panel in front of her. Thumping away she'd hit her head against the rear of the wardrobe. And then she realised, cheap furniture had plywood or hardboard backings that faced the wall, where they wouldn't be seen. 'Got to get it away from the wall,' she muffled. Mavis threw herself from side to side, thumping the rear panel and rocking the whole wardrobe. She positioned herself and gave another hefty kick at the panel, and then winced as her wrists jerked at the same time. '*Fuck you! You mother*,' she muffled again. It rocked heavily to the point, of nearly toppling over. A nightmare thought flashed through her head. *If it falls on its back, I'm well and truly fucked!* She took a breather and tried again. Mavis screamed with exertion, the rope cutting into her mouth as she flung herself from side to side, rocking the wardrobe, until suddenly she lost all sense of orientation as it toppled over and landed heavily on the carpeted lounge floor. She breathed in deep snatches through her gag. Thank God, she'd landed the right way up. She could see a strip of light above her from a damaged corner. With difficulty, Mavis wriggled and turned herself onto her stomach, and then kicked back, yelling with the pain as her sore wrists jerked. The thin ply backing, held on only by panel pins, burst out with each thump, until both her feet were poking through. She wriggled herself around in the extra space now available, and then kicked out the other end. Finally, she flipped herself over. Mavis lay there staring up at the lounge ceiling. She was still in her four-sided coffin, but now at least with no lid. If he came back

230

now, it *would* be her coffin. She imagined his last act as an undertaker, making sure she was at peace before refixing the lid. And then manoeuvring the makeshift casket on his barrow through the hallway into his garage and van. And then onwards at night to Hampton Court Bridge, for her burial in the Thames.

Now lying on her back, she knew this wasn't the best position. Mavis twisted herself around, swearing as she banged her head and face in the process, until she was resting crouched up on her knees. From there, with great effort, as the plastic line stretched and cut deep into her wrists, Mavis raised her top half and then painfully rolled head first over the wardrobe edge, and flopped onto the carpet floor.

She lay there exhausted, catching her breath in snatches. And then she froze. The adrenalin was surging back into her. She was trying to work out how long he'd been gone. Her head jerked to one side as she strained to listen. Traffic noises! Was he back? It seemed like he'd been gone for an eternity.

Mavis waited, and heard nothing. She had to get untied and quick, if she was to stand any chance.

She started to inch along on her back, the rope cutting into her wrists as she winced with each push. Mavis continued pushing with her feet, until she'd slid out of the lounge into the hall. At the far end, she could see the front door. *Make it to the door, push yourself upright against the door and turn the handle. Get outside, get seen.*

She moved nearer, bit by bit. The only thing that

231

mattered now. Her whole life shrunk down to this very act of survival. And then she stopped.

Shit! The lock? The bloody lock's too high up. Mavis could see the handle clearly now. Even half-standing upright, no way would her tied hands get to it. Only if she stood on a chair would she reach the brass handle – and then he could have locked it from the outside.

Mavis didn't want to waste any more valuable time, and she turned back, dismissing the idea about the door, muttering three fast *fuck*s to herself. The clock was ticking. She had to get back down the hall. *Get into a room. Hide or something. Better still, find something sharp. Get yourself free, and with any luck, stab the cocksucker at the same time.*

Mavis slid along past two closed doors, until she came to one a quarter open. She nudged it and it creaked wider. Lying on her back it took a few seconds to get some orientation, and she realised she was in the lounge again.

She remembered the Persian rugs and the coffee table. Mavis stopped and stared for a second. On the coffee table was an expensive-looking bronze paperweight in the form of a couple having sex. *Just Pollack's style*, she thought. There was also a chesterfield studded sofa and, across from that, a giant television sitting on a fine French rococo reproduction glass cabinet. Behind its glass doors, porcelain figurines stared into space. She moved in further over the rugs, rucking them up as she went past the sofa.

'Fuck,' she muffled out. She lay on her back again looking at the ceiling. It was the most comfortable position. Her wrists, bloody and chafed, screamed out their pain.

The chances of finding anything sharp were looking remote. She could imagine Vincent Pollack arriving back, at first searching the rooms in panic, and then realising with a smile that she was still a prisoner. His little fly all exhausted now. More tangled up than ever in his sticky web. And then a thought occurred: *the fancy artificial log fire?* With her hands tied she could still switch it on and reach through with some of the newspaper left around. And then lay something to burn and move away quick. Get up to the front door. Break a few windows. Hope people might see smoke coming out, smell burning. And then it dawned. What if nobody comes? End up a charred mess. Or pleading to a grinning Vincent Pollack to put her out of her misery. And the worst scenario, the prospect of a quick end by drowning or a slow death from being barbecued, soured any further plans with the fire.

And then Mavis had an idea as she looked at the reproduction glass cabinet. *The glass doors?* She pushed off and slid her way across until her feet were in range. Wincing as the rope cut into her wrists, she turned her face away, and with a few heavy thrusts kicked out the glass. Mavis manoeuvred herself around the glass shards on the floor, until she had her back to the cabinet. Straining her neck to look behind, with the bit of slack she had, she slowly began to saw through the plastic washing line using the jagged bits still attached to the frame; cutting and nicking herself at the same time.

She could feel her wrists getting looser. Now and again she would stop and strain hard, trying to force them apart, and then back to the sawing, until, with a sudden ping of ecstasy, the line parted.

Mavis rubbed her wrists, which were stinging badly with the burn from her bindings. She pulled at the tied handkerchief gag with both hands until she levered it over her chin. She tried to untie her feet, but it was difficult, because the knot was too tight; she had to admit he'd made a good job. She tried a shard of glass, but like the wrists, it was slow going and she didn't have the time. He could be back any minute.

The kitchen, get a knife. Mavis slid to the nearest wall, and then, using her back, she pushed herself upright. Hopping out of the lounge into the hall, she spotted the glass-panelled kitchen door. She opened it and saw the knife-rack on the work surface. Using the smallest one, she cut her feet free and then slipped the stiletto into the back of her trouser belt. Mavis went to the front door and tried to open it, but it was locked. No surprises there. And then she gave it a couple of half-hearted kicks out of frustration; it was too sturdy to have a go with her shoulder. She'd end up breaking her shoulder instead.

A quick look around revealed no telephone. No surprise again. All the windows had bars, but she could still smash the glass and start yelling.

The strong urge to do this was overtaken by the fact that her present situation probably offered her one and only chance of surprising him. Mavis went to one of the bedrooms. She could hide under the bed. She ducked down and suddenly jerked back with fright. She'd spotted a body.

Mavis gingerly peered under the bed again, and then slowly and with astonishment pulled out *Luscious Lita* – a scantily clad blow-up doll in half-cup black bra with suspender belt and fishnet stockings, and including orifices. The large box it had arrived deflated in, clearly displayed Lita's name. Mavis held it up with a smirk as it bounced around like a balloon. It was nearly as tall as herself. Mavis tossed it onto the bed; it lay there with its legs open, ready for action.

Now she had to sort out how to jump him, and quickly. He was going to be back any minute, and probably not in a good mood when he realised he'd been sent on a wasted errand, and Gertrude wasn't waiting at the pub.

Mavis had to hide from him, and quick.

No more than three minutes later she heard the front door slam, and then swearing. *'You lying slag, I'm gonna teach you–'* Pollack reached the lounge. *'SHIT! Fuck, wait till I get hold of you.'* And then he went to investigate the kitchen and the bedrooms. Suddenly it went quiet. Mavis froze.

Pollack came back onto the landing. 'Now come on, Mavis, I know you're in here somewhere. You can't get out. I made sure of it. Don't make me come after you.'

The last room he checked was the bathroom. Pollack held the pistol ready; he didn't want to use it unless he had to. It was far too noisy, and might attract attention. He'd corner her, and then use the knife to finish her off.

Pollack gently pushed the door open, in case she jumped out with her own weapon. She'd had time to find

235

one. The bathroom door creaked as it swung wide open. And there she was, hiding, silhouetted behind the shower curtain. *Stupid bitch*, Pollack thought, *as if I couldn't see her. Still, it'll keep all the mess in one place and make it easy to clean up.* He slipped the pistol in his pocket, and pulled the knife slowly from its sheath, strapped to his lower leg. He smiled to himself; the shower scene from *Psycho* briefly crossed his mind.

And then, like his Norman Bates counterpart, Pollack lunged forward in a mindless, stabbing frenzy, grunting with each thrust through the curtain, and then falling headlong into the bath on top of the hissing and deflating *Luscious Lita*. The last thing Pollack saw was his blow-up doll wearing Mavis's clothes.

Then *THWACK!* She hit him smack on the back of the head with the heavy bronze paperweight of the couple making love. And then she hit him again.

Finally, Mavis put a finger to his neck and checked; just to be sure. He still had a pulse.

She tugged away at the deflated doll until it was free of Pollack, and then she put her clothes back on. She had to get away quickly in case he woke up, and get back to Gertrude, otherwise she'd start worrying.

First things first. She needed proof of what she'd discovered downstairs. As he'd smashed her mobile phone, she hoped he'd have one of his own. Mavis searched through his pockets and pulled out a mobile phone, a set of keys and her own pencil torch. She couldn't find the identity bracelet from the girl, and that was hard evidence. '*Shit!*

Shit! Shit!' Mavis cursed. She found the plastic washing line and cut a length to tie his hands and feet. Satisfied he wasn't going anywhere for a while, Mavis congratulated herself. 'That went as sweet as an Anzac biscuit, and you're cactus for a while, mate.' She prodded him to be sure but he was still out cold.

Moving to the front door, she found it locked and tried the keys. None of them fitted. He must have hidden it for safety. Along the hallway she found the garage entrance, and thought with a sigh of relief, *Freedom at last.*

Mavis pulled the garage light switch, and could see he'd had a clearout. The meat hooks and wire nooses were missing from the beam. The crucifix had gone from the wall. Using the crowbar she lifted the wooden manhole cover and descended the iron ladder. The beam of her torch revealed that Vincent Pollack had been thorough. The steel drum and the woman's body were gone, as well as his collection of colourful DVDs. No doubt all transported in his van, which was also missing.

*

While Mavis escaped to make her way back to the Wimbledon agency office, Vincent Pollack managed to free himself from the poorly knotted washing line. And then he immediately took a cab to Gatwick Airport. After that, it was onwards to his hotel in Majorca.

NINETEEN

Ginger

That evening, Mavis was explaining to her secretary what had happened. 'He was havin' a right blue;, tell yer what, Gerty, I was out of there like a dingo with a squid up its arse. Thought I had Buckley's chance of getting out alive. That Pollack fella froitened the shits owt of me, he had a face like a fuckin bunyip; worse in fact. That garage of his smelt like death.'

'Argh! Vot did I tell you? All Jews smell.'

Mavis laughed. 'I don't know about that, Gerty. You should try yer luck Australia Day, sitting next to a stinking Abo on a crowded Bondi tram.'

'We'll have to ring his nibs. Get DI Faversham round here.' Mavis sighed. 'Even if it means listening to the old bandicoot whining on about contaminating evidence or disregarding police procedure.'

Reaching for the Rolodex, Mavis found the Wimbledon Police Station card and dialled the number. 'Can you put me through to Detective Inspector Eric Faversham? Would you tell him it's Mavis Bone from the agency?'

There was a pause, then a man's voice. 'DI Faversham.'

'Ah. Inspector, it's Mavis Bone,' she laughed, 'you know, with the Kraut sidekick.'

'So what have you got for me?'

'I did a search for one of our clients on a house in Wimbledon at number twenty-three Marryat Road. It belongs to a Mr Vincent Pollack.'

'A search? On whose authority? Without a warrant?'

Mavis rolled her eyes to her secretary. 'No forced entry. Just snooping around his garage. You have no idea what I found. He's got a torture chamber in the basement. All set up to make snuff movies, S&M, bondage and all that shit. There's a pile of DVDs.'

'Listen, you stupid Aussie cow. I don't give a flying fuck what you've found. You shouldn't have been in there.'

'Eric. That Pollack tried to kill me; he knows I know after what I found in his lair. There was a sheila's body in a steel drum. I'm sure it was a missing au pair called Anna that my client Mrs Clifton told me about. She had an engraved identity charm to prove it.'

DI Faversham sighed. 'Have you any hard evidence?'

'Not really. That bogan Pollack sculled it with all the evidence, when I was tied up. Even the dead sheila was gone when I was free to look. Probably taken in the white Ford transit van that was parked in his garage. I did get a make on the tags though. Got a pen? LR60 HWY.'

'Okay, okay. We'll do a forensic search of the property.

Just remember though, anything we find incriminating could be deemed by the CPS as fruit of the poisoned tree, and couldn't be used against the defendant, especially if Pollack highlights your break-in to his defence council. That's the idea of an organised, supervised search warrant, dummy. Stops them saying evidence could be planted or tampered with.'

Mavis cringed. 'Shit, didn't think of that one, Eric.'

'Do you and that Kraut sidekick of yours ever stop to? You're like a pair of prize heifers in a china shop.'

*

Three days later, DI Eric Faversham made his way up the stairs to the Mavis Bone Detective Agency. After intercom introductions, he pressed the buzzer and was allowed in. The DI shuffled in wheezing, hunched over and short of breath. He cursed under his breath, 'Those stairs will be the end of me.' The silver-haired fifty-four year old DI was looking his age, wearing as usual his sober pin-striped suit with matching blue waistcoat. This set off his Dickensian looks of a thin, severe face with wrinkled features and protuberant ears.

The DI winced as his elevenses found their way to his mouth from the twelve-year-old single malt stored in his silver hip flask.

Mavis Bone and Gertrude Stick were sitting in the agency office, singing along to a CD of Mario Lanza's 'Be My Love' on their music system.

'Such a vonderful singer.' Gertrude dabbed her eyes with a handkerchief. 'I alvays get emotional vhen I listen to him.'

Mavis agreed. 'Me too, Gerty.'

They were sitting at Mavis's office table, having lunch on a recently delivered meat feast pizza. Gertrude continued nibbling a large triangular slice, while Mavis reminisced. 'I remember my mother was a big fan, God bless her; taking me and little Caroline my sister, to the Rialto in Sydney to see *The Toast of New Orleans*.'

Twiddling her pearl necklace, Mavis carried on. 'I was waist high to an Abo's nipple then. Mum knew the sheila in the ticket booth, so we only paid for two seats. Little Caroline used to sit on her lap, and we'd share a choc ice together. That's all Mum could afford, on her farmer's wife allowance. Not a lot of wonga around in those days, what with Dad being laid off the farm, with his bad back. Can you believe, at thirteen years old, I had a job picking onions around some local farms, outback of Sydney.'

Mavis was lost in thought. 'I was saving pocket money to buy a pony called Ginger. I remember, we'd moved to a hostel in Heathcote farms, where the onion picking was good. The farmers there paid a good price to onion pickers. Rates of pay per box were the best in the county. Mum and Dad needed the money.

'In the afternoons, the school bus drove past an unkempt bay pony called Ginger. She was ginger by name and colour. Her stable was a disused dairy. The noise of the bus's diesel engine and the tyres screeching along the bitumen would set her off. She would take off down the paddock, with her tail up and her nostrils flared to the wind. She had such great spirit. I dreamed of sitting astride her in a paddock on her own. I didn't understand why she was alone. I knew one day I'd somehow set her free. I dreamed of riding her through the bush, camping under the stars and living off my wits, travelling from town to town – that was going to be the life for me. You could say, typical thirteen-year-old nonsense. However, every night I went to bed dreaming about the adventures Ginger and I would have.

'Dad had flatly said, "No horses." They were too expensive to keep, what with me and my sister to feed, and only one income. We'd learned not to harp on when it came to money. "We can't afford it" covered everything from "We're too busy" to "We're not wasting money on that." I already knew one thing about my life. If I wanted something, I'd have to get it myself.

'I wondered whether, if nobody wanted the pony, I could have her. At least look after her, and take her for rides. I thought that would be the same as owning her.

'One afternoon when I was visiting the pony, the old farmer called me over. He was in his late sixties, slightly hunched; his face was worn with heavy sagging lines, and he smelt of alcohol and tobacco. He could see I was keen, and said, "Wanta horse, hey? I'm sellin' her. She's hard in the mouth and she's foundering a bit." He lifted up Ginger's leg and showed me. Her hooves were splayed, with the fleshy parts hitting the ground. The farmer added, "She'd go lame quickly on the road. She needs a bit of lookin' after

– not in perfect condition, but nothing that couldn't be fixed. You can have her if you buy the extras as well, like the saddle, bridle, halters and the whole lot. I won't split 'em, understand me? Well, girl, do you want her or not?"

'I jumped at the chance, and told him, "I want her, but I haven't got any money yet." And then I tried to soften him up, and told him I could do onion picking for him, and work off the price, if he was agreeable. And I'd ride her for exercise, and groom her. I told him I'd brush her and take good care of her. I asked the farmer how much he wanted.

'He said, "A hundred dollars for the pony, and a hundred for all the gear."

'And I could work it off onion picking, as well as clean the paddock, and clean and sweep the sheds after school, and on weekends.

'I checked with Ma and Pa, and they were agreeable, but warned me it mustn't interfere with schoolwork.

'The farmer told me the onion-picking season was about to start. And the first lot would be ready to pick around mid-December.

'I called in to see the farmer late one afternoon. He was on the tractor in the onion paddock, turning a row into a wave of earth and onions, ready for picking. From then onwards, for the next three weeks, I picked all day, row after row, until I picked the paddock clean. It worked out that if I could pick and stack a hundred boxes a day, I could earn ten dollars a day, which also worked out at three weeks' work to buy Ginger. That would leave me a couple of weeks to ride her before school started.

'It was while I was on my second week of picking, the farmer told me Ginger was dead. It looked like she been startled by something, and run headlong into an electric sheep fence. When I saw her for the last time, the farmer had to pull me off. I didn't want to let go of her. After losing Bess, my farm dog. I made a vow never to get close to pets again.

'You could say that went for people as well. The farmer never paid me for the work I did. The last I saw of him, he was pulling a lifeless Ginger, who'd been tied to his tractor, for transport into the glue factory pickup truck.

'After that, as a family, we always seemed to be hard up.'

Gertrude scoffed. "Ard up, you don't know the meaning. You should tvy living in East Berlin in the nineteen sixties. I vemember in my mid-thirties climbing up a steep embankment in all veathers to steal coal from the vagons. With father killed in the vore and mother viddled with arthvitis, it was up to me to find fuel and stand in line for vations. It could be hours before a lovvy turned up, and then you 'ad to be quick while the Vussians threw out loaves and vegetables fom the back of it.' Looking into space she also began to reminisce. 'I vemember father taking me to the opera for the first time to see Wagner's *Siegfried* with Ernst Kozub. Like Mario, he also 'ad a vich, dark, powerful dramatic voice. He vos called an 'eldentenor. I also saw 'im vhen he played Erik in *Der fliegende Holländer, The Flying Dutchman* as it vos known in the Vest. He tvuly vos also a gveat singer.'

The DI glanced at the *Student Prince* film poster on the

office wall. 'Mario Lanza is my favourite too. I listen to his CDs in the car while I'm out chasing villains.'

'Ah! My favourite as well.' Mavis wrung her hands in admiration at the film poster. 'He was a great tenor. His voice was like burnished gold, and such sustained power with that high C of his. I loved how he used to sway when he sang "The Loveliest Night of the Year". He was so famous that, like a pop singer, he got mobbed everywhere.' She went to a filing cabinet and pulled open the drawer. 'Gerty and me have all his RCA seventy-eights in here.' She picked up a clutch to show the inspector.

'Wow!' he said, 'If you have "With a Song in My Heart", then I'll borrow it. It's the only CD I'm missing, and we'll forget about your break-in,' he jested.

Then the DI turned serious. 'Our team found nothing concrete in the forensic search of the Pollack property, apart from some plastic granules on the garage floor.'

Mavis jumped on this detail. 'I told you, Eric, the shufti bugger had that au pair sheila down there, all packed up.'

The DI shook his head. 'We need hard evidence, Mavis; a jury can't hang Pollack on that.' He looked at his report notes. 'The white Ford Transit you saw with LR60 HWY plates was picked up by traffic cameras that day near Wimbledon Common. It had been leased for hire from Peacock's in Balham, in a false name and using forged licence documents. And they automatically carry out a wash and valet of their returned hire vehicles. So our boys found nothing on the van.'

Mavis enquired further. 'You say it was spotted near

Wimbledon Common? Could he have dumped the contents somewhere?'

'Jesus, I never thought of that,' Faversham mocked. 'I'll have to tell the chief constable I want you on my team.'

Mavis ignored his sarcasm.

The DI went on impatiently, 'To relieve your anxiety, Mrs Bone, Wimbledon Common rangers and a small team of local police have been put on alert to look out for suspicious items, and to investigate any ground disturbance on the common. So far, nothing has been found or reported.'

Mavis sighed. 'That cunning bandicoot Pollack could be anywhere. You can bet that bogan is not within a cooee. To find where he is now, yer get more sense asking an outback steakhouse waiter.' The DI nodded in agreement.

Gertrude pulled out the Clifton file. 'Vait a minute.' She glanced at her notes. 'Missus Clifton said she 'ad an adopted gvanddaughter called Helen that lived in Majorca at a hotel that Pollack had bought. Perhaps the cunning yid is hiding out there?'

The DI winced at her racism. He considered for a moment. 'Could be, Gerty. However, if Pollack was standing in front of us now, we still don't have anything on him for a charge. It'd all be deemed circumstantial by the CPS.'

Gertrude snorted indignantly. 'I zink the CPS are vrun by yids as vell, that's vhy 'ee's still free.'

Mavis picked up on what her secretary had suggested earlier. 'Majorca? Yer might have something there, Gerty, well done.'

Detective Inspector Eric Faversham levelled a stare at

them both. 'Now listen, you two. No more breaking in, or taking the law into your own grubby hands. Is that clear?'

'Yes, yes, we'll be good girls just as you want,' Mavis mocked.

Gertrude Stick added her thoughts. 'This Vincent Pollack is alveady on our vadar, Inspector. I'm sure 'e is a Jew. You mark my verds, 'e vill come a cropper vun day. Cunning Jews alvays do. That's why 'itler 'ad them sorted.'

Mavis added, 'Now now, Gerty. He could be a smelly Abo, although it's unlikely, but I don't tie that dog shit smelling native Aussie crap, to every other Bruce that gets out of order.'

Gertrude Stick reminded her. 'You vink Jews don't smell? Believe me. The Vussian commissar wearing a Star of David pendant, that vaped me in nineteen-vorty-vive at the fall of Berlin, when I vos Hitler Youth, stunk like a votting cabbage. 'e said it vos my punishment vor stealing coal from vailway tvucks. Vith my parents and small brother, alveady killed by a Vussian Jewish battalion zat had overvun our Berlin apartment block. Ve 'ad no windows due to bomb damage. It vos freezing.'

Gertrude dabbed her eyes. 'Zee only lasting memory I 'ave of my little brother vos ven vee ver both at a Hitler Youth Vally in nineteen virty-eight, 'eld in zee Berlin Olympic Stadium. That Zaturday, there 'ad been over eighty-thousand Hitler Youth in their separate legions, amongst zee drumming and waving of flags. Ve 'ad marched in step as the band played the "Horst-Wessel-Lied". Then my brother 'ad performed military-style manoeuvres, ending with a night-time grand finale, vich included spelling out the name of Adolf Hitler with vlaming torches.'

Gertrude dabbed her eyes again, while Mavis put an arm around her shoulder. 'I vemember my brother, bless him, with his light brown hair combed over Führer style, and vearing the summer uniform of black lederhosen, with brown short sleeves and party svastika armband. 'e'd got a good place to view the Führer, near the concrete podium with its giant svastika. And then came the tumultuous welcome, as the Führer stepped up to the microphone, it vos unbelievable.'

Gertrude continued with a faraway look in her eyes. 'Hitler gave a speech in vich 'e spoke candidly about 'is own youth and painful adolescence. Ven 'e'd finished, ve all shrieked in a vipped-up frenzy, *Sieg Heil.*' With the same faraway look, Gertrude finished off, 'Vose ver the days.'

At that moment, Adolf, the agency office monk parakeet, who'd been dozing in the overhanging sheet-covered cage, suddenly woke up. 'Cunning Jews, cunning Jews, who's a pretty boy then?'

Mavis tapped the cage in annoyance. 'Shut up, Adolf, we've got company.'

'Who's a dirty dyke then? Who's a dirty dyke then?'

She tapped it harder this time. 'Will you shut up, Adolf, or I'll stuff you for the Sunday roast.'

The threat seemed to do the trick, as silence prevailed.

DI Faversham laughed. 'Don't fancy his chances as a mascot for the Golders Green Station.' He nodded a goodbye and made a move for the door.

'Not gonna stop for a cuppa, Eric? Gerty, be a dear and put the billy on, I'm as dry as a nun's cunt.'

'Vill do.' Gertrude offered, 'and you, Inspector?'

He shook his head with dismay, cringing at the profanity.

TWENTY

Bar mitzvah

Mr Joseph Wiseman, a silver-haired, seventy-five year old German Jew, arrived at the shared business entrance for the office of the Mavis Bone Detective Agency on Wimbledon Broadway SW19.

He pressed the third button down, and heard a buzzer as the door unlocked to allow him through to an entrance lobby. From there he took the stairs to the first floor as indicated by a business list board.

At a half-panelled glass door stencilled with **Mavis Bone Detective Agency – An eye for an eye makes the whole world blind,** he pressed another buzzer. Immediately Gertrude Stick, the agency secretary spoke through the intercom. 'Can I 'elp you?'

'It's Mr Joseph Wiseman. I have a ten-thirty appointment to see Mavis Bone.'

'Come through please.'

Another buzzer unlocked the door, and Mr Wiseman entered a small and cluttered outer office. He was immediately confronted by a smart sad-faced secretary who was wearing a blue trouser suit with big gold earrings. She was sitting at a desk covered in files. A chic lavender blue head scarf hid her platinum blonde dyed hair.

Mr Wiseman couldn't help noticing that high above, strategically placed between empty spaces on dusty shelves, filled with files and ledgers, a few sets of glassy eyes peered at him from stuffed animals. These were from two squirrels, with a fox about to pounce on them, and a suspended tawny owl that twisted slowly in flight.

The secretary nodded to the animals. 'Our last office tenant was a mortician, and liked to keep his vinger in.'

The German secretary's heavily lined and tanned face, which was mostly the result of visits to a sunbed salon, was further made up with pink lipstick and green eye shadow. She indicated for Mr Wiseman to take a seat, and spoke into the intercom. 'Mr Viseman to see you, Mrs Bone.'

'Please show him through, Gertrude.'

Gertrude Stick came round from behind her desk, and escorted the prospective client to a larger, brown-carpeted office, that contained three large sash windows and four filing cabinets. There he was greeted by the private detective.

Stocky, Australian-born Mavis Bone, with her jet black hair full of tiny curls, was wearing a smart red trouser suit. She raised herself from behind a leather-topped desk, and extended her hand. 'G'day. Please take a seat, Mr Wiseman.'

After introductions, Mavis said, 'I understand you

want to report your grandson's stolen year-old Golden Labrador.'

'Yes, this month, he's thirteen years old, so it was bought for his forthcoming bar mitzvah. He's very upset about it. I did report it to the local police, but they didn't seem that interested. So here I am, after reading some of your client investigation reviews, which were full of praise.'

Mavis responded, 'That's very kind of you, mate, and would you mind if my secretary sits in on this, and takes notes? That way we make sure to capture all the vital information.'

Gertrude Stick sat herself down with a notepad at the end of the desk, and reassured Mr Wiseman. 'Everything vot I write is fully confidential, my dear. It vill not be disclosed to anyvun else.'

Mavis rolled her eyes, knowing how Gertrude always trotted out her same introduction line. 'Yes, thank you, Gerty.' She turned to Mr Wiseman with a big, cheesy grin. 'I wouldn't know what to do without my Gerty. She's my Girl Friday, as you poms call it.'

Gertrude Stick took down his details, and then opened a client account for him. They assured him that details and photographs of his dog would be distributed to the police and on local noticeboards, as well as to the RSPCA and local councils that handled strays. They would also carry out street and local park searches.

In conversation, Joseph Wiseman chatted to Gertrude Stick. 'From your accent, it sounds like you come from Germany?'

'Zat is tvue. I lived in Berlin during the vor.'

Joseph replied, 'I did as well. What part of Berlin?'

Gertrude responded, 'I lived in Dorotheenstrasse in the Mitte district.'

'No way,' Joseph said, amazed. 'So did I. What a coincidence.' And then he lost himself in thought. 'Hang on a minute, I remember a family named Stick, living in the same block of flats where my family lived in on Dorotheenstrasse.'

Gertrude beamed a surprised smile, and fondly fingered the picture frame on her desk, which proudly showed a family group photo of her parents, with herself and her brother.

Joseph went on. 'I remember the Stick family well. they had a daughter named Gertrude who was a BDM member of the Hitler Youth. In fact she used to play with my daughter Frieda.'

Suddenly, Gertrude became hesitant. 'I'm sorry, but I don't remember playing with a girl named Frieda.'

Joseph Wiseman's tone was barbed. 'Oh I'm sure you do, Gertrude, and for good reason. That being, if you're the same Gertrude Stick who killed my Frieda, along with a crowd of Hitler Youth girls, when they set fire to her tent at a Jewish Youth Aliyah campsite.'

Gertrude shook her head in denial, 'Nein, nein, you have the vong Gertrude Stick, sir.'

Mavis looked shocked at the accusation.

And then he took out from his wallet a feathered black-and-white photograph. He showed it to Mavis Bone, and

253

pointed out a girl who was clearly a young Gertrude Stick, smiling and posing with his late daughter Frieda.

Before Gertrude could put away her family picture frame, Joseph grabbed it off her desk and made the comparison, pointing out to Mavis Bone the damning similarity.

Gertrude Stick still denied it was herself in his picture.

Wiseman explained what had happened. 'My daughter, along with four other girls, were on a Jewish Youth Aliyah activity weekend. Under the current Nazi law, all other religious youth groups had been banned. This meant they were Jew bait and at the mercy of local Hitler Youth hostilities. It was later learned at the trial, in 1946, that security around the campsite where they were staying had been compromised by threats from the Gestapo to the group leader's families.

'This meant the six Hitler Youth girls had a free hand to operate under orders from their BDM troop leader. They were instructed to set fire, using cans of gasoline, to the tent my daughter was in, along with the four other Jewish girls. Whereupon all of them were burned to death.'

While dabbing his eyes, Joseph Wiseman continued, 'After the war, the atrocity was held to account by a secondary war crimes tribunal. The BDM troop leader was caught and arrested. Under threat of severe prosecution, she had to reveal the names of the Hitler Youth girls responsible.'

At that disclosure, Joseph Wiseman withdrew from

his jacket a German court proclamation dated 1946, and showed it to Mavis Bone. 'For sentimental reasons, I carry this with me at all times.'

While Gertrude turned away, ignoring him, Mavis read the court ruling, which sentenced Gertrude Stick and the five other girls, taking into consideration their teenage years, to serve five years in Westerberg Reformatory Detention Centre for Girls, north of Berlin.

'Due to the aftermath of war, and the lack of security involved, the sentences were never carried out,' Wiseman explained. 'However, under current German law, the sentences are still legal and have to be served.'

He turned on Gertrude Stick and made it clear to her. 'My daughter's awful death has never been avenged, and I still want justice.'

Gertrude protested, 'I told you, you 'ave zee vong person, and it vos such a long time ago.'

He reminded her with a mocking laugh, 'That's what all war criminals say. Listen, Stick, I will go to the authorities and the police with this information, and show them the incriminating photos.'

'You are vasting your time, Mr Viseman.' At that, Gertrude stormed out of the office in a huff, while Mavis tried to reason with him.

*

Later that afternoon, Mavis talked over the ramifications with a worried Gertrude Stick, of her being held to account for his daughter's death. It was then they decided that Joseph Wiseman had to be silenced.

*

The next day, Mavis got a lucky break. Joseph Wiseman's lost dog had been found wandering in a local park. She telephoned him with the good news, hoping it might soften his decision about Gertrude. However, he was quite adamant, and his mind was made up to have Gertrude Stick prosecuted for his daughter's death.

However, being over the moon that his grandson's Golden Labrador had been found, and as a way of showing his gratitude, Joseph Wiseman invited Mavis Bone to his grandson's bar mitzvah celebration. This was for the coming Saturday at Golders Green synagogue. From there it was on to festivities, and a kosher celebration barbecue, in the back garden of Wiseman's large house. Mavis thanked him, hoping she might get a chance to persuade him to change his decision about Gertrude.

In the synagogue that Saturday, Mavis was wearing a smart blue summer suit with a matching headscarf. She'd attended the first part of the bar mitzvah celebration, during Shabbat morning services. This included Joseph Wiseman's grandson chanting from the Torah.

At the conclusion of prayers, the guests regrouped and made their way to the Wisemans' house for a festive bar mitzvah barbecue in their large back garden, which contained a decorated marquee.

*

As Mavis passed through the back garden gate into the marquee, she encountered numerous guests. Some were sitting in groups at tables with parasols. Bunting stretched like a canopy overhead, crisscrossed from parasol to parasol.

The music had been turned down, while people dined. Efraim Webermen continued to pour gently from the speakers, with an assortment of Israeli folk music. Around the tables, jackets had been discarded to the backs of chairs, while rolled-up shirt sleeves revealed expensive gold watches and chunky bracelets. Women fanned themselves with catering cards left on tables, left in case anyone else would like to hire Zimmer's for bar mitzvahs or weddings.

Imitation gold menorahs formed the centrepieces of the tables where groups conversed, some in Yiddish, some in English.

The music started up again with 'Hava Nagila', and people left their tables, already clapping and moving in rhythm as the first dancers in the circle made way for them. And then came the hora, another popular Israeli dance.

Over the sound system, an announcement was relayed. 'Ladies and gentlemen, the buffet is now open. Please observe N'tilat Yadayim. Bon appetite.'

The smoke from the spit roast caught Mavis's attention. She looked in that direction, where Joseph Wiseman was in charge and looking agitated. He was waving frantically at swirling clouds of smoke, and backed away rubbing his eyes.

Mavis approached him with a smile. 'Lots of smoke coming from that barbecue, Joseph.'

'I've had problems with this fire all afternoon, Mavis; my fault,' he confessed. 'The wood is damp. I should have stored it away in a dry place.'

Mavis was feeling peckish and noted that a long queue had gathered at one end of the buffet, and was inching its way slowly along. Black-clad waiters wearing kippahs stood to attention, helping to serve or top up dishes.

The buffet table heaved with Vienna sausages, kreplach, rollmops, grilled salmon, garlic chicken and a mound of chopped liver, topped with grated hard-boiled egg.

As Mavis edged her way nearer to Joseph's spit roast, she could see it was still underdone, with pink juices running, when he prodded the lamb with a fork. Mavis suggested, 'Do you have any barbecue fuel to squirt on the damp wood?'

'That's a good idea, Mavis.' Joseph picked up the plastic fuel bottle and gave it a squeeze. When nothing came out, apart from a dribble, he cursed, 'Damn! It needs refilling.'

She asked him, 'Do you have any more?'

'There's another spare bottle in the marquee by the generator lobby.'

'I'll get it, so you can concentrate on the spit roast and stoke up the fire.'

'Thanks, Mavis.'

On her way through the marquee, she passed tables that issued roars of merriment from groups all cramped together. Flushed faces from too much wine jostled and knocked elbows with each other while devouring buffet plates piled high with food.

Four empty bottles of Yarden Cabernet Sauvignon stood witness to one table's enjoyment, while numerous empty bottles of wine were to be seen on others.

A quieter table bowed their heads in prayer, saying a blessing for the food and wine. One of the elders chanted aloud as he rocked backwards and forwards.

*

Mavis approached the marquee generator lobby, and noticed it only had a few windows, which was handy.

The gasoline generator chugged away, giving the marquee its artificial lighting.

At the time, the lobby was quiet and deserted. Mavis spotted the plastic barbecue fuel bottle. She also spotted the generator top-up petrol can, and the funnel used with it.

Keeping a watchful eye, she quickly tipped away the contents of the barbecue fuel bottle, and then refilled it with gasoline from the can.

Mavis washed and scrubbed her hands thoroughly in the temporary restroom tent that had been set up for guests. Checking all was clear, Mavis quickly walked to the main party entrance, where the music and crowd noise became louder. She cast a careful glance both ways.

With no one paying attention, Mavis stepped onto the outdoor carpet and made for the buffet. Grabbing a fresh glass of wine from a waiter's tray, she disappeared amongst the many guests picking their way along the food table.

*

Mavis returned as Joseph was surveying the uncooked neck and middle section of the lamb on the spit roast. She handed him the bottle of barbecue fuel; he thanked her and busied himself getting more wood burning.

To Joseph's relief, the guests were now queuing at the spit roast, and hadn't yet filled themselves up with the remaining buffet.

Joseph raked the wood under the spit roast, and then stuffed some paper into the pile. The paper caught, and flames slowly began to curl and lick up.

Joseph read the label on the plastic barbecue fuel bottle. *Safe, odourless and instant. Get your barbecue off to a sizzling start with* CPL SUPAGRILL LIGHTING FLUID. The safety instructions were too small, and he didn't have his glasses. All he could make out was the fire hazard warning symbol.

Joseph removed the cap from the fuel bottle and squirted the damp wood. Smoke instantly billowed up, and he wave his arms frantically as the stinging sensation reached his eyes. He backed away and cursed under his breath. Around the other side, the paper had done its job. The crisp black charred pages glowed as the wood above it crackled into life, with yellow and blue flames peeping through the pile.

Joseph leant away and pointed the bottle warily. And then he squeezed the liquid onto the naked flames.

People instantly turned towards the sound of a loud *whumph!* It was followed by a piercing scream as an orange fireball exploded into a rolling inferno of flames. Mavis ducked as the explosion flashback of the bottle engulfed Joseph, turning him into a human torch. He began to run around in circles, waving his arms like a headless chicken, screaming as smouldering embers fell from him. And then he fell, got up, still screaming, ran, and then fell again, rolling over and over in a boiling mass of flames, his mad path traced by the sick aroma of burned flesh and areas of smouldering outdoor carpet.

His body writhed like a firework display caricature, jerking into life now and again, and then dripping and dissolving with the heat. The smell of burned flesh rose up with crackling sparks from the bits of woodpile and clothing melting into his skin.

A pitiful, gurgling '*Help me*' was finally heard. His movements decreased to short spasms and twitches. And then came a long-drawn-out groan, as if exhausted and resigned to his fate.

One of the guests spotted a red fire bucket of water near the demolished barbecue. He raced to pick it up. It was heavy and knocked against his legs as he ran towards Joseph. The heat coming up as he approached made him shield his face. He edged forward as near as possible, and then swung the pail. The liquid hit Joseph, and his body shuddered with the force. Sparks and smoke flew up, sizzling and spitting. Some guests turned away and threw up. Othes looked on, unable to move, transfixed. Not wanting to go near.

Another guest, claiming to be an off-duty paramedic, grabbed the fire extinguisher that had been next to the barbecue and squeezed the trigger. As the jet of foam found its target, a monstrous hissing was followed by a huge plume of steam, and everybody ducked back. People began to edge nearer as the paramedic continued to spray Joseph.

The speakers were still playing 'Hava Nagila' for the third time, but no one was dancing.

To prevent him from seeing the tragedy that has befallen his grandfather, the bar mitzvah boy was quickly led away into the house by relations.

Mavis Bone approached the pile of smouldering rags that had been Joseph Wiseman. Wiping her mouth with a handkerchief, she stopped to look at what was left of him, and bit the knuckles of her hand, trying to stem the urge to throw up. However, Mavis knew that Gertrude Stick's problem had just gone up in smoke.

The paramedic was taking charge, and moved people back while he pulled out his mobile phone and called for an ambulance. He crouched over the smouldering mass, and called to the crowd, 'Someone help me get his clothes off. I need a knife or scissors. He's cooking with them on.'

An overweight lady wearing a headscarf came waddling forward through the loosening knot of spectators with her handbag open. 'I've got some scissors.' She recoiled at the steaming mound. The lady wouldn't come any nearer.

The paramedic reached over and took the scissors. 'Thanks.'

Joseph had finished up face down, smouldering, on his stomach. His hair had gone and most of his ears. He smelt like a damp bonfire. The paramedic flinched as he knelt down and touched what remained of his clothes. Pulling the cloth taut, he ran the scissors all the way up the back of his steaming jacket to the collar. He cut quickly and waved away the smoke rising up in his face. He paused, and then carefully parted the flaps of the jacket. Skin peeled away with it. Although hardened to such scenes, bile still gagged the back of the paramedic's throat as he stemmed the urge to vomit. He realised that Joseph was burned a lot more on his front, where he'd taken the full force of the inferno.

The paramedic cut the jacket sleeves, but had to stop. He realised he was cutting through skin, as most of the material had melted in, and was lifting away like well-done pork crackling.

Using two hands on the scissors for the trouser turn-ups, he cut all the way along the legs, past the buttocks to Joseph's waistline. His face contorted with the resistance of the belt, and he cursed as he persevered, until the scissors finally cut through the leather. He tried to separate the steaming trouser halves, but again the skin came away. He stopped, and that was as far as he would go. The rest would be a job for the other medics when they arrived.

And sure enough, after the wail of an ambulance was heard, two men in green uniforms approached. One took off his gloves and knelt beside Joseph. He felt around his neck for a pulse, and then tried his wrist. The medic looked at his buddy and shook his head. And then they spoke quietly with grim expressions.

A rubber body bag was unzipped and laid out on the stretcher. With protective gloves, they lifted Joseph, wincing at the smell.

Part of the plastic fuel bottle had landed near Joseph's body. The older medic walked over and picked up the charred container. *Odourless and instant* could still be read on the brown-and-yellow singed label. He sniffed it, and then sniffed again. He looked at his colleague with a knowing nod. 'Petrol. It's been filled with petrol.'

His colleague shook his head and said aloud, 'How many times are we called out for this mistake? Especially in the summer, but thank you, Jesus, not as bad as this.'

The sweet smell of burned flesh had become nauseating to Mavis. She felt queasy, and was hunched over the fire bucket, holding tissues to her mouth.

The medic said to his partner, 'We'd better let the police know, and fill out a report.' His partner nodded in agreement and zipped up the body bag.

The music had been switched off. The laughing and party atmosphere had ceased. Now there were serious faces. Guests stood huddled together and spoke in low tones, some shaking their heads, while others looked mystified.

A few said a prayer, chanting slowly. Many kissed their shawls and talliths as a mark of respect as the medics passed them. The black body bag on the stretcher jolted with their footfalls as they tried to keep a dignified procession as they made their way to the ambulance outside.

A trolley was rolled into place. And then the motorised platform of the ambulance lifted them up. Finally, the pulled-back doors swallowed up the two medics and the remains of Joseph.

In the explosion, the lamb had fallen into the fire. Burned and charred it lay there, like a pagan sacrifice. The gods had not been satisfied today with just one offering.

Amongst the crowd, a discreet, thin smile appeared, Mavis Bone quickly pasted it over, before anyone noticed.

TWENTY-ONE

Thwack!

Forty-eight-year-old Vincent Pollack was busy at his hotel in Majorca. It was July 2012 and he had the decorators in for an early pre-season facelift. While getting very frustrated, trying to explain in pidgin Spanish to a large and overweight floor-tiler how some tiles should be laid diagonally, he fumbled for his mobile as the ringtone started up. It was his twelve-year-old adopted daughter Helen. She had a cold, and was staying at their rented villa next to the hotel.

As she'd been off school the last two days, Vincent had suggested that if she was feeling better she could catch up with some revision. Amongst a few reluctant sniffs and grunts, Helen had agreed.

She had her own computer in her bedroom, but needed to use the internet. Vincent had made sure the internet could only be accessed through his own computer, as he had installed child protection software.

'Dad, I phoned Bianca to check for weekend homework. I need to use your computer to search for a topic. I've got to finish a piece on *El Cid*.'

'Okay, but keep to *El Cid*. No listening to pop music. You've got some important exams coming up, young lady.' Vincent Pollack held up his hand to shush the tiler, who was still talking excitedly.

'Okay, Mr Grumpy, anything else?'

'Yes, make sure to take your cough syrup and keep indoors for today. I'll take Zita for a walk when I get back.'

Helen groaned, 'But can't I take…?'

'No!' he said impatiently. 'You don't want to get worse. I'll see you later.'

With that, the mobile went back inside his pocket, and he continued his argument with the floor-tiler, both of them now engaged in a heated exchange and waving tiles at each other.

If only that was all he had to worry about. At the time of purchasing the hotel, Vincent Pollack had been advised by his buildings insurance company to install a night security service, to deter vandalism and theft, as this would secure the validity of his policy certificate. Vincent had taken their advice and fitted security lights, as well as hiring a nightwatchman with five Presa Canario guard dogs. They would patrol the hotel grounds in the early morning hours, while the guests were asleep. These guard dogs were part of the bull mastiff breed, with an aggressive temperament and very unpredictable. Their massive heads and jaws, together with cropped ears, made them look very formidable. Vincent had fitted warning signs around the perimeter areas, advising people to beware.

Helen came down the stairs sniffing and dabbing a red nose. She went into the kitchen and poured herself a glass of milk. She turned on the radio and was greeted with the early morning news in Spanish. As she reached for the biscuit tin, on cue, Zita, her one-year-old Spanish Terrier, jumped up with a couple of excited barks, wagging her little tail. Helen broke a couple of chocolate biscuits onto a plate and reached down, with Zita already nibbling at them before they reached the floor.

After some toast and milk, Helen made her way into the lounge and switched on the television. Zita followed, her tongue making large sweeps around her mouth, licking off the remains of the treat. Helen nestled herself onto the sofa, between four small cushions, and patted her lap. Zita didn't have to be asked twice. She leapt up, wagging her stumpy tail, and licked Helen's chin.

They watched a *Friends* episode in Spanish. Zita fidgeted every time Helen laughed, and looked up to see what all the fuss was about.

After twenty minutes, with the credits rolling up, she sighed. 'Oh well, Zeet, I suppose I'd better get down to some work.'

With the homework folder tucked under her arm, Helen made her way to her father's study. The computer hummed into life and booted up. With a click of the mouse, she was on the internet.

As she sat in Vincent's swivel chair, Zita looked up

at her with a *what about me?* expression. 'Come on then, but only for a while, Zeet. I must get a move on.' Zita jumped up, nestling herself into Helen's lap and sniffing the keyboard. As Helen grabbed her school pad, a pen rolled off the edge of the desk. 'Shit,' she mumbled, trying to reach down, but her arms weren't long enough. 'Go find, Zeet,' Zita ignored her; she was comfy and wasn't budging. 'Come on, Zeet, off you get.'

Helen sat up and Zita jumped down to the floor. She got on her hands and knees, and saw the pen was underneath the desk. Ducking down she grabbed it, sat up quickly, and bumped her head. 'Shit! Bloody pen.' She rubbed the spot hard. Zita moved under with her, thinking it was great fun, but making the space even more cramped.

It was then Helen noticed the writing; faint, in thin black felt tip above her head. She craned her neck to get a closer look. Helen reached up blindly, her hand searching for a pad that had been near the keyboard. Her fingers probed until she felt the wire ring coils. She pulled it down, flipped a couple of pages, and began to write down the letters and numbers, *SP24915.*

She got back up and sat in the chair. Zita, without any prompting, jumped back up to her cosy position. 'Now keep still, Zeet, or you can get down again.'

Helen stared at the pad for a while. She thought, why would anyone write something under there, where it couldn't be seen? She'd helped Vincent put the two flat-pack desks together with the replacement computers, some months ago. Hers had been a Christmas present.

She'd been all excited, knee-deep in cardboard boxes and polystyrene packing bits.

Helen looked at the screen. The cursor ticked away, beside a box asking for a password. 'No harm in trying,' she mumbled. Zita raised her head nonchalantly, and then lowered it.

Helen typed the characters into the box. And immediately the screen dissolved into an assortment of headings: *Hotel inventory for the first months of 2011, Scanned purchase orders, Advice notes, End-of-year accounts* and *Personal*.

Helen hesitated for a moment and then clicked *Personal*. A file headed *PHOTOS* appeared with numerous JPEG icons. Almost instinctively, the arrow from her mouse clicked on the top one. A photo came up showing a bonfire on firework night. The made-up guy was strapped to a wheelchair, missing its head amongst a starburst of fireworks.

Zita looked up and fidgeted uneasily in her lap.

Helen hesitated with the mouse, and then clicked on another file. She was confronted with a scene of a barbecue. Gas bottles and outdoor heaters were scattered around, including an upturned grill heaped with coals. And then, to her surprise, a naked couple standing on a balcony. The woman, lifted up in her lover's arms, looked familiar. Unzipping her schoolbag, Helen pulled out a magnifying glass. With a sharp intake of breath, she realised it was her mother. The man she didn't recognise. Helen's mind was swimming in confusion. She didn't understand... what was her late mother doing in such a compromising position?

Clicking a further JPEG icon, curiosity seemed to wash over Helen as she leaned forward in anticipation. A photo of what at first looked like a war zone scene appeared, with smoke and flames and the complete devastation of a building. And then came the horror! A close-up of two badly charred bodies. The one still wearing a charm bracelet, she recognised as her late mother. Helen whispered to herself, 'Dear God.'

At that moment, Zita had become unsettled, as if she sensed something. Her ears pricked up. Helen looked at her. 'What's up, Zeet?' Zita gave out a whine but her ears stayed up.

Zita was now fidgeting, getting restless. She started to whine. 'Sit still, will you!' Helen said impatiently.

Zita was now barking at the window. She had seen or heard something.

Helen took out her mobile from her dressing gown pocket, and began to push the buttons to call her adoptive dad. Suddenly she turned to meet his face at the window. The face of Vincent Pollack behind her had seen it all, and he knew that she now knew.

In those seconds, Helen already feared she had meddled in something she shouldn't have, and might have to pay the price.

Without thinking she sprinted out of the room and down the hall, with Zita barking behind. Helen heard the key turn in the large mahogany front door. She dashed through the kitchen to the back door with Zita following, her tiny paws skidding on the marble tiles.

Helen slid the top and bottom bolts and then tried to push it open, but it didn't budge. 'Shit, for fuck's sake,' she whispered under her breath, and then realised that she hadn't unlocked it. Zita jumped up and down, barking at the door. Helen fumbled with the key, conscious of running steps approaching. The key was stiff to move, and wouldn't turn. She kicked the bottom of the door – that had worked before when it had swollen up with the rain – and put pressure on the mortise. With a jolt, the key clicked in the lock and the door burst open into the back garden, making Helen stumble over onto one knee and wince with the sharp pain.

Zita had been first out, but stopped and was now barking at Helen. The rush of warm July air hit the young girl's face. Blood formed at the tear in her pyjamas where the knee was grazed. She got up and ran for the hotel perimeter fence, shouting at Zita to follow, the pain in her knee causing her to limp the last ten yards.

She turned at the crash of the back door, as it was flung open and smacked against the brick wall. Helen started climbing the perimeter fence, Zita barking at her ankles, not wanting to be left behind. She grabbed the dog and started hauling it up with her. At the top of the seven-foot fence, Helen cursed as the wire ends stuck into her hand.

With the sound of running and heavy breathing getting nearer, Helen hoisted the dog over the fence, and then followed. Trying to climb down, she screamed with pain as the ragged end of the wire fence cut into her shin. She tried frantically to unhook her pyjamas, eventually tearing them away in a frenzied tug.

Leaning down, she dropped Zita to the ground, and then pushed off, letting herself fall. As she crashed onto her shoulder, she cried out, '*Shit!*' Helen tried to get up using her good shoulder. Zita whined, hesitating, seeing Helen on the floor and not wanting to run off.

The fence heaved as Vincent Pollack hit it with a flying leap. '*Come here! I want to explain!*' he shouted.

Holding her shoulder and limping, she dragged herself into the hotel gardens. Her dog had stopped and was again barking at her. Helen shrieked at Zita to come on. The dog faltered. And then she heard the muffled thump of Pollack, jumping down from the fence behind.

Helen ran until her temples pounded, ran until her eyes pulsed inside their sockets, ran until she had a hot stitch in her left side, up to the bottom of her ribs and armpits, and ran until she could taste blood in the back of her throat.

She was slowing, and the crunch of earth and twigs with heavy panting was getting nearer. Zita, now some way behind, barked at Pollack's feet. Helen limped, still trying to run with the smell of damp earth thick in her brain. She started to scream, '*Help me someone – please!*'

A large hand picked up a broken fence post. Blood dripped through Vincent Pollack's fingers, unfelt, from a hidden nail. As he lashed out at the dog, Helen turned to the injured screech of her pet. It was hit mid-body. And then she tripped, and went sprawling to the ground in a flurry of earth and twigs.

Vincent Pollack stood over her, legs astride his cowering daughter.

Helen cried out, *'Daddy! Daddy!'* still trying to crawl, sobbing and moaning.

A foot rested on her back. 'Stop screaming, you bitch!'

'Please don't hurt me. I won't tell.'

Zita, her spine broken, whimpered. She tried to drag her back legs away. For Vincent Pollack, it was in easy reach. Helen knew what was coming. As he raised the fence post again, she turned away and covered her face. And then came the screech, with a dull thud, finally quietening the animal for good.

Pollack's hand gripped Helen's pyjama jacket and he yanked her up, her legs kicking and sliding to get a grip. Helen cried out, *'Don't hurt me!'* She started screaming. *'I won't tell – please don't!'*

'Shut up, you bitch!' His hand dropped the fence post and covered her mouth to stifle the noise. Helen's head jerked from side to side, trying to shake it off. And then his other hand began to squeeze her neck in a vice-like grip of rising pain. Helen was gulping for breath as the pressure grew tighter and tighter.

All at once, Vincent Pollack started blinking repeatedly, and his face began to twitch in a convulsive tick. And then there was silence, broken only by Helen's intermittent final whimpering.

Helen's body was limp and lifeless. His hands let her slump to the ground like a rag doll, spilling out leaves and earth on impact.

Vincent Pollack's glazed eyes focused, and he was back to being ten years old, looking down at his stepmother Doreen, her twisted head at right angles; blood oozing from her mouth and nose. Vincent Pollack cried out, 'Oh, God! What have I done?' A line of spittle leaked from the side of his twitching mouth.

He surveyed the scene. It was quiet. Only the wind sang softly overhead. The afternoon shadows drew longer through the trees. The panic was softening now. His rapid breathing slowed.

From inside his jacket he removed a crucifix and a leather cat of nine tails with sharp metal thongs. Pollack stripped to the waist. The scars on his back stood out and glistened with sweat.

'I have placed my trust in false teachings and substitutes for God.' *Thwack!*

'I have broken a solemn vow and promise.' *Thwack!*

'I have neglected prayer for a long time.' *Thwack!*

'I have abused drugs and alcohol.' *Thwack!*

'I have killed and discriminated against others because of greed, race and gender.' *Thwack!*

'I have not been chaste in thought and word.' *Thwack!*

'I have used sex outside marriage and not to procreate life.' *Thwack!*

'I have given myself sexual gratification. I have deliberately looked at pornographic films and magazines.' *Thwack!*

'I have permitted sexual thoughts about someone to whom I am not married.' *Thwack!*

Blood was now running down his back as the thongs bit deep from his self-flagellation. And then he fell to his knees and held up the crucifix, begging for forgiveness.

Finally, as realisation dawned of what to do with his daughter's body, the worry lines in his forehead began to smooth. Vincent's eyes fell on the hotel's apartment block 2, which was having extensive building work carried out, and might provide an opportunity to conceal a body somewhere.

He knew, sooner or later, Helen's absence would draw suspicion. He didn't want the place crawling with police. It was the school holidays at the moment. A letter to her head teacher should square it, to say she'd gone on holiday to Rome, to do some sightseeing with a friend and parents. And then a quick flight abroad to Rome. Send out postcards in her handwriting to her friends, and that bitch of a mother-in-law. Rent out a bed and breakfast there, and use it as her holiday address in case anyone telephoned. Hopefully it would give him time to do a runner and disappear before she was ever found. However, if she was found, he could always say she must have been attacked by the guard dogs and dragged there.

*

One day later, Pollack made plans for his trip to Rome, which was to create the cover story of Helen's holiday there to account for her disappearance. He then carefully explained to Albert, his hotel caretaker, and to Ernesto, the nightwatchman, that he would be away for the next few days. Ernesto was seventy-two years old and partially deaf. He also limped slightly, which was a leftover from a stroke.

Pollack gave Ernesto a list of daily instructions that had to be adhered to. He was excused night duty, and he stressed to Ernesto the importance of keeping the guard dogs strictly in the kennel compound.

'Come with me to feed them so they'll get your smell,' Pollack said loudly, 'and I'll show you where to put their food and water.'

'Si, señor,' Ernesto said hesitantly and followed Pollack to the kennels. When the guard dogs had spotted them, they came bounding over, barking and jumping up at the wire fence.

'Now remember their feeding times, Ernesto, and don't forget the drinking bowls.'

'Si-Si, señor.'

Pollack stooped down and pulled out the metal drawer. He placed the bowls individually, and then slid the drawer home. At that, there was a snarling frenzy as the dogs fought over the bowls of food. This slowly subsided, until the only sounds were slurping tongues and the occasional spat when one dog encroached on another's meal.

Albert, the caretaker, also ran his own taxi for a bit of money on the side. Pollack had arranged with him a lift to Palma Airport, and a return pickup in four days' time.

The next day, with the promise of a bonus in his wage packet, and some freedom with his boss away, Ernesto purchased a bottle of Bulls brandy from the supermarket. He had fed and watered the dogs as per instructions.

And so, with the prospect of some free evenings ahead, Ernesto's hand clutched the neck of the brandy bottle; he wasn't going to trust the handles of a plastic bag with something so precious. Under his other arm he carried a French stick and a large chufa sausage.

That evening, Ernesto limped slowly back in the late afternoon to his watchman's site caravan. He was whistling a passage from *Tosca*. Puccini was his favourite, he'd seen the opera on his portable television the previous night.

By seven-thirty he'd poured his first large one, and taken a bite out of his French stick, with his eyes glued to the television. Mallorca had gone down one-nil to Real Madrid. The portable volume was up extra loud because of his deafness, so it sounded like the sixty-thousand strong crowd were actually sitting in his caravan with him. Ernesto raised his arms in despair, and uttered an obscenity concerning the bald referee, who was now surrounded by protesting players.

He took another large swig, with his mouth still full of bread and sausage. And then he stopped chewing as the first pains surfaced. *Indigestion*, he thought. The pain then spread to his arms. He dropped his glass and held his chest. He was feeling frightened now, and couldn't breathe properly. Ernesto rose from his chair. His heart thumped and spluttered, causing him to lurch into a jerky fit. He knocked over the side table, causing the brandy bottle to spill its contents onto the cheap rug. Ernesto stood with his legs apart, trembling.

The TV commentator was now shouting, as Real Madrid had scored again from a corner. The tin walls of the caravan reverberated with the cheering. Thick smoke from Roman candles lit up a sickly red haze over the screaming fans. Large banners rolled above the crowd's heads, like waves in a furious storm.

Ernesto's heart was slowly seizing up. It spluttered, and then started again, spluttered, started again, and then finally stopped.

As if on cue, with the referee's whistle blowing for half time, Ernesto crashed backwards into the cheap glass cabinet. His head lay amongst broken crockery. Blood was coming from his nose and mouth. His body twitched four or five times, and then came a final spasm. Ernesto's eyes were now wide open, staring at the caravan ceiling.

The players were making their way to the dressing rooms, with the commentator giving his ideas about possible substitutions. The referee moved off to the tunnel with his linesmen, and the crowd relaxed their excitement. While, from somewhere in the background, a death rattle rasped from Ernesto.

*

On his return from Rome, Vincent Pollack had landed at Palma Airport to be met by Albert the caretaker and his taxi. Albert dropped Pollack off at the hotel complex.

After giving him a generous tip, Pollack entered using the side entrance steel gate. Usually when it clanked shut, steel against steel, it was a signal for the dogs to start up. This time, only silence. Something was wrong.

He'd been gone four days, and had given Ernesto a contact number in case of emergencies. Vincent Pollack knew Ernesto didn't like using the phone. It wasn't surprising, because, being partially deaf, he'd always had communication problems using a telephone. On the rare occasions it was called upon, conversations with Ernesto were rather tiring and high volume. Although the dogs and his caravan were on the remote side of the complex, there was an skeleton staff on site, as a last resort for emergencies.

Pollack sniffed the air. Now and again he caught the scent of crag violets. The smell of their yellow flowers was always intense this time of the day. The evening light had faded to a late July evening. Its sky cast an eerie scene, as if muffling all noises except for the intermittent chatter of birds high in the olive trees.

Vincent Pollack cupped his hands and called, 'Ernesto?' He waited. Nothing stirred, still silence. *Perhaps he's in his caravan*, he thought, *maybe having an afternoon nap while the boss is away.*

It was the smell that made him falter. His steps slowed, and the awful stench was getting stronger. *Could it be a blocked toilet, or maybe the dogs had caught a fox or a rabbit, and it was now rotting somewhere?* Getting near the caravan, Pollack called out again. The putrid smell was overpowering, and it seemed to be coming from Ernesto's fanlight.

He knocked on the door. With a handkerchief over his

nose he muffled, 'Ernesto?' Still no answer. Pollack heard talking and then music. *Must be watching his portable.* He tried the handle. As the door swung open, he cried out, 'Mother of God!' A mass of flies exited past him, his arms swiping mindlessly in self-protection at the bloated swarm.

Confronted with the smell and the flies, Pollack stood back, not wanting to see inside. However, he forced himself to edge nearer. He clamped a handkerchief tight against his nose and mouth. With one foot on the caravan steps and the other inside the door, his right arm still waved off the flies trying to escape.

The first thing Pollack saw was the portable, with a hazy picture of a woman giving out the weather forecast. It was hard to see through the buzzing swarm. And then his eyes slowly adjusted to the darkness. There was a large shape in the corner. Something big on the floor. Something moving.

Nothing could have prepared Vincent Pollack to the sight he was about to see. When his brain had finally synchronised to the heap on the carpet, his eyes widened in horror. A moving mass of maggots had completely engulfed Ernesto. A writhing chain had formed through his mouth, and was crawling out of his nose and ears. One stiff arm was rigor mortised up in mock protest.

Pollack turned; he wanted to get away, get out, get anywhere, not here. He tumbled down the steps, coughing and retching, falling on his knees in the grass. With his sleeve he wiped his mouth. He kept repeating, 'Dear, God… Oh! Dear God.' Pollack got to his feet, his head reeling in a terrified daze. 'Must get the police,' he whimpered, 'yes, must ring the police, yes that's it.' He started to run to his apartment, and then slowed when he heard a sound. It was a low, pathetic whine; something in pain, maybe coming from the kennels. And then it struck him. His dogs! He'd forgotten about his dogs.

Pollack began to run in panic. Thoughts of his dogs swam through his mind. *What if he'd forgotten about the gate? What if they'd got out and killed Ernesto? Killed him while he was sleeping?*

Pollack reached the dog compound, and breathed a sigh of relief. The gate was locked. He cupped his mouth and whistled, his trembling lips distorting the usual sound. Usually they'd be bounding over by now, all around him, all excited, waiting for biscuits or tit bits. But now, nothing, no sign of them. And then he heard a pathetic whine again.

Pollack suddenly realised that the dogs hadn't been fed for days. That would mean they were ravenous and dangerous. And it struck him that if he could cement the disappearance of Helen by using the dogs as an excuse for attacking her, and dragging her away somewhere, then Ernesto's death wouldn't have been in vain. And another attack would certainly substantiate the disappearance theory.

Pollack decided to call Albert the caretaker. He made up an excuse for Ernesto.

With a handful of biscuits, he said, 'Albert, can you check out the dogs, and put these biscuits in their food bowls. I can't find Ernesto at the moment, but he's probably having a nap in his caravan.'

Albert responded, 'Yes boss.'

*

As Albert slid the bolt, and walked through the gate into the compound, the smell of excrement became overpowering.

It was then Vincent heard the first high-pitched screams and frenzied barking, with someone shrieking, '*Oh! God help me – no, please God – arhhhh! Mother, Christ – arhhhh!*' More growls and barking, and then ripping sounds, followed by the muffled snarls of what was undoubtedly a feeding orgy. And then came the faint choking sounds of a last desperate drawn-out cry, '*Help me... someone! Please...*'

Vincent Pollack made his way to the dog compound, and stopped at the fence. Looking through it, he saw the remains of Albert. The emaciated dogs were feeding on him, like vultures inside a carcass. They'd had their gorge, and were now pulling at his intestines, sucking and slurping on his blood. *Anything to staunch their thirst. Anything to staunch their hunger. Their last feed had been four days ago.*

TWENTY-TWO

Homophobic Cow

The middle-aged, grey haired woman, smartly dressed in summer clothes, wearing a light green cardigan, arrived at the shared business entrance for the office of the Mavis Bone Detective Agency on Wimbledon Broadway.

Mrs Joan Clifton pressed the third button down, and heard a buzzer as the door unlocked, to allow her through to an entrance lobby. From there she took the stairs to the first floor as indicated by a business list board.

At a half-panelled glass door stencilled with, **Mavis Bone Detective Agency – An eye for an eye makes the whole world blind,** she pressed another buzzer.

Immediately, Gertrude Stick the agency secretary, spoke through the intercom. 'Can I 'elp you?'

'It's Mrs Clifton. I have an eleven o'clock appointment to see Mavis Bone.'

'Come through, please.'

Another buzzer unlocked a door, and Mrs Joan Clifton entered a small and cluttered outer office. Similar to her last visit, she was immediately confronted by Mavis Bone's German secretary. The same chic lavender blue headscarf hid her platinum blonde dyed hair. She spoke into the intercom. 'Mrs Joan Clifton to see you, Mrs Bone.'

'Please show her through, Gerty.'

Gertrude Stick came round from behind her desk, and escorted Mrs Clifton through to their large brown-carpeted office. And there she was greeted by private detective Mavis Bone.

Australian-born Mavis Bone, wearing, as usual, a red trouser suit which complimented her jet black hair full of tiny curls, raised herself from behind her leather topped desk. She extended her hand. 'G'day. Please take a seat, Mrs Clifton.'

After introductions, Mavis said to her, 'As before, Mrs Clifton, would you mind if my secretary sits in on this and takes notes? You sounded worried when you phoned. You said you hadn't heard from yer granddaughter Helen recently,' Mavis Bone asked her. 'Is that right, mate?'

'My Olivia couldn't have kids, so she and her husband, Vincent Pollack, adopted one. Helen is her name. She must be around twelve years old now. She's living with this Pollack in Majorca, as he's her adoptive father. Although he never showed her much affection, well never in my company.'

Mrs Clifton said bitterly, 'I suppose he doesn't have the time, especially now, managing that hotel he bought in

Majorca, with the money from my daughter's life insurance policy. I'm sure the bastard had something to do with my Olivia's death.'

Mrs Clifton raised her hands in desperation. 'I tried phoning the hotel in Majorca, but that bastard Pollack keeps fobbing me off. He keeps telling me she's away in Rome on holiday with a schoolfriend and her parents. Although, I *have* received two postcards sent from Rome by her.'

'So why the worry, mate?'

'I... just... got a feeling... something's wrong. He sounded funny when I phoned. Although he did give me her bed and breakfast address in Rome.'

Mavis asked her, 'If you're worried about her safety, why not contact the police?'

'I would do. The last postcard I received from her was yesterday. I telephoned the bed and breakfast, and was told a young girl with the name Helen Pollack was staying there, but she'd left early with a group. They didn't have any more forwarding info than that. You can see my position, Mavis; I can't exactly report her missing to the police, can I? I'd look such a fool if I set them on a wild goose chase.'

Mavis contemplated. 'So what do you want us to do about all this?'

Mrs Clifton was adamant. 'I want you to check out this Vincent Pollack again and find my Helen. See if he's harmed her. I want you to go to his hotel in Majorca. I'll pay you well. I can afford it.'

Mavis squeezed her chin in thought. 'Yer on, mate.'

Mrs Clifton gushed her thanks and appreciation, and even became teary. With a handkerchief she dabbed her eyes. 'I'm so grateful. You have no idea how worried I am about Helen. She's all I have left now, since I lost my Olivia in that gas canister explosion.'

Mavis patted her shoulder in consolation. 'We'll do our best, mate, don't you worry. I'm sure your Helen is safe and sound, what with the postcards you received, and so on. Anyway we'll do as you want, and put your mind at rest.'

Mavis turned to her secretary. 'Won't we, Gerty?'

'Vee sure vill,' came the reply. 'And I vill 'ave to buy myself a new cozzee for the beach.'

'We must remember to pack the tennis rackets, Gerty.'

'I vill remind you, and some tennis balls.'

Mavis reassured Mrs Clifton with a smile. 'Don't worry, mate, we'll get some work done too. It's that we don't get a chance to go abroad much, what with our workload.'

Mrs Clifton sympathised. 'I understand. Running any business, one is always grateful for the odd break. And I should know, having worked for years in my late husband's plastics company.'

'I'm glad you see it that way, mate. Although you haven't seen your bill for this Majorca trip yet', she joked. 'But I'm sure our Gerty will sort you a discount for being one of our regular customers.'

'I vill do vot I can, Mrs Clivton, and then mail you a copy of our charges, vich you must agree to, and sign and veturn.'

Mrs Clifton extended her hand in appreciation, and thanked them both.

*

As Mrs Clifton took the stairs to the outside street, a Miss Russell, one of Mavis's upstairs tenants, appeared in the hallway and nodded to her in passing. Miss Russell, known as Rusty to her friends, was a slim and attractive middle-aged lesbian, who had ginger bobbed hair and usually wore a mustard-coloured trouser suit. Mavis rented her the top self-contained attic room in the agency building.

Rusty owned a domestic short-haired ginger cat called Raymona. Sometimes the cat made its way into Mavis's office. Mavis hated cats, because they brought on her hay fever. She put up with her tenant's cat, however, because her room was hard to let. Being in the attic, it wasn't everybody's cup of tea.

Now and again, Mavis had homophobic arguments with Rusty, telling her to keep her queer cat locked up, and she'd threatened many times to chuck it down the rubbish chute.

After a previous cat altercation, Rusty had given Mavis a peace offering of some cookies she'd baked. Mavis picked one up from the plate and cautiously took a sample bite, and then screwed her face up.

Rusty anxiously enquired, 'Is there anything wrong? They're fresh. I've only just made them.'

Mavis spat it out into her handkerchief. 'I would

normally have one, me darlin', with a cuppa … It's… It's just where yer fingers have been … you know… you being a dyke. What you lot get up to with all that foreplay and moist fingering, and havin' yer munch brunch.'

Rusty exploded. 'You homophobic cow.'

Mavis mocked. 'Me homophobic? Whatever that means it's rich coming from you. You're the only homo round here, mate.'

Rusty enquired, 'Oh yeah. So what was all that smooching and snogging with your Kraut lover at the Village People Bar in Soho last Saturday night? All dressed up with Nazi helmets and leather biker gear?' Rusty smiled. 'But I must say your joint karaoke rendition of 'Y.M.C.A.' was a new take on for me, especially the Hitler salute and goose-stepping to the chorus.

Mavis looked rather sheepish. 'Oh, did you like it? Me and Gerty had rehearsed a week for that karaoke night.'

Rusty enquired. 'So what's with the anti and denial bit?'

Mavis grinned. 'Politics, mate. Can't have the clients knowing they're working for a couple of poofs.'

Rusty shrugged. 'Who gives a fuck?'

It was then Rusty asked her, 'Oh, while you're here, Mavis, could you come up to my bedroom. I can't open one of the attic rooflight windows. It seems a bit stiff, I'll show you.'

Mavis followed her up the top flight of stairs. As Mavis entered her bedroom, Rusty was already sitting on her bed. She opened her arms to Mavis and said, 'Come here, beautiful.'

Mavis didn't need asking twice. Even after their altercations over the cat she'd always fancied Rusty, and wondered when a chance like this might come. She'd even dreamed about it, while lying in bed with her motorised dildo. And now here it was, and she was really in the mood.

Mavis straddled Rusty's legs and sat on her lap. Mavis took off her white blouse, revealing a sexy black bra that was barely up to the task of containing her well-endowed breasts.

Rusty swiftly removed it and tossed it aside. She held Mavis close, and buried her face between her breasts, while catching a whiff of her expensive Chanel cologne. Rusty felt Mavis's heartbeat against her flushed cheek. And then she ran her palms over Mavis's stiffening nipples, teasing them with her thumbs and tongue.

Rusty nodded to her bed and instructed Mavis, 'Lie down, and I'll give you a nice body massage.'

Mavis pulled her sterling silver snuff necklace from her bag, and cautiously tapped out the cocaine powder onto the attached silver spoon, making two lines. She said to Rusty, 'Have you ever fucked on coke?'

'Only marijuana,' she replied.

Mavis told her, 'You should try it on coke, it'll make you moan like a whore when you climax, believe me.' Mavis took two hefty sniffs and then licked her finger, after using it to wipe off the excess from her nose.

Mavis stripped down and stretched out on her stomach, while Rusty oiled up her hands with some kind of sweet-smelling herbal lotion. And then Rusty went to work. 'I love your shoulders, Mavis,' she purred into her upturned ear.

Only then did Mavis realise that Rusty had stripped off as well. She felt her stiff nipples brushing lightly against her back. Rusty dug her thumbs in and massaged her back muscles. 'You've got a lot of tension there, Mavis. All built up from sitting in that office of yours. Don't worry, I'll get rid of that for you.'

From a drawer Rusty pulled out and slipped on her battery-powered strap-on dildo. She tore open a Durex and rolled it over the veined eight-inch erection.

Working Mavis over with her slick fingers, she slipped them between the cheeks of her plump backside before moving on to her clit. Mavis moaned with pleasure as Rusty teased and caressed. And then Rusty climbed on Mavis's back, and thumbed the switch of her strap-on dildo. Mavis yelped like a hurt puppy as Rusty found her anal passage. However, after years of being double penetrated at college student lesbian orgies, this was nothing new for Mavis. In fact, she liked it this way. And she remembered she had even pleaded to girlfriends to climb on and enter her back passage, while on top of another girl.

And then Mavis finally bucked and moaned some more as she began to climax. Rusty hung on, like a rodeo rider, and tried to match her frantic hip rhythms. She could feel a storm brewing inside her own clit.

She knew the familiar signs of Mavis's impending orgasm, and then came the final shrieking and hollering as Mavis's thighs shuddered to a halt. Rusty groaned and twitched for one whole minute before she collapsed exhausted on top of Mavis.

*

After towelling themselves off, they kissed and cuddled. Rusty opened a bottle of wine and poured two glasses. Whereupon Mavis said jokingly, 'You know what, Rusty; I'll never moan about your cat again.'

Rusty replied, 'I should hope not, you fat old dyke.' With that, they collapsed with laughter and hugged each other some more.

TWENTY-THREE

Love Me Do

As the Thomas Cook brochure stated, there was a special late July offer for the Hotel Caterina in the resort of Port de Soller. Mavis Bone and her German secretary Gertrude Stick had been up since 6.30am, flying from Gatwick to Palma on a last-minute holiday deal that they'd seen in their monthly tennis magazine, boasting clay courts and coaching by a high-ranked tennis pro. Now, with tired relief, they put down their cases on the marble floor of the hotel reception.

Giovanna Piras, the attractive hotel receptionist, Spanish and in her late forties, informed them, 'You have rooms next to each other in apartment block two,' and pointed them out on a map of the complex.

Mavis, who'd nearly finished off her duty-free bottle of brandy on the plane and coach, had explained to Gertrude she needed it as a tranquilliser while flying. And so, while slightly tipsy, she thanked Giovanna, in her own inimitable and exuberant way. 'That's fucking champion, mate. Or as we say down under, as sweet as an Anzac biscuit.'

Giovanna looked puzzled and said, 'I'm sorry?'

Gertrude Stick stifled a laugh and said, 'Don't vurry, my dear. She's an Aussie. You'll get used to zee lingo, in time.'

Giovanna gave an understanding smile.

Mavis then turned more serious and asked Giovanna, 'Is it possible to speak to the hotel owner, Mr Vincent Pollack?'

With a sympathetic smile, Giovanna explained, 'I'm sorry. Mr Pollack is unavailable. He's in Rome on business, but he is expected back shortly.'

Later that evening, Mavis and Gertrude went to the hotel dining room for a hearty meal. Finishing off with a few more brandies, they both wearily walked to their rooms in apartment block two.

*

The following midday by eleven-thirty, the haze was beginning to burn off and make way for another cloudless afternoon. The waiters around the pool bar were telling customers it had been hot like this for nearly five weeks.

Giovanna joked with Mavis and Gertrude, while they were booking a tennis court at reception, 'The weather is too hot for us Majorcans, especially after a long summer. But good for business, as customers drink more at the bar, yes?' She laughed, and then they all laughed, as Mavis payed the twenty euros tennis court hire.

Halfway up the dining room stairs, Mavis informed Gertrude, 'Hey, you know what, Gerty, we forgot to ask that Giovanna for a map of the area. It would be handy, and we could browse the excursions on offer over lunch.'

Mavis added, 'Tell you what, Gerty, I'll nip down to reception. I won't be long.' Mavis excused herself, and quickly descended the stairs to reception.

Gertrude reminded Mavis as she left, 'Make sure you're qvuick, as they'll be no buffet left after veeding time. You know what this lot are like, similar to vultures veeding on a carcass.'

Mavis laughed and hurried down the stairs to reception, which was quiet, with no queue.

Behind the desk, Giovanna looked up with a smile. Mavis asked her, 'Hi, I forgot to get a map of the region. If you have any spare?'

Eyeing Giovanna up and down, Mavis felt herself becoming turned on. *Dear God, she looks so lovely*, she thought Her hotel staff trouser suit finished off what was a dead giveaway. Her boyish short back and sides haircut, together with the collar and tie, screamed out *I'm a dyke, and who gives a fuck?*

While she bent down to retrieve the map from a cupboard, Mavis couldn't stop looking at her shapely bum.

That's when Giovanna turned quickly, and caught Mavis ogling. Mavis immediately flushed up, and spluttered, 'Thank you,' while taking the map.

Giovanna smiled and held on to the map, teasing Mavis. She reminded her that one good favour deserves another in return. 'I'm on shift tonight, Mavis. And should I pass your room door, would you maybe invite me in for a coffee?'

Mavis flushed again and laughed nervously, while Giovanna still held onto the map, expecting Mavis to answer.

Mavis hesitated, uneasy, not quite sure if she was joking.

And then Giovanna repeated the come on, but more slowly this time. 'And should I pass your room door, would you invite me in for a coffee?'

Mavis swallowed, and realised the invitation was clear enough. An old cliché came to mind. *The hint was about as subtle as a circus seal taking a fish.*

Mavis agreed to invite her in, 'Yes… yes, Giovanna, that would be fine. I'll look forward to it.'

Climbing the stairs to meet Gertrude in the dining room, Mavis's throat was dry, and she was getting horny just thinking about it. Thoughts flashed in her mind, she was feeling excited, aroused. *Her legs wrapped around Giovanna, while she wore a strap-on, bringing her to an orgasm, her nails digging into Giovanna's beautiful shapely bottom.*

In the dining room, Gertrude waved to attract her attention. Looking slightly worried, she askd Mavis, 'Vot is up vith you? You're looking a bit vlushed and out of breath.'

Mavis assured her, 'It must be all that sun and the stairs.'

*

After lunch, they took the short stroll down to the local beach. And within twenty minutes, snores were drifting up from under Mavis's brolly, while Gertrude sat on her sunbed reading a biography of Joseph Goebbels.

Now it was mid-afternoon. The atmosphere was heavy and thick. Mavis reached for her beach bag and took a swig of mineral water. She squirted suntan lotion onto her legs, and then rolled back onto the sunbed and closed her eyes.

Mavis gently rubbed the sun cream in, and felt the hard line of the old scar below her left knee. Her mind began to wander as she thought of her tortured schooldays. Thoughts of Kirra flooded back. She touched the painted multi-coloured gumnut necklace that had belonged to Kirra. Mavis hadn't thought of Kirra for a long time.

*

Kirra was a sixteen-year-old Aboriginal school friend in Mavis's class, at the Sydney State Belonga School for Girls. She had surprised everybody, including her strict parents, by being expelled for stealing.

Mavis smiled to herself, as she remembered her own growing pains of youth; wanting to belong, wanting to be accepted, wanting to be friends with Carol Remington.

In 1964, at sixteen years old, Mavis had envied Carol Remington. Carol was tall and had been blessed with good looks; well, not just good looks, she was beautiful. On top of this, her parents were wealthy, and paying for her to attend a fashionable Sydney modelling school. And to cap it all, she was head prefect.

Carol was respected by all the teaching staff, and she was definitely the favourite of Miss Soames, the tweed suited, hair in a bun, starchy old headmistress of the Sydney State Belonga School for Girls. The school was built in the 1940s, and had a high academic record. This also compounded Carol's popularity, as she'd taken more 'O' levels than Field Marshal Montgomery had medals, or so Miss Soames had commented in the staff room; *and* she'd achieved top grades. She was down for good 'A' level predictions as well.

Carol, along with the other seven prefects', including Mavis and Kirra, was a huge fan of the Beatles. They had formed their own Belonga Beatle fan club. Carol, of course, was in charge as their leader, and one of the strict rules was to keep out undesirables and any riff raff, so only prefects could be members.

Carol had already seen the Beatles during the school holidays in June. This was at a concert in the Sydney Stadium, which was part of their Australian tour. Carol told the other girls that "They were hotter – hotter than molten steel," and she'd been in a state of near ecstasy.

Now all that hysteria was just a distant memory, Carol and the rest of her Beatles gang had to make do with the prefects' common room.

The school teaching staff did allow them an old second-hand record player, but on strict instructions that it was to be played only during lunchtime breaks, and it must not interfere with the daily duty rota. They were also allowed pin-up posters, with concessions; no Cliff Richard or Elvis, or any other pop star, should be displayed stripped to the waist.

So there they sat one lunchtime in the prefects' room, from twelve-thirty to one-thirty, with a window open, passing round a cigarette, chewing gum, drinking lemonade, pawing over Beatle magazines. This was in-between taking turns to kiss the occasional photo of George Harrison or Paul McCartney, with sudden shrieks of delight from the others.

The group's Friday and Saturday nights were taken up going to the Melody Ballroom. This was a young teens' non-alcohol venue, behind a local Sydney public house. There the disc jockey would play Beatle records, while the parents would drop them off around seven in the evening and then collect them at ten. This was apart from Mavis, whose parents were far too busy running the family farm. And likewise for her friend Kirra, whose Aboriginal parents worked as farm labourers.

As the group became tired of soft drinks and lemonade, the girls, promising a snog in return, would get the older-looking boys to forage for cigarettes and small bottles of rum from the pub's off licence. At that age, they wanted to look cool.

The ones whose parents could afford it bought them collarless Beatle jackets and wedge shoes, the fashion rage at that moment. At the Melody Ballroom, they'd chew gum and dance in a circle around their Mary Quant lookalike handbags, bursting into song with each Beatle record.

Although Mavis was a prefect, she sat on the fringes of the group. The only one wh really spoke to her was Kirra. They'd become friends, sitting near each other in maths and English.

Kirra had the looks of an Aboriginal, the giveaway being her nose and dark skin. But she was the only one who would listen to what Mavis had to say. Although Mavis declared her love for the Beatles, and pretended that like the others she had bought photos, mugs or badges from the official fan club, in fact the money wasn't there for such things. However, it was important to convince Kirra that she was just like the others. In reality, Mavis had to make do with a Beatles scrapbook, filled with comic and newspaper cuttings.

The truth was that the prefect group had never really taken to Mavis. Her clothes said it all. On Friday and Saturday nights, the school uniform stayed on in various dress combinations. She'd mix it up a little, to try and hide the fact her parents couldn't afford to buy her any trendy stuff. But the girls saw through it. Mavis was all too aware of the sniggers and remarks. How Mavis yearned to be cool, to belong, to be like Carol Remington.

Carol's father was the director of bookings at the Sydney Stadium. And it just so happened, the Beatles were performing there on 20 June 1964. Tickets were like gold dust, but her dad had managed to get eight complimentary ones. Carol, when she'd told the others, wallowed in popularity like a hippo in mud. But, she reminded them, after keeping a ticket for herself, there were only seven to spare for the Belonga Beatle fan club group. Of course, all the girls wanted a ticket; they all wanted to see the Beatles more than anything.

Saturday 20 June 1964 was also the release date of the new expected Beatles single, 'A Hard Day's Night'. Record sales were going to be *gi-normous* according to all the radio disc jockeys. Queues would be forming at record shops before they even opened.

Carol had an idea for the ticket allocation. She wanted it to be seen as a fair exchange, to test the loyalty of the group towards the Beatles. She suggested that those who wanted to go to the concert had to purchase the new Beatles single. This meant, in most cases, joining an early-morning queue. They had to bring the record into school on this coming Monday morning, as proof of purchase. The first seven girls who could show her the single would get a ticket.

In head girl mode, she stood in front of them in the prefect common room, and made it clear once again. 'Only the first seven girls with the record, will get a ticket.'

So this coming Monday was going to be an important date for seven Beatle fans, but not for Mavis. Mavis was given a flat 'No' by her mother. 'Maybe for your birthday in July,' she told her.

'But it's too late then, Mum,' Mavis frantically explained. 'I need the record by this Monday morning.'

'I don't care when you want it,' her unbending mother replied. 'Get yourself a part-time Saturday job. Then you can buy it yourself.'

With that the door had closed, with all her avenues of hope cut off.

Monday came, and it was raining. The bus platform was slippery, as Mavis found out. While she was getting off, she skidded and fell onto the kerb outside her school stop, badly cutting her knee. The bus conductor and some passengers helped her back onto her feet. Someone else picked up her satchel and a couple of schoolbooks, including her previously purchased Beatles single 'Love Me Do'. Mavis had brought it with her, to try to make out it was their latest release. She'd made sure the Parlophone paper sleeve stuck out of her satchel, to fool the others, hoping no one would look too closely. It was an effort to let the group know she wasn't a loser.

While Mavis cried with pain, and pressed a handkerchief against the knee wound, she held on to the bus conductor. The driver in his cab was looking around, concerned, trying to see what all the delay was about.

'Will you be okay, young lady?' The conductor offered his concerns. 'That's a nasty cut.'

Mavis gritted her teeth and stiffened, ready to take the weight on her knee. Choking back the tears with some sniffs and wiping her eyes, she concentrated on the matter at hand. This was to ensure the Beatles single was still sticking out of her satchel, so only the top two corners could be seen. It had to look as if she had been successful in buying the latest release.

All at once Mavis's face brightened. She saw Kirra walking briskly towards her, looking concerned.

'Mavis, what's up?'

'I just slipped, getting off.'

'Oh, you poor thing.' Kirra crouched down to take a look.

'Better get her to school, and let someone in first aid have a look at it,' the conductor said, as he eventually mounted the platform and rang the bell, to the other passengers' relief.

With her arm around Mavis's shoulder, Kirra helped her limp the short distance to school.

'Nurse should be in soon. Her car's not there at the moment,' Kirra said, glancing at the staff parking bays. 'Let's get you to the prefects' room, that's nearer. You can rest up then.'

'Thanks, Kirra.' Mavis winced as she adjusted the red-stained handkerchief, the blood still oozing down her shin onto her sock.

When they arrived at the prefects' room, no one else was there.

'First things first,' Kirra joked, as she opened her satchel and took out the Beatles single that she had purchased that morning.

'Did you get yours, Mavis?'

'Err, yes.' Mavis pulled out her own record, hoping Kirra didn't look too close.

'Better let Carol see it, so you're first in line to a get that Beatles ticket.'

Mavis winced her reply, 'I will in a minute,' and then she frowned as the pain came stinging back.

Kirra unpacked as usual, and put her stuff, including the new Beatles single, into one of the numbered lockers. The keys had been lost years ago, and so she just shut the door.

From the windows, the staff car park wasn't visible. 'I'll check out if nurse has arrived,' Kirra said. 'If she hasn't, I'll wait, and let her know about you. Will you be okay?'

Mavis nodded and forced a smile.

Kirra disappeared through the door. Mavis heard her humming the strains of 'A Hard Day's Night' as she made her way to the nurse's office. She'd be away for a while, as it was on the other side of the school, next to the canteen.

The next one in was Carol, looking gorgeous as ever, with the new Beatles single tucked under her arm. She looked at Mavis, mildly concerned, and then listened with a plastic sympathetic smile as Mavis unfolded her accident.

Carol winced and put her hand to her mouth when Mavis showed her the wound. 'That does look nasty. Can you walk on it?'

'I guess so,' Mavis said glumly.

'Look, don't move yet. I'll check to see if nurse is in,' Carol said, turning to the door.

'Kirra's gone for her,' Mavis cautiously replied.

Carol spun round, 'Kirra! What she doing poking her Abo nose in?' Carol had turned nasty. 'It's my job as head girl to sort out first aid.'

Mavis tried to make light of it. 'She helped me to school, she was only thinking of…'

304

Carol ignored her. She unpacked and then slammed her locker door shut. Mavis flinched and then heard her mutter, 'Trust that dirty Abo to try to look good in front of me.'

Carol made for the door. She said with a mocking sneer, avoiding Mavis's gaze, 'I'd better see if the nurse is in. Get myself involved before miss flat nose really throws her boomerang.' With that, she slammed her way out of the room.

And then there was silence. It was still early. The others hadn't arrived yet. Mavis looked at her knee. The blood had congealed at last. She dabbed the wound, and flinched as it smarted.

As more pupils began to arrive, she heard the clacking of shoes on the stone passageways, and then the opening and shutting of doors. All of this was mixed with excited exchanges and squeals of girlish delight, peppered with running footsteps. Someone was singing the Beatles hit, 'She Loves You'.

Mavis felt alone. She looked at the prefects' room door, and then she looked out of the window. Rivulets of rain made their way down the glass in ever-changing patterns. She looked at her concealed attempt to countefeit the new Beatles single. Her feeble effort to convince the group it was the latest Beatles release. Just so she could be like one of them.

She'd let the others show theirs to Carol. She'd hang around last, and pretend she got mixed up by mistake by putting the wrong Beatles single in her satchel.

She'd let the others collect the concert tickets. Mavis didn't mind not going. As long as they thought she'd made a genuine mistake, which was better than the truth; her parents couldn't afford to buy it for her. That way, she could get home with her dignity intact. *How these things mattered so much.*

Finally, Mavis looked at the locker doors, and she continued looking. She looked at them so hard her eyelids could have been nailed there.

*

Mavis had spent most of the morning in first aid, with the school nurse, Sister Watkins. It was suggested she should go to the hospital. However, by lunchtime she was feeling better and she could walk on it without limping.

So, with a generous bandage around her knee, she made her way back to the prefects' room. As Mavis entered, she was confronted by Miss Soames, the stern-looking headmistress. Carol and Kirra were at her side. The other five prefects stood to attention with grim expressions.

'Ah! You're just in time, Mavis.' Miss Soames turned to her. 'I'm afraid you have to be included in this.' The headmistress put her arm around Carol's shoulder, and then she continued, 'We have a thief amongst us. Someone has stolen Carol's Beatles record and Kirra's gumnut necklace from their lockers.' She looked at both girls for confirmation, and then added, 'I understand these items were discreetly hidden, as there are no keys for the locker doors.'

Miss Soames paused, and then continued, 'It's highly unlikely other girls have been in here, as this room is only for prefects, and out of bounds to the rest of the school.' The headmistress looked accusingly at the six remaining faces. 'The thief knew where to look.'

No one moved; it was deathly quiet.

'Right, all of you, empty out your lockers, and then your pockets,' Miss Soames said, with a no-nonsense tone. 'I don't want to call the police, but I will if I have to.'

After a few minutes, everything was out on the large table in their individual piles. Miss Soames walked around the belongings, and sifted through the usual schoolgirl items: gym clothing, books, magazines, hair brushes, combs, hair spray, mirrors, nail varnish, lip stick, tampons, bubble gum, cheap cologne, small change, keys, diaries, and of course the latest Beatles single.

Carol leant forward and whispered something in Miss Soames's ear.

'Are you sure?' the headmistress said.

'Yes,' said Carol. 'I always mark my own. I decided, after losing so many at parties.'

'Sensible girl,' Miss Soames said, with a half smile. And then she turned to the other girls with a serious expression and continued, 'Will all of you who brought in the latest Beatles single, please remove it from the sleeve.'

The girls muttered under their breath at the continuing accusations. '*She can't do this … I'll tell my parents … don't like being accused … my dad'll sort 'er out…*'

The girls began to fumble with their Beatles records.

Miss Soames caught a few whispered threats. 'Now listen, you can moan all you like,' she said, countering the remarks. 'Better this way than in front of the police.'

And then she nodded to Carol, to verify the records in their paper sleeves.

Carol slowly moved along the table, picking them up, one by one. Beneath the centre hole, she scrutinised the pound sign trademark of the Parlophone label. And then she stopped. She held one up with a look of disbelief. Carol looked at the owner.

Kirra shuffled uncomfortably, and then asked, 'What's up?'

'You know what's up, you thieving Abo.' Carol held out the record for her to see.

'That's *my* record, I bought on Saturday,' Kirra snapped.

'You lying Abo,' Carol said with a dark, sweet smile. 'Look, my initials are on it, see, CR.' Her finger pointed to the spot.

'Now, Carol,' Miss Soames interrupted, 'there's no need for those racist remarks.'

Carol wasn't listening. She slid the record out from its paper sleeve, with a smug expression. At that moment something fell onto the floor. All eyes looked down. Carol stooped and picked up the multi-coloured gumnut necklace. She held it in her palm.

'You conniving Abo,' Carol said to Kirra.

'Now that's enough, Carol,' Miss Soames reminded her. 'We can't have…'

Carol held out the gumnut necklace to Kirra and said,

'You reported it was missing, but you hid it in the sleeve. You said it was stolen, so nobody would suspect you.'

'*That's a lie!*' Kirra exploded. '*Somebody put it there.*' She looked in desperation at the headmistress. 'It's a sick joke. I'm not a thief.'

Carol said, with a sneering grin. 'Oh yeah! So where's your record, you thieving Abo?' The other girls looked at Kirra.

Suddenly, Kirra lunged at Carol and grabbed the record, knocking two other girls off balance at the same time. Kirra threw herself onto Carol, kicking, screaming, clawing. '*You fucking bitch, you set me up!*' Carol rolled with her on the floor, fending off punches and blows.

In all the commotion Miss Soames desperately tried to break them up, with the other girls shouting, '*Bundle – go on, Miss Soames, give it to 'em – put the boot in, Miss.*'

'Girls, stop it!' The headmistress rounded on both of them.

Kirra stared at the initials in biro beside the record hole. 'You could've written that on my record and hidden my gumnut necklace. You've never liked me.'

'Because you're a thieving smelly Abo.' Carol spat out the words. 'My dad says all Abos…'

'Carol, *that's enough!*' Miss Soames held them apart.

Kirra screamed, '*I didn't steal your fucking record!*' The tears started to flow. '*Someone's playing jokes! Setting me up.*'

She looked in desperation at the headmistress. With tears streaming down her face, she said, 'Honest, Miss Soames, I haven't stolen anything.'

The headmistress held up her hands to quash any further arguments. 'I don't want the police involved, Kirra, but I'm going to have to phone your parents.'

Meanwhile, in all the commotion, Kirra's gumnut necklace sat neglected on the table.

With no one looking, Mavis slipped it into her satchel, along with Kirra's latest Beatles single, 'A Hard Day's Night', which she had stolen that morning when she'd been left alone in the prefects' room.

Later, during the afternoon break, after Kirra had left with her parents, Mavis sat with the others showing off her Beatles single. The pain in her knee didn't hurt so much now.

On that 20 June evening at the Sydney Stadium, Mavis and Carol did a high five amongst the screams as the Beatles s launched into 'I Saw Her Standing There'.

They were red and sweaty from the shouting and excitement. They stood with hundreds of other girls singing the lyrics, sometimes breaking off and yelling, *'Paul! Paul!'*

After the show, they were all going back to Carol's house for tea. Her parents would be out visiting until later. Carol had smuggled in some booze, and then there was the promise of some boys turning up.

Mavis felt good. Mavis felt wanted. She was now really one of the gang. *How these things mattered so much.*

TWENTY-FOUR

Barbara

That evening, after dinner and drinks, Mavis said goodnight to Gertrude. It was now gone one o'clock in the morning. Mavis had made a special effort. Standing in front of the full-length mirror in her room, she admired herself. Standing at five feet nine inches in flat sensible shoes, Mavis knew she was blooming with the soft fat of post fifty, and no hope. However, she'd brought on holiday her garter belt and suspenders with seamed silk stockings, just in case she got lucky. Although she was AC and DC, Mavis over the years had had mostly women lovers.

She stood looking at her reflection. Her sexy black panties lost themselves up the crack of her bum. Her thumb gently twanged a suspender. She kidded herself that nylons still made her look leggy. And then she leant in closer, and pushed up her large breasts to accentuate them in the matching brassier. Her hand went inside her panties, and she already felt moist and damp with arousal.

Mavis pulled from her bag her sterling silver snuff necklace, and cautiously tapped out the cocaine powder, making two lines. She liked to fuck on coke, Mavis thought it doubled the climax and made her moan like a whore. And then she took two hefty sniffs, licking the finger that wiped the excess powder from her nose.

Mavis looked at herself in the mirror again. She suddenly felt foolish; mutton dressed up as lamb. Would Giovanna laugh at her? Would she even turn up? Giovanna had the looks that meant she could have any woman she wanted. Mavis wondered if in fact it was all a joke on her? *What are you doing here? An overweight spinster dyke with a plain face and big tits; all tarted up like a middle-aged brothel whore.*

Mavis put on her dressing gown and sat on the edge of the bed. She lit a cigarette and inhaled deeply. She'd been here before, over the years. Waiting for a phone call, and then, when it got late, realising she'd misread the vibes.

Her thoughts went back to her first true love, who she met as a part-time temp, working in Sydney when she was twenty-one. Barbara was her name, an eighteen-year-old college student, petite with long blonde hair, working her holiday break in Mavis's office.

They'd linked up one hot summer. It was on a blind date that Cupid's arrow struck. Barbara had suggested going to Bondi Beach in a foursome for the day. The guy she was seeing said he'd bring a friend along for Mavis. It turned out he wasn't Mavis's type. However, Mavis wasn't going to kill the day stone dead. She didn't want to hurt Barbara or her boyfriend's feelings. She'd just have to smile and be pleasant, for Barb's sake, and it was only for a day.

It was hot, sunny and cloudless. They'd bought some beach knick-knacks, including *Kiss Me Quick* hats and a blow-up dolphin. So, with their towels and swimming gear, they headed for the beach. It was heaving as usual. A sunny weekend at Bondi brings on a migration, like thirsty wildebeest galloping to a river's edge.

They'd found a sunbathing spot at the back, but there was nowhere to change, at least not while keeping one's modesty. Barbara suggested the changing huts. They could take it in turns. The boys first, as they were going to be quicker.

Once the lads had changed, the girls giggled as they shut themselves in. The rum and blacks at lunchtime were taking effect. Barbara was the first to undress; she had no inhibitions. She'd been to a posh girl's boarding school, played tennis, netball and hockey. Years of communal showers, while chatting away to other girls stark naked, was nothing new to her.

Mavis slowly followed, pretending it was all quite natural for her as well. She turned her back to remove her shorts and panties. Barbara had already sensed she was shy. That's when Mavis felt the kiss on her shoulder. She swung round, startled, and saw Barbara was wearing only a bra. Mavis tried to shield her nakedness, but Barbara's arms embraced her, stopped her from covering up. Her hands slipped down around to Mavis's buttocks, fingers probing. Then came a soft moan, as Barbara's experienced fingers found the spot and massaged. Mavis melted towards the embrace. They kissed and her tongue twisted and darted inside Mavis's mouth.

She helped Mavis onto a canvas chair and then positioned her legs up behind her head. Barbara gently massaged her mound, kissing and licking. Mavis was so moist, her mind swimming with ecstasy as Barbara's tongue worked inside her, probing. And then the heavy breathing and moaning quickened, while Mavis began to kick and jerk as she climaxed. Barbara held on, tongue still inside pressing deeper; Mavis eventually shuddered and then collapsed.

Barbara cuddled her and kissed her cheek. They kissed tenderly this time, like lovers after the seed was spent.

From that day onwards, Mavis couldn't think of anything else. She was infatuated, hook, line and sinker. Barbara was so young, yet so experienced. Mavis had never felt this way with other girlfriends. She was so happy, so in love, in fact they spent the whole summer together; a happiness Mavis Bone had thought was only possible in novels. She couldn't get enough of Barbara. She bought Barbara presents and clothes. Treated her to lunches and dinners. Mavis was so in love that it hurt. She couldn't think of life without Barbara.

And then one day Mavis's boss asked her to step inside his office. He always used her first name, but this time he addressed her over the phone as Miss Bone. Mavis felt uneasy as she knocked on his door.

As she entered, his face was looking stern. Sitting to one side of his desk were a middle-aged couple with matching expressions. They were Barbara's parents.

Mavis listened in horrified silence at the accusations. In-between pauses, the parents glared at her. And then the mother, with a face growing redder by the minute, took off like Typhoon Annie. With pursed lips, and a thin line of angry froth forming, the most scalding abuse erupted from a furnace inside her mouth, as she launched into a savage and malicious attack.

Pointing her finger at Mavis, she shouted, '*My daughter was led on by a filthy lesbian like you! You're a shame to your sex. Women like you should be put away. You're a danger to young girls. Your type are disgusting! Why don't you keep to your own filth?*' Her husband nodded with approval while she continued, '*You come anywhere near my daughter, and I'll report you to the police for sexual assault!*'

The mother stopped, wiping her mouth with a tissue. But she hadn't finished. With that, she was out of her chair and lashed out at Mavis, striking her face. Mavis leant back, fending off blows. The husband and her boss got to their feet and tried to restrain the woman, shouting at her to stop. Eventually they forced the mother to sit down.

Her boss composed himself, not able to meet Mavis's eyes. He told her he was sorry, but, under the circumstances, they would have to let her go. He explained she had to understand the company's position, as a family-run firm of solicitors in the community. They couldn't afford any scandal, so it would be better if Mavis handed in her

315

resignation. Her boss glanced at the parents, confirming their joint decision that had already been taken before Mavis had arrived. Her boss assured her she wouldn't be financially out of pocket, provided she agreed and promised Barbara's parents never to see her again.

Mavis stood up and protested in tears, telling them it was a consensual relationship, and they loved each other.

The mother, half out of her chair again, shouted her down, yelling, '*Shut up, you disgusting bitch!*'

Mavis never saw Barbara again. The parents had money and sent her away to a high-class finishing school in Perth. For her own good, they told their daughter.

*

It was the laughing and talking drifting in from outside that interrupted her thoughts. She recognised the voice. Mavis slid open the patio door and walked out onto the balcony. The cold marble floor made her catch her breath.

In the garden lights below, she could see it was Giovanna. She had her arm around the shoulders of a stunning Swedish woman, with long blonde hair; she couldn't have been more than thirty. They were kissing and whispering and giggling together.

It was two am. Mavis went back inside and took off her dressing gown. And then, with her lipstick, she started to deface the mirror. She slashed at it, red stripes of hate across her reflection; building up to a frenzy until her image couldn't be seen. The lipstick broke with the pressure and rolled onto the floor. And then the tears came, as she continued to smear the glass using her hands. Mavis heard Giovanna laugh again. Perhaps she was laughing at her? The red fingers, the smudged make-up, the little whore outfit she was wearing.

Mavis stared at herself in the other wardrobe mirror, and then she slowly smeared her lipstick to a down-turned smile. Suddenly, she started to laugh through the tears at her new reflection; *a sad clown, all dressed up and nowhere to go*. As she lay on her bed, and sleep took over, the contents of her handbag littered the quilt. Her credit card wallet lay open, while a feathered black and white photo of Barbara looked up at the ceiling.

*

The following day, tennis wasn't until four thirty in the afternoon, which was just as well. Their midday lunch had consisted of minestrone soup with French bread, roast suckling pig and sauté potatoes, followed by pistachio ice cream, and then cheese and biscuits. Mavis and Gertrude groaned as they descended the dining room staircase.

By five o'clock in the warm cloudless afternoon, they were three-all in the first set, and taking time out, sitting on the courtside bench drinking mineral water.

Gertrude informed Mavis, blinking as perspiration stung her eyes, that they'd lost a ball. Mavis pointed to a cluster of bushes and trees, indicating where it had landed.

Beyond the clay courts, the scenery gave way to a

clearing of unkempt grassland and then dipped sharply towards the woods. This marked the end of the manicured complex.

Mavis opened the tennis court gate to search for the ball, and told Gertrude she wouldn't be long. And then she frantically searched her cardigan and patted her pockets, realising she didn't have her mobile phone. And that's when Mavis remembered, she hadn't packed it for the holiday. Mavis cursed, realising she'd left it behind on the bed at her Wimbledon flat.

Walking into the clearing, Mavis picked her way through a thick clutch of pine and wild olive trees. A flutter of birds scurried away at the crackle of her tennis shoes as she trod carefully, crushing leaves and twigs.

Mavis felt she was entering a secret world, one that contained whispering trees, with lingering smells of fresh earth, all mixed with the July warm air.

She scanned the floor for the tennis ball. The ground was pin pricked with dancing shards of broken sunlight. Tall branches softly creaked in the afternoon breeze.

Mavis looked up into the trees. The redundant twilight of a Majorcan summer was beginning to tremble on the edge of autumn. She stood still, as the quietness and eeriness of an enchanted world began to leech into her mind, only interrupted with the soft clacking noises of branches losing their leaves.

Late mosquitoes began cruising around her neck, and she became conscious of her heart thumping uneasily in her chest. Mavis detected the faint smell of her duty-free

Chanel, mixed with perspiration. She kicked some patches of foliage in a careless motion, half deciding to go back to Gertrude and continue the game without the ball.

And then a deep, blood-curdling growl came from behind. It had a chilling primitive sound. Mavis instinctively knew it was already too late to run. The back of her neck burned with fear.

Whatever was behind her, a wolf or a bear? She could feel its warm panting breath on the back of her legs.

Mavis froze. Sweat was pouring down her face, stinging her eyes. It growled at her again, as if wanting to be noticed, wanting her to acknowledge its presence. She slowly began to turn, her face twitching, her heart in overdrive, thumping the walls of her chest. A scream for Gertrude lingered in her throat. How she wished she had her mobile phone.

And then Mavis saw it. Her eyes locked in silent terror with those of a huge wild dog. It was a male Presa Canario, weighing around one hundred and fifty pounds. The piercing, urine-coloured eyes stared at Mavis from the broad square head with its cropped ears. Saliva dripped from its savage jaws. The sagging lips were drawn back to reveal powerful yellow teeth. There was blood around its mouth and on its dark fawn coat, as if it had been gorging on a kill.

And then its right leg began to paw the ground, as if undecided whether or not to attack. Mavis's whole body shook. She became transfixed, hypnotised by fear in a trance that gripped like a vice, unable to move, not wanting to move.

At that moment there came some awful high-pitched screams, from somewhere deep in the woods. They were screams for help, begging for mercy. The sound jolted her concentration, and Mavis reasoned that the dog standing in front of her was one of a pack, which meant there were more of them.

It sounded like the pack had found a victim. She heard the frenzied sounds of a feeding orgy, growls and snarls and the ripping and tearing of flesh. All mixed with the desperate gurgling calls of despair, until the cries gradually became fainter.

Mavis knew what was coming. She closed her eyes and clenched her fists so tightly, that the nails dug in and made her palms bleed. 'Not me,' she sobbed, 'please, not me.' Mavis went into an uncontrollable shivering fit. 'Not me, pleeeese!' Her face contorted into a mask of petrified agony. 'Pleeeeeeese!'

Suddenly a hand touched her shoulder. Mavis screamed and pulled away, sprawling headlong onto the forest floor, kicking, writhing and shrieking amongst the leaves. Gertrude was trying to grab hold of her. 'Mavis! Mavis, it's me.'

She lashed out blindly, screaming, 'Keep away...don't kill me!'

'Mavis, vot happened?' Gertrude was wrestling with her, trying to grab her arms. 'Calm down, Mavis, it's only me... calm down.' She had managed to grab an arm, while Mavis screamed and continued shaking her head.

'Keep away from me, keep away from...' A hard slap

across the face stopped her and she focused on Gertrude. The mark of a handprint was beginning to flush up on Mavis's left cheek.

'Sorry, Mavis, you ver in shock. What happened?'

'The dogs, Gerty… the dogs, they were going to kill me.' Mavis burst into tears.

Gertrude put an arm around her shoulder. 'Vot dogs, Mavis?'

'Didn't you hear them?' Mavis said angrily through gulps and sobs.

'Hear vot? I've been looking for *you*.'

She had calmed down but was still shivering. Gertrude helped her to her feet, brushing off the leaves and twigs that were stuck to her tennis outfit. And then she took off her Fred Perry cardigan, and put it around Mavis's shoulders.

'We've gotta get away, Gerty, quick, there's … there's these wild dogs … they've killed somebody.' Mavis took a step and then whimpered with pain. 'My ankle, Gerty, I think I've twisted it.'

'Let's get you out of here. Hold on to me.' Gertrude supported her as they made their way back through a swathe of bushes and tangled undergrowth. Mavis's head constantly turned, looking wide-eyed, jerking Gertrude at the slightest forest sound, until eventually they came to the clearing.

Safely back within the confines of the fenced tennis court, they sat together on the courtside bench. Mavis was still shaking while Gertrude held her hand.

'We'll have to tell that Giovanna Piras at reception, Gerty. It's not safe in those woods. They need someone with a gun.'

'Calm down, Mavis, tell me what you saw.'

Mavis gulped her mineral water and then started coughing. Gertrude patted her back. 'Easy… easy… now, tell me what happened?'

'Dogs… great big dogs… ripping people apart, Gerty… someone's dead out there… it was horrible.'

Mavis took another gulp. 'Do you know what, Gerty, I've always been terrified of dogs, ever since I was eighteen years old, when I went on a road trip through the outback, and met up with some wild dingoes. It was the first weekend of the summer holidays, and we were excited.

'I was with three girlfriends, and it was our first road trip into the outback! No parents for a week! I was with my best friend Ruby, she was the oldest, and had borrowed her dad's car. I'd always been quite the worry wart, and wasn't sure this road trip was a good idea. Three girls going camping into the outback? We were heading for Goobang National Park, which was about two hundred miles west of Sydney. But it was summer, college was over, so I didn't care. I should have.

'Three friends left together on that Sunday, and three friends returned to Sydney a week later. But not the same three people.

'In the early morning, we put our tent and camping gear into the car, and our road trip started off. I remember I was very tired, but when we were sitting in the car, the others began to sing and laugh, and that made me happy. I enjoyed the pleasant air stream on my skin.

'It was on our second day, and we'd travelled about a hundred and fifty miles. However, I couldn't even have imagined what would happen next.

'I was so happy. A road trip with my cute girlfriend Ruby, and my two other best friends. I couldn't believe it! It was so wonderful! A much-needed break as well, from working on my parents' farm. The mood was perfect. Everyone was as happy as ever.

'We'd been driving for five hours, and then we finally arrived in the outback territory, which stretched out right in front of us. All we saw, was the endlessness of the red dusty parched rocky ground, and nothing else, which was so breathtaking for us.

'And then suddenly, as we were about to unpack and tent up; out from nowhere, a pack of dingoes appeared, less than two hundred metres away. We forgot everything around us, and just stared at this wonderful spectacle, having never seen dingoes close up before.

'Normally, nothing can unrest me, and I always thought I had everything under control. But this was something different! Right in front of us were a group of dingoes, howling their heads off! I looked to the right, and they were heading straight for us. Some were baring their teeth, and circling the car, as if they planned to attack. We all raced for the car and scrambled inside. There was absolute silence from us all.

'And then we started the car up, for the air conditioning,

which ensured it wouldn't get too hot inside. Suddenly the engine began to misfire, and then there was a loud *bang!* which stopped the engine completely. We were all shocked! Which meant, no more fresh air from the air conditioning! In the faces of my friends, I saw they were terrified; two of the girls were crying in fear. And then disaster, as we realised the only water we had in the car was one bottle that Ruby had brought with her. The rest was locked in the car boot, guarded by the dingoes.

'How could this have happened? What would happen to us? Trapped in the outback without any civilisation and nobody to help. These terrible thoughts haunted us, and we felt so helpless. The sun burned down on the car roof, making it hotter inside. We managed to wind the windows a quarter open. But the dogs sensed we had a problem, and would leap in numbers at the windows, and they were still surrounding the car.

'I had such misgivings, that it was a big mistake to go on this road trip into the Australian outback. We were stuck here in the heat, in the endlessness of this desolate parched land, with a broken-down car which we couldn't repair. We didn't see a way out.

'We were sitting around for hours, and nobody said a word. I looked into the painful faces of the others, and nobody did anything. The evening passed by, while we shared Ruby's bottle of water. And then the night came, and there was silence, apart from that awful howling of the dingoes. We tried to sleep but nobody was able to. All we could do was look out of the car windows into the starry sky, and try to forget our terrible predicament. Every single minute seemed like an hour. My only thought was, when will this nightmare be over?

'Finally I must have fallen asleep, because as I opened my eyes, I had to blink, because the sun was shining through the car windows so brightly. I looked at my friends, who were sitting huddled, leaning near the gaps of the car windows. Our spirits were low, and I wanted to lie in my comfortable bed, and have all the luxury of my home.

'And then, it was about mid-afternoon, the dingoes moved off somewhere, and just disappeared. Dear God, were we relieved.

'Suddenly, I couldn't be sure if it was a hallucination, because of the climate and the dryness? But it was real, I was sure I saw somebody out there. I informed the others. And then, with the car windows open, we screamed for help. I was surprised how loud I could scream, but this was an emergency. And then the figure in the distance came nearer, and nearer, and then I saw it was an Aboriginal young man. He had some tribal markings on his chest and forehead.

'In silence I inspected the man, he looked so fascinating with his tribal markings. Living in the outback, I'd only seen them dressed as labourers and servants.

'The Abo had a weapon in his hand, a spear, but he acted in a very harmless way. When I heard his voice, it was gentle and calm, and so we all relaxed. A feeling of joy and relief came over us. We had found help! At last. It was the best thing that could have happened.

'He beckoned us to follow him, we assumed to his tribal settlement. And so we followed the Abo through the desolate landscape. We all felt so tired and strained. It seemed as if the way would never end, but suddenly, after we had walked for nearly two hours, we saw little thatched houses between some trees. I had the impression that our steps got faster and faster. We were eager to arrive in the cool shadows which the trees threw on the ground. We had never felt so happy about trees! And then we were there. We'd made it! We were safe!

'In one of the thatched houses, the Abo showed us all where to sleep. We slipped into beds made of leaves and other natural materials. I was surprised how the Abos could live out there, without electricity and all the other things of civilisation. A life without basic luxury. Inconceivable for me! But not for long! These little houses were so strange, and the beds so uncomfortable, but I was so tired, I couldn't think any more. And I fell asleep very fast.

'In the morning, the Abos made us work, collect wood for fire and stuff. The next few days, the nice Abo who'd saved us, prepared food from nature, and showed the three of us what we could eat, and how to survive in the outback. Every day we learned more and more, and the next two days passed very quickly.

'At first, we realised the experience of everyday life wasn't that bad any more. We learned to live with less and without all the luxury. It was a great feeling.

'But one morning we asked ourselves how we could get home, because we knew we couldn't live in the outback forever. Our parents would be worrying. However, this problem was solved when the village elders came to us and said we couldn't stay there any longer, because we didn't belong to them. This was clear, and so we thanked them for all they'd done.

'After they'd explained how to get back to civilisation, we said our thank-yous and goodbyes. We had a long way to walk, but after half a day we arrived at the outskirts of the nearest town. And then finding our way home wasn't a real problem any more.

'Back home, none of us could decide if the trip had been a great or a terrible experience, but one thing was clear: we did begin to value our homegrown luxuries.

'And from then onwards, Gerty, I've always been terrified of dogs,' Mavis added with a laugh, 'And especially fucking dingoes.'

TWENTY-FIVE

Sweet Dreams

Mavis insisted she had to report her near attack, and tell hotel reception they needed security or police out there with a gun, in case the dogs killed somebody. Gertrude calmed Mavis down, and walked with her to report the incident to Giovanna, who was filling in as hotel manager while Vincent Pollack was away in Rome.

In Giovanna's outer office, Mavis explained to her what happened. She was given a small brandy from the reception drinks cabinet to calm her nerves, while Gertrude sat with her for support.

Giovanna Piras sat on the edge of her desk and continually motioned with both hands for Mavis to slow down. When Mavis had finished, Giovanna offered her sincere apologies, and then added that she didn't understand how there could be wild dogs out there. She explained that the current hotel owner Mr Vincent Pollack, used to keep

Presa Canario guard dogs, the type she described. That was until they attacked and killed the hotel caretaker. After that, all the guard dogs were put down.

Giovanna hesitated and then explained to Mavis and Gertrude with a wry smile, 'The Hotel Caterina is renowned to be haunted. The hotel was built on the grounds of a thirteenth-century leper colony, which later became a monastery. The story goes that, to make way for this change, the monks of Santa Caterina had the lepers burned alive, as they were deemed unholy.' Giovanna continued, 'Stories embedded in middle-ages Majorcan folklore are rife in this area, with reports of ungodly sightings and noises. Since then, tourists over the years have reported similar stories, and made this area of Port de Soller a haven for ghost hunters and people with paranormal beliefs.'

Seeing their expressions, Giovanna hastily added, 'Although we have no complaints, as the extra trade this makes us in tourism is very handy, especially in the out-of-season months.'

Mavis listened to Giovanna in-between sips of brandy, and let her eyes droop when she wasn't being watched. The brandy, combined with her near-death experience, was making her feel drowsy.

To show Mavis and Gertrude how responsibly the hotel treated such incidents, and to alleviate any further anxiety, Giovanna told them she would erect warning signs and put up boundary tape immediately. And with her grounds staff, she would initiate a full search of the area. Also, she hoped the incident hadn't caused too much upset to their holiday. And as a gesture of goodwill, all their further tennis court bookings would be free of charge.

Mavis and Gertrude beamed at Giovanna's generous offer.

*

That evening, Mavis and Gertrude changed and showered in their hotel rooms to get ready for dinner. They decided to give each other a knock on the door and meet up at seven-thirty in the downstairs bar.

In her bathroom, she noticed a strong smell of something putrid or that had gone off. Mavis screwed up her face. She sniffed the drain hole of the wash hand basin, and did the same, stooping down, with the shower.

The bathroom door slowly shut without her noticing, and the final click of its engagement made her turn round with a start. But she dismissed it, as most hotel doors closed on their own to comply with fire regulations.

Mavis reached for her cheap cologne and squirted some down the drain holes. She showered and dried herself, and then slipped on her fancy hotel bathrobe.

Despite the cologne the putrid smell had become stronger. Mavis sniffed around the bath panel, and her head jerked back as the stench became more concentrated. She opened the bathroom door to get rid of the steam, and to get some fresh air. It was then Gertrude knocked, and Mavis invited her in with an offer of some duty-free brandy. Gertrude didn't need to be asked twice, and sat watching the wide-screen television.

Mavis shouted over it, 'There's a really bad smell in here, like something's found a place and died.'

'Vots died?' Gertrude called back. 'I can't hear you.'

'I said it smells like something's…' Mavis felt the warm sensation of breath on her neck. All at once her body stiffened and tingled as though electrocuted. Something was shuffling behind her. But there was no reflection in the mirror. Mavis couldn't move; sheer terror had made her legs feel they were set in cement. The breathing had a blood-curdling whistle, like flaps in a release valve. She could hear sucking and blowing from somewhere, like the noise in a throat. Mavis slowly arched her head round, shaking, twitching and swallowing hard. The back of her neck was burning with fear. And then she saw something standing there, like a medieval figure dressed in rags, wearing a sack over its head. The eye and mouth slits of the sack were stained with green pus. The hands were disfigured, the fingers swollen and black with lumps and boils. Mavis screamed, '*Let me out! Fuck's sake! Let me out!*' She wrenched the door handle, but it had locked. '*Get away from me! Gerty, for fuck's sake help me!*'

Gertrude ran to the door. 'Vots up, vots the matter?' She grabbed at the door handle with both hands. 'Open zee door, Mavis!' She pulled at the door handle again.

Mavis pounded the door with her fists. '*Help me! Get it away from me – open the fucking door!*'

Gertrude began to panic and shouted, '*I can't. It's locked!*'

Suddenly the door burst open, knocking Gertrude to the floor. Mavis ran out, yelling, *'Get it away from me!'* She tripped over Gertrude and fell sprawling on top of her. *'Don't let it get me! Please.'* Gertrude was underneath Mavis, fighting with her, trying to grab her flailing arms. They wrestled on the floor. Mavis broke away and got to her feet, and then ran out of the room screaming. Running down the corridor shrieking in terror, she collided with a young German couple coming the other way. Now the three of them were on the floor, with Mavis lashing out and kicking as she continued to yell hysterically.

*

It took a full twenty minutes to calm Mavis down. She came to her senses on a stretcher. The paramedics had given her an injection. Mavis Bone looked lost as she gazed up at the gathered crowd through heavily sedated eyes. She was softly mumbling something incoherent. Passers-by peered through with their questions. 'What's happened? Who is it?'

Gertrude was kneeling, holding Mavis's hand. She spoke to a man in green overalls holding a medical bag. 'Can I go vith her to the 'ospital?' He nodded approval.

Once the back doors had closed, the ambulance made its way out of the complex, its rotating orange light sending out signals for attention. Cars stopped in respect as it swung out of the main entrance, and then down the outside line of motorists, who had pulled over in response to its harsh wail.

The 'vacated today' label was still hanging on the door of room twenty-two. The sign spoke the truth to some degree, but inside was something different. The bathroom door slowly closed, and with its final click came the whispers, like someone calling from inside a tunnel, 'Over here... we're over here...'

The smell had gone. All that remained was the odour of disinfectant. And then, silence.

*

The following morning, after being checked over for shock, Mavis Bone was released by Port de Soller General Hospital, and arrived in a taxi with Gertrude back at the Hotel Caterina.

Later that evening during supper, Mavis ate and drank for them both, including a whole bottle of Rioja. She told Gertrude her experiences the previous day had made her ravenous. As Mavis overindulged, she repeated what she saw in the woods, again and again, to Gertrude.

By ten forty-five that evening, they were sitting in the quiet hotel bar. Mavis had calmed down and was slumped on a couch by a corner table, brooding in a semi-drunk stupor over her third Bacardi and Coke. Gertrude had given Mavis a couple of her non-prescription tranquillisers, the ones she took whenever she flew on holiday.

As Mavis carried on again about the massive dog and the horrible screams, her eyelids began to flicker and close. Her head would begin to droop, and then all of a sudden she'd wake herself up with a start and slur out, 'They gosh a do shomething, Girshy, they jush can't forgesh about ish. They'll hash to hire an exorshist to get rid of the dogsh and shlepers.'

'They vill, Mavis, don't vorry.' Gertrude tried to look interested. She glanced at her watch. 'You've made out a 'otel complaint veport. They said they'd investigate it vurther, perhaps inform zee police. Just leave it to them.' But Mavis wasn't listening; she was gone. Her head was slumped to one side, and she was snoring.

Gertrude wondered how she was going to get Mavis up to her room in this drunken state.

And then, with a bit of luck, a distinguished-looking but somewhat drunk German hotel guest sitting nearby offered assistance. He politely bowed and introduced himself as Herr Vincent Petzoldt.

It took ten minutes to get Mavis to her room. They had to stop twice on the way, once to get a better hold when her legs buckled, and then when he strained his shoulder.

Supporting her under each arm, and with Gertrude leading, they hauled Mavis, with her feet dragging, back out into the humid summer night.

'Where now?' the tipsy German hotel guest asked, panting heavily and no doubt thinking this perhaps wasn't such a good idea after all.

'We're in that block over there,' Gertrude said, pointing, 'between the gardens and the swimming pool.'

They started off again and had gone about thirty yards when distant lightning flashes made them look up in unison. The humidity of a summer storm was brooding. Crickets in the floodlit garden chirruped mindlessly. Smells of honeysuckle were strong, as well as the damp odour of pine and grass.

The first small gusts of wind, as if on cue, skidded ripples across the top of the swimming pool.

'She's lost a shoe,' the German tourist said.

'Vot?' Gertrude turned to the voice. 'I'm sorry, meester.'

'Call me Vincent, please. Your friend's lost her shoe,' he said, pointing.

Gertrude glanced where he indicated, and noticed the *Vincent* tattoo on his wrist.

'We'll vind it on the vay back,' Gertrude said, scanning the ground. 'Mavis 'as got vore shoes than Dolcis, on this 'oliday.'

'Let's get her to her room before the rain starts,' the German tourist suggested, looking up at the sky, clearly becoming bored with all the hanging around.

The first few spots could be heard ticking on the plant leaves, while ever-increasing circles rippled out from the drops that hit the pool's surface. The lightning flashes were getting brighter and nearer. They lingered like a faulty neon sign, amongst the faint rumble of thunder.

With Mavis propped up outside her door, Gertrude thanked the tourist with 'Danke, danke schön' as he shuffled off muttering in German, and massaging his upper arm.

After fumbling in Mavis's handbag for her door card, and using some tricky manoeuvring, Gertrude eventually hauled Mavis onto the bed and took off her remaining shoe. She rolled Mavis onto her side and positioned the waste paper bin nearby, just in case she needed to throw up.

Switching the lights off, she whispered, 'Sweet dreams, Mavis,' and closed the door softly behind her.

*

By 12.30am the storm had taken off, big time. With the curtains still open, lightning lit up the bedroom with intense, strobe-like flashes. Mavis flinched with each burst, as if she could see them in her sleep. Rain sheeted against the windows, as the wind gusted around the balcony doors, making them chatter and vibrate simultaneously. The scene was reminiscent of an old horror movie.

Mavis was in the middle of a bad dream, laid out on a marble slab: *Somewhere a generator sparked into life, drawing current, dimming lights, all with the dull buzz of laboratory equipment. And then, suddenly, a current arced across two electrodes; its sharp crackle twitching the thing into life.*

The monster opened its eyes for the first time, trying to move its arms, only to find them strapped down. The implanted brain was then awakened by deafening thunder, the booming trailing off into an awesome rattling echo. Now the monster was trying to free itself, the face lit up with white flickers of lightning, showing crude surgical stitching around the forehead and neck. It began to wriggle and moan with anger. Suddenly the straps gave way, and it was free.

Stiff, disjointed, moving heavy footed, one lead boot in front of the other, it came towards Mavis. The arms outstretched –

hungry for its first touch, eager to caress, to kiss, to squeeze, to choke.

On the slab, it then saw Mavis, its creator, its tormentor. It grunted with anger and flexed its fingers. They moved like worms sprouting from stitched-on hands, hooked into claws, coming closer and closer.

Mavis began to moan. She was shaking her head. 'Keep away. Don't hurt me.' Her arms began to flail, trying to swipe away the evil thing in front of her.

At that moment, the latch on her balcony sliding door was unhitched by the vibration of the storm. The door slid open with the wind and smashed against the stop. The curtains billowed as the rain hosed in. It was like a bad day out at sea.

With a jolt, Mavis woke from her nightmare, lashing out blindly, shouting, '*Don't kill me! Don't kill me!*' She froze for a moment, trying to take in where she was. The noise, the flashing, the thunder. What had happened?

She tried to swing her legs off the bed, but the effort made her feel dizzy and nauseous. With a push up, she was on her feet, swaying, holding onto the bedside table, trying to focus. The floor was wet, and Mavis could feel rain spray on her face as it sheeted in surges with every gust.

Mavis took a step. '*Shit!*' She skidded and grabbed blindly at the billowing curtains, hanging on, trying to steady herself. She inched forward, feeling her way along the balcony doors, until she got to the opening. And then she felt the full force of its fury. It was like a gateway to hell. Rain lashed against her face. Her hair was stuck to the sides of her cheeks. The brown trouser suit she was still wearing stuck to her and made her look like a wet Cuban cigar.

She pulled at the door, but it was stuck. She pulled again, muttering some profanities, but it still didn't budge. Mavis's patience started to deteriorate. '*Don't fuck with me, you mother.*' Gritting her teeth and counting, 'one – two – three,' she wrenched at the door, letting out an awful screech of exertion. As it came free, Mavis skidded along the floor with the momentum, grabbing hold of the curtains to steady herself as it finally slammed shut.

It was as if she'd sealed the tomb of a Pharaoh with herself inside. The silence was numbing, peppered only by muffled gusts and the rattling of windows.

Behind the drawn curtains, the room still flickered into life with sudden white flashes.

Mavis needed the bathroom badly. She edged her way around the bed and fumbled for the handle. The door opened, and she clutched at nothing as she tried to find the pull-down light switch. Groping, her hand snatched at the cord. The light came on, blinding her like a supernova, making her screw up her eyes.

Mavis steadied herself and looked into the mirror. A blurry reflection looked back. She opened the bathroom cabinet and rummaged along the shelves for stomach settlers, spilling some of the contents into the basin. It was too late for that. Mavis turned and lurched for the toilet. She leaned over, gripping the seat with both hands, feeling she was going to be sick. She heaved, but only a small amount of bile came out. She heaved again and got on her knees, wincing with the effort. This was going to be a long night.

It was then she twitched her shoulders in surprise as the door clicked shut behind her. Mavis lifted her head. And then came the strong smell again, as if something was decaying, a really putrid stench. It acted like smelling salts, clearing her brain, sharpening the senses. She tilted her head and sniffed again.

A deep, primitive growl came from behind her. Mavis stiffened. Her heart began to thud loudly in her chest. On her knees still, she slowly turned. A swooning mad terror struck her. Her flesh began to creep in waves, moving up and down her back, along her arms.

With its teeth bared, the eyes locked on to Mavis's. It was a massive dog. The same type she'd seen in the woods – a Presa Canario. The piercing eyes in the broad head with the cropped ears held Mavis's gaze. Blood from its thick sagging lips dripped onto the bathroom floor. There was more blood on its head and shoulders, as if it had been feeding on a kill.

Mavis rolled her eyes in revulsion. Its breath smelt like a corpse decomposing in rotten food. With her face twitching and her body shaking, she waited for it to attack. It pawed the floor and gave a long low growl. And then it turned, as if distracted by something. The head cocked to one side. Mavis heard it too – crying… a girl's cry. The sound was distant. It echoed from somewhere hidden. Buried?

The dog's front legs started scratching the bath panel, its nails leaving criss-cross marks. And then it stopped. It looked at Mavis and barked. But it wasn't intimidating any more; it was too preoccupied for that. The dog returned to the bath panel and scratched it again, and then it looked at her and whined. Mavis flinched and cried out as it grabbed her sleeve in its mouth and pulled her along. The dog scratched once more, and then looked imploringly at Mavis again.

She began to understand. The bath panel… it was after something behind the panel.

Still on her knees, she wasted no time. *Humour it*, she thought, *maintain its attention away from you. If it wants to look behind the bath panel then…* Mavis started pulling at the bottom edge of the plastic panel. She tugged again, and it started to come away, and then with a judder and some scraping it eventually flopped out.

The dog panted with excitement and actually licked her hand as she pulled the bath panel clear. Mavis thought, *Please, oh God, don't lick my face.* And then the dog shot into the space under the bath.

Gritting her teeth from the soreness of her knees, and with her face nearly on the floor, Mavis crouched and peered into the empty void where the dog had gone. It was dark, but in the bathroom light she was surprised at the depth of the cavity inside. Behind the bath was a crawl space, which allowed room for plumbing maintenance and repairs.

Mavis heard dragging, and suddenly, out of the

340

blackness, the rear end of the dog appeared. It was pulling something with its jaws. She covered her nose. The stench was overpowering. The dog stopped and panted, waiting to get its breath. After a pause, it continued dragging the large canvas builder's bag, the type used to carry sand. Eventually, with great effort, it hauled the bag out in front of her. The dog looked at Mavis, its tongue hanging out and panting hard. And then it pawed the bathroom door wanting to be let out.

Mavis winced as she pulled herself up; her legs ached from cramping. She let the dog out of the bathroom, and it padded ahead of her to the room door. She opened it, wasting no time, wanting it to go away, just in case it might turn on her again.

As Mavis let it out, it stopped and looked up, holding Mavis's gaze, as if communicating. She used the door as a shield, still unsure, apprehensive. And then it dropped its head and padded off down the corridor.

Mavis shut the door and leaned back on it, closing her eyes with a sigh of relief.

*

A clap of thunder jolted her back to reality. Flashes of white lightning danced through the curtains. The balcony doors clattered as the wind gusted again.

She made her way back to the bathroom. This time Mavis wedged the door open with a chair. 'You're not closing on me again,' she said to no one.

341

The bad stench had gone. Now there was only the smell of disinfectant left by the maids.

Mavis stooped over the canvas bag. She gripped the wire tie and started to unravel the knot. It cut into her hands. After a minute, her fingers ached. She rubbed and flexed them, and then started again, easing, tugging, cursing softly as she slowly forced the wire curls to unwind. And then they eventually began to come away, until the kinked piece of wire dropped to the floor.

Mavis tentatively began to pull open the twisted neck of the bag, not really wanting to see inside. She knew deep down it was probably going to be something awful. However, as always curiosity had its way, and drew her in like a magnet.

The canvas was stiff and unyielding, but finally Mavis had the opening big enough to peer inside. She flinched back from the smell, with a hand to her mouth.

What Mavis found was the partially decomposed corpse of a child. The body was clothed in pink pyjamas. There were bloodstains on the pyjama jacket collar, and the hair was matted with dried mud and leaves.

Mavis Bone stepped back, biting her knuckles. And then nausea overcame her again; she reached for the toilet and vomited. She vomited again and took a deep breath. Wiping her eyes, she leant across to the sink and poured herself a glass of water. Mavis rinsed out her mouth, and then gulped down half a glass.

She stood, hesitated, talking to herself, undecided what to do. 'Reception… that's it… get down to reception… tell them.' Mavis moved quickly into the bedroom and then ducked as a tremendous thunderclap shook the whole room. *'Fuck me!'* she yelled. Glasses clinked in a cabinet, and a painting fell off the wall, the glass smashing. The storm was getting worse. She heard sunbeds by the pool moving around, sliding along the patio and flipping over with a *thwack* as the wind surged.

Mavis carefully picked her way around the glass and picked up the painting. She rested it on her bedside table by the phone. And then it dawned on her. *Of course, the phone, you stupid cow.* Mavis pressed zero and waited.

Giovanna Piras replied almost immediately. 'Reception.'

'Hello, it's room twenty-two. Listen… I've just found…' Mavis started to gabble. 'I've found a skeleton – a – a – body – in my bathroom – hurry – you've gotta come up – quick.'

'I'm sorry, can you repeat that?'

'Listen – you've gotta come quick – get the police. A dog found it.'

'A dog in your bathroom you say. Guests aren't allowed pets in the hotel.'

'No – no – listen. There's a body, in a bag.'

'One moment please.'

Mavis heard muffled speaking, as Giovanna, covering at reception, informed Vincent Pollack, gesturing to him by tipping her hand, that she had a guest on the line who had clearly drunk too much.

TWENTY-SIX

Jekyll and Hyde

Vincent Pollack had just breezed past, clutching his sixth Jack Daniel's. He was all smiles after having just returned from Rome, and he'd been drinking late with some guests and enjoying himself. He didn't usually get a chance to relax like that, and he felt he deserved it, well at least once in a while, and they'd had a good season. Also, it was the usual midweek cabaret night, and a chance to let his hair down.

Vincent Pollack took over the phone call. There was a pause, and Mavis Bone heard, 'Hello, Vincent Pollack here, the hotel director.'

'I've found a body – I mean a dog found a body – in my bathroom…' Mavis wasn't making sense; she was shivering with shock.

'I'm sorry…?' Pollack said. 'Did – did you say you found a dead dog in your bathroom?'

'No, *no, you idiot!*' Mavis bit her lip. 'I'm scared.' This time she slowed her voice down, and spelt it out. 'There's a body in a bag in my bathroom. Looks like a child's body, it's been hidden. A dog found it, like the one in the woods.'

There was silence. Mavis listened, the pause continued, and then she said, 'Hello… hello…'

'Which room are you in?'

'Room twenty-two.' She heard some talking and then papers being shuffled.

'Room twenty-two?' Pollack asked her.

'Yes – yes!'

'You're saying you found a child's body in your bathroom?'

'*Yes, for Christ's sake!* I've just told you, in a bag, tied up, behind my bath. It's been there some time. Mostly… mostly bones and a skull. You'd better get the police.'

'I'm coming up now,' Pollack said.

Mavis heard the receiver being put down. She made her way to the room door and waited nervously, wincing as the curtains lit up with a thunderous boom, rattling the cupboards and glassware.

After two minutes, three crisp knocks made her jump.

Mavis let him in, and said, 'Come through,' while still shaking, trying to control her nerves, her voice trembling as she led the way into the bathroom.

And it was only then that he recognised her. Pollack gasped and thought, *Dear God, Mavis Bone. That stupid bitch Giovanna had put you down as Mavis Rone in the guest register. I never twigged.*

Mavis Bone, feeling dizzy and nauseous, never twigged

345

Pollack either. Vincent Pollack tentatively peered into the bag. And then he cupped his mouth and nose, and leant against the wall, closing his eyes. *'Oh! – Oh, my God! It can't be?'*

Mavis looked at him in astonishment, 'Can't be? You mean… you know who…?'

'How did you find my daughter?'

'Your daughter? Jesus Christ! The dog – the dog dragged it out.'

'What dog?'

'The dog in my bathroom, I told you. I found a dog in my bathroom. The same type I saw in the woods.'

Pollack glared at her angrily. 'Don't be stupid, how can a dog get in here?' He looked at the gaping hole where the bath panel should have been. 'Who else have you told?'

'Nobody, I've just found it. Why?'

Pollack grabbed Mavis's arm and pushed her up against the wall. With a menacing look he said, 'You must have known she was there? Who else have you told?'

Mavis was terrified, and pleaded, 'Nobody, I swear.'

'Someone must have told you, bitch.' Pollack snatched her other arm and pinned her back.

'You're hurting me!' Mavis cried out, trying to pull away.

'Now tell me, how did you know a body was there?' he demanded.

'Let go of me, you idiot!' Mavis twisted in his hold. 'How would I know? I'm just on holiday.'

Pollack yelled at her, 'You're a liar!' He was nose to nose with Mavis. His breath reeked of alcohol. Pollack generally avoided drink, as it brought out the Jekyll and Hyde in him. On the few occasions he had succumbed, he could change from nice to very nasty, and he was very nasty now. His eyes bulged with fury as his hands applied more pressure.

For some reason, Mavis fixated on his wrist tattoo, spelling out *Vincent*. It stood out amongst his rippled blue veins.

Wincing with pain, Mavis's wrists burned in his grip. Even though he towered above her, she managed to get her back off the wall and physically pull him along. They grappled, and Mavis pulled him out of the bathroom and then into the bedroom.

Lightning flickered in white flashes as a boom of thunder rattled the balcony doors.

Mavis stepped back on a shard of broken glass. She flinched as it cut into her feet. Her heart was racing. She was breathing in snatches. The hangover was gone, and she was wide awake now, adrenaline whipping through her body. She wrestled with Pollack and spat into his face. It made him stop. He cringed as the phlegm ran down his cheek. He released one hand to wipe it off. He looked at her in astonishment, as if he'd never been so insulted.

Mavis saw her chance and tried to break free, but Pollack held on. She backed into her bed and fell on it, dragging him on top of her. 'Get off me, you arsehole!' she shouted, trying to push him away.

Mavis felt the full force of Pollack's weight as his body thudded into her. He pinned her arms down. She tried to struggle but it was useless. 'Well, well, well, little miss meddle,' he said with a sarcastic sneer. 'Now the cat's out the bag, or should I say that kid is. Trust you to find it. But now I'm going to tuck her back, just where I put her, with you included.'

Mavis looked up at him, terrified, too shocked to speak.

'Can't let anyone find her, Mavis. You see it's got my blood in her hair and on her clothing. Cut myself when I killed her. Flaming nail in some piece of wood.'

'Killed her? But why... why did you kill her?' Mavis bit the back of her hand trying to keep calm. *Try and keep him talking.*

'Little Helen had found out things, found out I'd murdered her mother for the life insurance to buy this hotel. She could have grassed me up. I couldn't have that, so far down the road now. This hotel is like a little goldmine. I'm living the Mediterranean dream, Mrs Bone, and nothing but nothing is going to make me give it up.'

Holding her down securely, Vincent reached across and pulled the belt from Mavis's dressing gown, and then snapped it taut.

Mavis flinched and leant back. 'Please, I won't tell.' Mavis tried to pull away. 'It'll... it'll be our secret, just the two of us.'

Pollack wasn't listening as he wrapped the dressing gown cord around Mavis's neck.

She started screaming, '*Help! Help! Someone help me, please!*' Mavis was reliving her nightmare. The monster coming towards her, arms outstretched ... greedy ...

348

wanting to be satisfied. Its fingers hooked into claws. White flashes of lightning arcing and buzzing, the lights dimming. She could hear a solitary door banging down below. But it was no use, she couldn't move with Pollack's body on top of her. The tension of the cord was tightening. She began to choke. Her last vision in consciousness was Pollack's lips pulled back, showing spit on his teeth as he gripped the cord – tighter and tighter.

The massive crash jerked both of them. The balcony door had slammed open again. The rain sheeted in, spraying their faces. The curtains billowed horizontally, like a pair of vampire cloaks riding a hurricane. Pollack stopped. He stared transfixed, completely spellbound. He released his grip, not even noticing.

Mavis was coming back, coughing and choking, pulling at the cord, feeling the tension ease. She looked up as the lightning highlighted Pollack's face. His startled contortions made him look like a waxwork monster in some old horror movie. The solitary door was still banging beneath them. The room floor, wet and glistening in the flashes, was like some enchanted lake in a fairy story.

Mavis hauled herself up on one elbow. Behind Pollack, she saw three pairs of urine-coloured eyes. She knew instinctively that the dog was back, and this time it had brought some friends. Their thick lips hung down, dripping with blood. Their deep primitive growls turned his head. Three huge Presa Canarios started inching towards Pollack, crawling on their stomachs.

He began to move off the bed, lifting himself carefully,

held in their captivating stare. Slowly, he shook his head; not believing, disbelieving as they inched nearer.

With his back to the balcony entrance, the curtains billowed and wrapped themselves around him. His wet suit clung to him as if he was mummified. The rain sheeted against Pollack's face. His wavy ginger hair stuck in strands to his forehead, like claws spread out and clasping their prey.

Pollack quickly looked behind, as the dogs moved forwards, backing him out onto the balcony. In-between the flapping curtains and spray, Mavis could see him silhouetted against a backdrop of throbbing white lightning.

He had climbed onto a plastic chair and was standing high on the balcony rail. The wind and rain lashed into his face, as he held onto an outside wall lamp to steady himself.

The dogs moved in closer, snarling, baring their red-stained teeth. Pollack was cornered, with nowhere to go. It seemed they wanted revenge for the blame of his daughter's disappearance.

He looked down at the drop, and then up into the night sky. Pollack's face began to distort into convulsions, as though epileptic. He started to blink uncontrollably and began shrieking and gibbering something incomprehensible.

'I have placed my trust in false teachings and substitutes for God. I have broken a solemn vow and promise. I have neglected prayer for a long time. I have abused drugs and alcohol. I have killed and discriminated against others because of greed, race and gender. I have not been chaste in thought and word. I have used sex outside marriage and not to procreate life. I have given myself sexual gratification. I have deliberately looked at pornographic films and magazines. I have permitted sexual thoughts about someone to whom I am not married.'

And then he suddenly stopped.

At last, Vincent Pollack knew his time had come. He raised his arms as if to embrace God, and then he jumped.

Mavis heard the blood-curdling screams and frenzied barking. And then he was gone.

The curtains flapped lifelessly, as if expecting, waiting perhaps for an encore, on some empty stage.

Only muted silence now, broken by the distant rumbling and flashes of a storm beginning to fade away.

Mavis tore at the cord, still coughing and choking, massaging the red weal around her throat. She got to her feet and then collapsed, feeling the glass from the broken picture cut into her knees. 'Ouch! Jesus, shit!' She got up again and moved cautiously, gripping the balcony door, looking for the dogs, ready to shut them out. But there was nothing.

Mavis blinked at the scene and then turned back. She limped across the room and then hopped with pain. 'Fuck! Fuck! Fuck!' She stopped to pick some glass out of her foot. And then she opened her room door and lurched out into the hotel corridor. Mavis had to get away. 'Fucking anywhere,' she whispered to no one.

With her left foot dragging, leaving a trail of blood on the marble tiles, she made her way to the lift. Mavis hurriedly pushed the call button, watching the numbers count down. 'Come on, for Jesus sake,' she shouted, pushing the button again in panic.

And then, with an audible *ping*, the doors opened. Mavis moved to step in, and then she flinched back, covering her nose from the stench.

'Hi, Mavis!' Vincent Pollack, with a chewed-out throat, wheezed through a bloody flap in his Adam's apple. The one eyeball staring at her had no lid. It looked stuck on, detached like a crab's. Next to it was the gouged-out mess of an empty eye socket. There were no lips or nose, only grinning tobacco-stained teeth from a half-eaten face.

His clothes were shredded, and his left hand was bitten in half. One leg had no calf muscle; Mavis could see the meatless bone clearly showing through his torn trousers. Some intestines hung out of his ripped belly, the entrails swinging near his ankles, while foul-smelling juice puddled on the lift floor.

'Guess what, Mavis? Those dogs attacked me, would you believe it?'

A green bubble of snot grew, and then burst from a hole above his mouth, where his nose should have been. Pollack grinned inanely at her. 'Some people shouldn't own pets if they can't control them properly. You know what, Mavis? I think I'll stick with cats.'

All of a sudden a ruptured vein broke, spurting blood from his throat onto Mavis's foot. Mavis flinched back in reaction.

'I'm terribly sorry, Mavis,' he said. 'I thought sooner or later it was going to burst.'

With that, Vincent Pollack gathered his entrails and tried to stuff them back inside his stomach. It was pointless; they weren't going to fit. 'Never mind, saves me dieting.' His chewed lips moved over yellow teeth to form a grin.

And then a stunted fingerbone from half a hand reached for the lift buttons. 'Well, got to be off now, Mavis. Got to see a man about a dog,' he wheezed with a chuckle. 'Can I give you a lift?'

She slowly shook her head.

'Oh well, perhaps another time. Going up, anybody?' Pollack paused, and then pressed the button for the top floor. Abruptly the elevator doors snapped shut.

As the lift trailed off, Mavis could hear him singing, '*How much is that doggie in the window? Arf! – Arf! The one with the waggley tail. Arf! – Arf! How much is that doggie in the window? Arf! Arf! I do hope that doggie's for sale. Arf! – Arf!*'

Mavis leant against the lift doors and closed her eyes. She slowly slid to the floor.

The chameleon of changing colours behind her lids finally hardened into a pulsating sweep of amber. It was the increasing wail of a siren getting nearer that brought Mavis round.

She looked up, all vacant, at a smiling medic dressed in green who was holding her arm. Mavis was puzzled, trying to take in how she came to be on a stretcher.

'This will make you drowsy, yes?' he said in broken English.

353

She watched, mesmerised, as the needle came nearer, and then she felt the twinge.

As the sedative kicked in, she slowly started drifting again, and then saw more bright colours.

With a final effort, Mavis slurred out to him, '*No shmore dogsh.*' And then her head slumped to one side as the medic checked her pulse.

TWENTY-SEVEN

Knot of Fear

Detective Inspector Eric Faversham had arranged to come to see Mavis in order to help Interpol with their enquiries. The inspector was now at Mavis's bedside. She'd been kept in overnight for cuts and shock at the Hospital de Manacor on the eastern side of Majorca.

Gertrude had been with her all morning. She was using the public phone at hospital reception to lodge their travel insurance claim and cancel their return tickets at the Palma airport check-in. She had managed to get them both a hotel for two extra nights near the airport. Mavis had categorically told Gertrude she wouldn't stay another night in that evil hotel, not for a million pounds.

The doctor had told Mavis she would be okay to leave in the afternoon, but not to fly for another twenty-four hours.

Among the usual hospital smells of disinfectant,

bleached linen, alcohol and waxed floors, Mavis was propped up between some fluffy green pillows, helping Inspector Faversham with his enquiries. She had explained what happened, and asked nervously if they'd found the man who had tried to kill her.

Inspector Faversham, wearing a smart beige suit with matching tie, told Mavis, 'Vincent Pollack's body has been found in the perimeter woods. It was thought, after his fall from the hotel balcony, some wild dogs must have dragged it there.'

The inspector looked at his notebook, and said, 'Along with your statement, Mavis, this seems to confirm the previous sightings of dogs roaming the area. And it appears to be the most likely course of events.'

Mavis looked anxious. 'But is he dead though? Please say yes. I don't want him coming back to hurt me.' She bit the back of her hand and looked at him with moist eyes.

The inspector leaned across from his visitor's chair and patted her shoulder reassuringly. 'Don't worry, Mavis, he's very dead. The old scar lacerations on his back, and the *Vincent* tattoo on his wrist, confirmed it was definitely Vincent Pollack.'

'But I saw him, Eric, when he came out of the lift, ripped to shreds, as large as life.'

'Mavis, you were probably in shock. You thought you saw him. The mind can play tricks.'

Inspector Faversham read from his notebook, 'Vincent Pollack was found badly mutilated, to the extent that the dogs had decapitated him. Run off with his head somewhere. Believe me, Mavis, he looked like he'd been through a meat grinder, and he'll never hurt you again.'

'Oh! My God.' Mavis covered her face.

She didn't want to hear any more, her face was still covered by her hands.

A nurse approached and gave the inspector an icy stare, pointing to her tunic fob watch. Inspector Faversham held up five fingers, the number of minutes more he would like with her patient. She nodded and responded with the same sign – *and only five* – giving him a cold sideways glance as she left.

*

A few days after their flight home, Gertrude Stick was holding the fort at the Wimbledon agency office while Mavis Bone flew back out to Majorca, having been asked by Detective Inspector Faversham to help the police with their inquiries and to tie up a few loose ends.

Because Mavis had found Helen's body, she felt it was her duty to attend the funeral. A memorial service for Helen was held at the *Tanatorio* in Port de Soller.

The presence of press and television made it big news.

After the service, many locals followed the hearse to the cemetery for the interment. Amongst the mourners was her grandmother Mrs Clifton, as well as a reception of teachers and pupils from Helen's school. Her schoolfriend Bianca read a moving poem to a solemn audience, all clutching a single white rose. With the others, Mavis stood among the congregation and laid a rose on Helen's coffin. Afterwards she slowly filed away with the crowd, dutifully stopping and reading the messages on the flowers and wreaths.

*

After her flight home that evening, Mavis Bone returned to her flat on Wimbledon Broadway. Settling down in bed, she sat up on one elbow, reading *Fifty Shades of Grey*, the holiday paperback she'd purchased at Palma Airport. And then her eyelids drooped, while her head slumped forward. As she collapsed into slumber, with a slight snore developing, her discarded book lay among the bed sheets.

The following morning, Mavis made breakfast for the two of them. She shouted from the kitchen through to Gertrude, who was showering in the shared bathroom. 'Gerty, breakfast is ready, I'll put yours under the grill.'

Receiving no answer, Mavis shouted again, and guessed she couldn't hear. Mavis moved herself closer, to yelling distance, and tried one more time. Still no answer.

She carried on with the breakfast and dished it out. It was a sunny morning, and the golden rays were streaming through onto the kitchen floor and table. The smell of bacon from her sandwich made Mavis peckish again, and she nibbled at the tiny remains of crispy fat dotted around her plate.

She sat down and poured a coffee, and, becoming impatient, she shouted through again, while putting Gertrude's breakfast onto the hotplate.

Mavis moved out to the lobby and heard the shower running, and then she hesitantly tried the door. As it opened, she called Gertrude again. Mavis saw her shape through the steam, behind the curtain.

As she edged nearer, she noticed a puddle forming. Part of the shower curtain was hanging over the side. Through steam and the sound of running water, Mavis yelled to her again. However, the figure behind the curtain didn't move or respond. Mavis's hand tentatively moved to draw the curtain. She hesitated. Something was wrong.

It was then she heard the bathroom door click shut behind her, the same click she'd heard in her hotel bathroom.

The first knot of fear began to screw up in Mavis's stomach. She called again, aware this time that no sound was coming out of her trembling lips.

Steam and beads of sweat began to gather on her forehead; they ran down the sides of her face, leaving glistening trails.

Mavis clutched the shower curtain and then stopped, freezing in disbelief.

Looking down she saw a pair of men's shoes, poking through, stained with blood. The shoes were motionless, waiting, together in harmony.

Mavis's hand, clutching the shower curtain, began to shake. The steam now, so intense, that her face was covered in matted hair. A nervous tick began to flutter on Mavis's cheek. She started to whine and keen like an injured animal. Mavis couldn't hear herself. The fear, the steam, everything was muted, as if she was in a thick London fog.

Mavis had to know, what was behind the curtain. She bit her lip and braced herself. There was no turning back.

And with an almighty wrench, she tore open the shower curtain, and then, *'AARRGH! JESUS, NO! IT CAN'T BE. NO! NO!'* Mavis screamed at the grotesque image of a smiling Vincent Pollack. The one eyeball that stared at her had no lid. It looked stuck on, detached like a crab's. There were no lips or nose, only grinning yellow teeth from a half-eaten face with a chewed-out throat. Vincent Pollack's clothes were shredded, and his left hand was missing, as if it had been bitten off.

As he stepped out of the shower tray, some intestines and entrails were hanging out of his ripped belly, swinging near his ankles. Mavis tried to scream but nothing came out.

She backed off and pulled frantically at the bathroom doorknob. It was locked, and so she pulled again, rattling it in panic. Vincent Pollack, with his arm raised, began to approach. Mavis flinched away, and saw he was holding something. In a sudden realisation of horror, she saw a jagged shard of glass in his hand. Mavis put up her hands in defence, but Vincent Pollack towered over her, as if he was smothering her with his shadow, engulfing her like a shroud. And then Pollack plunged the glass dagger into Mavis's chest, grunting with pleasure, and then *'AARRGH!'* Mavis reacted as her blood spattered the white dressing gown she was wearing.

Vincent Pollack was ready to strike again. Mavis tried to staunch the blood with one hand, and punched Pollack's eyeless socket with the other. She began to scream, '*Help me! I'm dying!*' Pollack fell on top of her, the glass dagger plunging again and again. Her dressing gown getting redder and redder. Mavis started screaming, lashing out in wild swipes. '*Help me! For fuck's sake, help me!*'

'Mavis! Mavis! Vake up!' Gertrude was wrestling with her, trying to grab her thrusting arms. 'Vake up, Mavis! Vake up, you're dveaming.' They wrestled until Mavis came round. Her unplugged look slowly evaporated.

'Oh God! He was trying to kill me again.'

Gertrude put her arm around Mavis's shoulder. 'It vos only a nightmare, my darling.' Gertrude kissed her on the cheek. 'The doctor said the nightmares vill eventually go. Anyway, I love you, Mavis. Nothing nasty is going to happen to you, I promise. I von't let it.'

Gertrude kissed her tenderly again. And they both cuddled up together, their naked bodies giving each other warmth.

TWENTY-EIGHT

Vincent Petzoldt

Forty-eight-year-old Giovanna Piras couldn't believe her luck, even though she swung both ways. Still, he didn't have to know that. It was security she was looking for, and Vincent Petzoldt could give her plenty of that.

Working as a hotel receptionist in Majorca, she'd met German tourist Vincent Petzoldt. In his late forties with a polished bald head and distinguished handlebar moustache, he'd immediately swept her off her feet. And now she was so in love. He had a few bob as well, and told her he owned and ran a wildlife reserve with its own lodge, among the Majorcan wetlands. This fitted in well with Giovanna's career plans, because she was studying, as a mature student, for an environmental biology degree.

*

The elderly grey-haired woman, dressed in summer clothes, arrived at the shared business entrance for the office of the Mavis Bone Detective Agency on Wimbledon Broadway SW19.

Mrs Laura Piras pressed the third button down, and heard a buzzer as the door unlocked to allow her through to an entrance lobby. From there she took the stairs to the first floor, as indicated by a business list board.

At a half-panelled glass door stencilled with **Mavis Bone Detective Agency – An eye for an eye makes the whole world blind,** she pressed another buzzer. Immediately, Gertrude Stick, the agency secretary, spoke through the intercom. 'Can I 'elp you?'

'It's Mrs Piras, I have an eleven o'clock appointment to see Mavis Bone.'

'Come through, please.'

Another buzzer unlocked a door, and Mrs Piras entered a small and cluttered outer office. She was confronted by a smart sad-faced secretary, who was wearing a blue trouser suit and big gold earrings. A chic lavender blue headscarf hid her platinum blonde dyed hair. The secretary was sitting at a desk covered in files.

Mrs Piras couldn't help noticing that high above, strategically placed between empty spaces on dusty shelves, filled with files and ledgers, sets of glassy eyes peered at her. These were from two stuffed squirrels, a fox about to pounce, and a suspended tawny owl that twisted slowly in flight.

The secretary nodded to the animals. 'Our last office tenant was a mortician, and liked to keep his vinger in.'

The German secretary's lined, tanned face, which was mostly from visits to a sunbed salon, was further made up with pink lipstick and green eye shadow. She indicated for Mrs Piras to take a seat, while she spoke into the intercom. 'Mrs Piras to see you, Mrs Bone.'

'Please show her through, Gertrude.'

Gertrude Stick came round from behind her desk, and escorted the prospective client to a larger, brown-carpeted office. And there she was greeted by the private detective.

Mavis Bone, with her jet-black hair full of tiny curls, was wearing a smart red trouser suit. She raised herself from behind a leather-topped desk, and extended her hand. 'G'day. Please take a seat, Mrs Piras.'

After introductions, Mavis said, 'Would you mind if my secretary sits in on this and takes notes? That way we make sure to capture all the vital information.'

Gertrude Stick sat herself down with a notepad at the end of the desk, and reassured Mrs Piras. 'Everything vot I write is fully confidential, my dear. It vill not be disclosed to anyvun else.'

Knowing how Gertrude always trotted out her same introduction line, Mavis Bone rolled her eyes. 'Yes, thank you, Gerty.' She turned to Mrs Piras with a big, cheesy grin. 'I wouldn't know what to do without my Gerty. She's my Girl Friday, as the poms call it.'

Gertrude as usual chimed in. 'Vot to do? You could give me a 'vise for a start, if you 'vont to do something. I 'aven't 'ad a—'

Mavis interrupted. 'Yes – yes, thank you Gerty.' She

364

turned to Mrs Piras. 'You indicated on the telephone you wanted to see me about your missing daughter, Giovanna.'

Private Investigator Mavis Bone, wearing white make-up with faint pink cheeks, black eye shadow and heavy red lipstick, adjusted her thick, black-framed glasses. She fiddled with her chunky pearl necklace as she prepared to listen.

There was bitterness in Mrs Piras's voice. 'Yes. I'm sure her disappearance is down to that smug bastard she was engaged to. Her fiancé, Vincent Petzoldt, told the police they'd broken up and called off the engagement.' She showed them her daughter's break-up letter to him. 'However, I reckon he forged it, when he found out that my Giovanna and his environmental biologist, Maxine Garcia, were lovers. My Giovanna worked for Vincent, as part of his Vincent Petzoldt Wildlife Management team.' Mrs Piras dabbed her eyes and wrung her hands with distress. 'And now, would you believe, he's even got himself engaged to Maxine Garcia. I think it's some sort of twisted revenge on his part.'

'And you think this Vincent Petzoldt has harmed your daughter?'

'Yes I do, Mrs Bone. I'd like you to check if he was involved.'

'Mrs Piras,' Mavis sighed, 'I'd like to help you. But you must face facts. You said the police have already carried out a thorough investigation concerning your daughter's disappearance.'

'That bastard is too clever for the police. He's very

methodical,' Mrs Piras added. 'No doubt he planned her disappearance to the finest premeditated degree. You see, my Giovanna is gay. In her emails, she told me she was having an affair with her work colleague Maxine Garcia. They were lovers. Maybe her fiancé found out about it and harmed her.'

Mrs Piras added, 'However, someone like you, Mrs Bone, could find something the police have missed or overlooked. I read the fantastic reviews on your agency website.'

She added, with pleading eyes, 'So will you take the case on, Mrs Bone?'

'Call me Mavis, me darlin', and you'd better know my agency rates before you commit yerself.' She turned to her secretary, Gertrude. 'Gerty, can you tell this lovely sheila our current rates of pay, and I'll put the billy on.' She asked Mrs Piras. 'Would yer like a tea or coffee, me darlin'?'

She responded, 'A tea would be nice with milk, no sugar, thank you.'

Gertrude chimed in, 'And I'll 'ave my usual. Black coffee and stvong vith three sugars.'

'Yes I know,' said Mavis, taking the kettle to the outside office sink. 'How could I ever forget you,' she said with a sigh.

Mrs Piras smiled at the office banter and enquired, 'If you don't mind me asking, how long have you been in business together?'

Gertrude pondered and said, 'It must be over tventy years now. My deceased 'usband was a private investigator, and I vos 'is secretary. Vhen 'e died, 'e left me comfortably off. I alveady knew Mavis, when she 'elped out from time to time with private investigations at my 'usband's agency. This was usually vhen ve vere overloaded. And then Mavis was looking to strike out on 'er own, and so ve teamed up. I do the accounts and filing, vhile she does the investigating. We even share the two-bed flat above the agency building. It vorks vell.'

'So you're partners then?'

Gertrude laughed, 'Yes, partners in crime, you could say.'

'Well the reviews on your website were full of praise,' Mrs Piras informed her. 'That's why I'm here.'

Gertrude assured her, 'Mrs Piras. Ve can never guarantee success, but you vill receive from our agency, a virst-class thorough investigation for your money.'

Mrs Piras's face darkened. 'All I want you to do is find out how where my daughter Giovanna is. The police have come up with nothing.' With a handkerchief she dabbed her eyes again. 'I still reckon it was her fiancé.'

Mavis asked her, 'So where is this Vincent Petzoldt now?'

'He's managing his wildlife reserve in Majorca. My daughter, who worked for him, did speak of a hotel he purchased in Majorca, the Hotel Caterina. She worked there once on reception. That's how they met; he was a hotel guest. The original owner, a Mr Vincent Pollack, had died accidently after falling from a balcony.'

It was then that Mavis and Gertrude looked at one another in astonishment. 'Err, you say your daughter Giovanna worked on reception there?'

'Yes she did, to save money for her university fees while studying for her bachelor's degree in environmental biology.'

'Mrs Piras, what a coincidence! We know your daughter, and the Hotel Caterina is well known to us. We were asked by a former client to find their daughter, who was murdered there by this same Vincent Pollack. Her body was found behind a hotel room bath panel.'

Mrs Piras looked shocked. 'Dear God, I remember my Giovanna telling me about that. So you helped to find the killer, this Vincent Pollack?'

Mavis explained, 'We did carry out an investigation, but Vincent Pollack died while trying to escape. And as far as I know, his body was badly mutilated by a pack of wild dogs that were roaming in the woods adjacent to the hotel.'

Mrs Piras responded, 'My daughter did say there was some sort of medieval curse on the hotel, and it had become a haven for ghost hunters and paranormal investigations. However, the Hotel Caterina is now part of the Majorcan wildlife reserve near Camino de Mallorca, which is between Soller and Port de Soller. My Giovanna was working there as a conservationist, part of her fiancé's wildlife management team. That was before she disappeared. She had already part qualified at the University of Palma, and was doing field studies for her degree. She had taken up the position, which meant living in an eco-friendly log cabin, in a remote location. And then, after a year, I never heard from her.' She dabbed her eyes again. 'According to Petzoldt's police statements, she just disappeared without trace. The police of course searched the area, but came up with nothing.'

Mrs Piras looked thoughtful. 'My Giovanna did say once, there were problems with radon gas in the wildlife reserve, which could contaminate all the wildlife living there. And she was worried at the degree of animals found dead or with deformities.'

Mavis and Gertrude stood up and offered their hands. Mavis assured her. 'We will be in touch as soon as we have something concrete, me darlin', I promise you.'

Mavis pondered and then said, very seriously, 'Mrs Piras, to find out the true reason for your daughter's disappearance, I would have to seek temporary employment at the Vincent Petzoldt wildlife reserve in Majorca. I would act as a plant, and be in contact with you.'

Mrs Piras beamed at the idea. 'Yes, someone on the inside is what this case needs. I could ask Petzoldt. Since the disappearance of my Giovanna, his environmental biologist Maxine Garcia has been looking for a field assistant. I could try and pull a few strings. And why not? That's the least he could do for me. I'll tell him you're my cousin and you're looking for employment in environmental work.'

Mrs Piras added, 'I'm still in touch with Maxine, and I'll tell her to take it easy on you, as you're still learning, just as a favour for me.'

Mavis added, 'That sounds great, me darlin', we'll give it a burl. And let's be honest, without me being there, we don't stand Buckley's chance of finding out what happened to your daughter.'

TWENTY-NINE

Flotation

While her secretary Gertrude Stick took control of their Wimbledon Broadway agency office, Mavis Bone filled in for forty-seven-year-old Maxine Garcia, as her assistant conservationist at the Vincent Petzoldt wildlife reserve in Majorca.

Part of Mavis's daily duties as her assistant was filing and recording the plant species that inhabited the forest grasslands, as well as ensuring wildlife habitats were free from disease and harmful insects, and monitoring local rivers for pollution.

Mavis asked her, 'So Maxine, still no news of your former colleague Giovanna Piras?'

Maxine's face darkened. 'Nothing, she just disappeared into thin air. The police have carried out countless searches for her.'

'Her mother is very worried, Maxine, in case she may have been harmed.'

Maxine scoffed, 'Don't tell me about it. I know she thinks my Vincent had something to do with it. She got the needle when I became engaged to him.'

Mavis asked, 'So when's your big day, Maxine?' Maxine was in the middle of dissecting the carcass of a cottontail rabbit, and looked up from the results of a chemical analysis. They were at work in the log cabin, slap in the middle of the Majorcan Camino Forest, about five miles from the Hotel Caterina.

'Just over four months' time. Saturday August the tenth to be exact,' Maxine Garcia replied, clearly excited. 'By then, Vincent should have finished redecorating his house. I've booked the honeymoon at S'Albufera Natural Park Hotel. My sister Tina is PA to the managing director, and she's wangled us a fantastic discount for this 2013 season.'

Mavis looked up. 'Wow, good for you both.'

'And Vincent's booked the church and reception.' She was now busy on the laptop, typing up some field reports. She stopped, took a swig of her coffee and then frowned. 'Trouble is, we need a new car. Well, not necessarily brand new; anything that's better than the one we've got. Even the guy in the garage told Vincent there's no point in throwing good money away on repairs. The cylinder head's leaking or something.' Maxine sighed. 'That's all we needed with the wedding expense.'

'Better to get it replaced now than have the old one pack up on you when you're setting off on your honeymoon,' Mavis replied.

'I know, I sound like a moaning Minnie, don't I? I'm cribbing, and there's me with an apartment of my own, all paid up for, and moving into Vincent's old house, with no mortgage, and he's paying for the wedding breakfast.'

'Lucky you,' Mavis said. 'Wedding breakfasts don't come cheap, I guess?'

'Yeah, you're right, but I'd like to find an extra part-time job in the holidays to help out financially. I feel guilty with Vincent laying out for everything.'

Mavis pretended she was pleased for Maxine, and that it had worked out well for her and her fiancé Vincent Petzoldt. It was Vincent who'd helped Maxine when she first started working at the reserve one year ago. He'd shown her the important wildlife habitat including nests and dens, and where he thought forest and grassland areas required attention for healthy growth. Working together they had become good friends and eventually lovers. For Maxine, who'd previously had lesbian preferences, this was a change, although she hadn't told Vincent; not even her secret affair with Giovanna.

Maxine said, 'Of course, Vincent's lodger, Dan, will be moving out and shacking up at his girlfriend's place.' Her expression was serious. 'Vincent reckons he was okay about it, but I do feel guilty. By marrying Vincent, I'm forcing him to leave. Mind you, as Vincent said, he's only got himself to blame there. Gambling all his money away on stocks and shares and then losing his house to creditors. Vincent said it was his own fault, what with his drinking and chasing women. He was lucky to have a landlord like Vincent, who could put a roof over his head as well as get him that forest ranger job.'

In the two months she'd been working at the Vincent Petzoldt wildlife reserve, Mavis hadn't seen a great deal of Dan the forest ranger. On the few occasions she had, he'd struck her as a younger Bruce Forsyth lookalike, with receding hair and a prominent chin.

Maxine's petite, pale face turned into a puzzled expression as she glanced at the chemical analysis results. 'You know, that's funny? The solutions of rabbit skin I've put through the photometer show very high readings of radon-222. I mean, it's a standard solution I test on everything we find dead, because of the EPA regulations. I know we live in a radon area, but Christ, this is ridiculous.' She was half talking to herself, and half to Mavis Bone. And then after a brief pause, her face lightened up with a thought. 'Do you know what, Mavis? I'm gonna suggest to the director we check out the area with those radon detectors.'

'Don't try to tell me,' Mavis scoffed. 'It's all double Dutch what I type up for you. You're the boff with the degree.' She took a bite of her blueberry muffin and carried on typing. Mavis liked her cakes. Her full, stocky figure gave away her weakness for the sweet things in life, and betrayed her desire for pastries.

Maxine continued, 'And look at the size of the thing. I mean, most rabbits I've seen aren't bigger than eighteen inches in length and weigh no more than three to four pounds. But this thing is huge. It's twenty-six inches and weighs over seven pounds. And the puncture marks in the skin. If they were smaller, I'd say a timber rattlesnake had got it. That would make sense, since we now know how they can multiply and breed from eggs. All from that prat of a zoologist who let two rattlers escape from his tank two years ago. But the bite dimensions are far too big for a rattler.' Maxine picked up another set of analysis results. 'Then again, the machine never lies. This baby was wacked by a timber, with a canebrake toxin way above the average bite yield. In fact nearly three hundred milligrams of crotaline venom. It doesn't make sense.'

'You're dead right, Doctor Einstein,' Mavis joked. 'You lost me at the cake tin toxin bit, whatever.' Mavis took a swig of coffee and then asked, 'Being stuck out here, does it worry you at night? You wouldn't catch me alone in this place after hours, for love or money.'

Maxine smiled, 'You get used to it, and with so much work on, I'm usually too busy working my butt off in the evenings to worry about the bogeyman.'

*

In the boardroom of the S'Albufera hotel chain, based in Alcúdia, Majorca, the directors were discussing the new eco-friendly hotel development. Planning permission on a private area of farmland had been given, provided the hotel would be run and maintained on a self-sufficient basis. This included using the river to drive a large waterwheel to power the electricity supply, in conjunction with discreetly

374

placed wind turbines and solar panels. The hotel water supply would be tapped off the river, using pumps and purifiers. Also the style of the hotel would have to be built in keeping with the natural surroundings.

The hotel chain were pushing this new concept in tourism, to attract eco-friendly customers who were climate conscious and cared for the natural surroundings and wildlife. They would have the benefit of knowing that all the hotel food would come from locally farmed livestock and river fisheries, together with fruit and vegetables grown within the locality.

The board of directors were sure this was the way ahead to attract tourists who wanted to go green on holiday. Tourists who wanted to live off sustainable energy and organic food during their stay.

To finance this new hotel, the board would be offering the public a share flotation on the stock exchange. They confidently predicted that once the project had been finalised, the share price would rise drastically. At the moment the share flotation was highly confidential. The board knew that if it should leak out, many investors could make a killing, buying low and then selling when the flotation was made public.

Thirty-seven-year-old Tina Garcia, PA to the managing director, was taking the minutes of the meeting on her laptop computer and feeling hungry. The meeting had started early, which meant she had missed her breakfast, and now the morning was dragging as she typed away. Her midday salt beef on rye with two doughnuts and coffee, at

Gerry's Diner across the road, couldn't come quick enough. And she could have her usual chinwag on the mobile, to her sister Maxine.

They were very close and phoned each other every day. This lunchtime they were both excited to be discussing Maxine's wedding. In-between snippets of chit-chat, Tina told her about the new hotel plans to build on the S'Albufera Natural Park area, which was near Alcudia, where she and Vincent were going to live. Tina knew Maxine was looking for a part-time job, and once the hotel was up and running, the S'Albufera hotel chain might be recruiting for secretarial vacancies. 'I'm telling you, Max', they've got money to burn. It's coming out of their ears. Do you know...' She looked around carefully and then continued, 'I'm even down for a share bonus when they do their flotation thing. They'll be offering shares on the stock market or something, to finance the deal. And they'll be as much as eleven dollars each after flotation, I heard. But keep it to yourself, this share launch thing is all hush-hush.' Tina took another bite of her doughnut and listened while Maxine changed the subject and talked about her wedding preparations.

THIRTY

Radon

In conversation over dinner that evening, Maxine told Vincent about the hotel development that Tina had mentioned. 'I'm telling you, she's down for a big bonus once the shares are floated, she told me. After flotation they'll be eleven dollars a share, and that's double what they are now, she reckoned. We might even get that new bed from her as a wedding present; you know, the one I hinted about.' They both laughed and carried on eating the delicious meatloaf she'd cooked.

Vincent's mid-forties lodger Dan had come downstairs just at that time, carrying boxes from his room. He was moving out and going to live with his current girlfriend at her apartment. It was a drag, as he was planning to finish with her soon. But in the present circumstances it was a roof over his head. He was already helping her with some of the bills, as she was unemployed and living on welfare. Still, it had seemed the right thing to do at the time, until she found a job. However, the relationship had since become platonic, and Dan realised he was being used as a meal ticket. She wasn't getting out of bed until lunchtime. But the prospect of Maxine moving in had forced him to shack up with her.

*

Later that evening, Vincent fired up his laptop and went online to check out the hotel group share price. It was at $5.46. Looking back through the stock history, it had stagnated around that figure for the last eighteen months. Although he'd seen first-hand how stocks and shares could backfire and ruin you financially, his lodger Dan being an example. Yet, he still liked to gamble and take the odd flutter from time to time on the horses at Palma racetrack. So when Maxine had highlighted a share flotation at eleven dollars each, it got him thinking. Vincent Petzoldt smelled a possible killing. If he got in now and bought up as many as he could afford, it could be the end of his money worries. He'd have to borrow big to make it worthwhile, but he felt smug and confident. He considered himself privileged to have access to insider information.

After some deliberation, he knew there was only one course of action. To raise the money to buy the shares, he'd have to take out a few personal loans, and borrow on as many credit cards as he could. Paying off the minimum balance for a short while would allow him time to wait for the flotation, and then sell the shares. With the profits from the share sale, he could repay the credit cards and loans, perhaps even buy himself a new car and boat, and hopefully still be left with a healthy bank balance. Maxine didn't have to know the full amount he borrowed.

The whole thing hinged on the share flotation price. Maxine had said eleven dollars each. What if she'd misheard, or they decided last minute to set them lower? He knew it was a risky undertaking. Then again, what successful investor didn't take risks? Petzoldt satisfied himself with the thought that he was doing the right thing.

He checked out the local brokers online, and then telephoned Mutual Investments over in Palma. Petzoldt acted casual, enquired about the S'Albufera hotel chain share price, and asked if there were any for sale. The broker informed him there were indeed. At least three hundred and eighty thousand were available for sale, at the current price of $5.22, offered in blocks of fifty shares. They also told him their fee was one per cent of the sale price.

Petzoldt enquired what the biggest purchase was that a single investor could make. They told him up to 55,000 shares was the limit placed by the hotel chain for a single investment.

That was good, he thought. He had plans of buying 46,000. That meant an outlay of just over $240,000. He knew this was make or break for him. If the hotel chain deal didn't materialise, then the existing share price would probably go down, and he'd be left with a worthless investment. No doubt Mutual Investments would buy the shares back, but at a much lower price. However, planning permission had been given, he knew that for sure.

Petzoldt had arrived early at the ranger's office a few times, to intercept the post for the wildlife reserve. This made sense, rather than have his PA open the mail. The letter addressed to him confirmed plans for a new eco-friendly hotel development in the S'Albufera Natural Park area. And the common aim of working together was to ensure the protection of all wildlife and habitat would remain paramount, while excavation and building works were ongoing. It also highlighted the more than generous donation the S'Albufera hotel chain would be making to the Vincent Petzoldt wildlife reserve, for the use of their wetlands area and wildlife management expertise.

For the next two weeks, Petzoldt checked his post and went online for any confirmation emails from the loan companies he'd borrowed from. And then, at the beginning of the second week, his prayers were answered. The cheques began to appear on his doormat. After a further week, he checked his bank statement again. There it was printed in black and white: **Credit $240,928.**

Going online, Petzoldt checked the share price again and immediately phoned his brokers. Within an hour they had his cheque, and as soon as it had been cleared, the shares were placed in a brokerage account they had set up for him.

*

A week later, Petzoldt decided it was about time he investigated Maxine's strange test results. His fiancé's investigations revealed high yields of radon gas on some of her wildlife reserve field trips. This was confirmed with tests on dead animals with abnormal deformities.

With a map of the area pinned to his office wall, and ten radon detectors set out on his desk, he explained to Dan, 'These devices are to be placed around the reserve at the locations Maxine revealed, that showed high yields of radon gas. Apparently some hotel chain chairman is a bit worried. Something big is going down. The hotel chain are interested in building on some of our private land here. That's all I've been told.'

Petzoldt explained to Dan, 'You'll see the exact positions where the counters are to be placed, and instructions for their installation.'

Dan looked at the map and asked Vincent, 'When do they plan to start building?'

'I don't know at the moment. All I know is, a hotel chain are interested in the area, and want to make sure, Radon gas results come within the normal safety band. This is before they stake a plot. Seems like this radon gas is some sort of natural radiation from the ground.' Petzoldt picked up a safety leaflet on his table and strained his eyes. 'It says here it comes from the decomposition of uranium, and lung cancer is one of the side effects, that's if someone was exposed to radon in high doses. Especially in a confined space, such as a house or a hotel.'

Alarm bells began to ring somewhere at the back of Petzoldt's head. He noted on the map that five of the counters were to be placed around the S'Albufera Natural Park area.

That evening, he went onto his laptop and read up on radon gas. He noted the US EPA safety levels were set at 4.0 picocuries per litre.

The following morning, Petzoldt and Dan set off with the radon counters. The devices were the digital reading type, with a window showing the concentration levels. This meant high levels of radon were easy to spot at source. Using the map location, each counter was identified with a numbered sticker.

Driving the Ford Ranger pickup, they covered an area of four square miles. Following the instructions, they hammered in the bright red wooden stakes to within ten inches of the ground. And then they primed and placed a counter into the small lidded box on top of the stake. The counters would then be collected twelve days later to have their readings assessed.

Petzoldt knew he was at the point of no return. If the counters showed high readings above the safety level at the S'Albufera Natural Park area, then it was unlikely they would build the hotel. It stood to reason that no one would stay in a hotel with high levels of radioactive gas swirling around, no matter how good the discount deals were. And it could take months for the hotel chain to find another safe site. And meanwhile, he didn't have the salary to pay back the money he'd borrowed. The whole deal hung on making a short-term killing, to quickly sell off the shares at flotation.

Petzoldt wished he'd waited before making the deal. Of course, being the nature reserve director, he'd known about the high levels of radon in certain areas of S'Albufera Natural Park; however, he never realised it would become such an issue that it could spoil his plans.

Knowing the counters would be collected in twelve days, he decided to check them out earlier. From the manufacturer's specification, he knew it took a couple of days for a radon reading to stabilise. He'd give it nine days, and then sneak out to check them. If they showed high levels, he'd remove the detectors and store them high up somewhere safe, well off the ground, until the readings had dropped to within the safety parameters. And then he'd replace them early in the morning on the day they were to be collected.

*

It was nearly six-forty-five and quiet, on this warm, early evening in mid-June at the Vincent Petzoldt wildlife reserve. Suddenly the desk phone started ringing. And then the answerphone kicked in: *'I'm sorry, Vincent's not here right now to take your call, but if you'd like to leave your name, number and message I'll get back to you as soon as possible.'* A woman's voice came on the line. She sounded anxious: 'Vincent, it's Maxine! You're not answering your mobile. I'm out at Old Garrison Road about a hundred yards from the Declan Lane turn-off. The car broke down again just as I got here. I haven't got the breakdown number, and my mobile's low on battery. Can you call them out? I'm exercising Coco.' The voice went faint but could still be heard. 'Coco, come here, boy. What you got there, boy?' And then a note of panic. 'Oh my God! It's an arm. He's found a human arm. Vincent, for Christ's sake… you listening?… the dog's found —.' The mobile cut out and there was silence. A finger pressed the replay button, listened, and then deleted the message.

*

Vincent Petzoldt was out of his mind. His fiancé Maxine had been missing for over three days. Her car had been found. However, after numerous police searches, including help from friends and neighbours, there were still no clues to her disappearance or any sign of her dog, Coco.

Today, Mavis Bone had organised another group, made up of friends and locals, to help in the search for her missing work colleague. It was a cloud-free Thursday, and forest smells of island sage wafted across the twelve hikers as they picked their way along the banks of the Torrent de la Vall Mar. Mavis had instructed them to keep in a line, prod the earth with their sticks, and then smell the end for signs of putrefaction.

It was just after one o'clock and she decided to rest up for lunch. 'Okay,' she said to them all, 'let's take a break here for forty-five minutes, and then we'll make our way to Clements Point.'

Some of the more overweight hikers looked glad of the rest. The temperature had already climbed to seventy-eight degrees. In turn, some of them removed their rucksacks and spread out small groundsheets. And then out came paper plates followed by an assortment of sandwiches, Scotch eggs and chicken drumsticks. The tops of cans hissed off, heads went back, and gulps and burps permeated the little camp.

Fifty-six-year-old Wally Dolmen, one of the largest in the group at eighteen stone, didn't sit on the ground. Once down there, he knew he couldn't get up unaided. A bit embarrassing amongst strangers. Instead he leant on the shooting stick he'd brought along. Finishing off his third chicken drumstick and the remains of his second can of beer, he needed to pee.

Wally, with his bright lumberjack coat tied around his waist, discreetly excused himself and took a short walk. Safely out of vision, he stopped near the riverbank. As he was about to unzip, he caught the smell. Wally winced as the stench filled his nostrils. He mumbled under his breath, 'What the fuck is that?'

Taking a step backwards away from it, his right foot disappeared down a rabbit hole, and he keeled over, hitting his shoulder hard on the muddy ground. 'Shit, shit, shit,' he cursed as he rolled over onto his stomach. His right hand had landed in something foul and slippery.

Wally tried to push himself up, and as he did so, he yelled in panic. A black, decomposed face, hidden beneath some ferns, groaned with his pressure and spurted brown slime from the nose onto his sunburned cheek. Wally instantly froze. He began to shake, and as he slowly looked down, he saw beneath some ferns that his right hand had gone right through the ribcage of a rotted body, and was resting on the spinal column.

At that point all hell broke loose. Wally emitted a high, piercing scream and started thrashing around on the floor, 'For fuck's sake help me! Keep it away from me... help for Christ's sake, the fucking thing's dead... Jesus Shit, I don't wanna die.'

Mavis Bone was the first to reach him. She thought he'd been attacked by some wild animal. She grappled with his flaying arms, while the others gawped in shock. Eventually, by sitting astride his chest, she brought him under control. Wally was incoherent, still whining and softly mumbling, until a hefty slap from Mavis woke him out of his shock.

Wally blinked at her, and then nervously said, 'I think I found a body, over there.' He nodded in its direction.

Mavis, with the help of two others, got Wally to his feet. While he rested on his shooting stick, a couple of the women in the party brushed him down, and then one of the men offered him some brandy from a hip flask.

Mavis instructed everyone to keep where they were, while she went to investigate. She trod carefully to the cluster of ferns, and then reeled back with a fist to her mouth. The stench was overpowering. She crouched down, aware of disturbing a crime scene.

With a handkerchief over her nose, she leant over the remains of a corpse. Her brief wildlife experience and studies had shown her pictures of decayed animals, such as deer and the occasional fox. The volume of remaining flesh and the decomposition of body fats, before animals finished off the pickings, gave an indication of how long a carcass had been in the wild. So although this was a human who'd been out in the open, she made a rough calculation that it had been out here for more than six months.

She instantly knew it couldn't be Maxine. The body was far too decomposed. It was only two days ago she'd put up the missing person posters on some of the hiking trails, showing a picture of Maxine Garcia. She remembered the police had found her pickup near Declan Lane, a popular dog-walking area.

Mavis's eyes scoured the ground and stopped at something caught on the protruding stump of a young fir tree. Moving closer, she recognised what it was.

Picking it up carefully, she held it out to ascertain the full length. The dark black chevron cross-bands along the body, set in a background of brownish yellow, determined it was the shed skin of a timber rattlesnake. However, the skin was *far* too long.

Using her own height as a gauge, she judged it to be around seven feet. She knew most adult rattlers grew to no more than four feet, so this was clearly another abnormality she'd stumbled across.

As she was about to turn away, she noticed something odd. She crouched down and then realised. The left arm of the corpse was missing.

Within an hour, the area was crawling with local Majorcan police. A crime scene had been established and was cordoned off with tape. The body had been covered over by a large white tent, and a police photographer with a forensic pathologist went backwards and forwards through the tent flaps, making notes on a clipboard.

As more police turned up, a senior officer began to organise them into groups, to carry out finger searches on their hands and knees. Further out, others walked slowly in a line, foraging with sticks.

That afternoon, Mavis Bone had given her full cooperation to the police, including a detailed statement of how the body was discovered. However, the snake skin was tucked away in her rucksack for further observation.

THIRTY-ONE

Mutating

After finding the body, and with Maxine still missing, Mavis Bone decided to arm herself. Whatever had caused these tragic events, be it a crazed serial killer or some mutant rattlesnake, she wasn't going to take any chances being alone out in the reserve. She had asked Dan for his advice, and he suggested she should have one of the forestry shotguns.

They kept three twelve-gauge Mossberg over-under shotguns, locked up in a strongbox located in the office. These were mainly used by the rangers for controlling vermin.

As Vincent Petzoldt was busy helping the police to find Maxine, and with the general running of the reserve to cope with, he'd assigned Dan to take over the shotgun requisition duties. Dan signed out the rifle with ammunition for himself; and then he gave it to Mavis, with strict instructions not to tell anyone, and to be careful.

Finding more high concentrations of radon in the snake skin she'd discovered near the body, Mavis decided to check out the radon readings on the remote detectors. With a copy of the map and the shotgun by her side, she climbed into her Toyota Yaris and made her way to the Torrent de la Vall Mar River. This was the area nearest to the log cabin where some of the detectors were located.

At seven o'clock, Mavis parked her vehicle and then trekked over rough scrubland containing buckthorn, rosemary, wild olive and dwarf fan palms until she reached the first radon detector. The evening smells of pine and sage nudged their way into her senses.

When she arrived at the red-coloured stake, she flipped the lid of the wooden protection box to reveal the orange plastic detector. She was slightly relieved to see that the digital display showed a reading of 1.2 pCi/L. This was well below the EPA safety requirements.

Mavis moved on to the other four detectors, and one by one she scribbled the readings onto the map locations. With the highest reading being at 1.9 pCi/L, she was satisfied the area could have had no influence on the mutated animals and reptiles that had been found. Her next stop was at Ses Puntes, where the other five detectors had been placed.

Mavis turned off the Torrent de la Vall Mar River Road, and took the narrow lane. At 7.45 there was still plenty of light. She parked the car and checked the map, and then, with the shotgun slung over her shoulder, she set off again by foot through scrubland and ferns to the next radon detector. Just as she got to the red-coloured stake, she stopped and listened. Something was wrong. It was deathly quiet. The normal night-time sounds of the forest had vanished, apart from the odd creak of a thick tree bough, as it contracted from the hot day sun. She'd never known it like this before. It was spooky. Mavis slid the shotgun from her shoulder. She had it loaded with three-inch twelve-gauge buckshot, and according to Dan it was powerful enough to take down an elephant at twenty yards.

Mavis surveyed the area for a while, and then, satisfied it was clear, she flipped the lid of the wooden protection box. For a few seconds she looked in disbelief. The digital reading in the window showed the radon concentration way above the safety level. It was 8.2 pCi/L. She made a note on her pad, and then proceeded a further half a mile on foot to the next stake.

Lifting the lid she could see the level was high again. This time the concentration reading showed 7.9 pCi/L. Mavis breathed a heavy sigh. This wasn't good news.

Moving on to the next detector, after a quarter of a mile she heard a rattle. And then with about two hundred yards to go, the noise seemed to be all around her.

Suddenly, Mavis froze at the distinct sound of a rattlesnake hidden in the grass to her right. And then she jerked at the sound of another rattle to her left. At that moment, just five yards ahead, a very large snake slithered across her path. It had to be six feet long or more. It looked like a timber, but she knew they didn't grow to that length. This was crazy, she thought, to find so many of them. Although Mavis was in her thick hiking boots and had a gun, she felt uneasy. In her brief career as a wildlife conservationist, she'd seen her share of timber rattlesnakes, but not so many concentrated in one place.

Mavis proceeded carefully to the counter. The increasing rattle of so many snakes fuelled tension into the evening atmosphere. To her it sounded like they were agitated about something. The noise was incessant, but collectively varying in intensity, as though their anger was being orchestrated by a conductor – a single leader of the nest.

As Mavis flipped the third lid, she raised her eyebrows and mumbled, 'Mother of God!' The Radon reading was 9.3 pCi/L. This was a major alarm. Way above the safety levels. She ran her fingers through her black curls and pondered. There were two more detectors in the Ses Puntes area, and she guessed they would probably be high as well. She decided to check the others the following night, as it was getting dark and too risky with all those timbers around.

It was now 8.50 and the light was fading. An early moon was out, with a clear sky on this warm evening, and so she could see some distance along the return trail. Mavis relaxed a little and began to walk back to her vehicle, but she was still ready with the shotgun in case she stepped on a snake, or one got too close for comfort. She was aware of rattlesnakes sounding off, as though they were following her.

It was just as she passed the second detector. Mavis slowed as a dark shape in the distance blocked her path. She raised her gun. Whatever it was, it was big and moving slowly across the trail. Mavis reasoned it could be something wounded, maybe a deer. Being wary, she stopped within thirty-five feet, and then curiosity got the better of her. Mavis inched closer, and then she couldn't believe her eyes. She clearly saw the dark chevron pattern of the markings against the yellow background of the massive scales. It was one giant of a timber rattler. The snake's girth was at least eleven inches or more; an anaconda sprung to mind.

Mavis did a quick calculation and estimated it had to be around thirty feet long. She was mesmerised by the caterpillar movement of the scales as it slowly moved across the path.

There was something else she hadn't noticed until now. Smaller rattlers were moving along the side of it. Like bees guarding their queen, they slithered close, as if in some pecking order of obedience.

Mavis's jaw dropped; never had she seen anything so bizarre. She thought, *What in God's name could have produced anything like that?* And then, it was as if someone had switched on a lightbulb inside her head. 'Dear God, no, it couldn't be,' she said aloud. She looked at the radon readings she'd scrawled on the map locations. 'You gotta be kidding me,' she mumbled under her breath. 'Jesus Christ, are you telling me it's mutated, like in a B horror movie?'

It took a few minutes for the entourage to cross the path, including stragglers. Even the smaller ones were six feet or more, as they moved in a rear guard action, rattling their presence. They looked organised and purposeful, and seemed to be giving out a warning of a territorial claim.

*

Mavis wasted no time. When she got back to her cabin, she frantically telephoned Vincent Petzoldt, the director of the wildlife reserve, leaving a message on his answering machine. 'Sorry it's after hours, sir, but I thought you should get this message as soon as possible. I've just been to check out the radon detectors and they're way above the safety level. Some are as high as 9.3 pCi/Litres in the S'Albufera Natural Park area. That's well into the danger zone. Also I'm sure we have a problem with the wildlife in that area, sir. Some of the animals and reptiles are being saturated with radon, and it looks like they're mutating to an abnormal size. In particular the timber rattlesnakes. I've just seen a giant one as big as an anaconda, sir. This supports my test results on some of the dead rabbits and snake skins I've found. I suggest we rope off the S'Albufera Natural Park area to tourists and hikers, until we've established the root of the problem. Anyone who goes inyo that area could be killed. We may even need state troopers to carry out a cull on the wildlife, to stop it from spreading. I'll type up my report and findings, and bring it over to you first thing in the morning, sir.'

The call had been heard. Petzoldt's office door was open. His fingers moved to the replay button, and while he listened, he frowned, then immediately deleted the message. And as he did so, he was thinking. *Interfering bitch. sticking her nose in. She has to be removed tonight, can't afford to wait. Got to look like an accident. Shut down her generator. When she comes out to inspect, jump her. And then soak her log cabin with gasoline. Leave some scented candles burning, and tip one over, that should do it. A quarter full bottle of bourbon on the coffee table, with her on the sofa, or what's left of her, clutching a glass.* He grinned. *No one will see the fire in the middle of the reserve. After that, fix the detectors. The snakes can wait until last. Carry out my own cull on them with the vermin flame torch.*

*

Mavis kicked off her shoes and went to the fridge. She poured herself a large glass of white wine, and at the same time nibbled on a plate of cold ham. Making her way to the bathroom, she showered, put on her dressing gown and then switched on a Carole King CD. Mavis collapsed onto the sofa exhausted, with her report notes by her side. As she began to scribble, the wine and the hot shower kicked in. Her eyes became heavy and eventually closed. The pen slipped from her fingers and rolled onto the floor.

An hour and a half later she woke with a jolt. Mavis was disorientated. For a fraction of a second she thought she'd gone blind. The place was in darkness. She felt for her mobile and it lit up. Fear and adrenalin swept over her, and then she realised with a curse what had happened. 'That bloody generator.' It had been giving everyone trouble for the last couple of years she'd heard. Usually the circuit breaker popped out from overheating. That meant trudging to the warehouse and pushing it back in again. She really didn't feel like doing it now. *Can't it wait till the morning?* She rolled it over in her mind. That would mean no hot water when she got up. And the report needed finishing; she'd promised her boss delivery first thing.

The luminous hands on her wristwatch showed it was eleven-thirty. Using the light from her mobile, Mavis reluctantly made her way to the dresser in the kitchen and fumbled in the drawer for the torch. Switching it on, she played the beam around. It was strong, with no flickering.

Sliding the bolts of the back door she peered out. The night was warm and humid. The stars were out and the moon shone, its glow flooding an eerie mood over the surroundings.

The large warehouse with the generator and propane tank inside it were to one side of the cabin. It was dark there, even with a torch. Not forgetting the snakes, Mavis went back for the shotgun. Breaching it, she could see the loaded shells. Feeling slightly edgy, with the gun raised and the torch beam pointing ahead, Mavis eased herself along the gravel path until she reached the wooden double doors of the warehouse.

It took Mavis a few seconds to realise. The large black area on one of them. The light from the torch confirmed it was a hole. Someone or something had smashed the bottom of the door through. Whatever it was might still be in there. With the shotgun ready she eased the door handle and slowly pulled it open.

The smell hit her and she cupped her nose. 'Mother of God,' she murmured. The torch beam lit up the inside. The floor was covered with droppings. Mavis knew instantly what they were. Her torch picked out the regurgitated pellets of animals. As she stepped in, she could make out the undigested carcasses of rabbits, squirrels and birds still waiting to be eaten. They'd been dragged here. Something was using the warehouse as a food larder. Perhaps a family of foxes or timber rattlers. The best thing was to get the generator running and get back to the cabin.

Mavis nervously played the torch up among the rafters in the roof. It looked all clear as far as she could make out with only a small pencil beam at her disposal. Next, she shone it on the control box. As Mavis moved towards it, the mound of rubbish in the corner caught her eye. It was banked up about eighteen inches in height with leaves and brush. She spotted rabbit fur and feathers spread over it like a blanket for something. Mavis moved towards it, and using the barrel of her gun, she prodded and poked. And then she froze. Mavis couldn't believe her eyes. She knelt down and pulled away some more brush, to reveal giant reptile eggs. They were pure white.

It didn't make sense. She thought, *What in the name could have laid these?* The rattle of a timber snake quickly cleared her mind. *Oh my God! Jesus, I've gotta get out of here. Report this. There could be more.*

She played the torch around the floor but nothing twitched or slithered. The snake had to be outside. Mavis forced herself to the control box. *Get the generator working, I'm not spending the night in the dark with Godzilla on the prowl.* She rested the gun with her free hand and opened the cabinet door. The beam shone on the protruding circuit breaker. Mavis pushed it in and then pressed the green start button. Immediately the generator chugged into life. She relaxed a little and then cursed again. *'Fucking torch.'* The beam had gone very weak. *'Shit.'*

THIRTY-TWO

Timberr!

Mavis groped for the pull-down light switch, and then remembered it was over by the doors. As she inched herself along, she heard something dislodge above her. At that moment something brushed her face. Mavis yelled in fright and swiped it away. And then it thumped her in the back. She screamed and lashed out. '*Fuck off! You mother—*' At the same time, her fingers found the cord and she pulled hard.

Like a supernova, the fluorescent tube was blinding. But Mavis never blinked. In front of her, swinging, not more than a foot away, was Maxine's face. She was suspended upside down. The outstretched arms swung in a pendulum motion. One hand had been gnawed off, while congealed blood surrounded a large gash in her throat. A glassy eye stared. The other was missing. The near decapitation made it look as though she was grinning with a second pair of smiling, bloody lips.

Mavis looked up. One of the feet had got caught in the vee of the rafters. Mavis spoke softly to no one, 'How on earth could she have got…? What in God's name could have dragged her…?' At that moment the foot slipped out of its shoe, and the body crashed to the floor. Mavis cried out and backed off. She pointed the gun upwards. She could see the shoe still lodged in the vee of the rafters.

Mavis bent down. She winced at Maxine's mangled features. Around the bloody neck, she recognised the gold chain. Mavis carefully examined the identity locket. *Maxine*, in copperplate writing, stared back at her.

A muffled voice spoke. 'I'd been wondering what happened to her. I searched for three whole days. Just assumed something had dug her up and dragged her away for their lunch.'

Mavis spun round to see him standing by the door. He wore a balaclava and was holding a flaming torch with a propane gas tank strapped to his back. She raised the shotgun. She was confused. She couldn't recognise the voice behind the mask. 'So you killed Maxine, but why?'

'If only that stupid dog hadn't found the arm. I knew she wasn't going to keep her mouth shut. Miss Goody Two-shoes could never keep a secret, including what her sister told her about the share flotation. When I heard about it, I was like a dog with a bone. Even Dan, my lodger, said I was a fool. Hadn't I learned from his experience, what had gone down before? A lesson learned with fingers burned.' He laughed at his own joke. 'But the hotel investment was too good to be true. That's until you stuck your nose in.' He mimicked her Aussie accent. 'I must do my duty and tell everybody about the high radon count. Keep in my boss's good books.'

She levelled the gun at him. 'So you'd be happy to grab the money and let the others die of cancer? Let the wildlife become infected?'

'Of course, my dear. Who gives a shit about the wildlife? Mind you, on that message you left, I liked your hysterical outburst about a giant anaconda. Made me chuckle. Sounded like you'd been smoking that ganja. Doesn't make any difference to me what you do out in that forest. Hell, even I sniff a bit of Charlie from time to time.'

'You think what you like,' Mavis said, 'it doesn't matter to me. And if you've got any ideas with that torch thing, forget it. I've got two up the spout aimed at your chest. All I want you to do is put your hands up.'

'Now that's what I call bad planning, Mavis. You see, who in their right mind would give a loaded gun to a woman? Apart from one that fires blanks, yes.'

He raised the flaming torch and moved closer.

Mavis stood firm. 'Don't make me kill you.' She aimed the rifle at his head in case he was wearing a bulletproof vest. His last remark niggled. *What did he mean?*

And then he lunged at her, squeezing the flame torch. As she ducked, she screamed as a blue sheet of fire shot out and scorched her face and hair. Mavis raised the shotgun and got off two rounds into the side of his head. The deafening blast from both barrels blinded her. She felt the powder burns stinging her face. Mavis couldn't see or hear

401

anything. She crouched to one knee in the smoke. *He must be very dead after that*, she thought. *Even decapitated.* Mavis rubbed her eyes and found blood on her hands, not sure whether it was from her powder burns or what was left of his brains.

She leant down and heaved a little, which brought up some acidic bile into her mouth. Mavis spat it out, and then she saw his shoes.

As the smoke cleared, Vincent Petzoldt was grinning at her. 'Twelve-gauge black powder blanks. I told you so.'

It was too late to duck. The jet of lighter fuel caught her full on the face. She was covered in it. It was stinging her eyes. As she crouched moaning with the pain, she could just make him out as he stood over her, soaking her with the last squirts from the can.

'Now it's my turn again.' He stood back carefully, knowing she was going to make one hell of a blaze.

In her blurred world, Mavis saw the flame of the torch raised, and braced herself for the terrible pain that was to come.

Suddenly, as if from nowhere, a huge, gaping mouth enveloped his head, right down to the shoulders. The hand dropped the torch, all too near to where she was standing. Mavis edged back, blinking, disbelieving. She could hear his muted screams as the fangs bit down on his face and neck. It was the massive head of a giant timber rattlesnake; the Queen herself. Mavis realised the thing must have been curled up in the roof space. And then it slowly began to lift him up. Now Maxine's location made more sense.

A food store in the rafters. His feet were twitching while his muffled screams sounded in its mouth. As his body inched higher, it shook him like a rag doll, as if annoyed with his noises. And then a sharp crack was heard. Mavis realised his neck had just broken. Higher and higher the lifeless legs inched upwards, until they disappeared among the rafters.

Mavis had to get out. The flame from the torch had caught some of the fuel spillage, and the dry brush shielding the eggs was already on fire. And then, one by one, they started slithering in through the damaged door, as if they knew their colony, their future existence was in jeopardy. Timber rattlesnakes, all of them at least six foot or more. The Queen's guard had arrived. They rattled out their agitation when they saw Mavis. They reared up and hissed at her. They couldn't let her wreak any more havoc in their lair.

As they moved in, she carefully picked up the flaming torch, knowing she could easily end up as a fireball herself. She spun round, prodding the flame at them. They flinched automatically and then struck back, annoyed and rattling, wanting to get at her. Mavis was cut off. There were too many snakes. She was surrounded by them.

With her clothes still dripping with fuel, she took a risk and extended the flame to the maximum eight inches. She threatened them with the fire and singed one or two rearing heads as she inched towards the doors.

It felt like something had punched down on top of her shoulder. Mavis dropped the torch. Something had her in a vice-like grip, and the pain was immense. She tried to move but it was useless. Mavis turned her head and stared into a massive eyeball with a vertical black slit. The thing above her was back for more. The huge scales of the bony snout were almost touching her face. And then the timber dislocated its jaws, and bit down more on her shoulder for a better grip. Mavis punched it with her free arm, but it was useless. She felt herself weightless, her feet weren't touching the ground. It was hauling her up.

Mavis screamed, and as she looked down she stopped abruptly with a look of horror. She saw the torch. On the floor, the flaming torch had landed on a can and was sitting upright. The eight-inch flame was burning into the side of the large propane gas tank. A small orange glow had already begun to spread across the surface. The thing was going to blow up any moment.

As Mavis wrestled and punched at a coil with chevron markings, its eleven-inch girth began to wrap itself around her waist.

The shotgun explosion was both blinding and deafening. Bits of timber rattlesnake brains splattered her face as she crashed to the floor. Her ankle collapsed under her, and Mavis shrieked with the pain. The other snakes reared up to strike, seeing their chance.

Mavis never felt the hand grab. She was in too much pain. Someone was dragging her out. She couldn't see the face of who was pulling at her. Her head struck the door and cut her forehead. Fresh air hit her, but she was still being pulled. Mavis cried out for them to stop, but they weren't listening. Rough ground and stones cut into her side, and then the sky lit up.

The fireball was immense and was followed by a thunderous explosion. Charred bits of warehouse rained down on her. Her hair was alight, and then someone was smothering her, shielding her with their body. Mavis was moaning in agony as smoking cinders wafted down, scorching her legs and face. And then two powerful hands dragged her to her feet. He covered her head with his coat.

Mavis looked into his face.

A blurry vision of Dan smiled back. 'I'm sorry about the gun. Vincent must have swapped it for blanks.' He glanced over his shoulder. 'Looks like I got here just in time.'

Mavis smiled, then coughed up some blood. 'The fuckin' thing bit me.'

'Don't worry, I always carry a serum pack when I'm in the forest. Let's get you into the cabin, and I'll give you a shot.'

*

Detective Inspector Eric Faversham travelled to see Mavis to help Interpol with their enquiries. The inspector was at Mavis's bedside. She'd been kept in overnight for cuts and shock at the Hospital de Manacor on the eastern side of Majorca.

Gertrude had been with her all morning.

The doctor had told Mavis she would be okay to leave in the afternoon, but not to fly for another twenty-four hours.

Once again, Mavis was amongst the usual hospital

smells of disinfectant, bleached linen, alcohol and waxed floors. Propped up between some fluffy green pillows, helping Inspector Faversham with his enquiries, she explained what happened, and asked nervously if they'd found Vincent Petzoldt, who'd tried to kill her.

Silver-haired DI Faversham was looking his age, wearing as usual his sober pin striped suit with its matching navy blue waistcoat. With concern written across his Dickensian face, with its wrinkled features and protuberant ears, he told Mavis Bone, 'Vincent Petzoldt's body was been found badly burned and all chewed up by some giant reptile. This was confirmed by the forest rangers who found him. And would you believe, his DNA forensics and dental records show him to be none other than Vincent Pollack, who was already being investigated for murder.'

'Jesus no!' Mavis put a hand to her mouth in shock. 'So you mean Petzoldt was Pollack all the time?'

'That's right. He took on Petzoldt's disguise, after surviving the hotel balcony fall. And then he killed him and mutilated him beyond recognition, to make it look like the guard dogs had ripped him to shreds.'

Dan the forest ranger appeared at the end of her hospital bed. He apologised to Mavis with a big smile. 'Sorry for the rough treatment I gave you, while sorting out Godzilla,' he laughed.

'Sorry?' she gave a mock laugh. 'You saved my life. I was nearly a goner until you blasted Mister Anaconda into eternity.' Mavis focused on him, her eyes getting clearer. 'So how come you got to me just in time, Dan?'

Dan replied, 'I got a call from the police, about that body you found with a missing arm. It was a woman. Apparently they found a slug in her skull, and dental records identified her as Giovanna Piras. She was Vincent Petzoldt's former fiancé, who'd disappeared some time ago. She'd been shot from behind. No doubt she ended up like Maxine, because she wanted to spill the beans about the high radon levels in the area.'

'And he seemed such a nice man.' Mavis stared into space.

Dan joked, 'Ah well, that just proves you can't rely on first impressions.'

Mavis laughed, coughed up some more blood, and winced.

A doctor dabbed her mouth and said, 'You may have some internal injuries, but the paramedics will sort you out. A busted rib maybe, but it doesn't look serious. Just don't laugh too much,' he joked.

Dan considered for a moment. 'What you need, Mavis, is a good holiday. Perhaps a weeks' camping in the reserve?'

'You bastard!' she yelled, and slung a box of tissues at him.

For his published crime writing short stories and novels. B.P. Smythe was inducted into the Crime Writers Association for his achievements.

About the Author

Eight years ago, he self-published his first horror novel, *Sow and You Shall Reap* http://www.amazon.co.uk/ dp/145677171X which can be purchased on Amazon in ebook and paperback. Over 6,000 copies so sold so far...

In the year 2017, B.P. Smythe secured a three book deal from Bloodhound Books http://www.bloodhoundbooks. com/, which included, *From a Poison Pen* http://www. amazon.co.uk/Poison-Pen-collection-macabre-stories-ebook/dp/B01BKWT4EE. His second book of short stories *From a Poison Pen VOL II* has just been released and is available on: https://www.amazon.co.uk/Poison-Pen-ii-B-P-Smythe-ebook/dp/B01LFM1032

In the year 2019, B.P.Smythe released three full length novels – *The Medal of Purity* www.amazon.co.uk/ Medal-Purity-Barry-Smythe/dp/1911412884 and *THE EXPIRED* https://www.amazon.co.uk/Expired-Barry-Smythe/dp/1911412728 and *Then There Were None* https://www.amazon.co.uk/Then-There-Were-None-Smythe/dp/1911412612

Barry Smythe (barrysmythe@hotmail.com)

Amazon author page: www.amazon.co.uk/-/e/ B006MCGVNU

https://www.goodreads.com/author/ show/5043570.B_P_Smythe

https://en.gravatar.com/barrysmythe

Books by B.P.Smythe

Your Book Review

I hope you have enjoyed this book, and will share it among your friends and family. While making them aware of its popularity, I would be grateful for your Amazon and Goodreads review.

Kind Regards
Barry Smythe (barrysmythe@hotmail.com)
Amazon author page: www.amazon.co.uk/-/e/
B006MCGVNU
https://en.gravatar.com/barrysmythe